THE DAWNING

31000 BC

By

Richard W. Wise

BRUNSWICK
HOUSE PRESS

The Dawning:
31,000 BC

Published by: Brunswick House Press
P. O. Box 465, Ivy, Virginia 22945

Poem: Painters

Book design: Amit Dey
Cover design: Miladinka Milic

ISBN: 979-8-9864208-0-6 hardcover
ISBN: 979-8-9864208-1-3 paperback
ISBN: 979-8-9864208-2-0 e.book

Information: d.sage@secretsofthegemtrade.com

Names: Wise, Richard W., author.
Title: The dawning : 31000 BC / by Richard W. Wise.
Description: First edition. | Ivy, Virginia : Brunswick House Press, [2022] | Includes
    bibliographical references.
Identifiers: ISBN: 979-8-9864208-0-6 (hardcover) | 979-8-9864208-1-3 (trade
    paperback) | 979-8-9864208-2-0 (ebook)
Subjects: LCSH: Cro-Magnons--Europe--Fiction. | Neanderthals--Europe--Fiction. |
    Young adults-- Europe--Fiction. | Man-woman relationships--Fiction. |
    Abduction--Fiction. | Voyages and travels--Fiction. | War stories. | LCGFT:
    Historical fiction. | Romance fiction. | Bildungsromans. | Action and adventure
    fiction. | BISAC: FICTION / Historical / Ancient. | FICTION / Action &
    Adventure. | FICTION / Literary.
Classification: LCC: PS3623.I825 D39 2022 | DDC: 813/.6--dc23

PAINTERS

In the cave with a long-ago flare
a woman stands, her arms up. Red twig, black twig, brown twig.
A wall of leaping darkness over her.
The men are out hunting in the early light
But here in this flicker, one or two men, painting
and a woman among them.
Great living animals grow on the stone walls,
their pelts, their eyes, their sex, their hearts,
and the cave-painters touch them with life, red, brown, black,
a woman among them, painting.

Muriel Ruykeyser

For Katherine E., and William T.

31,000 B.C.

SOUTHWESTERN FRANCE

CHAPTER I

KIDNAPPED

Lada heard a twig snap, turned, saw the men and opened her mouth to scream. A large, hairy hand smothered her cry.

The day began as an adventure. It was the second day of the false thaw. The Ice Season lay like a sharp flint blade beneath the sun's comforting warmth. The people, cooped up in the darkness of their smoky huts since the first snows howled down from the north, greeted the Sunfather's return with rejoicing.

Lada was a tiny girl, with a bird's nest of black hair and skin the color of oak bark. She had just passed her first moon's blood. Lada sought out Ejil, the lanky, dark-skinned boy who was her best friend and secret love. She had hoped he would join her. But Ejil had puffed out his chest and informed her that he was too busy to go foraging. Besides, it was woman's work, and he was off trapping meat. She hated it when he acted that way. "Boys," she said and frowned. She stuck her tongue out at his retreating form and skipped off to find her girlfriend Tule, whose eyes lit up at the prospect of joining her.

After Lada had solemnly promised her mother that they would be careful and return before dark, and not wander beyond the forest that fringed the lake shore, the two friends set out with baskets and digging sticks. Picking their way down the steep, muddy footpath that led from the camp to the valley floor, they entered the wood and foraged through the damp pines, which spread like a verdant blanket that began at the lake's edge.

As the sun climbed the sky ladder and the day warmed, the two girls made their way deeper into the thick forest and, probing with their digging sticks, searched for edible roots and tubers. The forest was quiet. Cave bears still slept, and lions, cave lions and other big scary animals avoided the thick woods. Lada paused and sniffed the air. She loved the sharp smell of pine. Overhead, fat clouds drifted across a vivid blue sky, and birds could be heard singing and flitting from tree to tree.

Lada noticed a thick layer of ground cover that had been blown by the wind up against a large boulder. She knelt and carefully flipped over the wet, musty leaves that her mother had taught her often hid edible spring plants.

She uncovered a tangled mass of pale green stems with exposed white blossoms. Dark-green tubers dangled beneath the stems. The sight of green made her mouth pucker. She didn't recall the name but recognized it as an herb her mother used to add a little bite to her stews. Anything she found would, by custom, be shared between the two families. *Too bad, Ejil missed out. Oh well,* she thought, glancing at her friend who was scouring the ground near a fallen tree, *I found them!*

A sharp peppery taste filled her mouth. "Tule," she called, "quick, come see what I've found!" The fresh taste was so good after a hard season of living on smoked meat, tubers and fried cakes of deer fat mixed with seeds and dried berries.

"What is it?" Tule kneeled beside her friend. The older girl was taller and thicker through the body than Lada. She had bright eyes, and unlike most of her people who had broad, flat noses with flaring nostrils, hers was a long, thin blade which the boys made the object of endless teasing.

"Foxbite! Oh, how wonderful!" Tule giggled. "Catya will be so pleased." Catya was Tule's older sister. She had taken care of the girl since her mother's death. Tracing the thin stems, the two girls deftly untangled and placed them reverently in Lada's basket. Focused on her work, Lada saw and heard nothing beyond the comforting sounds of the deep woods.

The sharp sound sent a shiver of fear down her spine. Lada met the man's eyes and flinched. The man removed his hand from her mouth and grasped her roughly by the chin. She inhaled sharply and her mouth formed the beginnings of a scream, but the look in his eyes and a warning finger pressed to his lips silenced her. His eyes were strange: gray like a stormy afternoon sky. She could barely stand to look into them. She twisted her head, trying to break free, but the hand gripped her like a strong winter's chill. The man's ruined visage conveyed no particular menace, only curiosity and a touch of amusement.

Lada's breath came in ragged gasps. She had never seen such a man before: pallid skin like a snake's belly; a deep, ragged scar cutting down his cheek to his jawline. The dark, puckered flesh drew his lips into a crooked half-smile, revealing a row of flat teeth. The man had a strong jaw but no chin. Bushy eyebrows that nearly met outlined a protruding brow ridge that made his strange, glittering eyes appear deeply sunken into his face. A tangled mass of stringy hair, the color of red ochre, covered his head and fell halfway to his shoulders.

Another man had taken hold of Tule. There were two others. They were armed with heavy, flint-tipped thrusting spears. Pale-skinned and broader in the chest and body, they were shorter by a head than the men of Lada's tribe.

Encircled by one of his thickly muscled arms, her scarred captor made a quick gesture and the others gathered around. They were shorter but similarly built, with broad, hairy chests and massive thighs. The one holding Tule—who stared bug-eyed and shook like a captured hare—was black haired with a misshapen leg. Another, holding extra spears, was missing an ear. Their pale faces were tattooed with intricate patterns of black whirling dots.

Lada's mind churned. Her skin felt cold and clammy. *Who are these men?* She had never seen their like before. Their pallid skin made them seem unreal, almost ghostly. *What are they?* she wondered. *What do they want? Where are they taking us?*

Her hands and feet were quickly trussed. Lada was hefted, like a haunch of fresh killed meat, onto a pair of broad shoulders. At the leader's signal, the party set off at a pace that ate up the narrow game trail, skirting the lake. Tule had been draped over the shoulder of the man in front of her. Bouncing along on a hard, muscled shoulder with her head hanging down, Lada saw little other than the passing ground and the gathering afternoon shadows until the man carrying her flipped her off his shoulder and pitched her roughly onto the hard ground. Ignoring her yelp of pain, he leaned down and untied the rawhide strips that bound her hands and feet.

Lada blinked. It was dark as pine-pitch, but before long, speckled shards of firelight began to illuminate the scene. She could vaguely make out the lumpish form of her friend, lying with her head against a rock, a body's length away. A feeling of relief flooded her chest, but quickly faded.

"Where are we?" Tule whispered, eyes red-rimmed from crying.

Lada propped herself on her elbows and wiggled backwards until they leaned shoulder to shoulder against the rock. "I have no idea," she said, licking her dry lips. Her stomach ached. A low murmur came from the men gathered around a fire at the mouth of the cave. *Where am I? Who are these men?* Lada asked herself again. *I'm so hungry. What a stupid idea. I should have stayed in camp. If only I had asked Ejil to take me with him.*

None of the men seemed to be paying them any attention. Lada swiveled her head, her eyes frantically questing for an escape route. The rising flames gave her some perspective. Lada and Tule were in the rear of a shallow cave of solid rock. There was only one way out, and that way led past their captors. They were trapped.

Fat crackled and spit. The rich aroma of roasting meat filled Lada's nostrils. Her mouth watered; her stomach rumbled. They had eaten nothing since leaving their village just after sunrise. The thought of her snug little camp brought tears to her eyes.

"What do these men want with us, Lada?" Tule sobbed. Her voice sounded hoarse from crying. "Are they going to eat us? I want to go home, Lada."

"Shush, Tule," Lada whispered. She saw no point in crying. *Tule is such a baby.* Squinting in the flickering light, her mind worked furiously. *Are these the giants of the šamán's tales?* Great, ugly monsters, larger than cave bears, with dripping fangs, who skulked in the darkness waiting to seize foolish children who wandered from the family fire? Monsters who would crack open children's heads like bird's eggs and suck out the soft insides? *They are ugly enough, but they are hardly giants.* The stories were confusing, but these were most likely those she had heard Breda's father describe as "the others;" strange human creatures with outlandish customs.

Butchered and eaten? Maybe; but that will not be all. She remembered her mother's warning: "all men want the same thing from a woman." *Oh, Mother, I miss you. What am I going to do? I just want to go home.*

Darkened fully and framed in the firelight, the cave entrance yawned like a giant's open jaw. *We must get away—and soon. Surely by now, our people will be out looking for us.* Lada felt a shiver of fear dance down her spine. The night held many dangers. Demons and evil spirits. Off in the distance she heard hyena yelping and a wolf's lonely howl. She shivered and glanced at Tule. The girl's eyes shone pale and wide against her dark face. *Even if we escape, we have no weapons, no way to protect ourselves. How will we ever find our way home? No, we have to take the chance. This cave is just off the trail. I know the direction we came from. The search party can't be far off. Oh, how I wish Ejil were here. He would know what to do.*

"After they eat, they will fall asleep. We will wait until then," Lada whispered. It often happened at the end of a feast. After gorging on meat, the men would nod off, leaving the women to clean up the remains. "We must stay awake then sneak by them," Lada murmured softly into Tule's ear.

"Lada, I'm afraid."

Lada flinched. A dark shadow had blocked the light. It was the scarred leader, his eyes glistening in the firelight. In contrast to her tanned leather boots and well-stitched tunic, he was crudely dressed. Ragged furs draped and cinched with strips of rawhide covered him to just below the knee, and leg wraps covered his lower leg down to the ankle. His shoes were little more than foot wraps, stuffed with dried grass and held together with sinew.

He squatted, gestured with one hand and made a single sound—which Lada supposed was a word—and held out two thick slices of blood-red meat. The juices dripped between his thick fingers. Tule shrank back, her fingers clawing at her face. Then, reaching out a tentative hand, she snatched the largest piece and crammed it into her mouth. Tearing it in half with her teeth, she clutched the greasy remains tightly to her chest as she chewed. Blood ran from the corners of her mouth and down her chin.

Lada hesitated, her eyes fixed on the man's face. He nodded and his face contorted into a smile, his mouth distorted by his scar. She reached out and took the meat. The man grunted something and shrugged off the water bladder that hung from his shoulder, placed it at the girls' feet, and rose and returned to the fire.

Tule wiped the back of her hand across her mouth, removed the leather tie from the bladder and drank. She made a face, burped and yawned. "Well," she said, "maybe it will be alright. At least they're not starving us."

Lada turned toward her friend, her lips twisted, unconvinced. Tule was always hungry. She had been too, but the fear and rough travel had taken its toll on her appetite. She yawned, sat back and closed her eyes. She began to nod off, caught herself and straightened up. They must not sleep. "Stay awake, Tule!" she whispered fiercely. "We must get away before we get to their camp. Who knows what they will do to us then?"

Tule shook her head and sat up, eyes like a frightened bird's. "I'll be alright," she said.

Hugging herself for warmth, Lada propped herself up. She could hear the north wind's harsh voice as it brushed across the cave's mouth—how many nights had that song lulled her to sleep in the warm bosom of her family's skin-covered lodge? An image of her mother's smile formed in her mind's eye. *Don't worry, Mother. I'll see you again, I will.* She brushed away the tears and shook her head. "Stay awake," she ordered herself in a soft whisper.

Tule was little help. Her head gradually slumped against Lada's shoulder; her warm breath tickled Lada's ear. The fire had burned down to a bed of glowing embers. One by one, the hunters lay back and dozed off.

CHAPTER 2

THE BOY

The boy glanced up from his work. His mother, Lette, the wife of the tribe's leader, had sent him to set traps, hoping, after so many moons, for a taste of fresh meat. The boy's name was Ejil. He was preparing a snare on the narrow, rocky game trail that wove its way along the cliff above his people's camp and overlooked the canyon floor.

The day had begun in the chilly wolf's dawn, but as the sun climbed the sky ladder, it had turned hot. Though, the light breeze that brushed his face still held a hint of more cold weather to come.

The canyon looks like a giant's hand pried apart a stone ridge and left behind a deep valley, Ejil fantasized. He wore a light tunic and breeches of tanned deerskin. His mother had stitched the hide together. She was a woman who could weave magic with a bone needle.

The country, as far as could be seen with the sharpest eye, was a barren, windswept taiga. In the distance, the dark shapes of mammoth, ibex and auroch herds grazed the patches of dry brown grass that dotted the snowy landscape. It had been an odd season, bitterly cold but with little snow. Ejil closed his eyes. His mind pictured the shaggy mammoth, the great-horned rhino, the bands of hyena and the big, spear-toothed cats who ranged across the plain by night.

From where he stood, Ejil looked down on his people's home. The camp was set high, embedded in the rockface with its back to the frigid north wind. Huts were huddled together on the wide, flat apron that jutted out from the cliffside. Nestled between the twin cliffs, the sun glinted off the iced surface of a small lake, which had formed from the streams that flowed into the valley. A thick beard of evergreen forest, protected from the chill winds by the cliff, grew around its base.

The tiny village was well situated and easily defended. The small band of hunter-gatherers had discovered it after a long period of wandering, following their separation from the mother tribe. It had been the first place they called home, and the fish-filled lake allowed them to return to it often.

Ejil knew the story well. Under the šamán's watchful eye, he had learned to chant it around the nightfire. The mother tribe had grown too large and inbred, with more mouths than could be fed. At the Gathering of Tribes, a council was called. The drums pounded. The šamán chanted the blood ties. Three families, whose children who were too close in blood to mate within the tribe, were chosen and a few from the other tribes joined them. Tears were shed and many gifts given. This was now three generations past, and Ejil's elderfather's father had led them to their new home. The tribe called themselves *The Broken People*, in remembrance.

During the green seasons, the Sunfather had trod close to the earth. Meat and forage were plentiful through the Season of Painted Leaves. Whatever was not eaten was dried or smoked to sustain the Broken People through the long Ice Season. They had taken full advantage of the sun's kindness and filled their larders. The tribe had prospered.

The fingers of two hands were no longer sufficient to count the cooking fires. The people were well fed and happy, and "happiness," his father was fond of saying, "was sitting with a full belly around the nightfire with a woman who came willingly to your sleeping fur. Of course," he said with a wink, "it is best to have thick pelts."

Talog, Ejil's father, was their First Speaker—he who held the speaking stick and spoke first at council. Talog was a blooded warrior and a skillful hunter. As fathers will, he expected his sons to follow him; but

Ejil, unlike his older brother, the son of his father's first wife, was less a hunter than a dreamer with a thirst for knowledge. Physically, he favored his own mother, Lette, Talog's lovely, young second wife. His father and older brother looked much alike: broad and muscular with ebony skin, black hair, dense as a briar patch. They had wide, squarish faces, thick eyebrows and dark, brooding eyes. Ejil's skin was lighter brown. He was tall and wiry. Doe-eyed like his mother; his eyes, his mother told him, were the rich brown color of heartwood.

Unlike his elder brother, Ejil enjoyed but took little pride in learning the skills of the hunt. His father doted on his lovely young wife, and, for her sake, tolerated his youngest son's odd behavior. But to Ejil's sensitive eye, his father's disappointment was painfully apparent.

Since he was old enough to think about it, Ejil had been drawn to Pelas, the tribe's šamán. Pelas had known many winters. He tottered along as he walked, leaning heavily on his staff. His bird's nest of white hair grew long beneath his chin and in a wreath around his bare dome. His father, he told the boy, had been šamán, as had *his* elderfather and *his* elderfather's father in an unbroken line going back to the Great Journey.

Pelas was a wise man with much to teach, and little pleases a teacher more than an eager student. Ejil would come whenever he could to sit by the šamán's fire. Often, even after the Sunfather had topped the Sky Ladder, and day had passed into night, still would Ejil sit enraptured by the old man's teachings. He was amazed at the depth of the šamán's knowledge. Pelas kept the old stories and the lineage of each family tucked away in his vast memory.

The grizzled elder was the last of his line. He had no wife, and no children. An apprentice was required to succeed him, one with sufficient wit to absorb and memorize the tribe's story. He had been pleased when Ejil had approached *him* and asked to study.

"Have you spoken to your father?" the šamán asked.

The boy shook his head.

"Why do you wish to become a šamán?"

"A voice came to me in a dream," Ejil said.

The šamán nodded. "You have been chosen." He went to the First Speaker and asked for his youngest son.

"A šamán? Never!" Talog had said, shaking his head vehemently. "My sons will be hunters and warriors," he told Pelas.

"Father, there is so much Pelas could teach me," Ejil said later as they sat with their meat at the night fire.

"To be asked is a great honor," Lette added.

"Honor? Hah! Better he should be a hunter, like me," Talog said, tapping his chest. "Like my father and elderfather." He regarded the boy sternly. As the tribe's leader, the Speaker had butted heads with Pelas many times—a man must propagate the spirits, but he neither liked nor trusted him.

"Father, please!"

"Enough!"

Ejil's continued entreaties earned him a slap that set him on his back, hard on the rush-covered floor of the hut.

He picked himself up. Tears coursed down his cheeks. Ejil's mother took his hand, gathered him into her arms and glared at her husband.

"Do not start with me, woman!" his father shouted. "He will be a warrior, not some sneaking priest—a useless mouth that must be filled, wasting his days shaking old bones and mumbling nonsense."

Lette understood her young son. Ejil knew she favored the šamán's proposal, and like waves grinding against a rocky shore, she slowly wore down her husband's resolve.

Ejil heard them arguing. "But think, husband," she said. She placed her hand on his thigh and made her voice soft and soothing, "Pelas is an old man and must soon pass into the Shadowlands. As šamán, Ejil will be second only to the First Speaker. He will be a powerful ally to you. And if Baal succeeds you as Speaker, Ejil will be his ally too. As šamán, he will bring honor to our family."

"Hah, that old man will live forever," Talog said, pulled back the hide covering the door and exited the hut.

His father was a hard and stubborn man, but he loved his beauti-ful, young wife and gradually began to see the wisdom in her words. Ejil would be allowed to study the ways of a šamán; but to save face, his father insisted that he also learn his weapons and the skills of the hunt.

Ejil squatted and began setting his second trap. He raised his ham-mer stone and drove a sharpened stake deep into the ground on one side of the tell-tale game trail. He took hold of a sapling growing on the opposite side of the trail, stripped its branches, tucked it under his armpit and wrestled it awkwardly to the ground.

The boy closed his eyes. *Mother will be so pleased,* he thought, pictur-ing himself strolling through the camp with a pair of freshly killed rab-bits slung over his shoulder. At that moment, a black nose attached to a long, furred snout roughly nuzzled the boy's ear, almost upending him. "No Prat, no!" Ejil said sharply and pushed the dog away. Usually, a push was a signal for play. The dog sat up and cocked its head, but hesitated. Something in his master's manner warned the shaggy canine that this was not the time. Prat whined and settled himself a little distance off, dark-brown eyes fixed on Ejil, his long tongue lolling out of his mouth.

Ejil resumed his work. Holding the branch clamped tightly under his arm, he attached a rope of woven bark fibers to the sapling's tip. He then slid a wooden wedge under the notch, carved a finger's width below the apex of the anchored stake, and held his breath as he let the rope slide through his fingers. The rope went taut, and the wedge snugged up against the notch. Exhaling sharply through his nose, he draped a light lariat, woven from reeds that grew along the lake shore, artfully over the bare, stunted bushes that flanked either side of the trail.

The boy sat back on his haunches, backhanded the sweat from his brow and surveyed his handiwork. Once snagged in the loop, a struggling animal would jerk out the wedge and the sapling would spring upright, hoisting up the hapless creature and leaving it dangling helplessly in space.

A wind gust ruffled his hair. A snapping sound and a sharp pain set him down hard on the frozen earth. Gingerly fingering his stinging cheek, he eyed his blood-smeared fingers. Smiling to himself, he rubbed his cheek and recalled a similar accident, and how the power of the striking wedge had astonished him; so much so that an idea, a picture, had taken form in his mind.

He cut a length of sapling into a staff the length of his forearm and fastened several strips of birch bark to one end, as he had when he set the snare. He then plaited the supple strips into a rope, roughly the length of his arm. Fetching a heavy rounded river rock, he wove the bark around it and continued weaving until the rope on the other side of the stone was of equal length. Then, fastening the remaining rope end to the club, he formed a loop with the rock dangling at the center.

His hand gripping the club about halfway down its length, Ejil stood before a rotted tree trunk. Mimicking the action of the sprung trap, he drew back his arm and whipped the rock forward. It struck the dead tree with a loud thump, burying itself deep in the soft wood. Ejil tried it again, this time using all his strength. The rock hit the rotted wood with so much force the thick trunk exploded. Stroking his chin, he stepped back and considered. *With a weapon like this in one hand and a spear in the other*, he told himself, *I could keep off an enemy with one arm and with a quick step forward, sling the rock and crush his skull with the other. Sling, yes, a sling! That's what I'll call it.*

Practicing secretly in a dense part of the forest near the lake, he imagined himself a mighty warrior, the rotted trees fierce enemies of his tribe. Wielding his new weapon, he conquered several in quick succession.

In his excitement, he failed to notice that the strands woven around the stone had frayed. Facing off against another seasoned warrior, he drew back his arm and whipped the rock forward, but this time the weakened strands split and the rock broke free, striking a tree several spear-throws beyond his target. Gritting his teeth, he stood for a moment. Then, noting the distance the stone had traveled, another idea sprang to mind.

Working with a sharp flint blade, he stripped bark from a birch tree, peeled back the inner bark, sliced it into thin strips and dried them overnight. The next morning, he separated the strands and wove a new rope. This time he made an open hammock, wide enough to cradle but not bind a stone. He needed a way to launch a rock, so he fastened one end of the rope to the staff and wove a loop around the other end wide enough to fit over his thumb.

The Ice Season had come late, and he'd spent the next several days practicing. He found if he retracted his arm and whipped it forward letting the cord slip off his thumb, he was able to sling a rock much further than a spear thrown by the strongest man. Using lighter rocks, his missiles went even further. The stones, however, flew off in all directions, rarely hitting what he aimed at. Gradually, he found that by adjusting his stance, standing sideways holding the short staff in his right hand, pointing his left shoulder at his target, spinning the rock close to his side and throwing underhand, they flew straighter, and he began hitting his targets.

He recalled, after one practice session with his sling, seeing a young hind. The doe had appeared one late afternoon—like an apparition—by the lakeshore just before dusk. Crouched behind a tree, Ejil had watched her approach and drink. Animals are creatures of habit…He looked up at the westering sun. "Maybe!" he thought. Rummaging through his pack, he drew out his sling, the cord wrapped tightly around its staff. He had kept the weapon carefully hidden to avoid his brother's questions and the inevitable taunts. *Maybe, if I hurry, I can reach her drinking place before*

sundown. He quickly reset the trap and hurried off down the backtrail that led to the far end of the lake.

He arrived panting at the place he had sighted the fawn. A quick-running stream flowed into the lake, keeping a small pool free of ice. There were tracks, but not fresh. *Looks like I'm not too late.* He circled around a shallow elbow that faced the spot where the hind had come down to the water and hid himself behind some thick bushes. Drawing out a rounded river pebble from a sack at the bottom of his pack, he crouched, gazed up at the sun edging toward the horizon, and waited.

Moments later, he heard a faint footfall. It was the hind. His heart raced as she picked her way daintily through the trees and thick layer of leaves that carpeted the forest floor. She paused, nose testing; her large mobile ears twisted back and forth, questing for danger. Ejil held his breath as her weak eyes swept past his hiding place. She took a few steps forward, paused, and sensing no danger, bent her graceful neck and delicately lapped at the clear, cold water.

Ejil rose to his feet, and with a single practiced motion, whirled the cord. Alarmed by the noise, she raised her head—too late. Ejil's missile struck her forehead just above the eyes. She staggered, the long, elegant legs collapsed, and she dropped soundlessly to the ground.

The boy's triumphal cry echoed off the surrounding cliffs. Dodging through the trees, he knelt beside the dying hind. Her legs were still twitching. She was a beautiful creature with a tiny head, long ears, and a mottled, rich red winter coat. He stroked her head. Tears slid down his cheeks as he watched the spirit slowly drain from those enormous brown eyes. Bowing his head, he asked her pardon and thanked her spirit for its sacrifice.

Ejil entered the camp in in the thickening dusk. He saw that the people were taking advantage of the thaw, building cooking fires outside their smoky huts. He was surprised to see Lada's mother and Tule's sister standing by his hut, their heads together, talking quietly.

His father, pacing in front of the hearth, saw him first. Talog's eyes widened.

He was expecting I'd bring home a rabbit. The thought warmed Ejil.

"Well done, son," Talog said, eyeing the doe. He clapped his son on the back.

From where she sat cross-legged by the fire, his mother smiled up at him. "Marvelous, my son. How did you do it?" she asked, relieving him of the kill. She picked up her handblade, placed the hind belly-up and slid the blade from under the chin, down the belly to the tail. "I'll roast a haunch tonight," she said, up to her elbow in the hind's bloody belly. "We'll smoke the rest."

"The skin is supple. It will make a nice soft jerkin for you, Mother," Ejil said, puffing out his chest.

Lette ran her hand over the hind's soft flank. "A doe's skin is always the softest." She smiled at her son.

Ejil's brow furrowed. "Where's Baal? And why are Lada's mother and Tule's sister standing there?" He had hoped that his brother would be there to watch how all eyes followed his triumphant entry into the camp with the hind draped across his shoulders.

"It's getting late and the two girls haven't returned from their gathering," his father said and resumed pacing.

"Your father sent your brother and another man down the trail with torches. They should be back soon," his mother, Lette, said.

Ejil bit his lip and squinted at the darkening sky. "I should have gone with her, Mother. She asked me to," Ejil said. He regretted his words that morning. *I was being stupid.* He shook his head. *Why do I act like that?* He and Lada had been inseparable as children. She listened to him even when the other children laughed at his crazy ideas. She understood him even better than his mother. And lately, he had begun to feel differently about her, and think about her more.

CHAPTER 3

ESCAPE

Lada pursed her lips and nudged Tule sharply in the ribs. "Shhh," she whispered, pressing a finger against the girl's lips. She raised one eyebrow. "It's time."

Tule rubbed her eyes and nodded. Lada took a deep breath, dropped to all fours and crawled slowly toward the narrow gap between the sleeping hunters and the cave wall; the hard rock cut painfully into her knees.

One of the men, the young one who had carried Tule, lay sprawled on his back with his head resting on his arm, leaving barely enough space for the girl to slither by.

Lada slowly rose to her feet and pressed herself against the cave wall. With her eyes glued to the young man's face, she raised one foot and slid her body forward. One of the sleepers snorted. Lada froze mid-step like a long-legged waterbird.

Barely daring to breathe, she waited. Her heart pounded against her ribcage.

No one stirred.

Taking a long breath, Lada lowered her foot until she touched firm ground. Two more steps would bring her to the entrance.

The sleeping hunter's chest rose and fell in an even rhythm.

Lada looked back and beckoned her friend.

Tule was frozen in a crouch, eyes bulging, her hands flat on the cave floor. She had not taken a single step.

The fire's embers glowed brightly enough for Lada to see naked terror reflected in her eyes. Tule had ever been a shy and fearful girl. Lada bit her lip. She edged back along the cave wall and stretched out her hand while nodding encouragement.

Tule dropped to her knees and inched forward.

Lada moved toward her.

Tule's unblinking eyes stared ahead vacantly.

Lada ground her teeth.

Finally, Tule rose slowly to her feet and stretched out her hand.

Lada slid closer. Their fingers touched. Tule grasped Lada's hand with a fierce strength. Silent as shadows, the pair slid along the wall toward the cave's entrance. Lada peered out into the dark night. They were almost free.

A cold breeze brushed Lada's cheek. The girl shivered. *Was it a spirit?* All sorts of evil spirits, she knew, haunted the night. She swallowed painfully. The beat of her heart reverberated loudly in her ears. *Surely, the sound will wake them.*

Lada blinked and peered out into the night. The waning moon and bright stars illuminated a landscape of stark gray and black. Nothing was familiar. Beyond the cave's entrance, the land seemed to abruptly drop off. *It's so dark. What's out there?* She cocked an ear and listened but heard nothing, just the usual sounds of the night.

Staring, she could just make out the outline of an unfamiliar ridge-line, dim in the moonlight. Her eyes searched the cold night sky. Her heart leapt! There it was: *The Father!*

She remembered soft nights lying back on her father's sleeping fur, staring up as he pointed out the pictures spread across the night sky and named each one: *The Hunter, The Warrior, The Mother.*

He kept a treasure: a small pouch filled with smooth, round, white pebbles, gathered from the streams that fed the lake. He would smooth the dirt and place a pebble to show the position of each star in the picture.

Lada squinted through splayed fingers, as she had been taught, and measured the distance between the star and the horizon. Less than two fingers' breadth! She inhaled deeply. Somehow, she would find the strength to escape these men and follow the star home.

Lada's eyes met Tule's, and she gave the frightened girl's hand a squeeze. Tule's hand was slippery with sweat, but she slid forward.

We are almost clear. We are going to make it! Lada thought.

Then Tule's eyes widened, her hands fluttered up to her mouth and she cringed backwards.

A strong hand clamped onto the back of Lada's neck and her insides turned to water. A second hand took hold and shoved her roughly toward the back of the cave.

Her heart sank. It was the scarred leader, the eyes in his shadowed face blazed like lightening. Trussed up like a captured fowl, Lada spent the remainder of the night shivering on the cave's cold hard floor.

When dawn broke, she was shaken awake. Her hands were freed and her leg bonds loosened. The Sunfather hovered, pale and cold, a touch above the horizon. Wan dawnlight filtered into the cave's shallow interior. Stiff and chilled through, she rubbed her wrists and ankles vigorously, trying to restore some life into her numbed limbs.

"Tule," Lada whispered, but Tule just stared ahead and refused to look at her. *Wonderful!* Lada thought and shook her head. *She thinks we are in for trouble, and that, of course, is my fault. If you had moved more quickly, Tule, we might have made it.*

The scarred warrior tossed a strip of cold meat into the dirt at each girl's feet. They had barely enough time to choke it down before their hands were rebound. Unlike the previous day, both were leashed; a leather cord with a slipknot fastened around their necks. One of the warriors held the other end. Tears coursed down Lada's cheeks as she stumbled along ahead of her minders. The leader took point and the last hunter brought up the rear of the short column.

The hunters set a brutal pace. The day remained gray; large dark clouds brooded overhead. Lada did her best to keep up. Up ahead, Tule fell more than once, only to be kicked and jerked to her feet by her leash, choking and coughing. At midday, the men halted by a fast-running stream. Lada, with Tule beside her, dropped to the ground and scooped up the icy water with her hands. The march resumed.

Day melted into night, and night into day. Lada's mind replayed the day of the abduction over and over again. *What if Ejil had decided to go with her? Would he have seen the strangers in time? Just as well he wasn't there—what could he have done against these men? If he had tried to defend her, they would have killed him for sure—but what if…*

Stumbling along in the late afternoon of the fifth day, lightheaded and near exhaustion, Lada detected the faint smell of smoke. The leader signaled, and the group abruptly turned off the trail. Moving swiftly, they made their way over the hard-crusted snow, zigzagging across a series of rocky hills studded with low bushes.

Topping a rocky hillside, Lada stumbled into the hunter's camp. Two long, angular granite boulders leaned one against the other, creating beneath them a narrow triangular opening to a cave. Smoke issued from a narrow crack where the boulders overlapped, and a peaked roof made a natural smoke hole. Thin strips of meat hissed and crackled on a smoking rack set above the banked fire inside the cave's mouth. The smell made Lada's mouth water.

Prodded from behind, she stumbled up to the cave's entrance, so exhausted she could barely think. People surrounded her, shouting and dancing. Men gazed curiously at her and the women formed a circle around her and Tule. They were shorter than the men, with the same broad faces, deep set eyes and thick brow ridges. *Such ugly people. What are they going to do to us?* she asked herself, peering at greasy, tattooed faces shining in the last rays of the sun. Like the men, their squat bodies were wrapped in ragged skins that reeked of rotted meat and left their arms and their legs exposed. Lada squeezed her eyes shut and prayed. *Oh, Great Mother, please protect me. Oh, Father where are you?*

She opened her eyes. Tule was crying, her arms dangled loosely at her sides while the women pinched and poked at her. Like Lada, her dark skin had gone gray with exhaustion. Tule's numb acceptance angered the women. One, her stringy, coal brown hair streaked with gray, jerked Tule's leash and shouted in her ear. The girl cringed and stumbled backward, which earned her a push followed by a hard slap across the face. Tule cried harder. The clan women capered about, making crying noises, mocking her.

A stout woman—a huge, squashed nose mashed across her face—grabbed Lada and pressed her face against hers. Eyeing her like a choice morsel of meat, the woman ran her wet tongue slowly up Lada's cheek with a great slurping noise. Lada's stomach lurched from the stink of the woman's breath, but she refused to meet her tormentor's strange blue eyes. *Great Mother save me. They are going to eat me. I'll never see my mother or Ejil ever again.* The woman flashed an evil grin, shrugged and faced the others. The clan women danced around, laughing and hugging each other.

One woman stood back in the shadows and watched. She was tiny and thin, stooped with age, made to look smaller by a deformed shoulder and humped back. Her gray-white hair, entwined with bones, dripped like twisted cords past her waist. As she came forward, the bones clacked with the sound of falling rain. Strange symbols had been daubed on her vest and etched onto her sagging cheeks and twig-thin arms.

The clan women parted like a falling tide and the cave went silent.

Ignoring Tule, the Spirit Woman's dark, deep-set eyes burned into Lada's like hot coals. A stab of fear and a long, thin finger beckoned her forward. The woman reached out a bony hand and plucked Lada's chin. Like a fly caught in a spider's web, the girl stood frozen, unable to look away. The woman raised her other hand and Scar appeared at her side.

The crone began to sign and speak, her voice like the scraping of rock across rock. The words and gestures were strange.

The people remained silent, lowered their eyes and listened.

Abruptly, the Spirit Woman stopped speaking. She turned and walked toward a narrow gap in the cave wall. Lada's eyes followed her until her form merged with the darkness. She blinked several times. Like magic, the woman had been there, and then she was gone.

Like sleepwalkers wakened from a collective dream, the clan stirred. The women hustled Lada and Tule to another chamber, deeper in the cave. A burning brand was shoved into a niche in the wall and they were left alone.

Lada squatted and gazed about her. Little could be seen in the flickering half-light but piles of bones and the dark shadow of a solid wall. Lada swallowed; her throat was dry. *What kind of bones?* she wondered. The only sounds to be heard were the echo of dripping water, the faint sound of flapping wings and the murmur of people stirring at the front of the cave.

Tule finally spoke. "This place smells awful," she said, making a face. "Are we ever going to see our people again?"

"I don't know, Tule." Lada's mind summoned up images of her hut overlooking the valley, her mother and Ejil. She tightened her jaw, shook her head to clear her mind and wiped away the tears. "I think these are the people that Breda's father calls Fish or Snakebellies, because of their pale skin, when it is his turn to tell a tale around the winter fire. You remember; it's the only story he ever tells."

"Yes, I remember. They fed him and let him go. Do you think they will let us go home, Lada?"

"Maybe," Lada said. *But then why did they take us?* she asked herself, thinking back to that awful woman's tongue. She felt herself starting to break down, but she took a deep breath and squared her shoulders. She decided to keep those thoughts to herself. *It will just set her off on another bout of crying.* Lada had had enough of crying.

Sometime later, three of the women returned. One carried a thick auroch hide; another, a dished rock with a tiny burning wick; the third, a pine-pitch torch, spitting and crackling. Lada tensed, but the women, seemingly tired of their sport, ignored the two girls. The three gathered in a tight knot at the other side of what Lada could now see was a broad, low-ceilinged chamber. They laid out the hide between them and began scraping it with hand blades.

Sitting with her back against stone, Lada was just about to nod off when footsteps jolted her awake. The man with one ear sauntered into the grotto. He halted, stood with hands on his hips and stared down at the two girls. Like a covey of quail silenced by a raptor's shadow, the clan women quieted and watched.

Lada's ears prickled. She broke out in a sweat. *What does he want*, she wondered?

One-ear glanced at the knot of clan women and flashed a wolfish grin.

Pointing a finger at Tule, he made a sign that required no translation. He was ordering her onto her hands and knees. He would mount her.

"No!" Tule screamed. Eyes darting about like a frightened hare, she searched for a means of escape. There was no place to run. She scrambled backwards, crablike, and squeezed herself tightly into a shallow niche in the cave wall.

The clan women leaped about, pointing and chattering like sparrows in a tree.

One-ear grabbed Tule's legs and pulled her, kicking and screaming, away from the wall.

"Leave her alone!" Lada yelled. Lada had almost resigned herself to her fate, but if Tule was going to fight back, she would fight too. Boosting herself off a large rock, Lada launched herself up onto One-ear's back, wrapped her legs around the hunter's waist, buried one hand in his thick hair and began beating his head with her closed fist.

One-ear danced about trying to shake her off, but Lada dug in with her fingernails. His hair was so greasy she barely hung on. He reached back. Lada felt his hand intwine itself in her hair. She screamed in pain as he took a grip and ripped her off his back. She hit hard, sprawling across the cave floor like a half-chewed bone.

His attention shifted back to Tule.

Lada caught the shadow of movement behind him.

A heavy hand fell onto his shoulder. He spun around and found himself eye to eye with Scar. The leader gazed at One-ear's raised fist and smiled.

One-ear swallowed hard. His arm dropped nervelessly to his side.

Scar watched the smaller girl scramble on hands and knees over to the other and wrap her arms around her.

The leader gazed at One-ear. His face was calm. "You heard the Spirit Woman's words?"

The atmosphere in the cave had changed. The clan women had, once again, gone silent.

"Yes, Scar."

"'Yes, Scar'?" he repeated mockingly, shaking his head. "She said that the women are slaves and will work, but are not to be mounted unless they are willing. Within three moons, they must decide. At the turning of the third moon, the warriors will choose. If a woman refuses to join with a man of the Lion Clan, she will be a slave, and any man may use her as he wills."

"This one wants me," One-ear said. He grinned and gestured toward the sobbing girl.

Ignoring the girl who glared at him, Scar cocked his head and considered the other, who was sobbing. "She does not act like she wishes to join with you, One-ear."

"They are captives. I would use her. That is the custom."

Scar gazed into One-ear's face and grinned. "You challenge me?" he inquired with a gesture.

One-ear's face darkened. "No, Scar," he gestured and dropped his eyes.

Scar's smile disappeared. "Once they have joined with a warrior these women will make babies for the clan. We wish them to do so willingly. The Spirit Woman has spoken."

"But they are Blackdogs!"

"Dig the bear shit out of your ear hole, One-ear. Come! You will tell the Spirit Woman why you refuse her orders?"

One-ear's shoulders slumped. He shook his head. "No!" he said, shaking his head. "I will honor her words."

"Good. Now, go!" Scar signed.

One-ear turned and lumbered off.

Scar squatted in front of the small girl. *How do I make her understand?* He knew only a few words in her tongue. He remembered the name he had heard the other girl call her. "No more, *Lada*" he said, struggling with the unfamiliar sound, then made the clan sign for "no."

"Thank you," she said, speaking slowly and placing a finger on her breast, "I am Lada." She raised her head up and mimicked the sign Scar had made and smiled weakly.

Scar's eyes widened and he gazed at her for a long moment. He grunted. *The witch was right. There is something about this one. She is quick and has spirit. Her eyes are open; she is trying to understand our talk.* He had an idea. *The women will show her. I will speak to Ravenhair. She will make them understand.* Satisfied with his decision, he nodded to the girl, rose to his feet and walked back toward the cave entrance.

CHAPTER 4

SEARCH & DECISION

It was just after sunset when Baal and his two companions returned from searching.

Lada, lost? Ejil felt a stab of guilt. *I should have gone with them.* He leapt to his feet. "Father, there is still some light. Let me go. Lada is my friend. I know the places where…"

Talog gazed at his second son and shook his head. "Last night the moon slept. Tonight, it is but a thin blade. You would not get three spear throws down the trail. Even the best tracker cannot find a trail in the dark. We will find our girls," Talog spoke confidently, but Ejil could hear the doubt in his father's voice. All knew well the many dangers that stalked the night.

"Did you find any sign?" Talog asked his eldest son.

Baal shook his head. His thick hair was tied back with a leather thong. "We found plenty of sign, Father, but the snow melted and has re-hardened. It is difficult to read." Baal's eyes found the short, wiry hunter who was the tribe's best tracker, "Breda believes that they were taken," he said.

The two women turned to each other. "Oh, oh, oh!" Ceda cried out and raised her arms to the sky.

Talog raised his hand for silence. "Taken? Taken by whom?"

Breda's eyes shifted from the women and focused on the Speaker. "Men took them. I am sure. Others—a party of others."

The chief's eyes narrowed. "Fishbellies? We have seen nothing of them since the time of my father."

"Are these the people your father has spoken of?" Ejil asked.

Breda nodded. "There was sign of many feet—four men, maybe five. Men with wide feet and toes, poorly shod."

Talog rubbed his bearded chin and considered. The young scout's face was still beardless.

Breda stood stiffly, staring down at the ground.

"Father, Breda is our best tracker," Ejil said.

Talog nodded, his lips pressed tight. "I must think on this," he said.

Baal scowled at Ejil. "Father, call a council. We must form a war party, find the girls and punish the men who took them."

"Baal's right, Father, there's no telling how far away they've gotten," Ejil said.

The Speaker smiled at his two sons. *They are old enough to challenge their father. How old was I when I first…?* He wrenched his attention back to the matter before him. "I must speak with the girls' fathers and consult the elders. Before this night is through, the council will decide."

A sliver of moon rose and the stars spread across the dark sky like sparks from a nightfire. The council of The Broken People gathered in the shelter of the deep cave. The cold had returned. Ejil's breath merged with the people's like woodsmoke as he joined those gathered around the flaming hearth.

The eldest men, the šamán and the hunters occupied the first row. The First Speaker and Breda's father were the only two who had killed an enemy in battle. The other men, those who had become hunters and wore the tattoos of manhood, filled in. The mature women took the second row, Ejil, Baal and the younger men behind. Girls and young children clustered in the rear.

Talog stood and held up a hand for silence. "You have heard Breda's words," the chief said. His eyes narrowed. "We have not seen a Fishbelly band in many seasons," he said.

The white hairs murmured, their heads bobbing slowly up and down.

Fishbellies? Ejil had heard the talk. *Pale skin?* He tried to imagine what such people might look like.

"Now they have come and taken our two girls. We must get them back," the Speaker said. "What does the council say?"

Baal raised his hand to be recognized. Ejil bit his lips. *Baal never misses a chance to impress the elders. All this talk wastes time. We all know what must be done.*

There was a murmur around the circle. All men, once they passed the test of manhood, and women who had had their first moon's blood were eligible to speak in council, but were expected to wait until those of their elders who wished to had taken their turn.

The Speaker hesitated; his brow furrowed. "Forgive my son. The boy is anxious to prove himself. Is there anyone among the eldermen who wishes to speak?"

There were appreciative murmurs from around the fire, but no one raised a hand.

Ejil saw Baal's jaw tighten. Though he was barely three winters older than Ejil, the beginnings of a man's beard covered a face the dark color of hearth-mud, with his father's high cheekbones and dark, brooding eyes.

"Father speaks like an old woman. We have we been at peace for so long that he doesn't see," Ejil heard Baal mutter under his breath.

Pelas shook his rattle, gazed toward the cave's entrance, spread his arms and mumbled an incantation. "Let us hear the boy's words," he said.

Ejil turned to his master in surprise. Baal leaped to his feet and held out his hand for the speaking stick. By custom, before a member could speak, he must first be recognized by the First Speaker and handed the speaking stick. The stick itself was nothing special, except that it symbolized the First Speaker's authority. It was a tradition handed down from the mother tribe.

"Why do we sit and talk?" Baal glanced around at the gathering. "You all heard Breda. Do any of you doubt his words? Tule and Lada have been taken by a band of Fishbellies. While we sit warming ourselves around the fire, the trail grows cold. Who knows where these beasts are taking our girls and what they are doing to them? I have spoken to the young men; they are ready. We must rescue our girls and drive these Fishbellies from our hunting grounds," Baal said.

"My son is a young man. And like all of the young, he is impatient," Talog said, staring at Baal. "Yes, we must act, but not rashly and not without a plan. Fishbellies are fierce warriors. This is known. The legends say that they occupied this land long before our people came. Some of our people have made war on them. If they have come this close, they have likely scouted our village. What do we know of them? How many warriors? Where are they camped? Is the camp easily defended? Where are its weak points? Before we act, we must send out scouts and bring this knowledge back to the council."

There was a murmur of assent from around the fire.

Baal stepped forward. "Father, Breda and I will go!"

The Speaker shook his head. "Breda will go; he is the best tracker. I have work for you here. Ejil will go with Breda. The boy is quick and can be as silent as a serpent."

Ejil's sat up, eyes wide open, his face beaming with pride. *Thank you, Father. I won't disappoint you.*

"Ejil?" Baal's jaw dropped open. "Father," he sneered, "Ejil is barely more than a boy."

Boy? Who was it, Baal, who killed the hind? The meat that fills your belly comes from my hand, Ejil thought, fuming in silence.

Pelas cut in. "Ambition burns in your eldest son's heart, but he has yet to prove his manhood. If someday he is to become a leader, he must learn patience. Ejil is a good choice. He knows how to use the tally stick. We must know how many warriors the Fishbellies have to send against us."

Baal snorted. His face flushed.

"Enough," the Speaker said, holding up a warning hand and glaring at his son. "The council has spoken."

The young hunter shook his head and turned to go, but Talog reached out and grasped his shoulder.

"My son!"

Ejil watched Baal set his jaw.

"You will meet my eyes when I speak!"

Baal's face darkened. His hands tightened into fists.

Ejil's breath caught.

His brother's gaze was now level with his father's. The annoyance was obvious in Baal's voice, but his father chose to ignore it.

"Baal, you will take charge of readying the young men. Make sure their spearpoints are sharp!" Talog said.

Ready the young men? Ejil watched Baal's eyes widen and his lips untwist and broaden into a wide grin, Baal bobbed his head. "Yes father, thank you. We will be ready," signaling the other young hunters to follow, he hurried off.

CHAPTER 5

SCOUTING THE ENEMY

They set out at dawn under a gray sky. Clouds obscured the sunrise. Breda cleaned his nose with a wet finger and sniffed the wind. "Good," he said, "no sign of snow."

Breda found Ejil fussing with his pack. The night before, his brother had stomped around the hut mumbling to himself, making his dissatisfaction obvious, but Ejil didn't care. He was worried about Lada. He had barely slept. He was anxious to begin the search.

Ejil securely wrapped a quantity of dried deer meat from the tribe's larders and placed it in his deerskin pack. He rolled and lashed on his sleeping fur. A cold mist rose from the valley floor. The trail would be frozen hard. Sign, what there was of it, would be hardened and easier to follow.

Breda scratched his ear and grinned. "What's that odd looking stick you are stuffing into your pack?

"An invention. I call it a sling."

"Sling? Ejil, we are going to move fast. Best to pack light," Breda said.

"Don't worry, it doesn't weigh much. It will come in handy; you'll see." Ejil ached to show Breda his invention, but now was not the time.

Breda nodded and hiked his pack on his back. "Alright, let's get going. We've got some ground to cover."

That evening the moon waxed full, Ejil and Breda stumbled into the rocky niche and the cold embers of the Fishbelly camp just before darkness swallowed the sun.

"This is a good spot, well protected. We'll camp here," Breda said, sniffing the air. He sank down onto a small rounded boulder.

Ejil sighed deeply, sat and dug into his pack. "Oof," he said, passing Breda a strip of dried meat. "My legs are on fire." He chewed silently, eyes staring vacantly ahead. Finally, he swallowed hard. "Are we far behind?"

"We've gained on them a bit, maybe."

"Maybe?"

Breda reached down, grabbed a handful of dirt, held it up and let it trickle though his fingers. "This part of the trail is dry. Sign is faint."

"I saw a pile of mammoth dung a short way back. Looked pretty dry. I'll go get some if you'll start the fire?" Ejil offered.

"Alright, but then I'm turning in. I need some sleep."

After he had the fire built up, Ejil laid out his sleeping fur and burrowed into it. He reveled in its warmth, then dropped off to sleep, remembering nothing until he felt Breda poking at him in the grey predawn. He struggled to his feet, shook himself, grabbed a handful of crusty snow and rubbed his face with it.

"How do you feel?" Breda asked, a faint smile playing around his lips.

"Like I've been stomped on by a wooly rhino."

"Too much soft living around the šamán's fire?"

Ejil grimaced and tore off a piece of deer meat with his teeth. "How close are we?"

"Hard to tell, exactly. As I said, we've gained on them a bit," Breda said. "Is this deer? Tastes more like elk."

Early that afternoon, Breda called a halt.

"I've lost the trail," he said panting. Breda began walking in circles, bent over, his nose close to the ground. The sun was barely the breadth of two fingers from the western horizon when he stopped abruptly and squatted. "Found it," he said, motioning to Ejil. "Here is where they left the trail and set off across country."

"How long ago?" Ejil asked, squatting. "We must be getting close."

Breda scratched an ear. "One sun, maybe less. We've gained some ground. I've found both girls' footprints—prints show a normal stride. The ground is softer here. If the weather holds, the sign should be easier to follow." He glanced up at the sun. "Might as well make camp," he said, pointing at a copse of thorn bush just off the trail. "The light is gone, and we must not make any more mistakes."

"So, they haven't been mistreated?"

"No injuries, from what I can tell, though they must be scared to death."

"I feel like this is my fault, Breda. That morning, Lada asked me to go with her."

"These are tough men. What would you have done against five of them?"

"I don't know. Something!"

"Gotten yourself killed, most likely."

Ejil sighed. He began looking around for wood.

"No fire," Breda said. "We'll be safe enough under those pines."

"It's gotten colder," Ejil said, rubbing his hands together.

"We're close to the Whiteface camp. Firescent can carry on the wing of the wind a half sun's walk or more. We'll put our furs together. It will be warm enough," Breda said.

"Whitefaces? I've never heard them called that."

"That's what my father calls them. You remember, when he was young, he got lost and spent a winter with one of their clans," Breda said. "He says they fear the night spirits and stick close to their fires after dark. Tomorrow night, the moon's face begins to wane. That is good and bad. We'll have to be careful. We start at first light and get as close as we can to their camp, then wait until the moon sets and move in."

"Dogs…do they keep dogs?" Ejil asked. He thought about Prat. The dog had not been happy to be left behind.

"My father says they hate dogs. They won't even eat them, and he says they will eat anything that swims, flies or crawls," Breda said. "He also told me they eat the flesh of men."

"Breda, you don't think…?" *They wouldn't…*Ejil's mind screamed. He shook his head. The idea was so horrible, he clamped his jaw tight. *I can't even think about it.*

"No, only warriors they kill in battle. They have a ceremony and eat their hearts."

"Isn't eating human flesh a great evil?"

Breda shrugged. "Who says so? Pelas? Once the spirit has left, the dead are dead. If you are hungry, you must eat or die. The Fishbellies sacrifice their enemies to the spirits. After they eat the hearts they roast the flesh. Father says the flesh tastes like bird meat."

Ejil made a face. "He ate some?"

Breda shrugged, "It was expected, and he was hungry."

"We must get close enough to count their warriors and see the camp's defenses. The council will need to know so they can plan. It should be no problem, that is, if you move as quietly as I have heard some say."

Ejil bristled. "Don't worry about me; I am light as a spirit in the dark."

"Ha, like a spirit, you say. Well, spirit boy, perhaps you will tell me about the strange pole you have brought all this way?"

"I call it a sling," Ejil said, standing up straight.

"You said that."

"I call it that because it will *sling* a rock much further than the strongest man can throw."

"Ho, ho, a mighty boast! I won the throwing contest at the last gathering, you remember," Breda said thumping his chest.

"Yes, I remember," Ejil said. "It's a secret. I will show you if you promise not to tell my brother! Is it safe? It will make some noise."

"I promise, and the Fishbellies won't hear you unless your stick can throw a stone further than a man can walk between sunrise and noon," Breda said.

Ejil snorted, slid the pole out of his backpack and rummaged around and pulled out a pouch. "I got the idea setting a rabbit snare. Watch."

Placing the rock in the woven pouch, he flicked the loop out behind him until it was fully extended. He whirled the rock around his head several times and released his thumb. The stone flew up in a high arc. Breda shaded his eyes and watched until the small missile disappeared from sight. There was a sharp crack off in the distance.

Breda stared at Ejil with his mouth open. "That is something!" he said, scratching his ear. "But can you hit anything useful with it?" he asked, cocking his head.

"I killed that hind doe by the lake from three spear throws away, the day you and Baal went searching for the girls," Ejil said.

"Good meat! Your mother gave me some. So, that is how you gained your reputation for stealth."

"Yes, well…"

"Hah, I knew it!" Breda said. He picked a louse out of his ear, examined it closely then crushed it between thumb and forefinger and placed it between his lips. "No one can creep up on a hind in winter! Will that thing throw a spear?"

"A spear?" Ejil's brow furrowed. "I never thought of that."

"At the last gathering, I heard that one of the tribes had made a tool that could throw a spear much further than any man. I spied on their camp, saw them practicing with some kind of stick. I tried to get closer, but they were camped on open ground. They spotted me and chased me off."

Mouth set, Ejil gazed at his sling, deep in thought, before making a reply. "My father thinks I'll never make a hunter."

"Has he said that?"

"No, but I can tell."

"I heard what he said about you at council. He thinks you are a good stalker. Killing that hind impressed him."

"He and my brother Baal…Hunting—that's all they think about, all they talk about most nights around the fire. They never include me. I mean, I like to hunt. A man must hunt meat to feed his family, but there are other things…"

"Like becoming a šamán and making that—what do you call it, a sling? You're a pretty good hunter. No match for me, of course," he said grinning. "Every boy gets jittery before he is tested. You'll do fine."

"You think so?"

Breda punched Ejil playfully in the shoulder. "If you can kill a deer at three spear throws with that sling of yours, there is no doubt. Look, I know you are worried about Lada. If my Mata was taken, I'd feel the same way. We'll find them tomorrow. Now, get some sleep. We leave as the dawn breaks."

"You're sure?" Ejil asked.

"Pretty sure," Breda said. "I smell something on the wind."

Ejil's eyes flickered open. "Is it morning already?" He squinted into the rising sun.

Breda squatted next to him, absently gnawing on a thick strip of deer meat. "Get up, sleepyhead," he said. "Here." He handed Ejil a strip.

Ejil squinted at the greasy meat with one eye closed. "Humm, reindeer, again?"

"Rather have a grub? I found a couple of fat ones while you were sleeping."

"Grubs? Where? They're good roasted, but raw, no!"

"No time for a fire," Breda said, "we've got to get moving."

Ejil noticed that the thick gray clouds that had followed them for several days had vanished. The vivid red and violet hues of the rising sun were smeared against the morning sky. He stood facing the horizon with his hands propped on his hips, lost in its beauty—forgetting, for a moment, his worry over Lada. "Beautiful, isn't it," he remarked.

"What? Yes. Beautiful," Breda snorted. He picked up Ejil's pack and tossed it to him. "C'mon, we've got a lot of ground to cover. Let's get moving."

The wind had picked up. The snow had hardened overnight. It was slippery in places but held their weight. They slip-slid over the hard crust, leaving little trace. The way was punctuated in places by broad expanses of bare rock where the sun's warmth had melted away the snow and the trail disappeared.

Breda stopped and stood stroking his chin. "See, see how they try to hide their tracks? Even this close to their camp. They are canny beasts."

Ejil bit his lips and slumped forward. "Any sign of Lada and Tule?" he asked.

"Yes. The Fishbelly party is moving fast. From their prints it looks like the girls are having a hard time keeping up."

"But they're alright?"

"They're still on their feet," Breda said.

Ejil pictured Lada stumbling, being prodded along, tears streaking her face. He nodded and shifted his pack. "Let's go."

Pushing on, they covered a lot of ground in a flat country thick with bushes. As the day wore on, the sun warmed, and Ejil found himself floundering knee deep in the thick, wet snow.

Finally, Breda dropped into a crouch and raised a hand. Ejil knelt beside him, his leg muscles burning.

"We are close," Breda wheezed. "You see here the print of a foot, and there," he said pointing, "men have trod. We will rest here and close in at dark."

They crawled on their bellies into a narrow hollow between two thick evergreen bushes, where there was little snow and they could rest unseen.

"Try to sleep," Breda whispered. "It's going to be a long night."

Ejil opened his eyes to pitch darkness. "What?" Breda clapped a hand over his mouth and hissed in his ear.

"Quiet!"

Darkness surrounded them in inky silence. The moon had set, but bright stars peered out of a sky shaped like the inside of a black bowl.

Flitting like shadows from rock to bush, they crested a rise and found themselves on a ridge overlooking a shadowed valley. Breda grabbed Ejil's arm, pulled him to the ground and pointed. Firelight flickered through a lattice of bare branches.

At the far side, steep walls of bare limestone rose, glowing a ghostly white in the starlight. Broad at the mouth, the cave was set in a broad dimple in the cliff face.

Flat on their bellies, Ejil and Breda peered over the ridgeline. Ejil clutched his chest. *The girls are down there, somewhere out of sight.* Ejil felt a surge of energy. From his pouch, he drew his tally stick—the flat thighbone of deer—and a flint burin and began making marks. Peering through the dying half-light, Ejil couldn't see much. The women kneeled by the fire while the men came and went. They were certainly not giants, as described in some of the ancient tales. Tongue between his teeth, he twisted the burin, cutting his marks, one for each warrior.

"I don't see our girls," Breda whispered.

"They're probably well-guarded, deeper in the cave."

"Or, in the Shadowlands!"

Ejil lay silent rubbing his chin. "Why would they steal them only to kill them?" He lowered his head and touched the ground with his forehead.

"Did you notice anything odd about the camp?" Breda asked.

Ejil shrugged and stared into the darkness.

"Several women, but I don't see any children?"

"Inside the cave?"

"Maybe, but think about our home place. Babies squalling, children running around, getting into trouble. It's too quiet."

"It's late; they're all asleep," Ejil said.

"Yeah, you're probably right. I'm getting a little jumpy. Try to get some sleep. I'll wake you. In the morning, we will see what we can see."

Below them, the fire dimmed and the camp grew quiet.

The first kick woke her from a dead sleep. Reacting quickly, Lada rolled herself up into a ball then jumped to her feet.

The woman's second kick was directed at Tule. "Up! Stinking slaves," the clan woman screamed. Tule yelped and quickly gained her feet only to be rewarded with a hard slap across the face. It was their minder, a bow-legged, thick-bodied woman with dark, angry eyes. One of the younger ones—she was quick with a shove or a slap. Tule had named her Crowbait. She had a nose like a squashed bird's beak, and long straggly hair, dark as a crow's wing.

Each day was much the same. Punched, slapped, kicked, the girls were rousted before dawn and worked until after the evening meal, but aside from the occasional poisonous glance from One-ear, neither she nor Tule had been molested by any of the men. Lada was grateful. Scar was keeping his word.

When night came and their work was finally over, she and Tule lay down exhausted on a bed of whatever they could gather up: dry grass, filthy leaves or the ratty scraps of old hides crawling with lice in the deepest part of the cave. This area was also the garbage dump, and the air was filled with a smoky haze.

Reluctantly, Crowbait would sometimes teach them some of her language. Lada suspected this had been ordered by Scar. She would point out a thing and make the sign or sound. Lada learned that failure to quickly repeat the lesson would earn her a hard slap. She was quickly picking up the rudiments of her captor's speech.

There were two meals: one at sunrise and one after sunset. They waited while the clan ate and made do with the gristly scraps of meat their captors left behind.

Tule cried herself to sleep most nights. Lada tried to keep up her own spirits, and tried to comfort the older girl, but Tule seemed to sink deeper and deeper into despair. "I don't understand, Lada, why don't they let us go. I want to go home."

At the end of the day, her mind numb, Lada lay down on her pallet and fell into an exhausted sleep. Often, waking in the middle of the night, her mind would conjure up images of home. She missed Ceda, her mother, and quite often her thoughts turned to Ejil. She thought about the times they spent together and things she had left unsaid: her feelings for him and the dreams she was beginning to have about their future together.

"Yesterday, old Crowbait screamed at me," Lada told Tule. "Then, she pointed her finger at me and used their word for joining. Be careful, she understands a few of our words. Anyway, I heard that big, scarred man, the leader, talking and gesturing to One-ear. He used the same word."

"Yuck! Wife? Slave is more like it. I'll never join with one of them. I don't care what they do to me. They are ugly and they stink. I bet they stink worse in summer. Besides, I've already decided, I am going to join with Donal. He is beautiful and I love him!"

Are we ever going to see our home again? Shut up, Lada, it's been less than a moon since we were taken.

"Donal? Does he know that?" Lada asked. She had decided it was best to keep her fears to herself.

"Not yet."

"Donal is your mother's brother's son, isn't he? That makes him your cousin. That is forbidden."

Tule stamped her foot. "I don't care. I will ask Pelas. He has the memories. What about you? Haven't I seen Palo, the flint knapper, squatting by the entrance to your hut?"

Lada snorted. "Palo? He promised father a sharpstone blade if he was allowed to court me, but mother drove him away. She says I am too young and must wait until the next Gathering. Besides, he's older than my father. It's all Father's fault, anyway. Mother says he and his brothers were as randy as cave rats when they were boys, and most of our young men are probably my cousins."

Tule covered her mouth to stifle a giggle. "What about Ejil? You two spend a lot of time whispering together."

Lada shrugged. Her eyes darted around the cave. Crowbait was nowhere near and no one else seemed to be paying them any attention.

"Lada, don't these people have enough women of their own?" Tule asked, lowering her voice to a whisper.

"Have you noticed? There are only three children, and one of the boys just mopes around. I think he's the one they call Squint-eye's son. He is thin and pale, even for them, and he looks ill."

"Maybe they don't know how to make babies," Tule said, then burst into tears. "I hope you're wrong about what you heard. When will our warriors come? I hate it here!"

Ejil watched as Breda opened his eyes, shivered involuntarily and hugged himself. It had been a cold night, and a thick mist had risen with the dawn.

"Why didn't you wake me?"

"I wouldn't have been able to sleep."

"Why not?"

Ejil rubbed both eyebrows. "Thinking about the girls."

Breda clapped one hand on Ejil's shoulder and squeezed. "You think too much. Don't worry, we'll get them back."

Ejil nodded, but said nothing. He thought about last night's dream. Someone was dragging Lada away. She reached back and held out her hands, but even running as fast as he could, she drew further and further away.

He turned his attention to the awakening camp. Two women appeared and stoked the fire outside the cave's entrance, and soon enough, Ejil felt his stomach gurgle from the rich scent of roasting meat.

Ejil's breath caught. Lada and Tule suddenly appeared, prodded out of the cave by a stout, dark-haired woman. Ejil squeezed Breda's arm. Three armed warriors and another Fishbelly woman joined them. One guard led them, single file, down a rocky path with the other two guards bringing up the rear.

Breda signed, and they slid backwards down the ridge and followed. The party passed through a rock-strewn meadow and descended into a sheltered valley, thick with trees. Breda signaled again, and they made a wide circle, approaching the defile from the far side. They scrambled up a huge boulder that overlooked the valley floor. The Fishbelly party had split up. The men stood guard while the women scattered, gathering wood. They could see the two girls working together.

"Stay here," Breda said. He slid butt first down the rock's smooth surface.

"Where are you going?" Ejil whispered after him.

"Shhh, I'm going to get close enough for the girls to see me. They're probably really scared. I want them to know *we will* be coming for them."

"Wait! I'll come with you."

"No! One man will be harder to spot. If the Fishbellies do catch me, don't wait; get back to camp as quickly as you can and tell your father what we've seen. As soon as I warn the girls, I'll double back," Breda said.

"Your spear," Ejil whispered fiercely.

Breda shook his head. "It will only slow me down." He took off, dodging through the field of scattered rocks at a trot.

Lada was gathering dry wood and stacking it in Tule's arms. A flash of movement deep in the wood caught her eye…There it was again. She blinked twice to be sure she wasn't seeing things. *Breda!* her mind screamed. *No, it can't be, how did he ever find us?* But there he was leaning against a tree, grinning.

He gestured for silence and dropped from sight.

Lada felt the thump of her heart and a warm surge of hope. She glanced toward each of the guards. They had spread out in a semi-circle and stood leaning on their spears, looking bored. She squatted, gathered a few dry sticks, walked over and stacked them on the pile in Tule's out-stretched arms.

"Tule," she said putting her mouth next to her friend's ear. "Breda is here, I saw him over there by the tree," she said, cocking an eyebrow.

Tule gazed back at her blankly, then she grinned and stared wide-eyed at her friend.

"Breda? Where?" Tule asked, her eyes searching the woods until she caught sight of the scout. "I knew it! The warriors are here. I knew they'd come to rescue us!" she said, gleefully.

"Tule, no—shush. Don't look that way. Keep your eyes away from him!" She felt her hairline break out in a sweat. "The guards will see you," Lada said, but Tule wasn't listening.

Tule dropped her load of wood and with a yelp of pleasure yelled, "Come on, Lada, let's get out of here!" She broke and ran toward the scout's hiding place.

One of the guards shouted at her, but she ignored him. He signaled the other two warriors. The one closest to Tule hefted his spear and sprinted after her.

Arms pumping, Breda broke cover and sprinted off back toward Ejil. A guard spotted him, yelled to his companion and started off in pursuit.

Lada's hands fluttered up to her mouth like a pair of panicked birds. From the corner of her eye, another shape caught her attention from atop a rock to her left. The thin figure, outlined against the bright morning sky, was familiar. Lada squinted to see better. Her heart leapt. *Ejil!* The figure raised and swung one arm. She saw a flash. *It is Ejil.*

One of the guards had caught up to Tule and thrown her to the ground. Lada's eyes darted about her, but there was no escape. Shaking uncontrollably, she froze and hugged herself, rooted in place.

The forest cover was sparse. Ejil watched his friend enter and work his way through the woods.

Unpacking his rock thrower, he took the pouch of rocks he had gathered, stood up and shaded his eyes to get a better look.

He had heard Tule's shout and saw Breda break cover, dodging through the trees like a jackrabbit. Breda was fast, but Ejil could see that the guard who had spotted him had a better angle and was about to cut him off. Quickly closing the distance, he was almost on Breda's heels.

Ejil wiped his slippery hands on his jerkin, picked up a smooth river rock and placed it into the sling's hammock. Panting with excitement, he gripped the handle, whirled the heavy pebble in a vertical arc, once, twice, three times and let fly. He bit his lip and watched.

Breda was no more than six paces ahead of his pursuer who had angled in on him.

If the Fishbelly had kept running, Ejil's missile would have missed, but he stopped and as he cocked back his throwing arm, the heavy stone struck him hard in the temple. He stumbled. His upraised arm dropped to his side and his spear clattered onto the rocky ground. Staggering like a drunkard, he collapsed, burying his face in the dirt.

Breda glanced back, turned toward Ejil and pumped his fist.

The guard who had knocked Tule to the ground now joined the race. More than three spear throws behind, he halted to examine his fallen comrade. The man lay sprawled out unmoving. Shaking his head, he resumed the chase. With a nervous hand, Ejil selected another stone and launched it, but in his excitement failed to set his stance. The missile went wide, bouncing off a rock well behind the running guard.

Cursing himself, Ejil grabbed another stone, took a deep breath and adjusted his stance. The guard was quick. He had gained some ground on the fleeing scout and was almost within spear range. Ejil's shot slammed into his neck, just below his chin, shattering his collarbone. The force drove him sideways and sent him crashing into a tree. Ejil's heart fluttered. It was all he could do to keep from jumping up and down.

The third warrior, a lumbering giant, stopped to help the first guard who had risen to his feet and stumbled about like a bird with a broken wing. The wounded man gestured him forward. The big guard resumed his pursuit.

Ejil took a deep breath, gritted his teeth and carefully set his stance. The next rock took the big man full in the mouth with an explosion of teeth.

One moment he was in pursuit, the next he was sitting upright on the ground holding his broken jaw.

Ejil jumped down from his perch just as Breda rounded the boulder.

"By The Mother," Breda gasped, bent over panting, inhaling in wheezing gasps. "That first one almost had me."

Ejil peeked around the rock to check on Breda's pursuers. Ejil's first victim was limping slowly back in the direction of the Fishbelly camp. The other two were still down. Breda slapped his back. "I thought that snaggle-toothed boar had me for sure. I saw the surprise on his ugly face!"

Ejil grinned. "Lucky throw."

"Hah," Breda said, and pounded Ejil's back. "All three! That sling of yours saved me. You've got to teach me how to use that thing. Now let's get out of here before more of those ugly bison pricks are all over us."

"Ouch, stop!" Ejil said, laughing. "The guards are out of the way. Let's get the girls!"

Breda shook his head. "No! They'll just slow us down, and once that guard spreads the word, they'll be baying after us like a pack of wolves. Tule was stupid. What's wrong with that girl, anyway?"

"Maybe she thought you had all our warriors with you."

"Yeah, maybe. Those guards are still staggering back toward their camp. So, we'll have a head start, but if we stop to gather up the girls, they'll catch us and gut us for sure."

"But—"

"Hey, they may look ugly, but you saw them run," Breda cut in, still wheezing. "We've got a good chance if we start back now. The moon will go dark before we get home. With luck, it will take them a little time to figure out who we are before they come after us."

"Breda, how can we leave those girls? Who knows what those beasts might do to them."

"You're not listening," Breda said, with a baleful look. "Right now, they're confused, and we've got a head start. But if we try to take the girls, they'll catch us for sure. I don't know about you, but I am not interested in being slow roasted over a Fishbelly fire.

"We've stuck a stick in a wasp's nest, but they will be wary. It won't be just crotch lice they'll be scratching around that campfire. Everyone jokes about dumb Fishbellies. Well, they're not stupid—or so my father says—but they see the hand of the spirits in everything. Did any of those guards spot you?"

"I don't think so."

"Good! Maybe they'll think those stones of yours came out of the sky," Breda said, spreading his arms and gazing upward. "That's big magic! Might be, they'll decide the spirits are on our side and leave the girls alone. Maybe they'll wonder if we're scouts from a big war party and are trying to draw them into a trap.

"They won't leave their women undefended. They'll send out a small party of their best runners after us. As you saw, Fishbellies are very fast on short runs, but on a long run, you and I will make them eat our dust." Breda said, bending over to ease the stitch in his side.

"I don't like it," Ejil said. "We've made them angry. I might have killed that one guard. What if they take it out on Lada and Tule? This may be our only chance to rescue them."

Breda glared at Ejil. "Look, no more arguments. We're leaving. We'll gather the men and come back for them."

Jaw clamped shut, Ejil scrambled back up to the boulder's top. It looked like the girls and the clan women had gathered into a knot. One of the guards was moving toward them.

Swallowing hard, he slid back down, picked up Breda's pack and handed it to him. "Ready?" he asked, his voice soft.

Breda eyed him silently, took a couple of quick breaths and picked up his spear. Ejil hefted his pack onto his shoulders and patted his pouch to make sure he still had a few stones. They started off at a slow trot, Ejil's rock thrower gripped tightly in his hand.

Scar stood with his warriors in a circle inside the cave, gazing down at Firespark's corpse.

The dead man lay on his back on the muddy cave floor. His woman crouched over him. Digging her fingers into a stone bowl, she smeared the corpse's naked body with a mixture of animal fat and blood-red ochre, preparing him to enter the afterworld.

The two other guards still lived. Softcheeks lay by the side of the cave. His woman tended his broken shoulder. Big Hands sat alone, cross legged in the dirt, cradling his grotesquely swollen jaw in both hands.

The two girls had been herded into the back of the cave under guard.

Scar gestured toward the two injured men. He fingered his chin. His scar always stood out in livid red when he was angry. His cold eyes flashed. "Three clan warriors against one Blackdog!" His hand made the sign signifying failure. Why?"

Softcheeks shrugged. "It was a bolt from the sky," he said, scowling while his woman rubbed her cheek against his injured shoulder. "Why did we take those girls?" His free hand made the sign that meant *bad*. "I knew it would bring trouble."

Scar hawked and spit on the ground. "Ho, Softhead you sang a different song when we found them."

Softcheeks shook his head. "Maybe, but that was what I thought." The clan had named him Softcheeks because, unlike his brother warriors, whose cheeks and chin were covered with a briary beard, his were smooth, pink and hairless.

"Young men need women," a gray-haired warrior said.

"Aye, but it will bring war," another said.

"War has come!" Grayhair's hands formed the sign.

"Blackdogs attacked us? I saw nothing! The spirits sent that stone," Softcheeks said, gazing nervously upward.

"Yes, Blackdogs," Grayhair said, his hand waving Softcheeks's words away. "They wanted the girls."

"I saw only one. The big girl was hopping around like a rabbit. Maybe she called a spirit," Softcheeks said.

"Then the Witch Woman must conjure a more powerful spirit," Grayhair gestured.

Scar's gaze shifted to each of his men in turn. "Grayhair speaks wisely. The Blackdog scouts have found us. I know them. They will go back to their camp. They will talk. They are mighty talkers. When they run out of talk, they will gather their spears and come."

Scar let his eyes play over the group. "Who comes with me to seek the Spirit Woman's council?" his hands asked.

The men dropped their eyes and stood silently, shifting their feet and looking anywhere but at their leader.

Grayhair shook his head. "Her cave smells bad and her eye is stern. I will wait for the leader's decision."

"Scar should go," One-ear said.

"Ho! One-ear fears the Spirit Woman will cast a spell and make him a slimy lizard," Scar said.

"He smells like one already," Grayhair said, slapping the younger warrior's shoulder.

"I will speak to her. She will conjure spells, spells more powerful than Blackdogs' magic," Scar said.

"Why wait for them? Attack them now before they are prepared for war," Grayhair said.

"Yes, we will take their women and kill the men," Scar said. "Those that do not breathe cannot make magic."

"Firespark no longer breathes. Big Hands and Softcheeks cannot fight. What of their flying spears? If we give the girls back, we will not have to fight," One-ear said.

"Your ear holes are stuffed with bison shit, One-ear," Scar signed, sneering. "We have watched these Blackdogs. Flying spears? Have you ever seen flying spears? They are lies told to frighten children. While you whimper like a girl, the Spirit Woman prepares her spells. She will defeat the Blackdogs' magic. We will surprise them in their camp. Blackdog blood will slake the spirits' thirst."

The warriors exchanged glances, but no one spoke or made sign. Scar grinned wolfishly at them and fingered his lion's tooth. "Go! Take up your war clubs, your spears and axes. When the sun is gone, we dance the sacred dance. When the Sun Spirit rises, the Lion Clan goes to war!"

The men began to disperse. Scar placed his hands on the shoulders of two young warriors, signaling them to remain behind.

The appearance of Breda and Ejil had made Lada's heart soar. *They have come to rescue us,* she felt sure. Then everything happened so fast. Ejil stood high on the rock and twisted his arm and the guards fell. *Was it some new magic Pelas taught him?* Then, suddenly, Fishbelly warriors, armed and angry, surrounded the girls and they were herded back to the cave.

"Where are our men? I can't believe Breda and Ejil came alone," Tule said.

"No one saw us taken. Naturally they'd send out scouts to see what happened. Breda is our best tracker. Talog probably sent Ejil with him to find us." *Ejil came to find me.* The thought filled her mind. It made her happy. *But where did you go? When will you come back? Please hurry!*

"It's all my fault," Tule said and started to sob, drawing Lada out of her reverie. "Why am I so stupid? I got so excited, Lada. I thought our warriors were already here."

Lada stamped her foot. "Tule! Stop, please! Crying won't help. Start thinking about what you do. What if Breda and Ejil were captured or killed? How would you have felt then?"

Tule's sobs grew louder. Lada shook her head, folded her arms across her breast and leaned her back against the cave wall.

CHAPTER 6

WITCH WOMAN

Scar took a side passage and entered the Spirit Woman's chamber. The crone sat hunched above her fire. Lamps, wicks of twisted reeds dipped in deer fat, burned in niches around the walls, but did little to dispel the gloom or the cave's smell of herbs and must.

She raised her head, her eyes narrow slits. "So, my son, you have not visited my hearth in many times the moon's coming. Now you are a great man. You avoid my fire. Have you come seeking the spirits?"

Spirits? What are these spirits? Scar had always wondered. *She taught me that they are everywhere. In the lakes, the rocks, and in the trees. Everywhere. And, that the most powerful spirits rule over the Caves of the Fallen, where a warrior's shade dwells, and the men he slew in battle serve him and sing of his deeds.* All this the old woman had taught him. *But in all the many seasons of my life,* he thought, *I have never once seen a spirit.*

It was dark and dank, and sounds echoed from the cave's deep recesses. No clan dared enter unless summoned. But for Scar, the place held few secrets. In their wandering, the clan had visited this campsite when he was a boy. He had lived with his mother. The cave had, for short periods, been his home. Despite her warnings that angry spirits dwelt in its depths, on the dark cold days when the Ice Demon held the Sunspirit in thrall and no one ventured outside, he had explored its labyrinthian depths.

Once, while exploring, he had entered a deep chamber. Raising his pinewood torch high above his head, his eyes searched the darkness. "Spirits of the cave," he shouted. "Here I stand. I do not fear you. If you exist, show yourselves!" He smiled with the recollection. The cave had remained silent, and he had emerged untouched.

"The Spirit Woman knows why I have come." His hand clutched his lion's tooth.

The old woman slowly shook her head. "Come, come, my son. Sit! I have made a brew. It will make you strong. You must be strong for what is to come. Let us speak as we did when you were a boy."

"I am no longer a boy. I am a man. I come to you as leader of the clan."

"Very well," she said peering up at him. "You are a man. You have taken the Blackdog women. They will make war to get them back, and you fear their magic."

Scar bristled. He inhaled, expanding his chest. "I fear no man," he said. "I come to ask you to use your gift. That is all."

"Your father was wise. He feared the Blackdogs."

"My father's hands shook and he whined like a dog! He let the Blackdogs push the clan into the Ice Lands."

"There are many of them and few of us."

"Yes, and my father, your husband, no longer breathes. His flesh rots in the ground. I say we take the Blackdog women to make babies. We will strengthen the blood and make the clan strong."

The old woman stood. "You are not wrong; our people's blood is weak." Shambling past, her hand made a quick gesture above the fire. The flames shot up; their long-fingered tendrils stretched upward clawing at the darkness. Bone-white and blood-red figures of mammoths, lions and bison leapt off the cave walls.

Scar sneered. "Hah," he snorted, thumping his chest. "Save your tricks to frighten the women," he signed with a flick of his hand. He settled himself facing her across the fire.

Though he had seen this trick often and knew of the pictures, still, the sight of them—moving, almost alive in the flickering light—sent a twitch of fear down his spine. *Had the spirits made them?*

He fingered his lion's tooth. He had found it, one day, buried in the dirt below one of the pictures. It had taken him a while to work out the reason for the hole near its top. *Who made the hole? Spirits? A Blackdog?* Finally, he had cut a thin cord and suspended it from his neck. "Who made the pictures?" he had asked, but the witch would never answer. *For all of her wisdom*, Scar thought, *she does not know.*

Mumbling to herself, the old woman stooped and ladled a steaming green liquid into two delicate cups, each fashioned from the crown of a baby's skull. She gazed slyly sideways at her son.

"One man has stopped breathing, and two are useless," she said, handing him the cup. Behind the crone's right shoulder, the hollow eye-holes in the skull of a long-toothed tiger—the clan's totem—stared from a niche in the rough wall, the color of bison's milk.

Scar raised the cup and sipped. "Yes, Firespark has fallen, Big Hands and Softcheeks cannot fight, but they will recover," he said.

"They chased one man?"

"A Blackdog spy. He found our camp. Firespark staggered back to the cave. When he made words, his body shook. He fell to the ground. Blood foamed from his mouth and his breath stopped," Scar said.

"Did you see a wound?"

"Only a bruise on the side of his head."

"This is powerful magic! A Blackdog šamán has conjured a dark spirit." She drew a sign in the air. "It will take a mighty spell."

"Can you beat the Blackdog magic?"

She shrugged shoulders thin as bat bones.

Scar snorted. "You speak to the spirits?"

"Yes, I speak to them, but have you forgotten my teaching?" she asked, glaring across the fire. "I serve the spirits. I do not rule them. I feel their anger. Only heart's blood will soothe them."

Scar swallowed hard. Sweat broke out along his hairline. *Heart's blood! So, that is how it must be?*

From a sheath at her waist, she drew a long, slender knapped blade, set in a handle carved of mammoth tusk. She held it up in the firelight and gazed at Scar. Cackling, she drew its edge along her tongue then spat the blood into the fire.

His eyes widened as he watched it glitter, scintillating like a starry sky. *Black sharpstone!* His mouth went dry. *She taunts me.* His hands itched to touch, to possess it. Nothing matched the sharpstone blade. It would slice through a man's throat or open his chest before he knew the pain.

"The two warriors. A spirit struck them down. They must be sacrificed. The spirits demand it," she said.

Two warriors? Two fewer fighters. I should have known. He shrugged, *but I did know. The spirits demand what they always demand: blood, always blood.* He gazed into the fire. *What good will it do to argue? A man cannot fight the spirits. If new babies are born, I will lead a stronger clan and the sacrifice will be worth it.* He sighed and bowed his head. "It shall be as the spirits command," his hand gesture said.

"Good!" the crone cackled. She had read both the fear and the lust in her son's eyes.

"The spirits have chosen, but the sacrifices must be prepared. Tonight, before the Sunspirit flees, bring the men here to me," she signed. "I tell you this: if you attack the Blackdogs, kill the men and the boy children. Find their šamán and kill him. All must die! There must be none left to rowse the spirits against us," she said, her mad eyes glittering like sharpstone in the firelight.

CHAPTER 7

SAVAGE EUCHARIST

The cave had been abuzz with activity since early morning. At first, Lada thought it had something to do with them—the appearance of Breda and Ejil. But after gnawing on a breakfast of the leavings, she and Tule were set to sweeping the area around the firepit at the front of the cave. Once they finished, they were shooed into the back of the cave and mostly ignored.

"What are they doing?" Tule asked in a whisper, her eyes wide.

"Preparing some sort of ceremony, I think," Lada said.

"Oh, The Mother save us! They are going to eat us. After what happened, that warrior dying and—"

"Shhh, Tule, keep your voice down," Lada cut in. "You're being silly."

"Really? How do you know?" Tule whined.

Lada shrugged. The clan began gathering around the hearth. "Let's get closer and watch," she said.

Tule's eyes bugged out. "No! Don't be crazy, Lada. I'm going to find a place to hide," she said. Shaking her head, she clutched her arms to her chest and backed away.

Ignoring Tule, who retreated deeper into the chamber, Lada moved toward the cave's main chamber—as close as she dared. Busy at their tasks, nobody noticed her. She pressed herself into a narrow, shadowed niche and watched.

Night dropped like a black shroud. The members of the Lion Clan formed two circles, with the men closest to the fire. Except for a ragged skin skirting their waists, they were naked. As Lada watched, two large bowls appeared. The bowls were passed around the circles, and each warrior and each of the women drank. *Honey water?* Lada wondered. The potent drink, made from fermented honey, fruit and herbs, was sometimes shared by the men of her own people. From somewhere deep in one of the side tunnels, drums started beating.

Scar stood to one side. Lada watched the smooth muscles of his chest ripple in the firelight. He drank nothing. His face, like those of his men, was painted with red ochre. There were black slashes across his cheeks. He leaned against the wall with his arms crossed.

Lada had not seen much of the scarred leader. At first, he seemed to always be nearby, but since the passing of the full moon, he had become standoffish. She wondered about the change.

The warriors began to dance. In the leaping flames, their pale painted faces glowed hideously, and the grotesque symbols daubed across their bodies stood out against their skin. Snake rattles ringed their ankles. Sitting in a circle, the women chanted, slapping their thighs, beating time. The pace of the drumming increased. The dancers threw up their arms, brandishing spears in pantomime, slashing at their enemies, casting huge gyrating shadows against the cave walls.

The drum boomed like approaching thunder. Lada felt her excitement rise with the rhythm of the dance. She swallowed hard, her throat dry as dust. Sweat gleamed on thick muscled bodies. The tempo increased. The drums grew louder. The dancers' feet pounded against the hardpacked earth. As abruptly as it had begun, the drumming stopped. The women stopped beating time. The men stood still, chests heaving. All was quiet. Lada's shoulders slumped forward. Her chest heaved. She bent forward trying to catch her breath.

The twittering notes of a bone flute announced her coming. The Spirit Woman emerged from the gloom of the deep cave and stepped behind a flat-topped boulder that stood like an altar behind the hearth.

The site of this malevolent old woman made Lada's heart beat faster. Scar joined the Spirit Woman and stood at her side.

A pair of standing warriors dragged one of the injured guards into the firelight. It was the young one with the hairless cheeks. Two others hustled the big warrior, stumbling forward. To Lada, the men seemed numb. They stood naked, tottering, arms draped over the shoulders of warriors, standing at either side. Their eyes shone brightly. Pale faces and bodies daubed in black. A thick stripe of red ochre crossed their chests. *What are they going to do to them,* she wondered?

The drums resumed, the tempo slow and measured like a beating heart. The Spirit Woman signaled, and the big man was dragged before the altar-rock. Holding her palm under his chin, the crone blew a puff of dust into his face. With the watching clan, Lada gasped as the big body slumped. His head fell backwards, his tongue lolled out and his eyes rolled up, exposing the whites. The two attendants lifted and laid him on his back. His upper body draped itself across the boulder, his chest bowed outward by the rock's rounded face. Lada's hands flew up to her mouth. She began to shake uncontrollably.

Spreading her arms, the crone raised her eyes—eyes set deep beneath her brow ridge, outlined in black; eyes that spit fire. Her hair fell about her waist in a cascade of straggly tendrils. Her voice rose, making sounds in a tongue Lada had never heard before. She called forth the spirits.

A long, thin knife appeared in her hand, poised above the hunter's massive chest. The slim, black blade glittered wickedly. The flute screamed. The flames leapt. In a single motion, the dagger fell, slashing through flesh and sinew. It gashed open the chest cavity like a gapping red mouth. The victim's head dropped to his chest and his mouth sagged as the crone's thin hand snaked inside and long, gnarled fingers tore out his living heart. With a cry of triumph, the Spirit Woman thrust the pulsing trophy high above her head. The people moaned as blood gushed from the organ; a web of rivulets, black in the firelight, ran down her arm.

Mesmerized, all watched as one as the blood flowed like the spring flood across the dead man's chest, down the sides of the boulder, and gathered in shining black pools at the foot of the altar. Scar held a skull cup against the rock until the warm liquid overflowed.

The young one came next. Eyes wide, Lada cringed, her chest heaving, she pressed herself back into the shallow niche. *Oh, Great Mother, if they will do this to their own people, what will they do to us?*

The Spirit Woman's dagger rose and fell again in its grisly arc. A forest of hands sprung up and the people shouted. Lada covered her eyes.

The drums began again. Lada watched, hands clutching her throat as Scar drew his handblade and sliced the bleeding organs as, one by one, the warriors left the circle and kneeled before the altar. The crone placed a bloody cut from the still-warm organ on the tongue of each and raised a hand in grisly benediction as each warrior sipped from the skull cup washing down the meat with his brother's blood.

Exhausted, her stomach turning, eyes vacant as a sleepwalker, Lada stumbled back into the cave. The images of the horror she had witnessed replaying in her mind. *These are not people,* she thought, *they are demons.*

CHAPTER 8

HESITATION

As the Sunfather awakened, The Broken People gathered in council. Ejil's parents' eyes glowed with pride as Breda stood and recounted how their son had downed three Fishbellies and saved him with his sling. After Breda finished speaking, Talog beckoned the scouts forward and laid a hand on each of their shoulders.

"This was well done," he said, turning to face the seated tribe. "My son, Ejil, is now a blooded warrior!"

"Thank you," Ejil said, preening in the glow of his father's praise. Breda grinned at him and slapped his back. Out of the corner of his eye, he caught a glimpse of Baal glowering at him, but Baal turned away. *What is it with my brother? Why can't he be proud of me?* Ejil asked himself.

The people pounded the ground or slapped their thighs and gave voice in salute to the tribe's youngest warrior.

Remember, older brother: it was I who was first to be blooded, Ejil thought.

"Were you followed, Breda?" the speaker asked.

Breda nodded. "Yes, a small party trailed us, but we left them in our dust," he announced in a proud voice.

Ejil nodded and smiled. *You have a right to be proud, my friend.* Breda was Baal's age and was already acknowledged as the tribe's best tracker.

It felt good to think that he and Breda had connected. *I've made a real friend.* The thought warmed him.

"Hah, they crawled back to their camp to lick their wounds," one man said. Others murmured their agreement.

Catya stood and held out her hand for the speaking stick. She was a tall woman with a dark cloud of curly hair hovering above her thin face, and dark eyes that were rimmed with red. "What about my sister, Tule? Have those beasts hurt her?"

Breda stood. "Both girls were alive and unhurt when we last saw them. They seemed fine, but after we left…?" Breda shrugged. "I don't know."

Catya stamped her foot. "Why didn't you bring our girls home?"

Talog placed a restraining hand onto Breda's shoulder. "I sent them to scout, Catya. If they had tried to rescue the girls, they all would have ended up captives and we would know nothing."

Catya opened her mouth, but then lowered her head and sat.

"We know where they are camped. Why do we sit here and talk?" another man asked.

"We must kill a few of these animals," Baal shouted. "They will learn to fear us."

"How many warriors?" the Speaker asked, pointedly ignoring the two outbursts.

Ejil handed his father his counting stick. "These are all we saw. There are more than all the fingers of four hands," Ejil said.

"Less one or two," Breda said, grinning at his friend.

Talog studied Ejil's count. "They have more men," he said.

"Yes father, they do," Ejil said.

Baal stood up and pounded his fist on his chest. "There may be more of them, but we are the better fighters," he yelled gazing around.

Talog stared balefully at his eldest son. "How often must you be told, Baal! Before you speak, you must ask for the speaking stick," he said.

Baal sat down. Ejil suppressed a smile.

Breda's father rose. His face was haggard, his shoulders slumped. He held out his hand for the speaking stick.

"You all have heard my story many times. As a boy, I spent an Ice Season in the camp of a Fishbelly clan. I was on a hunting trip with my father. It was late in the season of the Painted Leaves. We were foolish to tempt the gods, but game had been scarce, and we needed meat.

"The third morning we awoke to a wolf's-wind howling down from the Ice Lands. The first blizzard of the season was upon us. In our haste to find shelter, my father and I were separated. I said a prayer to the Great Mother, and she took pity." He paused and shook his head slowly back and forth. "But I never saw my father again.

"Frozen and nearly blind, I stumbled upon a Fishbelly fire. They took me in and—in their rough way—treated me kindly. I joined their hunts, and I tell you they are skilled hunters and tough fighters."

"A spear in the guts will slow them down," one of the young men shouted.

Breda's father slowly shook his head. "They are powerful men. They ignore pain. I saw one hunter, his arm almost ripped from his shoulder by a cave bear, get up, grab a spear and fight the beast one-armed. It is best to meet them with long-shafted throwing spears. I say this meaning no disrespect to any here, but fighting chest to chest, I know few who could stand against one of them," he said.

Baal snorted, mumbling to himself.

Ejil's mother stood. Her tightly braided hair marched in rows from her forehead to the nape of her neck. As the First Speaker's woman, she led the Women's Council.

"There has been much talk," she said, accepting the speaking stick from her husband's hand, "but we have yet to hear from our šamán. Has he read the signs? Will the Venerable Pelas tell us what the spirits foretell?"

All eyes focused on the old man, his dark face wrinkled like the cracked mud of a dry stream bed. Pelas had always been šamán, as had his father and his elderfather's father, back to a time long past remembering. He thrust his long wooden staff onto the floor and struggled to his feet.

With a fringe of hair, white as a fresh snowfall, circling above his ears, his bare, black skull glowed in the firelight. His beard was long and streaked with gray like the last snow of a long winter. He wore breeches and a belted tunic. A cape of tanned deerskin trimmed with fur mounted his stooped shoulders. Necklaces of mammoth bead, tiger tooth and bear claw, layered down his shrunken chest. His crooked staff, topped with the carved head of an eagle, glowed with the rich patina of great age.

"I have consulted the gods, but the signs are confused, their meaning unclear. Many will die. This much I can see, but little more.

"The Fishbellies were here, on this land, long before our people came. The story of the Great Journey has been sung many times around the winter fires. We came in peace, and they left us in peace, but over the years things have changed. There have been many conflicts with our people." The old man shook his head sadly. "Now we have little choice," he said, shaking his staff. The skulls rattled. "The tribe must prepare for war!"

Ejil's mother snorted and shook her head. "Signs and shadows! Is that all the venerable one can tell us?" she asked.

"The gods speak as they will," Pelas said. He leaned forward and shook his staff. The tiny bird skulls attached to its top clacked together with a sound like flapping wings. "For them we are like dust. They do not quake in fear, as we men do," he said, a sly smile playing about his lips, "before the demands of women."

Several of the men chuckled softly.

Ejil smiled. He was used to Pelas's way of talking.

Lette slowly shook her head, folded her arms and waited as Pelas planted his staff and lowered his body ponderously to the ground.

"Ha! War is a grave decision. The women must speak together before a decision is made. That is the custom," she said, ignoring the men's amused faces. "We will meet again after the sun rises."

"Another sunrise," Baal asked. "What if they come? We need time to prepare," he said.

"They have scouted our camp," Breda said.

"That may be so, but you yourself said you left them far behind," the Speaker said. "The Fishbellies are tough, but they are hardly men at all. I too visited one of their filthy camps, many seasons past. They cannot even speak, and who can understand their hand talk. They never do things quickly. It will take many sunrises for them to prepare for war, if they come at all. We will send men and block the trailhead. If there is sign, they will send back a runner. When the Sunfather rises the council will come together and decide."

Ejil watched as his father surveyed the men sitting in the first row around the fire. The council acted by consensus. The Speaker knew his people. As his eyes swept over the group, Ejil noted a chorus of nods.

"What of the back trail?" someone asked. It was narrow, difficult and dangerous at night, and for those reasons, rarely used.

Ejil pulled out his sling. "Father, let me go! There are places along the trail where only one man can pass at a time."

Talog waved him on. "Go!"

Breda stood up.

The Speaker grinned. "Go!" he said and waved a hand in dismissal.

Breda hefted his spear and fell in step with his friend.

Ejil heard Breda's father mumble something. The old man dragged himself to his feet. He was shaking his head.

CHAPTER 9

ATTACK

The Fishbelly war party set out in the gray mist of the following dawn. Ignoring the groans and bleary eyes, Scar set a grueling pace and kept it up until it was too dark to see. They arrived at the trail leading to the Blackdog camp, two sunsets behind Breda and Ejil.

Scar led his exhausted warriors off the trail at dusk. They hid themselves behind a rocky outcrop in a forest glade thick with pines. They were about halfway up the trail toward the Blackdog camp. The place was familiar. This was the glen where they had found the Blackdog girls. Leaving his warriors sprawled out on a soft bed of pine needles—sleeping where they fell—Scar returned to the trail.

It was full dark by the time he settled himself behind a thicket of ferns in the shadow of a large boulder. High up in the cloudless sky, the thin blade of the Moonspirit cast a feeble light across the narrow path. Something pricked his ear. He rotated his head and sniffed the breeze. *Blackdogs! Not far off!*

From his hiding place, Scar watched the enemy's shadows as they flashed by his hiding place. *These Blackdogs make more noise than a boar, snuffling roots. They think guarding the trail is enough to keep them safe, but we are ahead of them and the night hides any sign of our passing,* Scar thought, nodding his head with satisfaction.

Scratching his cheek, Scar visualized the Blackdog camp: banked fires; children reluctantly stopping their play; men crawling into sleeping furs. *Before the Sunspirit shows his face, we will show them. Now I must sleep!* He eased himself back against the rock and closed his eyes.

Her head was thrown back, her face contorted in a rictus of pain. Pale lips curled back against a row of white teeth. Her mouth formed around a soundless scream. It was his mother's face. Ejil watched helplessly as the cold spearpoint pierced the soft flesh beneath her ribcage and the blood flowed.

The camp erupted in chaos. The attack came from upwind. Specters emerged out of the early morning mist, stabbing and smashing with spear and club. Half asleep, the people staggered from their huts. Dogs barked. Women screamed. Clubs rose and fell, cracking skulls open like acorns. Babies were spitted and raised up on spears quivering like fish. Ejil saw his father and his brother Baal, standing side by side, holding off a pack of Fishbelly warriors who ranged about them like ravening wolves.

Ejil's eyes flew open. His chest heaved. His body was covered in sweat. The first rays of the early morning sun streamed through the tangle of bare branches high above the trail. His eyes darted about frantically, not recognizing the place where he lay. The shrieks of the dying echoed in his ears.

"Where am I?" he shouted Then he remembered; he was on the back trail that led to the camp.

Breda sat back on his haunches gazing at his friend. "Bad dream?" he asked, frowning.

"Dream? Yes! I mean no; it is not a dream, Breda. It's real! I saw it! The Fishbellies are attacking our camp!"

Ejil leapt to his feet. "This is happening now! Somehow, they slipped by our trail guards and surprised the camp. Come on! We've got to help them," Ejil said, and sprinted off in the direction of the camp.

Spears poised, with their backs against the cliff, Baal and Talog thrust and feinted, desperate to keep the attacking warriors at bay.

Spears bristled, threatening them from all sides. Though this was Baal's first battle, he was young and strong and had practiced hard. He was ready. His father's back pressed hard against him, and he felt the ragged breathing. Exhausted, he was drenched in sweat. Blood leaked from many small wounds.

From the corner of his eye, Baal glimpsed a tattooed warrior facing off against his father. Bending forward at the waist with his spear held straight out, the broad chested fighter, teeth bared, skipped in and out, probing Talog's defense.

The Fishbellies had attacked boldly, easily slaughtering several waking men. But with three of their number sprawled in the dirt at their feet, they had learned a wary respect for the two dark-skinned warriors. Young and obviously anxious to prove himself, another young clan fighter shouted his war cry and rushed the speaker.

With a single practiced motion, Talog parried the inexperienced fighter's thrust. Deflecting his blade upward, he ducked under and stepped inside his attacker's defense. The young warrior jerked back his spear, but not quickly enough. Talog's vicious thrust pierced the soft skin beneath his ribcage and buried itself deep in his gut.

The man's eyes flew open wide and he staggered back, the speaker's spear lodged deep in his bowels. Talog tugged at his spear trying to retrieve it, but the frenzied warrior grasped the shaft, screamed and fell forward, tearing the weapon from the speaker's hands.

Now unarmed, Talog jumped back, slamming against a rocky outcrop. Father and son now faced their enemies side by side. With desperate fingers, Talog tore at the rawhide lacings to release the heavy stone-headed mace lashed to his belt.

Seeing his chance, a one eared warrior darted in from an angle and with a quick jab buried his spear into Talog's exposed side. Seeing his father's distress, Baal felt a stab of pain and gritted his teeth as his father staggered, hands still clutching at his war hammer.

The Fishbelly warrior ripped his spear from Talog's body and with both hands slashed across his throat with its knapped edge. Great gouts of blood fountained from his wound and flowed like a red tide down Talog's bare chest.

It happened so fast; Baal could do nothing to help. He saw his father stagger and crash to the ground like a fallen tree. His heart thumped and his spirit screamed, but he dared not take his eyes from the enemies who ranged about him like snarling wolves. Nostrils flaring, he bared his teeth and thrust right and left, slowly giving ground.

Baal's chest heaved. Strands of curly black hair lay plastered across his forehead. A gash in his left breast and another across his thigh oozed gore. Six men now, one his own father's bloody corpse, sprawled across ground, muddy from the carnage. Baal snarled and shook his spear, beckoning his attackers forward. The Fishbelly fighters growled and snapped like curs, but none dared come within range of the young fighter's dripping spear.

Baal snatched a few quick breaths just as a broad, hideously scarred Fishbelly warrior shouldered aside the men surrounding him. The man carried a heavy, flint tipped thrusting spear. The two warriors' eyes met.

The man pointed at Baal and thumped his chest. Baal nodded, accepting the challenge. He inhaled deeply, pushed the hair back from his eyes and stepped cautiously forward, ready to close with his enemy. The other Fishbelly warriors receded like the tide, clearing a space for the two fighters.

The two circled, eyes locked, spears probing, each seeking an opening but carefully protecting the brittle flint points. They were well matched!

Baal, taller and lankier with long-corded thews, had the advantage of reach. The Fishbelly was shorter, broader—a compact mass of bone, sinew and muscle.

The mist had cleared. Breasting the cliff on the opposite side of the valley floor, the early rays of the morning sun now shone full into Baal's face. He squinted and tried to circle away from the bright orb, but the Fishbelly grinned and held his ground.

Partially blinded, Baal shook his head to clear the sweat from his eyes, then without a pause, launched a frontal attack. The scarred warrior slipped sideways; saved by his tigerish swiftness as the point of Baal's spear passed within a hairsbreadth of his chest. Baal pressed his superior reach forcing the Fishbelly fighter to back closer the cliff's edge.

Eyes bright, the man parried. Baal saw that he was positioning himself for a counterattack. He flicked out his spear point like a serpent's tongue to keep the man off balance and force him backward.

The warrior crouched. Baal prepared himself to block, but the Fishbelly grasped his spear shaft in both hands and leapt forward, surprising Baal with a two-handed block that forced his spear skyward. With cat like grace, his enemy again dropped into a crouch and slashed right, the point of his spear ripping a long, shallow trench across Baal's bare chest. Blood spurted! The pain drove Baal back, giving his enemy space to maneuver.

Blood dripped from Baal's wounds. His breath came in short wheezing gasps. Squinting into the sun, his out-thrust spear trembled in his hand. *He's a much better fighter,* he thought. The sour taste of fear flooded his throat. The next attack, he knew, could finish him.

Gritting his teeth, Baal abandoned all caution. He tore the short-handled war hammer from his belt and leveled his spear. Bellowing like an angered bull auroch, he charged forward in a last-ditch effort to spear his enemy or force him back and over the cliff.

The scarred warrior sidestepped and spun, deftly avoiding a bone-crushing blow from Baal's hammer. Baal stumbled past his enemy. Scar grasped his spear in both hands, spun and struck Baal hard across the back, propelling him toward the cliff's edge. Baal staggered once and, with a guttural cry, tumbled over the edge.

Scar stood bent over at the edge of the cliff, panting, a hand on each knee, gazing down at Baal's prone body, head and arms dangling off the edge of a stony outcrop partway above the valley floor.

"Good fight!" One-ear said gazing down Baal's prostrate body. "Does he live?"

Scar shook his head and scowled. "He was a strong fighter, but no man can fall so far and still breathe! His shade will await me in the Caves of the Fallen."

Killing done, Scar and his warriors searched the bodies and dug through the remains of the huts, seeking weapons and plunder.

"Take what you can carry. Make sure the men and babies no longer breathe. We will gather the Blackdog women and burn the camp," Scar ordered. "We will bury our warriors along the trail. Each man will take at least one woman. We go!"

CHAPTER 10

AFTERMATH

The sun was a handsbreadth above the horizon. Ejil and Breda halted, panting at the edge of camp, and stared at the remains of what had been their home. Bodies were strewn like fallen leaves across the muddy earth. Dirty smoke curled from the ashes. The dead lay as they had fallen. Some had fought back, but surprise had been so complete that most were slaughtered as they emerged sleepy eyed from their huts.

Ejil ran in the direction of his family's hut. His stomach clenched. He doubled over in pain, beating his fists against his thighs. "Mother!" he cried, but she did not answer. Her body lay faced down, naked in a dried pool of her own blood, outside the hut's smoking remains. "Mother!" he cried again, kneeling, tears streaming down his cheeks. "What have they done to you?"

With gentle hands, he rolled over her still-warm body. There was a deep, livid gash across her throat. The blood had begun to crust around the wound's mouth. He stroked her forehead and stared into her sightless eyes. "Mother, come back, please come back," he whimpered. He remembered those eyes as they had been: stormy blue and vibrant with life. He stroked her brow as tears rolled down his cheeks, pressed her eyes closed and wailed.

He sat stroking her fine hair until Breda placed a hand on his shoulder and shook him.

"My father is over there," Breda said, pointing. His eyes moist and red-rimmed from crying. "He took a spear in the back. Never even touched his weapons. Those cowards cut him down as he crawled out of our hut. My mother and baby brother died beside him.

"Ejil, they crushed my brother's head with a rock. Such a tiny thing," he said. "I touched his little hands," he said, gazing down at his own hands. "I can't find Mata. I can't find any of the younger women and girls. The Fishbellies must have taken them. The men, the young boys, the babies and the eldermothers and fathers, all have gone to the Shadowlands."

Ejil, tears overflowing and choking on the pain in his throat, stood silently. The horrible shrieks he heard in his dream haunted him, he could hear them still.

Breda wiped his eyes and stood up straight. "My mother had father's broken spear in her hand. It was bloodied. She must have taken one of those beasts with her. Did your dream tell you where they took our women?"

Ejil shook his head, wiped his eyes and squinted at Breda. The hard lump in his throat made it difficult to speak. "Yes! No! I saw…I'm not sure what I saw. Snatches of things. Nothing after the attack. They, they seem to want the women. They must have taken them back to their camp. Any sign of my father and brother?"

"Not your brother…Your father's body lies over there by the cliff… He died fighting. He took several of those cave rats with him." Breda's hand gripped tighter. "They even killed our dogs," he said. "Prat is lying near your father with his head crushed."

Tears running down his face, Ejil nodded. "Your father was a good man," he said. Ejil stood and embraced his friend. Breda's tears felt warm against his cheek.

Ejil's father's face lay half buried in the mud. All around him were signs of death. His body had been stripped. Everything—his weapons, the ivory beads denoting his rank.

Breda shouted from the cliff edge. "Your brother! I've found him!"

Ejil raced to the cliff edge. The two survivors stood and gazed over the cliff at Ejil's brother lying face down on the rocky shelf several man heights below them, one arm dangling over the edge pointing toward the valley floor.

"Is he dead?" Ejil asked, his voice flat.

"Looks like. Hey! See that?" Breda said, pointing. "His head moved! He's still alive."

Clambering down the steep cliff face and onto the narrow shelf, they dragged Baal back from the edge and gently turned him over onto his back.

The young warrior groaned. "Water," he croaked.

While Breda went for water, Ejil checked his brother's body for wounds. A spear slash across his chest had bled down the front of his loincloth. The jagged wound on his thigh oozed blood. His left shoulder appeared to be swollen from the fall, but Ejil could feel no broken bones.

Ejil propped his brother's head in his lap. Baal groaned and tossed his head side to side babbling incoherently.

"Shhh…quiet now," Ejil said. "It's me, your brother. Try not to move."

Baal lay quietly. Ejil sat gently smoothing back his hair. His brother lay like a baby, helpless in his arms. Ejil recalled his father's words, "family is everything. There is family. Then there is the tribe. There is nothing more." An aching sense of guilt flooded his chest. *He is my brother, the only family I have left! You've always disliked me, Baal. Now, with all that has happened, I hope things can be different between us.*

Breda's voice interrupted his reverie. He dropped down a water bladder and a muddy sleeping fur. Ejil propped up his brother's head and tipped water into his mouth. He washed the dried blood from his face and tucked the fur around his body to keep him warm as Pelas had taught him.

While Ejil tended his brother, Breda rummaged through the camp.

"How is he?" Breda asked.

"He'll live. Find anything?"

"They took everything they could carry: beads, spear points, flint nodules, but they missed one of the food larders."

"Good! There was a lot of blood, but my brother's wounds are not deep. I'll need some herbs to make a poultice. Any sign of Pelas?"

"Yes! Outside his cave," Breda put his hand on Ejil's shoulder. "His skull is broken."

Ejil's voice caught. He had been expecting this, but to Ejil, Pelas had seemed indestructible. If anyone could have escaped, it would have been the wily old *šamán*. "Did they loot the cave?"

"I don't know! I didn't go in…I've never been in there."

Ejil nodded. *Of course, who would dare enter a šamán's lair without an invitation?*

Breda laid out wood and using an ember from the still-smoldering remains of the camp, fanned a flame into life.

"Watch my brother," Ejil said. "He needs medicines and I need tools. I am going to the šamán's cave."

Breda nodded and added another stick on the fire.

Ejil made his way to the cave. Pelas' broken body lay face down outside the cave's entrance. Ejil staggered and squeezed his eyes shut. The back of the priest's head looked like a crushed egg shell. His dead hand clutched a heavy club.

Ejil took a deep breath and entered the cave he knew so well. It was a wide grotto that narrowed at the entrance, shallow but dark. Thick bundles of reeds had been roped together and hung across the entrance as a barrier against the wind and snow. It was a place filled with memories.

Six winters had passed since he had begun his apprenticeship. Now, no longer a boy but not quite a man, he was alone. His respected teacher had entered the land of the spirits. Ejil's eyes filled with tears. *I have learned much, but there is so much I do not know—so much more I have to learn,* he thought.

He removed the lid of the auroch-horn fire carrier he had found in the remains of the family hut, and breathed softly on the glowing ember that lay nestled in a bed of fire moss until a small flame appeared. Twisting a bit of the moss into a wick, he dipped it into the fat residue in one of the small stone oil lamps scattered about the cave, then lit another.

The cave was undisturbed. The Fishbellies, too, had feared to enter, and the thought that there existed at least one place of sanctuary in his world gave Ejil a small sense of comfort. *Pelas could have stayed safely inside. He would still be alive. But no, that was not the šamán's way. He fought; he fought to defend his people.* Ejil squatted by a stone where his master used to sit and instruct him. *I will never hear his voice again.* He shook his head. *It hurts, it hurts to think about it.* He stood. "Enough! I've got to think about my brother. He needs my help," Ejil said aloud.

Raising a lamp to eye level, Ejil poked through the bunched herbs dangling from the cave's low ceiling until he found what he needed. He selected a large, ear-shaped birch mushroom to seal the wound against the fever demon, marigold petals, dried garlic, and some cooking herbs and sprigs of sage to clean Baal's wounds and prevent infection. Leaves of stinging nettle would brew a tea that would ward off fever.

He found Pelas's wound kit. It was packed in the small, round ivory box. He held up the box and examined it in the dim light. It was fashioned of hollowed mammoth tusk with an ibex head delicately engraved into its fitted lid. Ejil had always admired it. Various-sized bone needles and coils of deer-leg tendons were packed inside. He shut his eyes. "Thank you, master," he said, then placed it reverently into his leather waist pouch.

Back on the ledge, Ejil found Baal awake and Breda tending the fire. Breda had rolled a scrap of fur into a pillow to prop up Baal's head.

"I told him about your mother," Breda whispered.

Ejil nodded, squatted and hunched his shoulders against a chilling breeze off the valley floor. "How do you feel, brother?" he asked.

Baal snorted and glared. "How do you think I feel? I hurt all over. What's in the bag?"

Ejil had expected Baal to say something about his mother, but no. "Medicine, herbs to treat your wounds!" he said.

"What do you know about treating battle wounds, little brother?" Baal demanded.

Ejil met his brother's eyes. *Nothing,* he thought, *has changed.*

"Have you forgotten? I was Pelas' apprentice," he said, keeping his voice even with effort. "Those wounds must be cleaned and stitched, or they will fester."

Baal continued to glare at him.

Ejil sighed. "You choose!" he said spreading his hands. "I'm all you've got. I'm doing my best to help. But I warn you, if those wounds are not treated, they will turn foul, and the fever demon will come. His fire will twist your body and light a torch behind your eyes. Your death walk will be long and painful."

The blood drained from Baal's face and fear filled his eyes. He flapped his hand dismissively, rolled onto his side and looked off into the distance. "Get on with it," he said.

Breda caught Ejil's eye and grinned.

Ejil sniffed at the wounds. They were rimmed an angry red, but there was no sign of infection.

His brother's dark eyes followed him as he formed a piece of tanned hide into a shallow bowl, staked it out at each corner and filled it with water. Dropping in hot rocks from the fire brought the water quickly to a boil. Ejil crushed the herbs from the šamán's store and sprinkled them into the steaming liquid, then carefully pared the mushroom into soft, thin strips like cured meat.

Dipping a rag of soft deerskin in the hot brew, he gently washed the wounds.

"Here," he said holding out a stick, "bite down on this. I've got to sew up your stomach and that thigh!"

Baal snatched the stick and eyed his brother. He swallowed hard as Ejil removed a long, curved bone needle from the ivory box, squeezed one eye shut and threaded it with deer tendon from the šamán's store.

Baal shoved the stick between his teeth, turned his head away, and grunted for his brother to begin. Tiny beads of sweat broke out around his hair line and across his lip, and his jaw muscles bulged, but he made no sound as the sharp bone pierced his ragged flesh.

Finally, Ejil sat back and regarded the neatly stitched wounds.

"It is done," he said.

He squeezed the water from the sopping mass of herbs, applied the spongy poultice and covered and bound the wounds with clean deerskin scraps.

Meanwhile the nettle tea was steeping. He waited for it to cool.

"Roll over on your back and try to stay quiet or you will tear out the stitches. Drink the tea. If you escape the fever, all should be well. Tomorrow will tell the tale," he said.

"What if I need to piss?"

"Roll onto your side and use this," Ejil said and placed a broken wooden bowl beside him.

That night, the three dined on a stew made of dried deer meat and ground nuts from the tribe's store. Nobody said much. After eating, Baal fell immediately to sleep. Ejil sat with his back to the fire and stared at the star-filled sky. He had done this often, but tonight as he stared outwards, instead of seeing a sky filled with possibilities, he gazed into a vast emptiness. In the distance he heard a wolf's eerie howl.

Baal slept fitfully, muttering to himself. But as dawn broke, his color was better and his skin was cool. Ejil changed his dressings and fed him more tea. Two sunsets passed, and as the Sunfather peeked over the adjoining ridge on the third morning, Baal's head had cleared and he was able to roll over on one elbow to feed himself.

Breda and Ejil didn't talk much. They spent the next day rooting amongst the ruins. One sunset later, Alpa, one of the war party sent to guard the trail, limped into camp, his hair matted, his face covered in dried blood.

The young man's narrow face was gaunt and his cheekbones stood out sharply. Ejil cleaned and stitched his head wound, and after some dried deer meat and two bowls of nettle tea, he told his story.

When the Fishbellies came howling out of the wolf's dawn, they found the small party lying wrapped in their sleeping furs, sleeping peacefully.

The fight had been quick and vicious. The Fishbellies spared no one. Alpa had been knocked unconscious by a blow from a war hammer. Bleeding profusely from his scalp, he had been left for dead.

"I'm surprised no hyena or wolves found you," Breda said.

Alpa looked up at them with pain-filled eyes. "They found plenty of dead to feed on," he said, staring into space.

While Baal slowly regained his strength, Ejil, Breda and Alpa buried the dead. Despite the cold, flies buzzed. The pungent stink of death had begun to rise from the decaying bodies.

The sky remained clear. "Look, Doombirds!" Breda said, pointing up at the winged scavengers circling in the clear sky. Digging was arduous. They built fires to soften the frozen earth and scraped shallow hollows with antlers and deer-thigh diggers, then heaped stones over the bodies to discourage scavengers.

Ejil washed his mother's body. In a stone bowl, he mixed powdered red ochre with animal fat. To make her more pleasing to the gods, he smeared the paste evenly over her body covering her from head to toe. Then he laid her on her back in a shallow pit with her hands crossed at her breast. He had little in the way of offerings to ease her shade's path into the shadow world. The Fishbellies had taken all the people's wealth as booty.

Ejil reached behind his neck and carefully untied a thin strip of rawhide. Strung on it was a single ivory bead, carved by Pelas into the shape of a rabbit as a present to his young apprentice. He gazed down at it. Pelas had joked that Ejil was like a rabbit, his nose always twitching. The bead was slightly yellowed and almost round, with a groove on either side outlining the animal's hip and leg, the whiskered face tucked between them, the ears swept back. *Here, Mother. You always admired it.* Tears welled up. *Take it with you on your journey and remember me. I will always remember you.* He kissed the bead and tied the cord around his mother's neck and gently adjusted it, so it lay between her soft breasts.

Ejil stood silently gazing down at the grave. He blinked back tears; his eyes were sore from crying. His mind drifted back to the good times.

He longed to wrap his mother in his arms and beg her to come back to him, but her spirit had fled. He squeezed his eyes shut and tried to picture her face, her eyes alight with life, but that image was already fading into the mist of forgetfulness. Tears dribbled down his cheeks. An aching emptiness gripped his guts in a clenched fist.

What happens when someone dies? Does their spirit wander, or does it fade like a summer's breeze? he asked himself. Raising his eyes to the sky, he squinted at the blazing orb staring down at him. *Is my mother's spirit up there somewhere, or is it down below? Can she see me? Does she know how much I love her?* Pelas had spoken of a place where the shades of the dead gathered, a land of shadow. Perhaps that was all anyone could expect. Ejil kneeled, picked up a handful of earth and gently sprinkled it over her body. Baal did the same, then Breda and Alpa. When the simple ceremony was over, they built a mound, placing each rock carefully, reverently, on her grave.

The next afternoon, as Ejil sat at the hearth making tea for his brother, a shadow fell across his face. His breath caught. It was Breda standing above him holding the šamán's staff. "I found it a little way from Pelas's cave. It is yours now," he said, handing it to Ejil. "This is all we have left of the story of our people."

Baal hawked and spit. "That's the šamán's staff! Why do you give it to Ejil? He is still a boy."

"Hardly a boy," Breda answered. "A blooded warrior and a skilled healer. Without his tending you would be shaking with fever, puking and begging the death spirit to take you." He stared fiercely at Baal. "Who else should carry it? Your brother was Pelas's apprentice, and he has the sight. The morning of the attack, the spirits warned him in a dream. I was there; I saw it."

"He dreamed, I fought," Baal said and turned away.

Ejil picked up the eagle-headed staff with both hands. It was warm and smooth, and the dark wood glowed like living flesh. He ran his fingers over the tiny symbols engraved in its surface. Here were the six distinctive notches, each a reminder of a stage of the Great Journey. He squeezed his eyes shut and tried to empty his mind as Pelas had taught him. His fingers explored the staff's twisted contours, remembering its teachings. How many generations of hands—šamáns' hands—had held it?

Ejil reverently placed the staff on the ground in front of him. "I am not worthy," he said.

"Who else, then?" Breda repeated. "You are the šamán's heir. Without you, our memories are lost. Who will remember our lineage? Who will sing our songs around the evening fire? There is no one. We will be forgotten."

Baal snorted.

Once the Sunfather rose and they had broken their fast, Ejil stood before the group, the šamán's staff in his hand. "Our duty is done. We have given our people back to the Earth Mother. We have food and weapons. We will never forget, but we must leave this place of grief and seek out a new place." His eyes met Baal's. "Can you walk, brother?"

"Better than you," Baal said, struggling to his feet; his thigh still pained him. Alpa had cut him a thick-forked sapling, which he wrapped with scrap leather to make a crutch. "The sooner we leave this place the better, but where? We should follow the Fishbellies tracks. Find out where they've taken our women."

"We know where they went. What do we do when we get there? No, our best path—maybe our only path—is toward the mother tribe. They are kin," Breda said.

"They cast us out. Why should they welcome us now?" Baal asked.

"They had no choice. You know the tale. It has been told often enough. The people were too close in blood and there were many mouths to fill. The elders met and the tribe divided. Our father's elderfather led and brought us here where there was food in plenty and our people could eat and multiply," Ejil said.

"How do we find this tribe? And what of our women? Have you forgotten them? Alpa's mother? Mata? Are we to abandon them to be slaves? What of our dead?" Baal raised his crutch and stared up at the sky. "Their blood crying out for vengeance. Those filthy beasts will pay in blood for what they have done. I swear it!" Baal shouted.

"Am I a stone, brother? We all share your pain," Ejil said. "I will carry it always. You are a great warrior, brother, no one questions that, but look around. Our enemies are many. It will take more than the four of us to win back our women. If we are to have any chance at saving them, we will need help!"

"The mother clan's hunting grounds are there," Breda said pointing south. They call themselves The First People. I spoke to one of their young hunters at the last gathering. They live by a river so full of fish you can walk across the river stepping on their backs. It is far, two moons' walk, maybe three. There will be sign, and where there is sign, I can follow."

"Why are they called the First People?" Alpa asked.

"You remember the story. At the beginning of The Great Journey, we were all one people." Breda said.

"Yes, and as our people wandered, food became scarce, and small groups split off so the people would not starve," Ejil said.

"You think these kin of ours, these First People, will help us? My little brother speaks as if he knows the decisions others will make. Has he seen this in one of his dreams?" Baal sneered.

"Have you a better plan, brother?" Ejil asked. "Breda's plan is the best plan because it is the only plan."

"All this arguing is useless," Breda said. He squatted down and began stuffing his pack.

Baal glared at Breda. "I am the First Speaker's eldest. I have proven myself in battle. Have you forgotten how many of their warriors died by my spear? It is my right to lead."

Alpa grunted in agreement.

Breda raised his head. "Being the son of a speaker does not make you speaker. That has never been our custom. The speaker is chosen by the council."

"Being the apprentice of a šamán does not make you a šamán," Baal said.

Alpa spoke up. "Breda's is the best plan. Inside, I cry out for my mother, but the four of us have no chance against the Fishbellies. We should seek out the elder clan. They are our kin. They must help us rescue our girls and women."

"Good! We are all agreed!" Breda said staring directly at Baal.

Baal shook his head. Grunting, he stretched his free hand down and took hold of his pack. They had scavenged the camp and outfitted themselves with deerskin parkas, stout bear-skin-soled boots and long, woven waterproof grass capes, their war gear, and as much dried meat as they could carry. Ejil hefted the šamán's staff in one hand, his spear in the other. Breda leading, they set out in single file.

CHAPTER 11

THE SPOILS

Heavily laden with captives and plunder, Scar and his warriors began the trek back to their camp. The pace was slow and took many days. The warriors loaded the women with their booty, but when their eyes were elsewhere, many things were lost by the side of the trail.

Babyface knocked a captive to the ground and kicked her viciously in the ribs. "Where is my fur, woman?" Crying out in pain, she rolled herself into a ball. The warrior retracted his foot to deliver another kick but found himself face down on the trail. Spitting dirt, he scrambled to his feet in a rage and came face to face with the leader. Scar grinned, his fingers formed the sign of challenge. The young warrior dropped his eyes and stood quietly until Scar's hand relaxed.

"If a woman disobeys, slap her. Do not injure her. What good is she if you break her ribs? If her leg is broken, she cannot walk," Scar said, his eyes sweeping the warriors' faces.

"I gave this snake's daughter my new sleeping fur to carry. It is gone. She threw it away." Babyface signed and pointed at the cowering woman. "It was a good fur."

Scar's lip curled. He addressed the warriors.

"Hear me!" Scar said, his voice rising. "The women will do slave's work, but they are not slaves. You heard the Spirit Woman. They are not to be mounted unless they are willing. Will a woman choose a man who kicks her, Babyface? You must be sweet like sticky honey. Beat a woman too often and one night she crawls into your fur with a sharp blade and guts you."

Several of the warriors made sounds deep in their throats.

"You see, soft head," Scar said poking his forehead with a blunt finger, "they understand."

The young man's face flushed. "She must obey. I don't need a mate. I need a woman who will carry my things and spread her legs," he said.

Scar leaned down and offered the injured woman his hand. The girl drew back, hissed like a snake then leaped to her feet and spat in his face.

He jumped backwards; his face burned. Wiping his hand across his cheek, he stared at his open palm. "Now I see why you name her *Snake's Daughter*."

The warriors guffawed, slapped and punched each other. Babyface snorted and turned away to hide his smile. The captive women cringed back, exchanged glances and squeezed themselves together in a tight knot.

"Speak more, oh wise one, teach us how to handle a woman," Squint-eye signed, grinning.

Scar glanced at his warriors, the tips of his ears burning, then remembered: *I am Scar. I have won a great victory*. His chest expanded. He grinned and spread his hands. "Soft words are good," he signed. "Kicks are bad. The women are angry. We killed their men, but we have taken them to make babies for The Lion Clan. They hate us now, but when the wolves howl and the Ice Demon comes with his tiny knives, that will change. They will remember that a woman needs a strong man to protect her."

Lada raised her head and squinted into the long shadows of late afternoon. A low haze hung in the air, pungent from the smoking fires outside the Fishbellies' crude huts. Some distance away, a long file of men snaked down the hillside leading to the cave. Wiping her greasy hands, she nudged Tule who looked up from her task. Scar and most of the men had left in the early morning after the bloody ceremony some suns past.

Lada shaded her eyes. The party seemed large. They drew closer. Her hand flew up to her mouth and she shook her head in disbelief. *Mother? No, no, it can't be.* Her mother shambled along near the middle of the column. Her head was bowed, and behind her was Tule's sister, Catya, and many of the other women of her tribe.

Tule stood as if frozen, staring, her eyes bulging. Lada suddenly felt dizzy. *Where are our men and the children?* As they neared the camp, the warriors began to dance. Shaking their spears, they prodded the women along.

Pushing and shouting, the clan women surrounded their men, eager to celebrate. The captives, including Lada and Tule were herded into a tight knot at the crowd's center. Lada threw her arms around her mother. "What happened?" she asked. Both women were crying. "They attacked our camp," Ceda told her. "They killed everyone! Your father. All the babies." Lada's mouth dropped open. She stared at her mother in disbelief.

A hush fell. Lada twisted her head around as the crowd parted and the Spirit Woman stepped forward. Her face was reddened with ochre. She had rubbed charcoal in the hollows, so that her dark orbs seemed to peer out at the world from a deep tunnel. Her gray hair fell about her breast in a cascade of knotted strands.

"You have won," the Spirit Woman said, looking Scar up and down.

"Yes, the Blackdog clan is no more. Their warriors, their babies and old ones lie rotting in the dirt," Scar signed.

"The spirits led you to victory."

"Yes, Mother," Scar said. *The spirits, always the spirits. It was my plan and my warriors who triumphed.* He kept his face carefully neutral and did what was expected. His eyes raised to the sky; he made the familiar signs. "Spirits we thank you. You who gave us the power to destroy our enemies."

She nodded. "Show me what have you brought us." She eyed the captive women, and the rattles wrapped around her ankles made a sibilant hiss as she glided toward them. The women cringed, but the clanswomen had encircled them, hemming them in. None would meet that cold eye. The witch grasped one girl's shoulder, gripped her chin and searched her eyes. "This one has spirit," she said.

The clan women giggled and stared, prodded and poked at the captive women.

"They will learn our ways and bear us sons. The clan will grow strong," Scar said.

"It is a good plan," the old woman signed. "All things happen as the spirits will. Tonight, we feast," she said, addressing the assembled clan. "The spirits have brought our hunters a fat deer. They are pleased."

Scar's eyes narrowed. *Her attitude has changed.* Despite his suspicions, he felt his chest swell with her praise. *What is she after?* he wondered. He knew her so well, knew she never did or said anything without something more lurking in the shadows. Always, she spoke of his father. Nothing he did was good enough. *Soon,* he knew, *she will reveal herself.*

With much shouting and a few sharp blows, the clan women herded their captives into the back of the cave, set a guard then began preparing the victory feast while the warriors sitting around the fire boasted of their deeds. Scar kept apart. He sat, hand cupping his chin, his sharp eyes moving from face to face. *These women bring trouble?* Already, the men argued over the younger ones.

He had warned them with strong words, but he knew, men's needs were stronger than any words. Scar himself had no woman. His had died, long ago, of the burning sickness. Any woman would have been proud to be chosen by the leader, but none among the clan's few young girls moved him.

After the feast, he had Lada brought to him. Captive for less than a moon, she had already learned some of their words and could even make crude signs.

Sitting cross-legged before the fire, he could barely admit it to himself, that this girl, standing proudly before him—hands at her side, eyes defiant—moved him as no woman ever had.

"You have heard," he said.

"Yes! You and your warriors killed all my people."

Scar shrugged. "The Lion Clan made war. We are stronger. The weaker died. All is as it always has been."

Lada's lips trembled and her eyes filled with tears. "What do you want?" she asked, making the simple clan sign that she had learned signified a question.

The leader eyed her and nodded curtly. "You are learning to speak like clan. That is good. All must learn," he signed, and watched to see if she understood. "Your men have passed into the Caves of the Fallen. All women must now join with a man. Until the third moon, no man will mount you unless you wish it. Those who join with a clan warrior become clan."

The girl put her hands on her hips and glared down at the Fishbelly leader. "And if we do not wish to be *chosen?*" she asked, repeating the sign for emphasis.

Scar sighed. "You will be a slave, then you will *die,*" he said, emphasizing with the sign one of the clan's few spoken words. "A slave is not clan. A slave may be used by any man. You understand?" he signed, staring at her.

Lada raised her tear-stained face and gazed at him. *Has she more to say?* Scar wondered. But instead of speaking, she turned and strode away. Scar watched her graceful swaying hips. He felt a stirring in his groin.

Leaning back and staring at the fire, he brooded. This girl fascinated him; her shining black skin and soft curly hair, her big, doe-like eyes. *She is young! She is skinny and her hips are narrow.* He allowed his mind to consider what, up to that moment, he had refused to think about. *If I choose her, will she refuse me? And if I do take her, what will my clan think? Mother will call me a fool.* He shook his head trying to rid himself of the thoughts of her that kept returning. *I do not care,* he told himself; yet the thought of other men mounting her—using her—filled him with rage.

He scratched behind one ear and shook his head to clear it. *The lice are bad. I need grooming.* At the hearth, two women were cracking bones with rocks and removing the marrow. He adjusted himself to ease the pressure on his erection and looked around. *Humph, Raven-hair? Where is she? She is always ready.*

Lada walked toward the back of the cave half expecting to be stopped and put to work, but the clan women were busy preparing the feast and ignored her. She found Tule sitting alone by their sleeping place, sat down next to her and beat her clenched fists against the ground.

"What did he want?" Tule asked.

Lada's mother, Ceda, and a few of the other women gathered around.

"He's a beast! Now that all our men lie with their faces buried in the earth. He says we must choose mates from among the clan."

"I'd die before I'll choose one of them," Tule said.

"The choice is to join with a man and be adopted into the clan or be a slave until you die."

Several of the women began to sob.

"Their šamán is a woman?" Mata asked.

"Šamán? That horror! Ugh!" Tule cringed. "She might cut your throat and drink your blood."

Lada covered her face with her hands. Ceda stroked her head. "What is it, my child?" she asked.

"How can you ask, Mother? Father is with the spirits. Our people are dead, murdered by these animals, and we are their prisoners. I don't care what that hideous man says, I will never join with any of the men who murdered my father."

Ceda closed her eyes and shook her head. "Yes, I can hardly bear to think about it. They showed no mercy. It, it was horrible."

Lada tightened her jaw. "Did none of the men escape?" She stared hopefully at her mother.

"You're thinking about Ejil," Ceda said, and pulled Lada into her arms. "I did not see him, my poor girl, but no, no one escaped. Our dead lay scattered across the ground, like fallen leaves."

Lada buried her face in her mother's shoulder. She was thinking of Ejil, picturing his handsome face glowing in the morning sun. She loved that face, and she would never see it again. Ejil was dead. She thought about the times they'd spent together, in their special place, on top of the cliff overlooking the valley. Together, warming themselves on the big, flat rock. Shoulders touching, they looked up at the sky. "Soaring," he had called it. Ejil loved watching the birds, especially the hawks. "They are free," he had told her. "They soar, they float across the sky. They see everything, the whole world."

She began to sob.

CHAPTER 12

THE DISPOSSESSED

The setting sun hovered above the horizon, sending out glowing streamers of blood-red, deep violet and gold as Ejil's party approached a high cliff overlooking the plain. A cluster of massive boulders at the cliff's base promised shelter from the wind. The moon had waxed through two phases and began to wane since Ejil and the three other survivors had descended from the shelter of their rocky escarpment onto the open taiga.

The partially melted winter snows left spreading patches with exposed tufts of short brown grass spotting the plain. Here and there, narrow creeks filled with frothing, brown meltwater cut across the taiga. In the deeper defiles, the ground was wet and spongy underfoot.

Hunger forced a stop. Only a few shreds of dried meat remained at the bottom of their food bags. Herds of mammoth passed tantalizingly close. A small herd passed, led by a shaggy old bull with long, yellowed tusks that curled back so far that they almost touched. He raised his trunk, trumpeted and changed course as soon as he caught their scent. There were two small females and a calf, but for all their bulk, mammoths moved fast and even the little ones would easily outrun a man. Baal slammed the butt of his spear into the ground, but there was no place on the broad plain to set an ambush.

While the three others went off to gather dry wood, Ejil crouched behind a pair of huge angular rocks that his imagination told him had been placed by giants. He gently shook a hot coal from his fire horn into a nest of dry grass and breathing softly, coaxed the fire spirit to life.

He marveled, not for the first time, at how his breath restored the fire and spread the flame. Fire fascinated him. "All things, while they live, possess spirit," Pelas had taught him, "but fire is pure spirit." He missed the old man, missed his wisdom. *When a man dies, his spirit leaves the body with the last breath. Is that why we use the same word for death? What then? Where does it go? Is it scattered by the wind?* Pelas would just shake his head and smile. At times, Ejil felt that his head was full and ready to burst with all the questions stuffed inside it.

"Your eyes are filled with clouds again," Breda said, squatting down beside him, grinning.

"Where are the others?" Ejil asked.

"They'll be along." As he said it, Baal and Alpa strode into camp and built the pile higher.

"Catch anything?" Ejil asked.

Alpa shook his head. "I saw one rabbit, but he was too quick for me."

Baal just shrugged. He had said almost nothing since their journey began.

"Cave lion! I found tracks. A big one with teeth like spear points," Breda said.

Ejil jerked his head around and gazed at his friend in alarm.

Baal hefted his spear. "Where?" he asked, his eyes searching the taiga.

"In a hollow near the cliff, over there," Breda said, pointing. "Fresh tracks. It's a she-lion. Probably has a den close by."

"A lion's den! In these rocks? Alpa asked. "All gods protect us! The fire! We'll need to keep it burning all night."

"Even a cave lion would not dare attack four armed men," Ejil said.

"Have you ever seen a full-grown male?" Breda asked.

"No. Didn't father and the hunters drive them all off before I was born?" Ejil asked.

"Not all," Breda said, and exhaled sharply. "A grown male is twice as long as a man is tall. He weighs as much as three of us and, sitting, his head would be even with your brother's shoulder. A female is not much smaller. You remember, Baal?"

"Who could forget? Teeth like curved spear-points, two bottom and two on top. As long as a man's hand," he said, holding up his own, "and keener than a sharpstone blade! Gutted Tule's brother, sliced his belly open with one swipe of that great front paw."

"Nearly got father. I had just been given my first spear. I buried it in his shoulder. I'll never forget the way he glared at me. Those demon eyes! The smell! The hate!" Baal said

"The lion snarled, jerked out my spear with his teeth then leaped up onto a ledge higher than a man can reach and retreated into a wide crack in the rocks."

"What happened then?" Ejil asked.

"He disappeared. None of us dared follow him."

"Shouldn't we pack up and move on?" Ejil asked, looking from his brother to Breda.

"Move on? Where? It'll be dark before we make any distance. Lions are night stalkers. Out there on the plain he can play with us, come at us from any direction. We're better off here with our backs up against the cliff." Baal looked up at the cliff overhead. He can't get at us from up there," Breda said.

"What can we do?" Ejil asked.

"Torches might help drive him off if he gets too close. There are dry cattails over in that hollow. We'll build up the fire. Keep our backs to it and our spears ready and hope the wood lasts until dawn," Baal said. He squatted down and carefully added a few sticks to the fire. In his mind, Ejil pictured a pair of pale-yellow eyes staring down at him.

The night was damp and still. The weather had warmed and there was a scent of rain. The stars flickered dimly through the hanging mist. Ejil and his companions sat in a half circle in a natural cove between the rocks with their spears bristled outward like the spines of a stickhog. Long days of walking had left him exhausted. The others, he knew, felt it too. Eyes drooping, heads nodding, he watched as one by one, the men dropped off. Ejil was the last to succumb. The heat of the fire warmed his back, his eyelids flickered, his head drooped forward.

Alpa woke with a jerk. Had his sharp ears picked up a faint sound? Or was it a dream, or another nightmare of the Stonehead attack? He felt a stab of fear and gazed out into the darkness. All was quiet. He rose and blinked. "Anybody hear anything?" he asked the three dark lumps arranged around the hearth at his feet. No one stirred. He squatted and rubbed the sleep from his eyes. His head still ached from the blow he had taken from a Stonehead war club. He tossed a few of the remaining sticks on the glowing coals and stared numbly at the rising flames.

What was that? He thought he heard something, so he turned from the fire and stared out into the night, but all he saw was a black wall. The glow of the fire had taken his night vision. He shrugged and sniffed the air. It seemed musty. A sleeper stirred, mumbled and coughed. He listened for a moment, then feeling the urge, stood and, skirting his companion's sleeping forms, stumbled out a few feet beyond the rocks. Loosening his breeches, he arched his back, gazed up at the stars and released his stream. *Ahhh, feels good!* he thought with a long sigh. With a throaty growl and a flash of tooth and claw, death swept him up like a dry leaf caught in a gale.

A high-pitched scream tore through the night, followed some moments later by a deep-toned roar that echoed off the cliff face, shattering the night. The three sleepers leaped to their feet and backed up to the fire, spears thrust out before them.

"Did you hear that? Where did it come from?" Ejil asked, rubbing his eyes.

"Don't know," Breda said, "but that was a man's scream." His eyes darted left and right. "Where's Alpa?"

"That's whose scream you heard," Baal said with a snort. "Stupid fool! Must have wandered off." He raised his spear and savagely thrust the butt into the half-frozen ground.

"What are you doing?" Ejil asked, clutching his own spear. "That lion is still out there."

Baal laughed. "The roar you heard! He has made his kill. Lions kill to eat. He'll be back when he gets hungry; and when he does, we'd better be long gone," Baal said. "Come on, little brother, pack up. It's almost dawn. Alpa won't make much of a meal," he said, hefting his pack.

Ejil glanced at Breda. The scout nodded. "Baal is right. There is nothing to be done for Alpa now. Cave lions claim a wide territory. We'd best be gone," he said.

Baal started out. Breda started to follow but felt Ejil's hand on his shoulder. "Did you hear that scream? Alpa sounded surprised at what was happening to him."

Breda smiled a grim smile. "Death can be like that. A surprise!" he said. "If you are very lucky."

None spoke. By the time the sun sank below the horizon in a burst of color, the cliff had shrunk halfway into the flat expanse of the taiga. Gazing back, Ejil wondered why, as he moved away, the earth seemed to swallow whole mountains and why they loomed larger as you approached. *Where are they when I can no longer see them?* he asked himself, sighing.

The sky clouded over and darkened. That night, they made camp on the barren taiga. There was little wood, but plenty of dried bison and mammoth dung to fuel a fire. Ejil glanced around nervously. He couldn't stop thinking about Alpa. He felt exposed and vulnerable.

The night was frosty, and there was a scent of snow on the wind. The stars flickered dimly through the mist. A light snow began to fall.

"Good meat," Baal said. He was sitting cross-legged across the fire. He wiped his mouth with the back of his hand. Ejil noticed that since the encounter with the lion, Baal seemed to come back to himself. He had started talking again.

Breda gingerly pulled the thin slice off the stick he was using to roast it and held it up by two fingers. "Enjoy it! That's the last," he said.

Baal grunted. "We need a rest, and this seems like a good place to hunt. Did you see that deer herd we passed? I got pretty close. They're not as skittish as you might expect."

"Good," Breda said. "That means they haven't been hunted, not in a long time, and there's no scent of enemies on the wind! We'd better try hunting while we can."

"Yes!" Baal said, shaking his spear and grinning. Juice ran down his chin. "Tomorrow night, fresh meat."

Long days of walking had left Ejil footsore. His eyelids flickered and despite his fears, his eyes refused to stay open. He curled up in his sleeping fur. One by one, the others followed.

The next day's hunt went badly. The deer herd had run off. They saw a bison herd, big furry mounds far in the distance.

Ejil's sling brought in a brace of hare. Out of a deep crack between boulders, he dug some tender fiddleheads and tiny onion bulbs and managed a rabbit stew. The following day proved luckier.

Baal woke abruptly in the predawn darkness to find Breda squatting beside him chewing a stem of spring grass.

Breda jumped to his feet. "Shake off your dreams, my friend. We have to leave now if we want to be at that waterhole before the Sunfather peeps over the horizon," the scout said with a grin.

As always, Baal led. He had proven his hunting skills so many times that Breda always took up the second position whenever they went out. They made a wide circle downwind and crossed a game trail that led to a swampy shallow valley they had scouted the day before. They settled themselves in a stand of brittle, brown cattail that flanked the pond side of the narrow trail.

As the countryside took shape in the frosty light of the wolf's dawn, Baal spotted a tall buck, his nubs of antlers beginning to regrow. He and his pregnant mate picked their way down the rocky trail that led to a small pond. The buck halted mid-stride. His mobile ears swiveled backward then forward, and his quivering nose sampled the chill air. His mate halted a few paces behind him; her body shivered, her liquid-brown eyes darted left and right, then her head dropped to crop a quick mouthful of moss. Testing the air again, the big buck stepped off, the doe following closely behind.

Scarcely daring to breathe, the two hunters waited, hands tightly grasping their spear shanks. As the deer came abreast, Baal signaled, and they jumped to their feet. Breda took aim at the buck, but the startled animal reared, made a great leap off his back legs and charged right past the bemused scout.

Startled, the gravid doe turned to follow her mate, but unbalanced from the weight in her belly, she stumbled forward onto her knees. Baal's spear flashed in a short arc. The knapped point pierced the soft flesh behind her right shoulder, penetrating the heart. Eyes wide, she collapsed and rolled over, her life's blood pulsing onto the soft, mossy ground.

Kneeling side by side, Baal and Breda quickly dressed out the doe. Baal's flint hand-blade sliced open the womb. He wrestled out the unborn fawn and set it aside, then scooped out the entrails. Despite the warm stink, his mouth watered. "Tonight, we feast on veal," he said.

"Yes, with thanks for Baal's spearskill," Breda said.

Baal shrugged and asked—he had been waiting for the right time—"Tell me something, my friend…"

Breda eyed him and nodded. "If I can."

"We have been friends and companions on many hunts. We made our first kill together."

"I remember," Breda said.

"Why then have you taken my brother's part against me?" he asked, eyes studying his friend.

Breda's eye met his. "I have not taken against you Baal. I have only tried to read the signs and choose the best trail for us to follow."

"I don't care what my father said; my brother is not a warrior. To be a true warrior, a man must look his enemy in the eye. Ejil has yet to prove himself."

"He is young, yes, but there is at least one dead Fishbelly who would argue with you," Breda said. "Ejil is wise beyond his years and he has *the sight*. You saw him use the new weapon he created, what he calls a *sling*."

Baal snorted. "A toy! Good for hunting rabbits."

"He brought down three men with that toy. But for him, my bones would by now have been picked clean by the Doombirds. I owe your brother a debt of blood," Breda said.

Baal paused for a moment. *So that's it?* Baal had always respected Breda. *I need him on my side,* he thought. "It was my plan," he said, rubbing his jaw, "to make you Chief of Hunters when I became First Speaker."

Breda shrugged. "Who is the best tracker?"

"You, my friend; that is known."

"Who else then? Must I pant after you like a dog for a place I have earned?"

"Had you lived in the speaker's lodge, you would know that such things can be difficult."

"Difficult?"

"Talud was a skilled tracker, almost your match!"

"Yes, he was a good hunter and a fine tale teller. I miss him."

"He was also the son of my father's brother," Baal said. "It is natural for a man to favor his own blood."

Breda shrugged. "Ejil is of *your* blood."

"He is my second mother's son. Perhaps we share blood, perhaps not."

Breda snorted. "Lette had eyes only for your father. Even at a gathering, she never took another man."

Baal shook his head and stared up at the sky. *She could cast her spell on a man, my friend, even the young ones.* Thinking about her, he felt himself hardening. He shook his head, laughed and playfully punched Breda's arm. "I remember you mooning around our hut. Ejil was born not long after the last gathering, so who knows?"

Breda's face darkened. He scowled and gritted his teeth.

Baal's eyes never left Breda's face. *You are another of those who fell under her spell.* "I have sworn vengeance," he said.

"Yes, as have I, and your brother as well, but what can three do against an entire tribe?"

Baal thought back to the fight in the camp. His nostrils flared. A blast of hot anger surged through him. Baal's mind flashed back to the scar-faced warrior who had bested him. *We will meet again, and the next time…next time will be different,* he swore, teeth clenched. "Fishbellies, hah! Snakebellies is a better name. They are no better than cave rats infesting our land," he said and shook his fist, "I swear I will hunt them until not one is left to lift his eyes to the sun."

Breda slapped Baal's back, stood, cupped his hand above his eyes and scanned the horizon. "Haven't we all taken that pledge? Our people are dead, and I will not rest until we find my Mata and the rest of our women. That will come soon enough. But right now, we better get going before the blowflies come. It's a long walk. We can finish the skinning back at camp. I see a sapling over there," he said pointing toward the pond. "I'll go cut a carrying pole."

"Right, we'll talk of this again," Baal said, standing. "I'll gather a bunch of those cattail shoots."

When Baal and Breda walked into camp, footsore and burdened with meat, they found that Ejil had built a smoking rack. "I dreamed that you would have a good hunt," Ejil said.

Baal snorted. He noticed Breda attempting to catch his eye; he scowled and turned away.

Breda began skinning the doe. Grabbing a flap of hide, he carefully sliced at the membrane that held it to the skin, peeling it toward the deer's backbone. "Look," he said, smiling happily, "grubs!" They lay just under the skin—gleaming, bone-white and fat as a man's thumb. The scout took one between his fingers and bit off half. "Ah," he sighed, "tasty!"

Baal reached over, scraped another off the deer's sticky skin with his hand-blade and popped it into his mouth. "Good!" he said nodding.

"A feast!" Breda said. He scraped off two more and dropped one into Ejil's open hand. They all went to work cutting thin slices of meat off the doe's carcass and laying them across the rack to smoke.

Stomachs full, Ejil and his companions slept under a scintillating meadow of stars. But when they woke the next morning, they found a sky clouded over with gray and a freshening wind.

Breda shaded his eyes and gazed north. "I do not like this. I can see my breath and those—" he pointed, "—are snow clouds."

"This far into the budding season?" Ejil asked, shading his eyes.

"This early, you never know. The gods are tricksters. I knew this weather was too good to last."

"How long do you think?" Baal asked.

"Midday, if the gods are with us," Breda said.

"We'll have to run for it," Baal said.

"Run where?" Ejil asked.

"There," Baal said, pointing. "See that ridge? You can just see the tops of trees sticking up. There must be some kind of hollow. There should be a cave, or at least a hill to burrow into to make a windbreak."

The wind had increased. Breda spit dust, shaded his eyes and followed Baal's finger across the flat, barren landscape. The point where land met sky had completely disappeared. He shook his head slowly, hawked and spit. "The storm will catch us before we are half way there," he said.

"We still have unsmoked meat," Ejil said.

Baal snorted. "It won't much matter how much meat we have, little brother, if that storm catches us in the open."

"Baal's right!" Breda said. "The snow's already started. If we don't find shelter, we'll die. We'll divide up as much of the meat as we can carry. It's getting colder, so it'll keep, and in this weather, nothing will be hunting us. He rubbed his hands together. We can always pack some snow around it to keep it fresh. Let's get going."

The three donned their snow shields, a long section of a deer's hollowed legbone with a slit cut along the center and secured with a rawhide strap over their eyes. Baal uncoiled a length of supple rope made of twisted rush and passed one end down the line.

"Breda, you take lead; Ejil, you're in the middle. I'll bring up the rear. Hold tight," he shouted, his voice barely audible against the icy blast. "Don't let go! If you do get lost, keep the wind at the back of your neck. If we keep going, we might make those hills while there's still light."

Ejil clenched his teeth. *I should have listened to father more carefully,* he thought and got into line.

Breda's prediction proved true. The ridge began to take shape and loomed closer, but they were still a distance off as the world disappeared behind a howling wall of white.

The following wind bullied and shoved them stumbling along, fierce gusts at times almost knocking them off their feet. The snow, mixed with dust, was soon ankle deep. Ejil's mouth felt gritty. The prickling needles of snow cut into his exposed flesh. Even the thick bearskin soles of his boots couldn't keep out the wet.

Ejil saw Breda stumble. Baal grabbed him under the arms and hoisted him to his feet. "You need a rest," Baal shouted in his ear. "Get in the middle. Ejil, take the rear. I'll break trail."

Ejil stood panting and dejected. Clouds of his breath billowed out in front of him. He was grateful that it was not him doing the hard work of breaking trail, but he hated seeing his tiny store of hard-won authority slowly draining away as his brother, once again, took command in a crisis.

The wind appeared to moderate. It stuck to their woven rush capes and drifted around their knees, forcing them to lift their legs high. Thigh muscles screamed. Every step became an agony.

Head down, placing one foot in front to the other, Ejil's mind came unmoored and drifted like pond grasses riffling in the wind. His mother, humming as she busied herself around their hut, appeared before his half-closed eyes. She squatted by the hearth, preparing a meal, and smiled at him. He returned her smile and reveled in the fire's comforting warmth.

Suddenly, he couldn't breathe. He raised his head, opened his eyes, spit out a mouthful of snow. He looked around. *Where are they?* He pushed up his snow-shield, wiped his eyes and squinted into the storm. An icicle of fear slithered down his backbone. He was alone—his companions were nowhere in sight. Ejil scrambled to his feet and shouted their names, only to have the wind snatch away his words.

Fear now struck him like a blow from a hammerstone. His breath came in short, harsh gasps and his heart raced. He lurched forward in panic, tripped and sprawled head long into the drifting snow. He felt a grip on his shoulder. He looked up into the smiling eyes of Pelas, his old teacher. The old man stood leaning on his staff, one hand extended. The driving snow formed a whirling wreath all around his head.

"Help! Master, please help me!" Ejil begged.

The old šamán smiled. A spider's web of lines crinkled around his dark, clouded eyes. His mouth did not move, but his words were plain. *Control your fears, young Ejil. Panic is the messenger of death. Remember your lessons; breathe, breathe. Breath is the essence of life.* He reached out his hand.

Ejil blinked, rubbed the snow from his eyes and reached up, but the old šamán had disappeared. He scrambled to his feet. He was alone. The storm wrapped around him like a white shroud. He squeezed his eyes shut and forced himself to take a long, deep breath, then another and another until he felt his fear begin to ebb.

Recalling his brother's words, he turned until he felt the sting of the icy needles on the back of his neck. Part of him wanted to just sink down into the snow and rest. *I am so tired. Just a little rest.* He felt something beckoning. *Is this what death is? It would be so easy to lie down and accept its warm embrace…—no!* He sucked in a breath and stepped forward. Another breath—life began to spread within him like a warming breeze—another step. He was in a world with no beginning and no end. *Where am I? How can I? Forward!* he ordered himself. *Forward!*

A snow-covered apparition rose up before him. He blinked.

"Ejil?" It was Breda's voice. "I thought we had lost you. What happened?" Breda asked, his hands gripping Ejil's shoulders.

"Breda? Thank the gods!" Ejil shouted into the scout's ear. "I don't know, I think I fell asleep. I woke up. You were gone. Where's my brother?"

Breda formed his hands around his mouth. "Back there," he shouted, jerking his head. "Making camp! I came back to look for you. I was about to give up. We found a good place. "Come on, your brother should have a fire going by now," he said, turned and strode off.

Ejil squinted. The storm began to abate, and a ridge of low hills rose like a series of long, low wrinkles across the landscape with spruce pines sprouting like thick patches of fur out of the hollows. The wind wailed like a disembodied spirit, and the trees swayed back and forth like ceremonial dancers. But all was calm and peaceful once they entered the cozy nest that lay beneath the fragrant, needle-clad branches.

Baal stood and brushed off his knees. "What happened? Lost in one of your dreams, little brother?"

Ignoring his brother's sally, Ejil shrugged off his pack, crouched and flexed his frozen fingers above the crackling flames. He was embarrassed, feeling stupid. *Had Pelas really come back from the spirit world to rescue me? Or was it, as my brother says, a dream?* Ejil thought back and recalled his mentor's words:

"There is much to be learned from dreams," the old man had once told him.

"But where do they come from, master?"

Pelas's lips twisted. "Questions, always questions. From the gods, I believe. They are sent to teach or to warn those whom the god's favor. Such people have *the sight*, young Ejil."

Breda squatted down next to Ejil and wrapped his arm around his shoulder. "We were going to let you find your own way until we remembered that most of the meat was in your pack," he said slapping him on the back.

"This spruce," Baal said, gesturing toward the fire. "It'll burn hot, but not for long. Spruce burns quick. You two better fan out and find us more. I saw some bare trees yonder," he said, pointing.

They cut pine branches and laid them out. Pine needles made good insulation and a soft bed. After making tea and roasting strips of fresh deer meat over the fire, the exhausted Ejil crawled into his sleeping fur and fell into a deep sleep beneath the low-hanging pine boughs.

The next morning, Ejil opened his eyes, stretched and greeted a bright blue sky. He had slept well, and it was late. The Sunfather already sat a handsbreadth above the horizon. Icicles hung from the green branches and the sun sparkled like cave crystals off the newly fallen snow. He sat up. Baal squatted by the fire stripping long slender birch boughs.

"Where's Breda?"

His brother shrugged. "Scouting trail. There's a stand of birch," he said, jerking his thumb back over his shoulder. "You'll need snowshoes, if you don't want to be left behind." He held up a completed shoe and regarded Ejil with his cold, black eyes.

Properly shod, the travelers emerged from the trees' shadows onto a white, featureless plain, which stretched out and merged with the sky in all directions. After the hard labor of the previous day, with snowshoes tied to his feet, Ejil felt like he was floating. Giant shadows cast by the early morning sun stretched out before them as they skimmed across the snowy surface of a cloud.

Day followed day. The odyssey continued as the travelers worked their way South. The snows retreated into small patches, the land greened, and steppe grasses began to sprout. Herds of bison, of auroch, sloth, camel, peccary and elk grazed across the plain. From the extreme cold of the ice season, the weather turned steamy hot by day and frigid after sunset. The Budding Season had finally arrived.

One morning, early, with Baal in the lead, the travelers breasted a hill. Baal raised his hand to signal a halt, then crouched and gestured Breda and Ejil forward. Below them by a small, fast-flowing stream lay a huge male lion stretched out in the grass feeding on a freshly killed bison.

Ejil took a deep breath and slowly released it. He stared at the beast, awestruck by its size. *By the gods! Lying prone like that, it's longer than a man is tall.* Oblivious to the three men, front claws gripping the kill, muzzle dripping blood, the beast tore great gobs of meat from the bison's flank. The hunting had turned poor and they were once more out of meat. Leaning on their elbows, peering over the top of the hill, Ejil and his two companions waited, hoping to scavenge something from the remains of the lion's kill.

A pack of hyena—drawn by the blood smell—materialized on a low ridge just beyond the depression where the lion fed. Ejil watched, fascinated, as the wily beasts moved in and slowly surrounded the kill. Larger than wolves, their scruffy brown coats spotted with black, they circled, yipping and laughing. Whining, one of the members slunk forward, buried its salivating jaws in the fallen animal and attempted to claim a piece of meat. Ejil knew about those jaws. Once they clamped down, they were impossible to pry open. The lion roared and lunged, driving the scavenger back, but the hyena were persistent. Each time he drove one off, he'd turn to find another slinking in from the opposite direction.

Finally, the beasts backed off and sat waiting until, finally sated, the lion stood, licked his jaws, glared at the pack and ambled off, his swaying belly sagging almost to the ground. The pack closed in and began to feed.

"Well now, little brother," Baal said, "Breda has been boasting about this sling of yours. He tells me that you knocked down three Fishbellies with it. There is a lot of meat left on that bull. So, show us what your throwing stick can do. Killing a few hyena should not be too difficult."

"All right," Ejil jumped to his feet, ready to accept his brother's challenge.

"Wait!" Breda said. "There are a whole tribe of those dog fuckers. If they decide to attack, we'd have no chance out here in the open."

"I can do it, Breda," Ejil said, unwrapping the cord.

"Attack?" Baal snorted, "Those cowards? They go after the wounded and helpless. We each have two spears. A couple of bleeding corpses will drive them off. You ready, little brother?"

Ejil stood with his legs parted, sling dangling from his hand, and nodded. Breda gazed back at him somberly and shook his head. "Your aim better be good," he said, hefting his spear.

Ejil saw that Baal too had set his stance, and now stood with a spear ready to throw. *My brother has no faith in me.* Ejil knew that a man's ultimate test came when he faced the charge of a dangerous animal. He feared that test, afraid his courage would desert him. *I must stand. No matter what happens, I must stand.*

The wind was in his face. So far, the scavengers—laughing and ripping flesh—had barely noticed him. One of the beasts—the largest, raised her head, studied Ejil—glossy black eyes, sniffed as if in dismissal, and buried her dripping jaws in the bison's soft flank.

Ejil gritted his teeth. Sweat dripped down along his backbone. He whirled the sling over his head and let go.

The missile went wide.

One of the beasts gazed around then dipped his head and returned to his meal.

"Hah," Baal said, "not even close."

He's trying to rattle me, Ejil thought. Gritting his teeth, he placed another stone in the sling cup and adjusted his stance—took a couple of deep breaths to steady himself, spun and let fly. A big scraggly beast leaped into the air with an unearthly howl, ran off a short distance and fell to the ground. The big leader raised her head, panting jaws hanging slack. She studied the three hunters, then dropped her head and resumed eating.

Ejil's fingers grasped a big rounded pebble. Keeping his eye on the big leader, he carefully placed it in the cup and stretched out the cord. The missile caught the huge female solidly behind the ear. She leaped yelping, spun in a circle as if chasing her tail, then dropped to the ground unmoving.

"Good shot," Breda said, glancing at Baal, who avoided his eye.

"I've got the range," Ejil said, but the pack was now aware of him. Three of the beasts trotted forward, faced up the hill and glared. He swallowed hard, seeing the murderous look in their dark eyes. With their lips drawn back they seemed almost to be smiling at him.

"Get ready," Breda's voice warned.

But the pack hesitated, unsure. Ejil relaxed his shoulders, took a deep breath and launched. The middle beast fell.

Except for one male, the pack backed off. A deep growl emerged from between his slavering lips. Snarling, he surged forward to within the length of a few spears, stopped and stared—eyes ablaze—greasy rough standing on end.

"That's the leader's mate. Watch out! He's getting ready to charge," Breda's voice warned.

Ejil swallowed hard. The hyena was close enough to smell his stink. Ejil felt those jaws closing around his throat. Sweat broke out all along his hairline. *Did I load a stone?* He stumbled backwards a step, keeping his eyes glued to the crouching death. *Close, so close!* From the corner of his eye, he caught Breda edging forward—arm cocked—spear poised.

Hefting the cord, he felt the stone's weight and relief surged through him. Raising his arm, he twirled the cord. With a sharp yelp, the hyena charged. Ejil's world went still and soundless. He was aware of everything and nothing, his mother's soft breast, Lada's sparkling brown eyes. The cord's looped end slipped off his thumb, the missile flew…catching the big male between the eyes. The scavenger dropped to the dirt, rolled and stopped; Breda's spear sprouted like a weed from his bloody throat.

Bent over, panting, Ejil glanced at Breda. The scout grinned back at him. "Your kill! I was just making sure," he said.

What was left of the pack turned tail and disappeared over the ridge. Baal and Breda moved in. Ejil stood guard, sling at the ready while his companions chopped away with their hand axes, cutting away long strips of flesh and several large rib bones.

Soon, the sky turned blood-red, the sun fled over the horizon and night fell. The fire sparked and spit and the rich aroma of roasting meat rose up. Thin strips of bison meat dried over the fire. The rib bones were split; the men feasted on the soft, nut-brown marrow.

Baal tossed a bone over his shoulder and belched.

Breda carefully licked each of his fingers. "Admit it, Baal, Ejil's sling proved itself," he said.

"Nine hyena were about four too many," Ejil said.

"Those words, *four*, *nine*, what are you saying?" Baal asked.

"Old Pelas taught me to count. He had a name for each of a man's fingers," Ejil said.

"The tribe kept him well fed. He had a lot of time to think about odd things," Breda said.

"What names?" Baal asked.

Ejil held up his right hand. "Everyone knows *one, two, and three, four and five*," he said, wiggling one finger after another.

But after five, our only word is 'more,' or we make cuts on a tally stick.

"This one he called *six,*" he said, holding up the thumb of his left hand. "Then *seven, eight, nine* and then *ten*," he said and wiggled his little finger.

"What if there are more than ten?" Breda asked.

Baal snorted. "You start on your toes."

"Your toes!" Breda burst into laughter. He rolled over holding his stomach.

"Was it that funny?" Baal asked, his face deadpan.

"Name the toes? That might work," Ejil said.

Baal and Breda, eyed each other, broke up and rolled over on the dry grass.

After a while, Ejil sat up and wiped his eyes. "Two men with slings could have killed that whole pack," he said.

"This many?" Baal asked holding up both hands, fingers spread. "I don't believe it."

"You don't believe it?" Breda said. "I saw what that sling thing can do in battle and you saw what happened to those hyena. Suppose it was you instead of Ejil facing that pack."

Baal raised an eyebrow. "Are you saying I would have missed with a spear?"

"No, but Ejil had to kill one, wound another then kill that big female to discourage them," Breda said, ticking off three fingers. "You have two spears. Even if you killed the first two, you would have been one spear short."

Baal snorted loudly and turned away.

From across the fire, Ejil watched his brother. Baal's beard had grown full. He sat rubbing it, gazing into the flames. How often had he watched his father make the same gesture? Finally, Baal raised his eyes. "Could you teach other warriors to use that thing?" he asked.

"I could teach anyone, brother," Ejil said. "Like throwing a spear, it takes practice."

Baal gave a short nod. "If you could figure out some way to throw a spear like you threw those rocks, that would be really useful." His eyes glittered from across the fire like the eyes of a demon.

A yawn issued from where Breda lay prone beyond the fire's narrow ring. "I told him the exact same thing. Look, it's been a long day and it's your watch, Baal," Breda said. "Sunup is not that far off. Keep the fire up or those dog-fuckers will be back. I'm getting some sleep," he said, and rolled into his sleeping fur.

The next morning, they woke to find doombirds circling the kill. Several had landed and stood off in a group, waiting.

"We'd better get moving. It won't be long before a bear or another lion shows up.

CHAPTER 13

SUDDEN DEATH

"Lada, there is something wrong, daughter," Ceda whispered.

Lada looked up from her task. "What's happened?" she asked.

"That young boy—you know, the sickly one."

"The thin one they call Reed?"

"Yes, that's the one. I swear, child, I'll never understand how you've managed to master so much of their strange talk. Even when I learn one of their words, I can't get my mouth around it to say it. The signs are easier."

"When I came back from the spring, I saw several clan women clustered around his bedplace. The women were petting and shaking him. I think he's died. That awful witch woman was chanting and shaking a gourd and praying over him."

Lada brushed herself off, and cocking an ear, she edged along the wall toward the cave's entrance, with Ceda following a step behind. Most of the clan had gathered in a half circle around the little boy's bedplace. The boy's father, the one called Squinteye, held a torch above where the child lay. Scar stood back a few steps. He turned his head toward the two women. Lada flinched, but he said nothing, just nodded, his eyes sad.

The kneeling mother held the boy in her arms. Looking down at him, she rocked back and forth, moaning softly. The other women sat silently around her, gazing at the dead boy.

The Spirit Woman whispered in her ear. The woman shook her head vehemently. She looked down and stroked the boy's hair.

Leaning forward, The Spirit Woman placed a hand on the mother's shoulder. The woman looked up, her face covered in tears. The old woman smiled, nodded, took the woman's arm and raised her to her feet. The mother stood, head bowed, still cradling the boy.

Gently, she ushered the mother in the direction of the side tunnel, which Lada knew led to her chamber. The others rose silently and followed.

"Come," Scar beckoned.

Lada's eyes widened. "Me?" she said, pointing to herself.

"Yes, I wish you to see," Scar responded.

The two women meekly followed Scar into The Spirit Woman's chamber.

Several torches blazed from the walls. The young boy's pale corpse lay on a deer pelt by the fire. *He looks so thin, so vulnerable,* Lada thought, looking down at him stretched out by the fire. The crone and the dead boy's mother kneeled on either side of him.

So, this is the old crone's lair. Lada raised her eyes and gazed about the chamber. Her breath caught. Beautiful paintings of animals covered the smooth surface of the innermost wall. In front of her, a red mammoth and several other animals outlined in black.

The booming drum brought her attention back to the drama that was playing out in front of her. As she watched, the Spirit Woman picked a few nodules from a leather bag and placed them on a rock's curved surface. Using a heavy, rounded river stone as a pestle, she ground the nodules into a red powder and added warm deer fat from a bowl set by the fire. Using her fingers, she mixed a thick paste and began spreading it all over the dead child's tiny body.

Red ochre! My people also use it to prepare our dead to enter the afterworld. The blood color is pleasing to the gods and aids the person's entry into the Shadowlands, or so they say. I guess the Fishbellies must believe that too. What are they like, the shadowlands, I wonder? Ejil often talked about such things. He knew Pelas's teachings, but I remember him telling me that since no one had ever returned from that place, no one really knows.

Watching the preparations brought back memories. *My two baby brothers. Both dead before they were old enough to walk. It is always sad,* she mused, *but so many people die—especially babies.* She turned to her mother. Ceda's hands were clasped tightly to her breast. A single tear dribbled down her cheek.

The crone finished her work. She laid the child's body gently back on the deer hide. People started to rise. Scar gestured to Lada. The two women turned and quickly made their way back to the main cave.

Carrying the wrapped corpse, the child's mother passed Lada and placed the body on a waist-high rock just inside the cave's entrance.

"Is that?" Ceda whispered.

"Shhh! Yes, Mother, the same rock I told you about, where they sacrificed the two injured guards."

The clan gathered in a circle around the altar rock and held hands. The Spirit Woman and the baby's corpse were inside the circle. The mother raised up her eyes and began to keen. Another woman joined in, then another, while the men stood silently with their heads bowed.

Lada gripped her mother's shoulder and pointed. The two women stole quietly back to their chamber.

"What do you suppose they will do now?" Ceda asked.

Lada shrugged. "Bury the poor thing, I guess. She shook her head sadly. I think it's best we didn't stay and find out."

"Scar seemed to want you to see."

"Yes, and I have no idea why."

CHAPTER 14

THE FIRST PEOPLE.

As Ejil watched, the goshawk circled, balanced on a pair of out-stretched wings, gliding effortlessly across the cloudless sky. *To his eye, we must seem a ragged line of tiny dots*, he decided.

The ground was uneven, with tufts of short grass between rounded outcrops of stone that jutted from the ground like the sun-dried rib bones of a dead Mammoth.

A tiny rivulet of sweat trickled past Ejil's nose and down his chin. He slapped his cheek with the flat of his hand then fanned his face. A moon had passed since their encounter with the hyena. The dried meat was long gone, the game had disappeared and they were living off roots and berries. For days now, thick swarms of midges, tiny black flies, had plagued them. The pests arrived with the sun and worked their way into every moist crevasse, all throughout the daylight hours. Ejil's dark face was overlaid with gray dust and slick with sweat. He was barefoot, they all were, having long since worn out their shoes. Their ragged clothing hung from bodies lean with hunger and stinking from rough travel.

"Breda, what more do you remember about the place where our people live?" Baal asked.

The land had been slowly rising. Breda stopped to catch his breath, wiping his forehead with a bare forearm. "Their camp is in a deep valley. A river winds like a snake across the valley floor. Trees line either side of the river, and steep cliffs of layered white stone overlook it on the near side. The hunter spoke of a great stone bridge, shaped like a rainbow, with the river pouring through it. Beneath the stone rainbow, the river is so full of fish that a man may cross it by stepping on their backs. The First People's camp is off a rocky beach. The stone rainbow can be seen from the village."

"A rainbow of stone with a river running through it?" Ejil asked. He closed his eyes and tried to visualize what such a thing would look like and shook his head.

"Sounds like one of those stories told late at night around the fire. How much honey-water had you drunk?" Baal asked.

"Not much," Breda said, "but this is no taleteller's lay. The rainbow can be seen every day in broad daylight. He said that it is an awesome sight and the home of a powerful spirit."

"So, all we have to do is find this stone rainbow. We have been walking south for almost three moons. Our shoes are gone. We have no more meat. We have seen no one since this journey began. Maybe we are chasing rainbows," Baal said.

"Once we find the river, we can follow it up-current," Ejil said.

Baal shook his head. "My feet hurt. We keep walking, but we get nowhere."

"See over there in the distance, Baal," Ejil said pointing. "What do you see?"

"Nothing! I don't have hawk's eyes like you, little brother. Hills, ridges?"

"Ridges of white stone," Ejil said.

Baal shrugged.

The climb ended abruptly at the edge of a high cliff.

Ejil was well in the lead when he reached it. He looked out. Below him was a broad valley. *Could it be?* He turned and shouted. "I think we've found it!" Baal and Breda jogged up and joined him at the cliff's edge. At the valley's center, an undulating river glistened in the westering sun.

"Beautiful!" Breda said.

"That's it! That's it! That's the river," Ejil said, pointing.

"It seems right," Breda said. "What do you think, Baal?"

"I'm wondering how we are going to get down this cliff," Baal said.

Ejil put his hand over his mouth to stifle a cough. He nudged Breda and pointed.

"I think we have a more serious problem," Breda said, raising his chin. "Look there!"

Runoff from the rains had cut a narrow gully that eroded into a zig zag down the soft limestone of the cliff face. Partially screened by the tall, spindly pine and broad-leafed oak which sprouted from the crevasse, an armed party of men was working its way up the steep defile toward where the three travelers now stood.

Baal stepped back and motioned to Breda. "Fishbellies?" He asked in a fierce whisper. "Can you tell anything about them?"

"From here all I can see is the tops of their heads—and their spear tips, of course. Could be just a hunting party," Breda said in a normal voice.

"How many?"

"Ten maybe, plus a couple of toes," Breda said, grinning at Ejil.

"Maybe they're friendly. Maybe they can tell us where to find the mother tribe," Ejil said.

"Maybe, maybe not—but we'd better find out."

Baal regarded Breda with a sour look. "I say we hide over in those rocks," he said, pointing his chin toward a jagged gray outcropping. "If they are those bone-sucking Fishbellies, we stay hidden and hope they pass by without seeing us," Baal said.

"And, if they are our people?"

Baal shrugged. "Make ourselves known and hope they are friendly."

A hunter breasted the cliff, stopped and scanned the landscape. He was a short man, his brown skin burned black by the sun. His matted hair and scraggly beard showed no sign of gray. He had thick lips and regular features, but instead of the broad nose characteristic of his people, his was narrow and hooked. A long, sleeveless deerskin tunic over a shirt of the same material, belted at the waist. The tunic was daubed with red and white symbols. His heavy parka he carried lashed to his backpack.

One by one, the other hunters scrambled up the path, boosted themselves over the edge and gathered. Each man carried a pair of flint tipped spears.

"See anything?" From where Ejil crouched behind low lying rocks, the voices of the party were clear. The speaker was a tall man, his head a bush of tangled black hair. He had a broad, open face, a wide nose, as if it had been pushed into his face, and a full black beard which set off a mouthful of white teeth. A short necklace of matched fox teeth and another of bear claws layered down his chest.

"I don't see why we bother; it's a hard climb and there's never anything worth risking a spear throw up here," another man said.

Another hunter hawked and spit. "Four suns and no sign of meat. My waterskin is almost empty and my mouth is dry as dust."

"Maybe Salat can scare up some of his nasty old roots for dinner," the short man said.

The mouth of the man he addressed twisted into a weary smile. He wore a fox skin hat and carried a large, bulging, deer-skin gathering bag that hung by a long strap from his shoulder down to his waist.

"If Salat can make another stew like that one we had last night, he can gather all the roots he likes," Pelat said, a broad grin lighting up his face.

Peeking out from behind the rock a bit more than a spear-throw away, heart pounding, Ejil listened. "Their talk sounds like ours," he said, whispering into Baal's ear.

"I think I recognize the big one," Breda said.

Baal looked from Ejil the Breda, shrugged and stood up.

"Greetings!" he said. Bending over, he placed his spear carefully onto the ground then spread wide his arms. "We come as friends."

The hunters hefted their spears. Hooknose stepped forward; his arm cocked. "Who are you? What do you want here?"

"Our tribe was known as the Broken People. We seek help finding our mother tribe," Baal said.

"How many are you? Come out where we can see you," Hooknose said.

"There are three of us." Breda said. He and Ejil stepped out from behind the rock, placed their spears on the ground and stood up at either side of Baal.

The short hunter motioned them forward.

The big man placed a restraining hand on Hooknose's shoulder and pushed his spear toward the ground. "Calm yourself, Daga. You forget who is first hunter and leader here. I will speak."

He stepped forward, shading his eyes. "I know you. You are Breda, son of Breda. We met at the last gathering, though you looked a lot better fed at that time," he said with a smile.

Breda grinned. "Yes, and you are Pelat. Forgive me, I have forgotten your sire's name."

Pelat's mouth twisted. "He recently passed into the Shadowlands. He was called Talog, the same as your First Speaker."

Breda bowed his head. "May his song be sung forever. Our speaker, too, has made that journey. These are his sons, Baal and Ejil. We have travelled for more than three moons in search of your camp."

The short hunter cut in. "These are our hunting grounds. Why have you come?" he asked.

Breda cleared his throat. "Our tribe was massacred by Fishbellies. We come seeking sanctuary with our kinfolk."

Daga's eyes narrowed. "You say the Fishbellies massacred your people?"

"We are all who are left. They took our women," Breda said.

Pelat shook his head.

"You survived?" Daga asked.

"Yes. Ejil and I were posted as lookouts. We were guarding the back trail when the Fishbellies attacked. By the time we got back, they had gone and our people were dead."

"And you too?" Hooknose asked, staring narrow-eyed up at Baal.

Baal's face darkened. He drew himself up and glared down the shorter man. Ejil could feel his anger welling up. Breda put his hand on Baal's shoulder and squeezed hard.

"Baal, son of Talog, fought bravely. Together, he and his father made a slaughter worthy of a tale teller. Several of those murderers lay in the dust at their feet before Talog fell, and more fell to Baal's spear before he was surrounded, struck down and left for dead," Breda said.

"You have our condolences," Pelat said. "Do not mind Daga, here," he said, eyeing his short companion. "He is not yet blooded, and his tongue sometimes entangles his feet. As for sanctuary, I cannot speak for our First Speaker, but we owe hospitality to all who come to us in peace and claim it. That is known. So come; you are our guests, and we bid you welcome. My hunters and I will be honored to escort you to our village."

"Have you seen signs of a Fishbelly band?" Breda asked.

"Fishbellies? Do you mean those strange, pale-faced men with the heavy foreheads and no chins?"

"Yes."

"No, we have not seen them in many times the seasons turning. "We call them Whitefaces. They are as skittish as deer in the molting season. Usually, they run when they see us. I have never before heard of them attacking our people," Pelat said.

"Whitefaces, Fishbellies, whatever you call them," Baal said, "you would remember this band if you saw them. A vicious warrior leads them. He has a long scar that stretches from his eye to his chin."

A murmur of talk rippled through the hunting party. They eyed the three strangers with a new respect. Baal stared down at the short hunter. Daga's shoulders drooped. His eyes studied the ground at his feet.

Baal gripped the young man's shoulder. "I take no offense, Daga," he said. "A warrior should be suspicious of strangers." He gazed benevolently down at the young hunter.

Daga raised his head and gazed up at Baal, his eyes shining.

Ejil felt the familiar twinge of jealousy. *Baal always seems to know how to choose just the right words.*

"I remember your talk of the great stone rainbow; we are anxious to see it," Breda said.

"Yes, it is a sacred place and a great wonder. It was built by the gods. We cross it to reach our camp," Pelat said. "Pick up your spears. The Moon Goddess rises gibbous this night. It is a long walk. We must hurry to reach home before she sets."

The bridge was visible from a great distance in the moonlight. Ejil watched awestruck as it grew ever higher until it loomed above them. They climbed a narrow path. Broad and well-worn, it wove between the rocks and up the rainbow's shoulder. Below, the river flowed black as they crossed. Ejil could make out the camp sprawled across a flat sward with a fringe of beach, white as bleached bones in the moonlight. The village was tucked into a broad curve in the river, nestled against a backdrop of high cliffs. The hearth fires spread themselves out like bright beads winking across the dark landscape.

Their arrival caused a stir. As they passed through the light of each hearth, people stood and followed. By the time they reached the hut where they were to sleep, a small crowd had gathered. A few carried torches. Pelat managed to shoo them away with a brief introduction and a promise that all would be explained come morning.

Using a borrowed torch, he showed the travelers inside the empty hut and lit two small oil lamps. The flickering light revealed a simple dwelling, much like their former home, bowed ribs made of saplings covered with bark and hides. The hut had been unused for some time, and the floor rushes gave off a musty smell. But after so many months of travel, the place seemed to Ejil as if he had come home.

"The women will bring you food, and I shall inform the šamán of your arrival. I know she will wish to see you and hear your tale," Pelat said. "In the meantime, rest. No one will bother you. I will return in the morning. I bid you goodnight." He crouched to exit the hut.

"The šamán? What of your First Speaker?" Breda called after him.

Pelat glanced back over his shoulder. "Our First Speaker died after the last season of the falling leaves. Callas, our šamán holds the speaking stick. "Goodnight," he said. He lowered the flap and was gone.

Baal snorted. "A woman rules? What of the warriors?"

Breda shrugged and placed a hand on Baal's shoulder. "It would be best, I think, if we kept our eyes open and our mouths closed until we see how things lie," he said.

Ejil stood outside the hut and stretched his back while he made water, his tattered deerskin breeches puddled around his ankles. The sun had just peeked over the horizon. He had slept well enough, though he had strange, unsettling dreams of a great battle and of spears that flew so high that they reached the sky. He examined his stream as Pelas had taught him. *Bright yellow and pungent. A good sign.* Ejil stretched his arms back, expanded his chest and inhaled deeply, enjoying the scent off the river.

The great bridge floated high above the mist. *It truly is like a rainbow in stone. Is 'bridge' even the right name for such a wonder?* Ejil remembered making bridges by laying a fallen log over a stream. He shook his head slowly in reverence. It was indeed, as Pelat said, a wonder. *What sort of invisible magic*, he wondered, *holds it up?*

The camp stirred, stretched and came alive with the sun. Women scolded, babies cried, children ran in circles babbling happily while their mothers revived the banked fires and began preparing the morning meal. The sights and sounds were so familiar. Ejil pictured his own mother preparing the morning meal before the fire. His eyes began to mist. His chest tightened and he struggled to draw breath. *Mother!* he called silently. *Mother, I miss you. How can I still be alive and you are dead?* "No," he said. "No, I can't think about this right now." He wiped the tears from his eyes with the back of his hand and drew a long breath, and then another.

Embarrassed, he gazed around himself, but aside from the occasional furtive glance, no one looked in his direction and no one approached. The wind shifted, bringing with it the scent of roasting meat and the pungent odor of frying fish. Ejil's stomach rumbled. *Pelat promised meat and drink. I hope it comes soon.* He rubbed his stomach. It felt shrunken. He had eaten little in many days.

The mist had begun to clear and the sun sparkled off the river. The fishermen were hauling and emptying the night's catch from their long conical traps into big woven baskets. Hovering above, great white birds screeched and dived, plucking up any fish that managed to elude the men's quick hands. His stomach made a gurgling sound.

A woman šamán who is also First Speaker? Ejil almost laughed out loud recalling how the outrage had transfigured his brother's face.

He adjusted his clothes. He was about to wander over and introduce himself at the nearest hearth in hopes of being offered a bite when he noticed a group coming toward the hut. Pelat was leading. From their slender frame and distinctive walk, the other two were obviously women. Perhaps they were bringing breakfast…but no—Ejil scratched his head—it wasn't trays of food they were carrying. *What is this about?* Ejil wondered, his eyes narrowing. He pulled back the leather flap that covered the hut entrance. "Pelat is coming," he announced, "and there are two women with him carrying spears."

Breda scrambled out of the hut, followed by Baal.

"What the…?" Breda asked, handing Ejil his spear and the šamán's staff. The three stood together, spears planted pointing skyward.

The women were a strange sight, identically dressed in deerskin jerkins that fell to their knees. They wore wide leather headbands painted with red ochre and decorated with feathers and shells. Each had a familiar device tattooed on her right cheek. Ejil recognized the symbol of one devoted to the Cult of The Mother.

Ejil liked Pelat, liked his bearded, open face with its spider's web of squint lines at the corners of his eyes, eyes that locked onto yours when he spoke. This morning, however, yesterday's bright-eyed smile was gone, and when he caught the hunter's eye it did not linger.

"These are Zula and Penta, our šamán's two acolytes," he announced. "She has sent us to bring you before her," he said, biting his lips.

Ejil raised a hand in greeting. *Two armed women to guard a šamán? What is the meaning of this? Pelas never needed protection. Who feeds them?* The taller one, Zula, nodded curtly then quickly looked away; the shorter ran her eye up and down his staff then stared forward like the hollow-eyed clay figure which sat in a niche in Pelas's cave.

Pelat kept his eyes averted. He seemed embarrassed. The two groups stood awkwardly facing each other. Baal's eyes remained fixed on the two guards, his fingers tapping against his spear shaft.

Finally, Breda cleared his throat. "We are honored that your šamán has found time to speak with us so soon," he said. "Please, lead the way."

Pelat blinked then stepped aside and motioned them forward, "After you," he said.

Breda glanced at his companions and stepped forward. Baal and Ejil followed. The two spear-women fell in step behind.

People ceased work to gaze at the passing strangers as the small procession wove its way between the huts toward the center of the village. The dwellings were all similar, mound shaped and hide covered. The day was warming, and some had their sidewalls rolled up to allow the cooling breezes to waft through.

One old woman, her head a tangle of gray hair, met Ejil's eye. She cocked her head, grinned, then cackled merrily, her three remaining teeth glinting in the sunlight. A young mother gave her toddler's rump a slap and shooed him off to join a covey of boys and girls who ran naked, circling the huts like a flock of tiny scavenger birds. One man, gray beard down to his waist, sat cross-legged, his deft fingers artfully plaiting green willow shoots in a half-formed fish trap.

A drying rack, woven from thin branches, stood outside every hut. The odors of fish, offal and roasting meat mixed and drifted on the gentle wind. The day would soon grow hot, though a chilly undertone was always present, a reminder that what Ejil's people had always called The Season of Life was brief, and the icy winds would soon sweep down from the north.

They came to a halt at a long, narrow building with a rounded, sloping roof and flat sides. It was much larger than the huts surrounding it and set apart by a wide space, its construction a patchwork of bark and hide. A ribbon of gray smoke curled from a smoke hole at its center. Pelat gestured toward the entrance, a large arched opening covered by a deerskin curtain painted with black and red images of bison, ibex and auroch. Ejil studied the painting. The animals appeared to float in the air. These were spirit animals, and beautifully drawn, Ejil thought.

"Our šamán is expecting you," Pelat said. "I must warn you not to stare. Men are often made speechless by her beauty. The young šamán may keep his staff, but weapons must be left outside." He indicated a rack set at one side of the door. "No one other than her guards is allowed to carry weapons in the šamán's presence."

Baal regarded Pelat with narrowed eyes. "Yesterday we were your honored guests. Today, we are treated like prisoners," he said, eyeing the two women.

Pelat extended his hands palms down. "Please," he said with a pained expression, "we mean you no harm. You are our honored guests."

Ejil stepped forward. "Baal! Pelat is our friend. He is simply asking that we follow the custom."

Pelat caught Ejil's eye with a quick, grateful smile. "Yes, please," he said, nodding vigorously, "the Venerable Callas is waiting to speak with you."

Breda poked Baal's shoulder. "If these people wished us harm, what good would three spears be, hey?" He laid his spear on the rack. "Let's go meet this beautiful šamán," he said.

Baal shrugged, laid his weapon next to Breda's and entered the longhouse, followed by Ejil.

The light was dim, but the smoke from the fire lingered in the air, and thin rays of sunlight seeped through the plaited reeds that made up the inner walls and cast a distinctive pattern on the rush-covered floor.

Several women sat cross-legged by the fire, preparing hides. Another sat grinding nuts and wild grain on a mortar with a stone pestle.

Toward the far end of the hut, a woman dressed in a long, supple doeskin gown, open to the waist and belted with a dyed-red deerskin sash sat on a shelf set across the hut, holding a staff. The three visitors froze. Ejil's mouth dropped open. Enormous, with large, rounded arms and legs; huge pendulous breasts dangled almost to her waist, nipples gazing outward like round black eyes. Her head was smooth and hairless. She wore no headdress, but a necklace of boar's tusks hung about her neck. Her gown was slit down the center exposing bulging thighs and calves rippling with fat. The face was round and swollen like an oak gall. Long, slitted eyes made it appear as though she viewed the whole world with suspicion. The rounded cheeks were counterposed against a flat nose and full lips. Her chin hung down her chest like a bullfrog's pouch.

"I am Callas," she said, motioning the three travelers closer, "šamán and First Speaker of The First People. I am told you claim kinship and seek refuge among us. You," she said, pointing a finger at Ejil, "are very young, yet you carry a šamán's staff. Tell me your name and lineage."

Baal stood with his mouth gaping open.

Ejil's throat went dry. Callas looked like one of the clay statues of The Great Mother that was kept by his mother in a small shrine in one corner of their hut.

"I am Baal," his brother said, stumbling over his words, "I am the eldest son of Talog, ah, First Speaker of the Broken People, and I am a blooded warrior. We have come seeking an alliance. It is, uh, my place to——"

"Silence!" the šamán bellowed. Her deep, manly voice echoed off the hide walls. Her eyes stretched into narrow slits. She raised one fleshy arm and aimed her forefinger at Baal. "I am šamán and First Speaker of the First People, Baal, son of Talog. It is I who summoned you here and it is I who decides who will speak and when. You say you seek alliance…" She threw back her head and laughed. "The First People do not make alliances with men dressed in rags who come before us barefoot," she chided, looking pointedly down at Baal's dirty feet. "I will speak with the young šamán," she said, beckoning Ejil.

Arms hanging by his side, Baal's gaze dropped down to his dirty feet and curling toes.

Ejil stepped forward hurriedly and bowed. He cleared his throat noisily. "Venerable Callas, my name is Ejil; I am also a son of Talog. This is my brother Baal and our good friend Breda, son of Breda. I carry the staff of Pelas, šamán of the Broken People. The Venerable Pelas dwells with the spirits. I am—was, his apprentice."

Callas's chin pouch jiggled as she nodded. "I have been told of your misfortune. I knew your master. He was a šamán of great wisdom and power. Tell me what brought you to us and how the Venerable Pelas died."

Ejil bowed. "Our story is a long one. I am not sure where to begin."

"At the beginning, young man," Callas laughed. "That is always the best place to begin a story. I will hear it all."

Callas cupped her chin and listened, her left eye never leaving Ejil's face as he recounted the story. Only one thing marred the šamán's features: her right eye came unmoored and wandered upward and focused on the ceiling. She sat up and shifted her weight as Ejil came to the end of his narrative, and as she did the eye refocused itself on Ejil's face.

"A sad tale. Now, Baal, son of Talog, you wish to speak?"

Baal straightened his shoulders and cleared his throat. "You have heard our story. We come seeking your help, Venerable Callas, your help and the aid of your people to rescue our captured women and to take vengeance on a band of those you call Whitefaces, the beasts who killed our sons and fathers."

Callas stretched her arms and yawned. "You rightfully call yourself kin, and so long as you honor our customs you are welcome. As for vengeance, that is not our affair. We have lived in peace by this river since the time of my elderfather's father. Your story is a sad one. My heart reaches out to you, but we owe no blood debt to the Broken People. If we are threatened, we fight, but we are not about to start a war with people who have done us no harm."

The šamán's words shocked Ejil. He thought back to the journey. *All this way, seeking help with hope in our hearts. What of our kinship? Is she heartless?*

Baal pulled back his shoulders and widened his stance. "You will do nothing to help us, then?" he asked, his voice shaking.

"Tell me, son of Talog, do you know where to find this, er, Fishbelly band?"

Baal swallowed hard. "Well no, not exactly, but we did keep careful count. We left at the time of the waning moon and met your hunters on the night of the third gibbous moon since the massacre," Baal said.

"And, you know the place where these Fishbellies are camped?"

Baal signaled to Breda who scratched his head. "I could find the place from our old camp, but they had been there for some time, and I fear that they will have decamped and moved on by now," he said.

"Breda is a great tracker," Baal said. "Where there is sign, he will find it."

Ejil sighed. He felt all hope slipping away.

"So, Baal, son of Talog, we must take up our spears, leave our village unprotected and follow you where? The world is vast. Doubtless, you know the story of The Great Journey. The great fathers of the fathers of our elderfathers traveled for seasons beyond our reckoning to reach this country which ends some say at the great water with waves the size of mountains, though none here have ever seen it.

"Before two moons have passed, the cold winds will howl down from the north carrying ice and snow and the Season of Death will be upon us. There are fish to be dried and meat to be smoked. Our larders must be full if we are to survive the long, dark moons of ice and snow."

Baal stared silently at the šamán.

Ejil set his jaw. He had not expected the šamán to reject their plea, but he understood. *Baal's arrogance will get us nowhere.* He hated the idea of Lada remaining a prisoner, but... *The šamán is right; it is too late in the season. I will not give up, but we must prove our worth to these people.* He made a quick bow and spoke up formally. "We thank you, Venerable Callas, for your hospitality."

Ignoring Baal's hostile silence, Callas continued. "Since you have no women, one of our widows will wash and repair your stinking rags, cook for you and see to your needs," she said, pointing a finger at their tattered clothing. "You have our protection, but you must work. Baal, you will join the hunters. Breda, son of Breda, are you a fisherman?"

"I—" Breda began to speak but the šamán cut him off.

"No matter, you will learn," she said flapping a hand. "Ejil, son of Talog, I will decide about you once we speak further."

"Venerable Callas, I ask your pardon for the smell," Ejil said. "Perhaps, I should bathe before we talk. We have been together traveling hard for many moons, and since we all smell the same, we have ceased to take notice of it."

The šamán's lips spread. She sniffed the air, her chins jiggled and she threw back her head and laughed.

"You may go," Callas said, with a languid sweep of her hand indicating Breda and Baal. "Pelat will show you the way to the sweat hut, or the river if you prefer. My women will bring you soapweed. "But you, Ejil son of Talog, your bath can wait. I have questions, and I can stand your stink long enough to hear the rest of your story."

Ejil bowed his head. "As you wish, Venerable one."

The moon waned and then became new again, and the weather turned colder. Good to her word, Callas did all she had promised. Ejil and his companions did their best to show their gratitude. Baal joined the hunters. Breda was fascinated by the fishing. He was respectful. He seemed eager to learn, and was readily accepted by the men who worked the river.

Callas assigned Ejil to help in the šamán's hut. She was impressed with Ejil's knowledge of herb lore. Like all sámánok, one of Callas's main duties was treating wounds and administering to the sick, but she was so heavy she could not walk any distance without help. She soon began sending Ejil in her place.

Ejil took on any task the šamán asked of him, hoping if he proved useful, he might be able to change her mind about helping them. His mind kept returning to Lada. *How is she? Have they hurt her?* He pictured her walk, her lovely brown eyes. Those thoughts stirred him in ways he was unfamiliar. She had always been there. It never occurred to him that he could lose her. *I would gladly give up any thought of revenge if only I could have her back.* That made him feel guilty, but he knew Breda felt the same about Mata.

One day, waddling back to the longhouse, Callas startled Ejil, who was sitting back on his haunches studying the images on the painted hide that covered the entrance. "Beautiful work, isn't it?" she wheezed, out of breath from her short walk.

"Forgive me, šamán; I did not hear you coming."

"You remind me of Pelas," Callas said. "He would often sit alone, not sleeping, eating nothing for many days, communing with the spirits."

"He always said I asked too many questions."

"Questions, hah! When he was young, Pelas was a great one for questions. I believe he recognized a kindred spirit in you."

Callas words warmed him. Talog, his father, and Pelas, the two men most important to Ejil, were dead. He missed their comforting presence and their guidance. He still wished to become a šamán, but feared he was not worthy. Callas praised his work, but somehow it was not enough.

"The pictures Pelas made were beautiful," Ejil said. "But these seem almost alive. Whose work is this, Venerable Callas?"

She laughed. "Not mine? No! Your master used to say I was born with fingers more like toes. He was right. Pico painted those. Many years ago, he was also apprenticed to Pelas, but he was a poor student. He is absent minded and can neither memorize the sagas nor remember his herbs. He almost killed our last First Speaker with a poisonous mushroom, but his painting is god-inspired."

"Is Pico still alive?" Ejil asked, feeling his excitement mount. "Is it possible to speak with him?"

"Oh yes, he is very much alive. Pico stays by himself. He has a hut below the mouth of the sacred cave. It is high up in the cliffs, almost a half day's walk. There is a large chamber—paintings by Pico line its walls. That is where the tribal council meets. There are some, deeper in the cave that have been there for as long as anyone can remember."

"A sacred cave," Ejil said, his excitement rising. "Is it very deep, then?"

"It is the womb of the earth, sacred to The Mother. No one has ever found its end. None have gone so far in as Pico, but even he had to turn back when he grew faint and his torch refused to burn."

"His torch wouldn't burn? How strange."

"Yes, perhaps it is the fetid breath of the spirits that dwell deep in the earth. Pico believes the doorway to the Shadowlands lies in its depths. Powerful spirits protect it.

"When Pico is not painting in the cave, he keeps busy with tattoos, knapping, making beads and paintings like this one. Most of it he trades for food. The beads," she said, cocking an eye, "he trades for the women's favors, but the only ones who will have him are widows, old and toothless as he is, ha ha ha!

"It is best to start early when it is still cool, before the Sunfather mounts high on the sky ladder. Go at sunrise. I warn you, Pico is a strange one. He can be ill tempered and doesn't take to many. Do not be surprised if he drives you away."

CHAPTER 15

THE CHOICE

Tule was the first. One night, as the captive women gathered around their fire, she stood up, shyly staring at her feet. The women grew quiet and waited. "The three moons have almost passed. I am with child and…" she said, her voice soft, "and, I have decided…" She lifted her chin. "…to join with Spearpoint!"

Lada was dumbstruck. She jumped to her feet. "Join with one of those, those killers!" She stared openmouthed at her friend. "What? And be adopted by the people who murdered your father and mother?" she demanded, glaring at Tule across the fire.

"Spearpoint had no part in that! He is a good man," Tule said, her eyes blazing.

Lada looked around at the other women expecting anger and condemnation, but they remained silent. Shaking with rage, Lada stalked off to a dark corner to be alone with her anger. After a while, her mother came and sat down beside her.

"They lost fathers and husbands and babies. Have they forgotten?" Lada asked her mother.

Cooing softly, Ceda wiped away her daughter's tears. "No, they haven't forgotten, but what did you expect? We are alone. Our people are dead and we are slaves, dear."

The next morning, Tule sought her out. "Please don't hate me, Lada. It just happened," the girl said with tears streaming down her face.

"But he is one of *them*. You swore you wouldn't ever…" Lada said, her voice breaking.

Tule shook her head. "Spearpoint is a good man, Lada. He wasn't there! He's not like that awful Scar. He had nothing to do with the attack on our people."

"Nothing to do—how can you forget?"

"I haven't forgotten, but our dead are dead. They have returned to the Earth Mother. We are alive. I need a man. I want to have babies. I have always wanted babies. Don't you want babies, Lada?"

Lada shook her head and walked away.

Unlike the elaborate preparations common with Lada's people, joining within the Lion Clan required only a simple ceremony. As the moon waxed full, two women captives found partners. One joined with a warrior, the other with a clan woman.

Each evening, the clan gathered around the central hearth. Lada and the other captives formed a circle around them, hoping to catch the discarded scraps which made up their evening meal. Clan women, in particular, enjoyed humiliating the captives. They would toss bits of meat and laugh while the captive women scrambled and sometimes fought over the meager leavings.

One night, after the eating was done, Tule and Spearpoint stood before the clan. The young hunter held up Tule's hand and gazed around the fire. "Here is my woman," he signed.

Tule turned to Spearpoint and smiled. "This is my man," she said, making the sign she had been taught.

The clan beat their hands on their thighs to signify their approval, and it was done.

"My sister makes three," Catya said. The captives had been ordered back to their chamber after the joining. "At least now she will eat with the clan and get something she can chew," she said, staring at the piece of hard gristle she had been gnawing.

Lada sat cradling her head. "They enjoy humiliating us," she said.

"Yes, but what choice do we have?" Ceda asked, stroking Lada's hair.

"It's either that or starve." Catya stood and spun around. "Look at me. I'm a bag of bones. Whatever I eat comes out the other end. The cave stinks. They won't even let us go outside to relieve ourselves. It's disgusting."

Lada lifted her head and gazed at Catya. "What are you saying?"

"I'm saying anything is better than this. Look, all our people are dead. I caught one of the ugly brutes eyeing me the other day. I'd join with any one of them for a nice piece of liver."

One day, at the time of the waning moon, Lada was returning to camp with a skin of fresh water. She walked carefully, the heavy auroch bladder balanced on one shoulder. The narrow path from the stream was flanked by a cliff on one side and a stand of scrub pines on the other. The Warm Season was well upon them, and Lada was enjoying the shade and the cool pine-scented air. Halfway to the cave, she found Scar squatting by the side of the path.

"I will speak," he said, standing, making the clan sign.

Lada was becoming fluent in the clan language. She was used to Scar seeking her out with questions or if there was something he wished the captives to know.

The sun shining between the web of needle clad branches dappled the ground. Scar took hold of the water carrier and lowered it gently onto the bed of needles that carpeted the path.

She signed her thank you. "What do you want of me?" she signed.

"The women..." he stopped, seemingly unable to find a word to express what he wished to say. "No pain?" he signed, then grimaced and stretched his gaze beyond her off into the distance. Lada knew of no clan sign for *happy*, but she thought that she grasped his meaning.

She did not know what to say. "No man forces himself on us, but we are your prisoners. We are not free," using the word from her own language.

He tried, he pronounced the word, *fwree*, then frowned and shook his head. "Some women have joined with clan warriors. They are clan," he said, his eyes seeking hers.

"Yes, that is so," she signed.

His brow furrowed. "What, then?" he signed.

Lada shrugged. *He thinks that becoming clan is everything.* She found their language frustrating. So many things—feelings, particularly—for which there were no words or signs. Her intuition told her he had more to say. She waited.

"The chill winds soon come down from the north. A woman will need a man to protect her," he said. "I want you for my woman," he said making the sign for "joining."

She rocked back on her heels and met his eye. Lada remembered the sign well. It was the same sign a man used when he wanted to enter a woman. One-ear had made it to Tule that first night, but he had repeated it, which made it into a command. "Do I have a choice?" she asked.

He shrugged. His eyes regarded her's questioningly.

"I am…" She couldn't think of a clan word. "I am honored," she said, using her own language and signs, she hoped, would make her meaning clear. *Honored,* she thought. *I always assumed it would be Ejil who asked me that question. Stupid girl,* she thought, berating herself. *Ejil is dead, and the world has moved on. You must make a choice.*

Lada's mind was in turmoil. Scar was the clan leader. She dared not offend him or let him see where her mind was focused. She kept thinking of escape. *But where and to what?* She thought about her mother's words.

He shook his head.

"It is, it means, you are the leader and a great warrior," she said, searching for a way to explain and flatter him. Finally, frustrated, she shook her head. "Thank you," she signed. She put a finger to her temple. "I must think."

"Three moons are almost passed. You still have my protection," he signed. He raised his eyebrows and made a circle with his arms. "I will wait. Tell the women, we must leave this place. Game grows scarce."

"When?" she asked, her eyes wide.

"As the Sunspirit rises," he said, cupping both hands to make the sign. "We must go. The leaves begin to turn color." He stood and, without another word, walked off. Lada followed him with her eyes. His proposal had not surprised her. She knew, as women do, that he desired her. What did surprise her was that she was considering his offer.

He is an impressive man, despite that terrible scar. He saved Tule, and he has been kind at times, she mused. Lada had closely observed clan customs. A woman drew her status from her man. *If I join with Scar, I will be an important woman in the clan.* She thought of her mother. Ceda was beyond the age of childbearing. If no man chose her, she would forever remain a slave. *As Scar's woman, I will be able to protect her.*

And, if I refuse? Lada knew enough of men to know what that would mean. Scar was a proud man. He would be hurt and angry, and she would remain a drudge, dealing with Crowbait's constant humiliations, surviving on scraps and leavings. And worse if she ran and was caught. *No, I must either accept Scar or run, and there is no place to go. Ejil is dead. All of my people have gone to the Shadowlands.* Lada covered her face with her hands and wept.

CHAPTER 16

THE PAINTED CAVE

Ejil looked up the trail that led to the sacred cave. It was well traveled. Level for a short stretch, it meandered through tufts of browning grass and low-lying willows, their sprouted sprigs had shot up like rabbits' ears, signaling the coming of the Hot Season. Further up the cliffside, no grass grew on the steep, narrow path. The bright sun reflecting off the white stone made Ejil squint.

Winded and half-blind, he mounted a ridge and finally came in view of the painter's hut. It was perched on a windy shelf below the high cliff that led to the cave's entrance. Clearly visible from the trail, the narrow crack in the rockface brought to mind the soft opening of a woman's sex.

He called out but got no answer. He was standing outside the hut, studying the charcoal drawings on a deerskin pelt stretched across a frame made of lashed branches, when a gruff voice erupted from behind him.

"Who are you? What do you want here?" the voice demanded.

Ejil twisted around and stared. The voice's owner appeared to have stepped out of a bad dream. Short and scrawny, he was dressed in a ragged deerskin jerkin covered in dabs of paint—black, red and white. A filthy halo of white hair surrounded his baldpate like a bird's nest, upon which a pair of entwined snakes had been tattooed in red. A curtain of twisted strands of braided hair hung down past his shoulders. His skin was black. His pinched visage sported an equally straggly mustache and beard. Narrow of shoulder, his body bent forward. Long, bony arms dragged almost to the ground. One eye was bright while the other had a droopy lid, which, when viewed from one side made him appear half asleep.

Ejil stared dumbfounded.

"Well," the visage asked, its voice like a croaking frog, "are you deaf *and* stupid?"

"Uh, sorry, my name is Ejil," he said, as if he couldn't quite remember who he was. "I am the son of Talog, First Speaker of the Broken People. I am here, Venerable Pico, because I…I mean, well, because I admire your paintings. Callas sent me."

"Humph," Pico replied. "Callas sent you, you say? You have seen some of my paintings before, I suppose." He brushed his hair aside and scrutinized Ejil with one piercing eye. "Venerable, is it? Do I know you? What have you brought me? What, your hands are empty! Is it a tattoo you want? I'm constantly plagued by the young men about tattoos. They believe it makes them look fierce. Stupid nonsense!"

"No, Venerable One, I want to learn to make pictures like yours."

"You have come to see my drawings?"

"Yes, Venerable Pico, yes! I would like to see them very much! I was apprenticed to Pelas our šamán, but he was murdered, as was my family and the rest of our tribe. My brother and I and my friend Breda are the last of our people," *Well, not the last, I hope,* he thought with a twinge of guilt. "Your, ah, šamán has given us sanctuary. I admired the paintings at the entrance to the longhouse, and Callas sent me to you."

"Callas sent you. Oh yes, you said that. I have heard of you; you are the one they call the young šamán. Humph, young šamán, indeed! You look barely old enough to have stopped pissing yourself. Pelas, did you say? Yes, I studied with Pelas for a season," Pico said, fixing a fierce gaze on Ejil. "You've probably heard about that." He turned his face away. "Sorry to hear he died," he said, staring off into space. "The man knew his spells and his herbs, though he was never much of a painter. Now that you are here, do you want to see some real paintings?"

"Yes, Venerable Pico, I do," Ejil said.

"Yes? Well, as it happens, I'm on my way to the cave," he said, flapping one hand in the general direction. "Come along now, and stop calling me 'venerable,'" he said, shaking his finger. "You'll hex me. Words have power, you know. Didn't your master teach you anything? Besides, all the *venerable* people I know are dead, and I am in no hurry to join them." He strode off, then scuttled up the rocky path leading to the cave like the scrawny spider he very much resembled.

The sun was hot on Ejil's back. He couldn't quite decide if he should follow this queer old man or not. When he finally heaved himself, panting and covered with sweat, onto the narrow apron that fronted the cave entrance, he found the little man crouched by a small fire. At his back, far below and spread across the valley—the dark ribbon of the river undulated along in lazy curves. Off in the distance, across the river, a large herd of what looked like auroch grazed on the greening grass.

The old man selected a few curled shards of birch bark from a pile, dipped them in a large bowl hollowed out of softstone, then twirled them around a charred pine branch. Ejil watched him intently.

"Pine pitch," Pico said, raising his head. "It flows best as the leaves are beginning to color. Bind rolled birch bark tight around a torch head and it will burn, but it will last much longer if you soak it in pitch. Smells better too, but take care with the pitch, nothing will put it out. It'll burn a hole right through your hand. In the deep cave, I use oil lamps to paint by. Torches don't burn well; they poison the spirit. When a torch starts guttering, that's a warning, the spirits are near. Best get out quick or you'll find yourself dead—that is, if you can find yourself at all," he said. He bent over and slapped his leg and laughed until tears cut furrows down his grimy cheeks.

The laughter ended abruptly. The old man straightened, wiped away the tears with his forearm and shoved a torch head into the fire. It burst into flame. He studied it for a moment then lifted it above his head and, without a word, strode through the cave entrance.

Inside, a short passage led to an expansive chamber. The air was damp and cool against Ejil's face. It tasted earthy. Pico lifted his torch. Ejil craned his neck and gazed at the clusters of vivid-white, tapered stone columns that hung down like giant's teeth from high up in the cave's shadowed recesses. Others were attached to the floor. Some were quite small. *They look just like my penis and they are the color of spunk,* Ejil decided, his hand absently caressing his organ. *And over there on the wall, great frozen gobs of gooey spunk.* He smiled at his own little joke. *You don't suppose it really is spunk left by some spirit?* He asked himself. He stretched his neck looking at other stark white columns that soared upwards from the floor until they were swallowed by the darkness. As the torch swayed, tiny reflections winked and sparkled.

Pico paused then waved the torch back and forth. "You see that? See how they twinkle? Star crystals is what I call them. Same stuff, I believe. Sometime I'll show you my small one—green, odd shape,—this long," he said, extending his index finger. "Color of a leaf in the Hot Season. You can see right through it."

"Really? How do such things come to be?" Ejil asked before he could stop himself.

Pico regarded him with a sour look. "Only the gods know. Stop asking stupid questions."

"Yes, Venn—ah, Pico, sorry," Ejil said. He reached out. It was cold to the touch. *They are like huge icicles.* He had often watched icicles form, building droplet by frozen droplet. *But these, these are solid rock. Could stone melt and flow like water or spunk?* He would have liked to ask, but he feared he had already antagonized the surly old creature. *I'll wait,* he decided, *until he's in a better mood.*

The chamber walls were too uneven for painting, but on one side under a long undulating crack, Ejil noticed an area which appeared to have been smoothed over. A pattern of red dots stood out against the muddy brown background.

"What are those? Drops of blood?" Ejil asked, before he could stop himself.

The old man shrugged and smiled, the torch flames dancing in his dark eyes. "Come closer," he said, holding the torch high. "They're handprints! Painted, who knows how long ago?" He raised the torch and brought it closer to the wall. "There are more, they're everywhere deeper in the cave, but there we dare not go without first offering up prayers to still the spirits."

"How deep does it go? The šamán says it has no end."

"No end? Well, don't know about that," he said with a wink. "Everything has an end. It is called the womb of the earth. Some say it is the entrance to the Shadowlands.

"The maker of these prints had little art," he said, screwing up his face. "Deer fat mixed with red ochre. Makes the color brighter—lasts longer. Whoever it was, dipped his hand in the mixture and used it like so, he said pulling back his fingers and thrusting his palm forward. "Wanted people to know he was here." The old man shook his head. "Good ochre is hard to come by!"

"It looks like a mammoth—I mean, to me." Ejil said, cocking his head, shifting his angle of view.

Pico shook his head. "A mammoth? Nonsense! He stepped back, cocked his head and squinted. "Mammoth, humm…well, maybe made like a tattoo. Pierce the skin with a bone needle dipped in paint. Makes a tiny dot. A pattern of tiny dots set so close together make a picture.

"Sometimes I do the same thing on deerskin; but skin is soft, rock is hard. Some people's heads are just as hard," he said, and slapped himself in the forehead. "Ha ha, so they tattooed the walls. Come along now, we must get on."

They passed into a corridor through a second chamber and into a third. Ejil sniffed the air. It was cooler and the earth smell was more pronounced. The chamber was broad and commodious.

It was like standing in a giant mouth with pointed stone teeth hanging ominously down from inside the shadowed jaw.

In the moving torch's flickering shadows, grotesque shapes formed images. A mammoth; a woman's face with long, cascading hair. Pictures formed before his eyes—changed shape—and were gone.

Pico stepped up to the wall. "Observe," he said, raising his torch with a flourish. Ejil's breath caught. Spread out on the wall before him were the most beautiful charcoal drawings he had ever seen. To the left, a group of aurochs—tall as a man—ambled across the wall. A few precise uninterrupted strokes by someone wielding a burnt stick had brought them to life.

It was as if the chamber wall had, at one time, been as supple as a deerskin, folding over and in on itself forming three separate niches between the folds. The central panel was a deep, smooth-sided grotto.

At the far-righthand panel, a brace of lions—heads and necks only. The manes had been darkened with charcoal. Ejil had never seen animals depicted so. *One is partly hidden by the next, as if set deeper in the rock or side by side. They are hunting. The ones in back are prodding the others forward.* He felt the beast's arrogance and the vibration of padded feet as the fearsome killers sauntered across the plain.

On the far left at knee level, simply outlined in charcoal, paired bull rhinos engaged in fierce battle. The animals strained forward, toward each other, and the brittle sound of horn clashing on horn echoed in Ejil's mind.

"You see how I used the shape of the stone," Pico said drawing the torch from side to side. It moves with the torch. He grasped Ejil's shoulder, turned and pointed. "Here, you see I drew the bison around this point where the rock protrudes from the wall and forms the beast's shoulder and withers."

"Yes, wonderful."

"Hah, you think so? Watch this!" He brought the torch down to eye level and passed it the length of the panel from left to right. The play of light and shadow caused the animals to emerge from and then recede into the wall. "You see! You see! There are more, but these are my latest," Pico said, jigging excitedly from one foot to the other.

"Beautiful," Ejil said, his eyes alight. "They jump right off the wall! Who taught you about the shading and the…?"

Pico raised his hand. "Hold a moment, young fellow," he said, his face breaking into a smile behind its hairy curtain. "As you know, I apprenticed to Pelas. When we were both very young, Pelas apprenticed to Oda, son of Holsi. Oda was the better painter, and his mother was better still. Her name was Kata, I believe. The lions are her work, I think. Holsi was supposed to have been a great painter too, but he was long before me. I don't know his work. His sire was also named Pelat, I believe.

"Anyway, I took the idea from Oda's mother, though I have improved on it, if I do say so myself. I found that by rubbing in the charcoal with my hand, if I made them darker, they'd appear closer, if I rubbed off most of the black, they seemed more distant."

"I've never seen a painting like that," Ejil said. "One animal standing in front of another. You see the one with only the back end visible?" Ejil said, pointing. "It's walking right through the wall. Some say that cave walls are like skin and behind them is another world."

"You see all of that, do you?" The painter's eyes twinkled. "I started at the back. Once I had the back line right, I drew the hindquarters, and when I got to the crease I stopped. Couldn't figure out how to finish it without it appearing as if the beast was cut in two, so I left it," he said, and cocked his head sideways.

"He does seem to be walking through the wall, doesn't he?" He rubbed his scraggly beard. "Well, there is plenty of work to do. Humm. Did Pelas teach you to mix colors? Can you tattoo?"

"He taught me to mix the paints. How to grind the ochre and shake it up in water to separate out the sand. Pelas always said I made a powder fine as baby's hair. I know how to heat the yellow to make red, and to make red redder. I've watched Pelas make tattoos, but I've never done one myself. But you'll see, I'm a very quick learner."

"I thought you were apprenticed to Callas. Won't she have something to say about your coming up here?"

Ejil shrugged; thinking of Pelas had made him sad. "I told you, she sent me. I gather herbs for her and make potions for the sick, but there is no agreement between us. My father has gone to the Shadowlands and I am of age," he said, feeling his spirits lift. *I will not forget Lada; I will not forget my family or our plans,* Ejil promised himself to ward off a creeping feeling of guilt.

"Humm, well that Callas is a subtle one. Best be wary; if she does something, there is always some reason behind it."

Wary? Why should I be wary? Why would Callas have…"I believe fate directed me to you, Venerable…I mean, Pico."

"Ha ha, I see you have been infected by old Pelas's ideas. How did you get here? Did I miss something? Was there a spirit finger goosing you up the path? Did I see a god dragging you along by the ear?"

"Pelas taught me that life is like a thin rope made of thin strands of twisted reed, and our story was twisted together long before we were born. The gods are tricksters. They make us believe that we control our own lives."

Pico cocked his head. "Why did you say you came?"

"I admired your work and want to learn to make pictures."

"Exactly; on your own hind legs. We are ruled not by some god's desires but by our own. Why doubt it? Pelas was a great šamán, oh yes, but he did not know everything. No one knows everything, and hardly anyone knows as much as Pico, ha ha!" He pranced about as he chuckled. For an old man, he was very light on his feet. "The gods gave you a head," he said, patting his own, "to think with. Would they have done that if they did not expect you to use it?

"If you pick up a pebble and drop it, it will fall to the ground. That is the nature of a pebble and not even the gods can change it. You have a nature too."

Ejil was confused. "Yes, but surely the gods could make the pebble float up to the sky if they wished!"

"Ever seen such a thing?" Pico asked.

"No, but…!"

Pico held up a charcoal stick and pointed. "Here is Pico's first lesson, young man: never accept anything. Question; always question! Now take this charcoal stick and make me a picture here on this wall."

Ejil's mouth dropped open. "Draw? You mean, now?" he croaked; his throat suddenly felt dry.

"Here, take this torch and examine the wall. The picture is already there. All you have to do is draw it out."

Ejil hesitated, gazed at the cave wall for a moment, then, with a few quick strokes, drew the outline of the bull mammoth with the long curving tusks he had encountered on their journey. He remembered the tiny, intelligent black eyes and the bull's pungent odor. He drew his long trunk dangling toward the ground, stepped back, handed Pico the charcoal stick and eyed the old man nervously.

Pico held up the torch and, shading his eyes, studied the drawing. "Um, good…very good, young Ejil. You were able to see it. Pelas taught you well."

Ejil raised his eyes. "Yours are so much better."

"Better? Yes, of course. You copied Pelas and Pelas copied Oda. But Pico didn't copy anyone, no indeed," he said jigging foot to foot.

Didn't he just say he copied Oda's mother? Ejil was growing accustomed to the old man's odd behavior and decided it would be best not to mention it.

"Deeper in the cave there are paintings done in the same style. Pelas himself may have drawn some of them." The old man regarded the boy carefully. "Still, young Ejil," he said, "your lines flow like a flute's soft trill."

So began Ejil's association with Pico. The exact nature of their relationship remained unspoken between them, but on many mornings, Ejil would leave the village after his work was done and climb the trail to Pico's hut below the sacred cave and learn about painting.

CHAPTER 17

FIRST HUNTER

Above, on a ledge overlooking the shadowed ravine, Pelat and Baal lay breathing softly, the sun hot on their backs. The day was lovely; thick puffy clouds were strung like ivory beads across an azure sky. Baal wiped his eyes and peered through a crack in the rocks. They were hunting in the pine forest which fringed the cliffs on the near side of the river.

With a twist of his hand, Pelat signaled the other hunters where they crouched hidden in the trees. They had been stalking a family of boar and finally caught a glimpse. It was a huge female followed by a big male and their piglets, working their way upwind through the rock-strewn forest.

"You should see that sow," Pelat said, his eyes glittering. "She's a big one," he said, opening his arms wide. "There's enough meat on her to feast the whole tribe with leftovers."

"I've never seen bigger. What now, Chief?" Baal asked. Baal had an idea, but this was only his third hunt under Pelat, and this part of the forest was new to him. Already, the first hunter had singled him out and named him scout because of his ability to probe silently ahead without alerting their prey.

"If they keep going in that direction, they'll pass through that narrow ravine; you know, the one by the big tree," Pelat said.

"I know the tree. It's a yew," Salat said. "My uncle says it is so old it must have been planted by the Sunfather himself."

Pelat thrust his spear butt into the dirt. "Right," he said, sketching the sacred sign in the air, "maybe it will bring us luck. They are taking their time. If we are quick, we can block off both ends."

"I don't know the lay of the land around here," Baal said. "Is the ravine a good place to trap her?"

"It's the only place. The rest is open rocky ground. If a few of us hide in the rocks above the entrance, the rest can circle around and seal off the ravine from the other end. The other end is wider. The walls at the entrance are steep and slippery. They'll be forced to go through one at a time," Pelat said.

Salat shook his head. "We can hide in the rocks above, but once we slide down into the entrance, there's barely enough room for two men to stand, and as you say, the walls are too slippery to climb. If she decides to backtrack, we'll be the ones trapped. Somebody's likely to get himself gored!"

Baal snorted. He had been seeking a chance to exhibit his skills and prove himself. It had been expected that he would follow his father and become First Speaker of the Broken People, and his ambition had not cooled. *I will make my reputation as the best hunter. Then only one woman stands in my way.* "Two men at the far end should be able to take them both."

Salat's lips twisted. "Two men? You might get the sow, if you're lucky. She'll be in the lead, but the male?" He shook his head. "I say we climb the rocks and try taking them from above. That way nobody gets hurt."

"Yes, and a miss means a smashed spear tip. What if they make it out the other end?" Baal asked.

"Then they're gone!" Tanus said. "The ravine opens into a broad valley. We'd have no chance of catching them."

"I'll stand and block the far entrance if someone will back me up," Baal said.

"Two boar, two spears," Daga said, thrusting out his chest. "I'll stand with Baal."

Pelat clapped his hand on Baal's shoulder and grinned at Daga. "I am first hunter. I'll stand, and Baal will back *me* up. The rest of you block the near end. Once they enter your end, make a lot of noise. We don't want them backtracking."

Salat nodded.

"Right, Chief," Baal said, forcing a smile. *Now, Pelat will claim all the glory.* He had been watching carefully. Over the previous hunts, he had observed the men's skill. *None of you, not even Pelat, can match me with a spear.* He stood tall and grinned. "I'm ready," he said.

The big sow stopped, cocked an ear and sniffed the air. Her mate and six squeakers clustered about her. Just outside the entrance to the ravine, an ancient yew shaded the hollow where she stood, its exposed roots grasping with knurled fingers the thin soil between the rounded, half-buried boulders. Short tufts of grass and clusters of ferns had sprouted between the rocks, and thick mats of reindeer moss grew between the root's splayed digits, carpeting the deep shade beneath the tree's broad limbs.

The sow was massive, standing thigh high; she weighed more than three grown men. From either side of her lower jaw splayed yellowed tusks thicker than a man's thumb and as long as his first finger. They curved upwards, tapering to a wicked point. Another, shorter, pair thrust downward from her drooling upper jaw. Her deep-set, rheumy eyes blinked. The axe shaped head shifted from side to side. Her eyes were weak, but her ears were very sharp. She could scent danger further off than a strong man could sprint; but to hear, she must be downwind from the threat, and she was not.

The tiny, red-rimmed eyes surveyed the ravine's narrow entrance. Her breath whistled down her long snout. Whining, the hungry brood between her legs protested the delay, but the old sow was not to be hurried; her long survival was a testament to a cautious nature.

Lifting her head, she tested the air once more, grunted, then trotted through the entrance to the ravine. Following single file, close behind the lumbering male, the last of the brood disappeared around a curve a little ways inside the entrance.

From his perch, Baal could see the other hunters gathering in the narrow cleft at the far end of the defile. He couldn't tell from this distance, but he was betting that Daga had taken the center. He had learned to respect the diminutive hunter. *He talks too much, but he is clever and does not run from a fight,* Baal had decided.

Baal and Pelat waited, fingers drumming the smooth surface of their spearshafts. Then came the sound of scuttling hooves. "Ready?" Pelat asked. Baal nodded. They slid down the smooth rockface. Landing quietly, they blocked the boar's exit. Pelat stood in front, Baal behind him, looking over his chief's right shoulder.

Rounding a corner, the sow spied the two spearmen standing in her path. Eyes darted left and right. The smooth walls were much too steep for her stubby legs. She was trapped. Blood surged through her arteries. Baal looked into her pig-eyes and felt a surging wave of blind rage. Snorting a warning to her mate, she lowered her head and charged forward screaming her feral war cry.

Spear grasped in his sweaty hands, Pelat retracted his arm to throw, but the sow's size and speed unnerved him.

He hesitated…he threw—his spear skidded across the sow's back and clattered onto the rocky path in front of her mate.

The sow barreled forward, crashing full speed into the unarmed hunter. Whipping her head side to side, her tusks slashed through the bands of firm muscle between Pelat's thighs. Then, dropping her head, she hooked upward, and her lower tusks pierced his groin. Pelat screamed, his eyes on fire with pain.

Jerking her head skyward, the maddened boar boosted Pelat up above her head and shook him back and forth like a rag, her tusks grinding into his soft flesh. A toss of her head propelled him up and over her back.

Pelat sprawled face down across the narrow path. The boar shook her bloody snout, her tiny porcine eyes now focused on Baal.

Baal acted on pure instinct. He hiked his left foot onto a stony out-crop, boosted himself up and pushed off. Landing his right foot in a niche in the opposite wall he launched himself forward.

His timing was perfect. Baal dropped straddling the sow's back. Grasping his spear with both hands he drove the sharp flint point straight down between her shoulder blades, piercing her beating heart. The tiny eyes widened. With barely a whimper, her legs collapsed, and the huge boar rolled over in the center of the path.

The sow's mate skidded to a stop and stared. Baal's heart pounded in his ears. Reflexively, his hand tightened, but his spear was stuck firmly in the sow's corpse. His hand was empty, but luck was with him.

Seeing his dead mate, the big male spun around and tore off in the opposite direction, toward the group of advancing spearmen.

Baal sighed with relief, grasped his spearshaft and tried to tug it free. Then came the sound of clattering hooves.

He's turned back! Baal's entire body erupted in sweat. He had one chance!

Pelat's spear lay in the path beyond his fallen comrade, tantalizingly out of reach. Acting with tigerish speed, Baal dove over the sow and, somersaulting over Pelat's body, landed upright on his haunches. Grab-bing Pelat's spear, he wedged the butt hard against his instep and lowered the point into the path of the male boar's maddened charge.

The big male showed no hesitation. He came straight on, his driving force almost upending the panting hunter. The boar impaled himself, driving the spear's point deep into his chest, through his lungs and out his back. Hunter and hunted came face to face, a handsbreadth from the end of the spearshaft.

The beast's breath was hot and stinking. Baal could feel the unwavering hatred mirrored in those tiny eyes. He has seen that look before in the eyes of the men he faced in battle on an early morning that seemed so long ago. The boar's head jerked side to side, the jaws snapped open, exposing his great tusks. He grunted, gnashed his teeth; a final breath gushed through his snout like a fetid wind. The boar fell dead at Baal's feet.

Baal shook his head. It was like awakening from a dream. He swallowed hard, his throat dry as the winter tundra. Trying to stand, his legs wobbled—his muscles refused to support his weight. Daga reached down, grabbed his arm and hauled him unsteadily to his feet. Baal looked down at his hands, they were shaking.

Pelat lay on his back across the path, blood oozing from his wounds. The gash across his groin was a jagged mouth pulsing bright arterial blood. Tanus held his head propped up on one knee.

Baal blinked and shook his head again. The fog began to clear. He eyed his comrades with a feeble grin.

Pelat gazed up at his companions, then stared into Baal's eyes. "I panicked," he said stretching out his hand. Their eyes held, saying all that needed to be said.

Baal squatted, gripped Pelat's shoulder and grasped his hand. "You stood bravely. If you had not, I would be lying where you are now," he said.

"No, that big sow spooked me. You stood bravely."

Baal shrugged. "It happens." He smiled gently. "We've done for them both. They won't be goring anyone ever again."

"Not ever? How long is that, do you think?" Pelat asked, his voice a shadow. "I never saw a thing better done. The tale of this kill will live long amongst the winter fires. You have proven yourself, Baal, son of

Talog, to be a great hunter!" He stared up at the ring of expectant faces. "He killed them both. I name Baal first hunter," he said, and his face contorted with pain.

First hunter? Baal's breath caught. He swallowed, struggling to keep his face blank, to stifle his pride. He looked down at his dying comrade. *I am to be first hunter!* He had gained more than he had hoped for. Along with elation, he felt somehow guilty. He liked Pelat and respected him. *There was nothing I could have done,* he told himself. Baal took Pelat's hand. "Many thanks, Pelat, but you are still first hunter, my friend. Tonight, thanks to you, we feast on roast boar."

Pelat lips quivered. "I'm afraid I'll miss the feast." He squeezed Baal's hand and shivered. "It's cold," he said, his voice a whisper.

Baal patted his shoulder. "The wounds will heal, and tonight, yours will be the place of honor. You shall have the best cut. I will select it myself."

"I, I don't think so," Pelat said. "Tell my wife and—" His eyes widened, as if in surprise "—make sure the meat…" his body twitched violently—once, twice, then went limp, the light in his once-bright eyes fading slowly, like the setting of the sun.

Baal gazed up at his companions, then reached out and closed the hunter's eyes. Tanus and Salat were crying; tears tracked down their dirty faces. The hunters now regarded Baal expectantly.

Both boar were dead. The hunters had seen Baal tugging at his spear protruding from the sow's body. They had all witnessed the second kill and stood gazing at him in awe. Pelat had named him, as was the custom. There was no need to talk. Baal felt his world shift.

"What do we do now, Chief?" Daga asked, his hands propped on his hips, his eyes directed at Baal.

Baal paused for a long moment, his mind churning furiously. This was the moment he had waited for. His chest swelled. He must allow nothing to dim his glory. *If we leave the kills, the meat will spoil. Pelat can wait.* He pictured their entrance into the village. *The people must see these beasts.* "We've got to get this meat back to camp."

"What about Pelat?" Tanus asked, scowling. "We can't just leave him."

Baal turned to Salat. "How long will it take us to get home?" Baal asked.

The hunter scratched his head. "Until the sunrise, if we walk all night."

"You all heard Pelat's last words," Baal said, addressing the hunters. "This is Pelat's last kill. He died for it. He would not want the meat wasted. We'll lay him out and cover his body with stones to keep off the scavengers," Baal said, gripping Tanus's shoulder in a fatherly gesture. "After we bring home the meat, we'll come back, make a litter and bring our friend home with honor."

Stout saplings were cut for carrying poles. Tanus and Daga squatted down and began the gutting. They tossed away the steaming entrails. The livers they wrapped carefully with moss and dry leaves. Carry poles were slipped between the trussed feet and hoisted up onto brawny shoulders. With that, the hunters began the long trek home.

The day woke with the sky cloudy. Ejil emerged from his hut to a cacophony of bright voices. The village children had spotted the hunters as they descended from the rainbow bridge and made their way toward the low-lying huts.

Some ran back to alert their friends.

Others swarmed the returning hunters, peering at the beasts' dangling heads and making faces. They circled, pulled back the cold lips to examine the great tusks.

Monsters sprang from wide eyes.

Protruding fingers became make-believe tusks.

Snarling, they charged, heads down, pretending to gore each other.

The tired hunters eyed each other with weak smiles.

The gathering adults watched mutely or else pointed and whispered as the party trudged by, the animals' heads swinging jauntily from side to side. Word spread, and more people soon surrounded them. Callas came, carried in a seat made by the crossed arms of two strong men. People voiced their surprise. Ejil shook his head in disbelief. No one remembered ever seeing boar so large.

"All hail our hunters," Callas said, raising one fleshy arm. "Tonight, we shall feast," she said. She stood before the two carrying poles that were now resting in the wide crotches of a split pair of thick saplings.

Breda sauntered up from behind and stood next to Ejil.

Ejil raised his head and sniffed the air. "I thought I smelled something fishy," he said, grinning.

Breda smiled and pointed toward the šamán who resumed speaking.

"Who was the first to bury his spear?" Callas asked.

Ejil saw Baal hesitate, his brother's eyes roving from one hunter to another.

Daga stepped forward. "Baal! His spear alone killed both beasts."

Callas's eyes widened. "One man? Alone? Surely not. What of the rest of you? Where is our first hunter?"

"Pelat has drawn his last breath. The big sow gored him. His spirit has gone to the Shadowlands!" Baal said.

Callas' face fell.

Ejil shook his head. He thought back to their first encounter on the ridge overlooking the river. *Pelat was a fine man. Now he's dead, and Baal is the center of all eyes. It seems unfair.*

Behind Callas, a woman began screaming. "My son, my son!" Pelat's mother keened. She tore at her clothes and her long hair.

"After the sow gored Pelat, Baal killed her, then stood firm and defended our wounded chief against her charging mate." Daga gestured toward the carcasses. "Both died from a single thrust of Baal's spear."

A murmur of sadness mixed with appreciation rose from the assembled villagers.

"Pelat, dead? He was a good man and a fine hunter. I will miss him." Breda lowered his gaze and shook his head. He put a hand on Ejil's shoulder. "Looks to me like your brother has done it again. No one can equal Baal's spearskill."

Ejil's jaw tightened. *Yes, my brother has a demon's own luck. I wonder, did Pelat pay for it?* he thought, but said nothing.

"Yes, a great kill!" Callas said. "We will deal with that later. Where is Pelat's body? We must honor him."

"We could not carry both. Pelat wanted us to make sure these kills got to the village. Tonight, we feast in his memory," Daga said, his eyes moving from face to face. "Tomorrow we will bring back our chief's body."

Callas's face hardened. "And allow scavengers to defile him? That cannot be allowed. You will go back—now!" she shouted.

Baal squared his shoulders and gazed at the šamán.

Breda nudged Ejil. "Watch your brother."

"It was Pelat's last wish that we bring the meat home," Baal said in an even tone. "His body is well protected. Our men have walked all night. They need food and a night's rest. Pelat was our leader. We have not forgotten him. Tomorrow morning, we will go back and claim his body and bring him home with honor."

A pained sigh passed through the crowd.

"Look at the crowd. I think Baal's put her in her place, for once," Breda whispered in Ejil's ear.

Ejil kept his eye on the šamán's face. He had come to know her well. She seemed calm, but her slitted eyes betrayed a brewing anger. He watched those eyes flit from face to face and saw her anger fade away like a summer shower.

Callas spread her arms as if to envelop them all. "Of course, Pelat's first thought was always the needs of his people," she said. "Tonight, we will feast and honor Pelat's memory. Tomorrow we will send a party to bring our first hunter back to us so we may bury him with all ceremony."

You've won this time, brother, but beware! Like you, our šamán rarely forgives and never forgets.

Baal nodded. "We will bring him home."

Two of the older women took charge of the carcasses. Wielding sharp stone blades, for each pig they girdled the ankle and the back of the neck, cut off the head, then carefully slit up the center of the back of each leg and from the belly to the head, then peeled back the pelt.

Some brought wood and built a huge fire in the open space in front of the longhouse. Others dug a deep pit in the sandy soil. As the blaze burned down, they raked the glowing coals into the pit and covered it with a layer of damp riverweed. Stuffed with the leaves and tubers of wild garlic, onions and thyme, the sow's body was lowered into the pit. Garlanded with yams, caraway and mushrooms, it was covered over with earth. It would slow bake until nightfall.

Other women busied themselves preparing cakes of pulverized acorns that had been soaked in maple syrup and set them out to dry in the sun. Others worked on the male carcass, cutting thin slices and laying them across the smoking racks. The boars' heads were mounted on sharpened poles to oversee the feast.

By dusk, the rich aroma of roast boar permeated the village. Stomachs rumbled.

The rich smells reminded Ejil of other happier times—the people feasting around the fire after a successful hunt. He pictured it and saw Lada framed in his mind's eye. *Pelat is dead and the people are sad. But death,* Ejil mused, *is always a close companion.* Tomorrow they would mourn, but tonight they would celebrate with steaming bark plates, heaped with roasted boar and steaming vegetables dripping with grease.

Baal and the hunting party occupied the place of honor. The men congratulated them. The women competed to serve them the choicest cuts. Children stood and stared, and mothers came forward, bowed and asked to touch them for luck.

One toothless old woman, eyes sharp with hunger, watched the juices trickle down her daughter's chin as she chewed. The old mother raised her chin; her mouth gaped open like a hatchling bird, and her daughter dropped the well-chewed cud into her mouth.

Sunlight faded to a few red streaks above the cliffs and the purple shadows of night crept silently across the valley. Finally, after all had eaten their fill, the šamán rose. Someone threw a load of brush on the fire and the flames leapt and lit her where she stood between the two-mounted boars' heads, their long, curling tusks gleaming in the firelight. Callas raised her hands toward the heavens.

"Have we eaten well?" she asked, addressing the faces surrounding her that glimmered in the flames like a string of shiny beads.

"We have," the people cried out while they drummed their thighs to show their pleasure.

"Good! Tonight, my children, we are both happy and sad. We are sad for the loss of Pelat, our first hunter. He was a fine man and a good provider. When he led, our men never returned empty handed. We mourn with his family. But Pelat died like the brave man he was. We are happy because our bellies are filled, thanks to his prowess and that of our cousin Baal, son of Talog, warrior of The Broken People.

"You all know their sad story. The Broken People are gone—all but he and his brother Ejil and their companion Breda. They came to us seeking sanctuary. They have asked to be adopted into the tribe and be taken into the hearts of The First People. We could call a council, but everyone is here. Tonight, I say we take these men into our tribe and pray to The Mother to draw them to her bosom and suckle them."

"Yes, yes, yes," the people chanted. "Adopt them. Take them in!"

"We are to be adopted into the tribe," Ejil said.

"Why tonight?" Breda said. "Callas is up to something. Look, Daga's whispering in your brother's ear. That little man follows your brother around like a puppy dog—now, see Baal? He's eyeing Callas like a rat watches a snake."

"Callas is a subtle one. My brother doesn't trust her."

"Right, and Baal always repays a slight."

"Did you notice the little trick with the fire? She's up to something!" Ejil said.

Breda nodded. "Shhh! listen."

"Our hunters have brought us a pair of boars, bigger than anyone has ever seen," Callas said. "The story of the hunt will be told and retold. To honor our fallen friend, I have decided that the boars' tusks shall be offered to The Mother to ease Pelat's shade into the Shadowlands."

Baal's mouth dropped open.

Salat leaped to his feet. "By right, the tusks belong to the hunter who made the kill. This is known," he said.

Baal started to rise, but Daga threw his arm around his shoulder, pulled him back and whispered in his ear.

"Ha! Did you see that? Your brother is angry. I don't blame him. What is Callas playing at?" Breda said.

"She does love to adorn herself," Ejil said.

Daga stood. "Baal slew both beasts, each with one thrust of his spear," he said, facing the šamán. "The tusks are not yours to give, Callas, they are trophies of the kill. They are always awarded to the first hunter. It has always been so. Before he died, Pelat named Baal, son of Talog, to succeed him."

Each of the hunters grasped his spear and stood up next to Daga.

Callas drew herself up, but before she could speak an old man struggled to his feet and raised his hand. Thin and stooped, his hair like a white cloud, he pointed a long finger. "Daga speaks true, and well you know it, Callas." His thin form was bent forward like a reed in the wind. "Young Baal has proven himself a great hunter. The tusks are his by right."

Callas propped her hands on her hips. "Was he a member of our tribe when these beasts were killed? It was Pelat who led the hunters, old man," Callas said.

"Old man, is it? Have I lived so long that you have you forgotten my name and the name of my sire, Callas? Is that why you speak to me thus? Perhaps that is because I was a man grown when you dropped squalling from between your mother's bloody thighs. I am Tamo, son of Tamo. I am a blooded warrior and elder of this tribe. I have lived many winters and made many kills, but I have never seen or heard of a braver deed. What would you do this night, šamán? Do you ask us to adopt this worthy man into our tribe and at the same time, rob him? For shame!"

"I know your name, Tamo," the šamán said, her jowls trembled.

A loud murmur like the growl of a cave bear erupted from the crowd.

Baal stood and raised his hand. The people quieted. Ejil sighed. *It is Baal's night, and all now await him to speak.* "Callas has made a mistake," Ejil said to Breda. "The people are with Baal."

It was now full dark. The gibbous moon had risen and hung in the night sky, suspended like a pendant shedding light, surrounded by a bright necklace of stars.

"Our šamán speaks truly. Pelat was our leader. He was a great hunter. I never met a braver man. Had he not stood steady as a rock against the sow's charge, I would be dwelling now with the spirits. Pelat gave his life for a brother hunter. That was the man he was." Baal paused and gazed at the assembled villagers.

A warm murmur greeted his words.

Baal's head tilted back, as if he was holding back tears, then dropped forward. He stood quietly as if in prayer.

Ejil studied his brother. He had never seen Baal like this, had never even seen him cry. *Pelat was his friend. Is he really sad, or is he pretending?* He turned to Breda, but his friend had his head cocked. He was watching intently.

Slowly, the people quieted. Baal cleared his throat and continued.

"A large tusk shall be offered to the Sunfather, as god of the hunt, and another to the Great Mother. The sow's great lower tusks, those that claimed Pelat's life, shall be buried with him. Let the gods marvel at his prowess. Let them sing his praises and escort him to a hearth of honor in the Shadowlands. The small tusks will be pierced, and each hunter will wear one at his throat in remembrance of Pelat's bravery," Baal said.

The hunters smiled at each other and nodded in agreement.

A murmur of approval rose from the assembled. Baal raised his voice. "And one of the male's great tusks shall go to Nyla, Pelat's mother, in memory of her son's sacrifice. And another to his wife and son—his last words were of his love for them. They shall have a tusk as well."

A great roar rose from the assembled tribe. Pelat's mother ran forward, kneeled, grabbed Baal's hands and kissed them. The people beat their hands on their thighs. Baal kneeled and hugged her. Tears ran down his face. He took both her hands, kissed them, and raised her up. The new first hunter squeezed Daga's shoulder and took his seat.

"Baal handled that well, like your father would have."

"You think so?" Ejil asked.

"Oh, he is still the same wild boy I grew up with, but I see more and more of your father in him. Today he showed the people an honest heart and real leadership, and the people saw Callas for what she is: arrogant and petty."

"You mean, he humiliated her. I've been doing my best to change our šamán's mind about helping us find our women, but she's stubborn, and she already didn't like Baal. Now, I am sure she hates him," Ejil said, nodding toward the šamán, who stood with her arms crossed staring silently into the fire.

"You spend too much time in the longhouse, Ejil. I've made a few friends among the fisherfolk. Not everyone is happy with a woman as First Speaker, and the younger men want to help us. I grieve for my Mata every day. If it were not for Callas's stubbornness, the people would likely support us."

Ejil didn't like hearing praise of his brother coming from Breda's mouth. "I wonder. Many people follow Callas because they believe she is The Great Mother come to earth," he said.

Breda nodded. "True. But some of the men say she neglects the sacrifices and proper homage due the Sunfather. The gods do not like being ignored. That does not bode well for our tribe."

CHAPTER 18

NEW HUNTING GROUNDS

The summer solstice had passed. While the Sunspirit still smiled down and warmed the land, the Lion Clan set off to find better hunting. Lada marched with the women. Scar arranged them in a long single line, women in the middle, warriors at the front and rear.

Their few possessions were carried mostly by the women in slings and backpacks. The men carried their sleeping furs on their backs. Their hands remained free, and each carried a spear.

Crowbait saw to it that Lada bore a heavy load. Her pack-straps soon began to cut painfully into her shoulders. Complaints would be met with blows and derision, so she gritted her teeth and marched on. Her mind numbed, and as day followed tedious day, she focused on little more than placing one foot in front of the other.

The land greened as they descended onto the taiga. The sky remained clear and the sun beat down mercilessly. The plains were rich with the sights and smells of emerging life. Flocks of birds turned and dipped across the sky. In the distance, herds of deer, elk, bison, ibex, and onager could be seen grazing on the new grass.

They found a free-flowing stream late one afternoon and made camp next to a low-lying swamp nearby. The next morning, the women awoke to find an auroch herd had taken over the swamp during the night. Standing contentedly, the shaggy beasts chomped on the tender shoots of marsh grass, oblivious to their human neighbors.

"Tule, over there, the herd!" Lada said, pointing. "How I would love a smoking rib." She felt her stomach gurgle. The dried meat had given out several days before. The clan was subsisting on what they could forage.

"It's been so long since we've had any decent meat. If I have to eat another grub, I'll scream."

Tule, now big with child, waddled closer to the herd and propped her hands on her hips. "My man says the herds here have never seen clan hunters and they do not fear us. He is always out ahead of the hunting party, scouting. That's why they call him Spearpoint," Tule said.

Lada sighed and gazed at the grazing herd. She had endured Tule's constant boasting for some time, and it had become tiresome. Now that she had joined with the young hunter, she took every opportunity to display what little she knew.

One great bull with a wide spread of horn and dark placid eyes stood gazing about himself while the others grazed. Flies circled, his tail twitched, his head dropped and his flat teeth cropped the sweet grass. He was so close, Lada felt like she could almost reach out and touch him.

He must be the leader, she decided. She knew aurochs had poor eyesight. *What is he thinking?* she wondered. *He doesn't seem to be afraid. Does he see me as just another animal eating grass?*

Suddenly, the tiny birds grazing on the animals' backs exploded screeching into the air and flew off.

"Ho!" Tule said, pointing, "Look, our hunters!"

Lada cupped both hands above her eyes against the sun and stared. There they were, covered in mud to blunt their man-scent. Like specters from a nightmare, they rose from the grass surrounding the surprised herd.

The big bull stretched his neck—eyes wild—bellowing the alarm. The startled herd lowed, rolled their eyes, twisting their heads side to side seeking escape, but armed men surrounded them on every side.

Scar dashed forward, leaped onto the back of the lead bull and drove his spear down between the beast's shoulder blades. Bellowing in agony, the bull's front legs gave way. As he wobbled unsteadily, Scar leaned forward, wrapped his arm around the dying animal's neck, drew his hand-blade across his throat, then jumped aside as the great beast rolled onto his side. It had taken but an instant. Lada could only shake her head in wonder at his skill.

That was the signal. The hunters closed in and the slaughter began. Another clansman drove his spear into the side of a big cow who lifted her head and bellowed in surprise. Lada felt a stab of pity. The rest of the herd, now leaderless, stood rolling their eyes, awaiting their fate. The pitiless spears stabbed and slashed, dyeing the grass bright crimson.

Tule shook her head, giggling. "Did you see that, Lada? Quick, get your hand-blade. We will all have full bellies tonight. Come on!"

The women moved in and the butchering began. As usual, they divided; clan worked with clan and the captive women worked together. Some kneeled, slit open the beasts' stomachs and scooped out the steaming entrails. Others skinned, peeling back the animals' thick coats. A few gathered fuel and built fires to roast and smoke the meat. There was little wood, but luckily they had made camp near the remains of a dead mammoth whose bones had been picked clean. The greasy bones burned hot.

Lada and Tule attacked a dying cow. Lada sliced open her belly with a handaxe while Tule cut the throat to bleed her out. Long ropes of intestine slithered like a nest of snakes out onto the ground. Both girls were soon up to their armpits in gore.

Tule pulled out the liver and held the dripping organ up in both hands, then buried her teeth in the slippery flesh and began to chew. "Delicious!" she exclaimed. Lada pointed her finger and laughed. Tule's mouth and chin were smeared with blood. It reminded Lada of happier days with her mother and the other women, preparing meat for their men—of her father and of Ejil. She felt a sharp prick of sadness.

Tule stuck out her tongue, reached over and rubbed the still-steaming organ across her friend's face. "Now we both are the same," she said, laughing gleefully. "Here." She offered Lada a bite of the steaming liver. "It's always tastier before it cools."

Lada shook off her sadness. There was much to be done. For the next several days, the clan remained camped, gorging, smoking meat and working the hides. Jealousy raged! Clan women clashed with the captives over the most mundane tasks. With stern looks of disapproval, they watched the captive women weighting the hides down in a cold stream to wash them.

"Stop, stupid, mud-faced cow. You will ruin the fur!" Crowbait screamed. Hands propped on hips, she glared down at Lada from the stream bank. With one hand, she added a gesture that signified "dumb" in clan sign.

Fed up with Crowbait's constant carping, Lada glared up at the clan woman for a few moments then went back to her work. Lada understood the clan woman's anger. *It is not our fault we were brought here. Is it our fault they are dried up and barren?*

Crowbait jumped into the freezing water, pulled up one of the carefully weighted hides and threw it onto the grassy bank, then stood facing Lada with her feet wide, —her arms crossed—her eyes challenging.

Lada charged, lowered her head, and butted the astonished woman full in the stomach, knocking her backwards. She took hold of the sopping hide and pulled it off the bank.

The enraged clan woman surfaced, coughing and spitting like a half-drowned wildcat. Shorter but much heavier than Lada, she leaped up onto her back, wrapped her arms around the struggling girl, dragged her underwater and held her down with the weight of her body. Lada was furious and close to panic. *That jealous cow is trying to kill me.* Later, she wondered where the strength had come from.

She managed to get her feet beneath her. She grasped Crowbait's stumpy legs and propelled herself upward. She surfaced with the clan woman riding her shoulders. With a great heave, Lada tossed her backwards into the middle of the stream, turned, and stood panting. As Crowbait's face broke the surface, Lada cranked back her arm and punched her hard in the nose.

Blood spurted. Crowbait covered her face with both hands. The clan women gathered on the bank, pointed and screamed. Drawing her hands into claws—her face scarlet, her nose dripping blood—Crowbait attacked, her thick fingers questing toward Lada's eyes.

Tule, who was standing behind her, knee deep in the stream, grabbed the clan woman's long, stringy hair and dragged her backwards.

All the women were now gathered on the stream bank. Another clan woman, a big, sturdy girl called Rhino, leaped from the bank and landed on Tule, screaming like a demented spirit.

By the time the men arrived, it had become a melee. Pent up resentments burst into the open like lanced boils. Women splashed and thrashed trying their best to drown each other. They slapped, punched, bit, scratched, and wrestled in the stream and on the muddy bank.

While Lada dodged her enraged nemesis, Scar waded in, grabbed hold of Crowbait and dragged her out of the stream. Twisting around to break his grip, Crowbait punched the clan leader in the face.

"Why did you bring these black-faced women here?" she screamed at Scar.

Scar's wide eyes stared back with surprise.

"They are not clan. They will never be clan. They want our men."

Glaring, Scar pulled back his arm to strike. But to Lada's surprise, he hesitated, then turned and jumped back into the stream, leaving the cringing clan woman dripping on the stream bank. Lada was astonished. *Why?* She fumed. Lada gritted her teeth and hammered the water. Her hatred of the clan woman gripped her like a tightening fist.

Scar and another warrior separated two of the fighting women. Finally, the men corralled the women into two groups, placing themselves in between. The women, both clan and captive—soaked, bedraggled, covered in mud—stood, glared, and shouted at each other.

Scar paced back and forth, eyeing one group then the other, signing and speaking furiously. Finally the women quieted.

"Why are you fighting?"

"These stupid black bitches are ruining our pelts," Crowbait shouted, pointing at the huddling captives. She stared boldly at Scar. "Stupid black cows. Soaking the pelts will ruin the fur. They smear them with brains. They stink!" Crowbait said, gesturing wildly with her hands, her harsh voice a tad below a screech.

"Wrong!" Lada snarled, hands mounted on her hips. "We mix the brains with ashes to soften the pelt," she signed furiously. *They probably don't understand a thing I'm saying*, she thought, gritting her teeth. "Ask your men! Our skins are softer, and they shed water better. Crowbait smells her own stink. Wash that fat, greasy body once a moon. The smell will go away," she said, her lips curled, eyeing the clan woman.

"You lie," Crowbait screamed and charged at Lada, but one of the men intercepted her with a backhand that sent her sprawling on her back, her arms and legs kicking the air like an upended water bug.

"Enough!" Scar shouted, his fierce eyes focused on the women until each, in turn, dropped her eyes. "There is much to be done. Each woman may do it as she thinks best, but the meat must be dried and the skins tanned. Any more trouble and every one of you will be punished!" He signed slicing the air twice with one hand, the clan gesture signifying *pain* and stormed off.

Cowed for the moment, the women shuffled off in separate groups, mumbling to themselves. Lada stood as if rooted, her eyes spitting fire. But beneath her anger was a swelling sense of victory. *Crowbait, you snake-bellied cow. You are angry because, for once, we were treated fairly. Well, I know another way to show you, Crow…bait!* Lada raised her eyebrows, tossed her head, turned, and walked away.

Under the watchful eyes of the men, there was an uneasy peace, but the tension still crackled like the air after a summer thunderstorm.

Night fell, the moon waxed toward full. The Spirit Woman sat cross-legged, erect, and motionless before her hearth. A serving woman flitted about like a firefly. Scar squatted directly across the fire toying with a stick, drawing circles in the dust and avoiding those vacant eyes which never blinked and gleamed like boiled bird's eggs.

Scar had seen his mother sit like this for hours at a time, and it always unsettled him. *What was it she saw?*

It was hard to sit quietly without his mind wandering; he had tried it as a boy, but weird shapes rose up and passed before his inner eye. They scared him. Finally, the Spirit Woman's pupils rolled forward, her eyes refocused and widened in recognition.

Scar made the formal hand sign of greeting that meant, "May you eat well," in the clan language.

"So, the Leader has come seeking his old mother's advice?"

Scar stifled a retort and sat quietly.

"Walk with me," she signed, wiggling her first and second fingers. Neither spoke until they were out well beyond the night fires. The evening was clear and the stars sparkled. A fresh southerly wind moaned through the ripe grasses.

The Spirit Woman glanced back toward the camp. The fires flickered in the distance. "The Blackdog women make trouble," she said.

Scar shrugged.

"I warned you!"

"Yes, you warned me. But what choice if the clan is to survive?" he signed, spreading both hands, palm up.

"What happened by the stream was but a spark. Take care that it does not grow into a raging flame and consume you."

"It's Ravenhair. She makes trouble. I put her in charge because she is strong. It was a mistake. She has a temper," he said, rubbing his swollen cheek. "The Blackdog women call her Crowbait—some clan, too. It fits her," Scar said, suppressing a grin. "She challenged the Blackdog woman."

"The girl called Lada struck her."

"Yes, after Ravenhair tried to drown her," he said, somberly. *The girl has spirit,* he thought to himself, secretly pleased.

"Ravenhair is angry. She wishes to join with you. She knows you desire to lie with the Blackdog woman."

"This many Blackdog women have joined with our men," he said, holding up four fingers." Three bellies swell. Two more will soon join," Scar said.

"What of the others?"

"A few will not join with men who have women. It is not their custom. Blackdogs can be more stubborn than clan women, but the breath of the ice demon will soon blow down from the north," Scar said. "Then we shall see."

"You speak of one in particular?"

Scar dropped his gaze.

The Spirit Woman swallowed a smile. "What will happen when the new babies are born?"

"All good. Babies mean the clan will live. All know this!"

"They will share their mother's spirit. They will not look like clan. They will not *be* clan. Our women will hate them."

"What does that matter? If babies are born it means that the spirits are pleased?"

The crone pressed her lips together. "We will see," she said.

"The warriors will obey me. The women will do as they are told," Scar said and shrugged.

"Walk carefully, my son. The warriors grumble. I hear it on the wind. Your want for the girl clouds your heart."

Scar snorted and pounded his right fist against his breast. "Who would dare challenge me? I lead because I am strongest."

"Ravenhair has kin," she said.

Scar crossed his arms over his chest.

"Do not be a fool. A man is a leader only if his people follow him. Not every challenge should be met with force. You must find a way to pacify Ravenhair. Take her! You have juice enough to keep two women."

"You are the Spirit Woman," he said. "Where are your potions and spells?"

She shook her head slowly. "It is not the spirits, my son. It is the blood. I cannot be cured with spells. It takes many small streams to make a great river and keep it flowing. We have not met another clan in many seasons.

"There are no babies. The clans are dying. Soon there will be none left and the Blackdogs will rule the land." The Spirit Woman again shook her head. "Perhaps our people's time has passed. Something comes, my son. I feel it. It waits, broods, and grows strong. I warned you. Kill them all, I said. Did none escape? Are you sure that you destroyed the Blackdog clan?"

Scar scowled into the darkness. *Perhaps, it is your time that has passed, old woman. The Lion Clan will live, and I will make it strong.* "We left no one alive. The Blackdog šamán lay by his cave with a smashed head. Their shades flew howling like hyena down into The Caves of the Fallen," he said aloud.

"This is not over, my son. An angry spirit stalks us. I feel it, but my magic can do nothing to stop it, and I fear it. It is coming."

Work resumed at sunrise, and the clan raced to preserve the meat before it turned putrid. Lada and her friends laid their soaking-wet hides out in the sun to dry.

Lada's mother cupped her forehead and gazed up at the blue sky. A large, frothy cumulus cloud passed across the sun. "If this weather holds, the hides should be dry enough to work by tomorrow."

Lada did not respond. She stood gazing down at the hide spread out before her in the grass. *I'm sorry, Ejil,* she thought.

"Daughter," Ceda said, placing her hand on Lada's shoulder, "did you hear what I said?"

Lada raised her head. "No! Sorry mother I was thinking of something else."

"Oh?"

"I've made my decision. I am going to mate with Scar."

Ceda tilted her head and gently squeezed Lada's shoulder. "Are you sure?" she asked in a soft voice.

"What choice do I have?"

"After what happened at the stream?"

"Especially after that. The clan women hate us. I need a man to protect me, so I can protect you."

"They believe we are stealing their men."

"It was *their* men who killed our men and brought us here."

Ceda reached up and brushed away a strand of her daughter's hair that had fallen across one eye.

Lada's smile was dutiful, but her eyes remained distant. Over her mother's shoulder, her eyes roamed the open taiga. "Mother. Out there… it's so big! Does it never end?"

Ceda sighed and shook her head. "I'm sure I don't know, dear."

"When we were first captured, the only thing I thought or cared about was escape, but then you came, and…" *I feel like I am betraying our people, but what people? Father is gone. My Ejil is dead. There is no one left. There is no escape because there is no place to go.* "Scar is the leader of the clan. If I join with him and give him babies, I'll be safe and I can keep you safe. Being Scar's woman will bring me status. Crowbait and her friends won't dare to abuse you."

"You mustn't worry about me," Ceda said.

"No? If no man chooses you, you will be a slave forever."

"I am too old," Ceda said, smiling softly.

"No one will dare hurt the mother of Scar's woman."

Ceda wrapped her arm around her daughter's shoulder. "I am glad to see my girl all grown up, and I am proud that you will do what you must. You are lucky; you are young and lovely, and you have a strong man who wants you. He murdered my husband, and for that I can never forgive him. But he is a great hunter. You and your children will never lack for meat. He looks after his people, and he will keep you safe."

"I will never be able to care for him," Lada said.

"Perhaps not. That is nice when it happens. Your father and I were like red deer in heat. I'll always cherish the memory of our early seasons together." Her eyes sparkled like spring rain, then her face flushed and her eyes filled up with tears. "I still miss him, you know."

Lada took her mother in her arms and stroked her hair. "I do too, Mother. I do too."

The sun had risen above the horizon once for every finger on Lada's hand before the clan resumed its trek. Every pack was full to bursting with dried meat. The beautiful colors of the Season of the Painted Leaves had arrived, and with it the rain, turning the ground slick and making walking difficult. They marched every day from early morning until dusk. By day's end, Lada's shoulders were rubbed raw and her deerskin tunic stuck to her body and stank so badly she could hardly bear it.

Scar stood atop the hill, shaded his eyes with his hand, and squinted at the land toward the eastern horizon. Two warriors, One-ear and Grayhair stood with him.

The old man's long hair was pulled back in a horse's tail. "The sky grows pale," he said, gesturing upward. "The ice is coming. We must find shelter."

One-ear nodded. "The leaves will soon fall. The wind will shift north," he said.

"Hah," Scar snorted and stamped his foot. "You tell me what I know."

"We passed a likely camp yesterday a little past midday, as the Sunspirit began climbing toward the west. You remember?" Greybeard asked.

Yes, he thought, and nodded to Greybeard. *It was in the shape of a cupped hand. The cliff faces south. There is overhang enough to make dry hearths. A stream wanders the valley, and the cave is deep enough.*

Grayhair knuckled his eyes and blinked owlishly. "My eyes see only mist in the distance."

"There is nothing; only emptiness," Scar said.

"No shelter, then?" Grayhair asked. "My bones feel the ice on the wind."

"We have meat," One-ear said.

Scar made a face and rubbed his chin. "Not enough."

Grayhair shrugged. "We can make camp and still hunt. The herds are not yet wary."

Scar thought about his joining with Lada; he looked forward to it. He thought about her and felt himself hardening. "We will make camp," he said.

The joining ceremony began after the evening meal. The cave grew quiet. The Spirit Woman stood before the hearth and began to sway and gesture, her arms and hands moving in graceful arcs. This was something new. Lada marveled at the deft grace of the old woman's movements. Suddenly she understood. It was more than a dance; it told a story: the tale of the Lion Clan's beginnings.

The gestures spoke directly to her—and judging from the rapt expressions on the faces surrounding her, to the rest of the clan, as well. It reminded her of Pelas chanting her tribe's history around the nightfire.

The old woman's movements drew her ever deeper. Pictures began to appear, one after another, before her eyes. Some were bright and clear, others like the view through a fog. She saw a cold, barren world, driving snow, and a line of men—like tiny black beetles—trudging along between great jagged walls of blue ice.

Then it was over. The Spirit Woman sighed and slumped like an old leather sack down next to the fire and the people began to stir like those just awakened from a dream. Lada stood up with Scar and joined hands. No one spoke. The silence sat like a weight on Lada's shoulders.

"This woman is now my woman," Scar announced, looked down at Lada and made the sign for joining.

Lada's eyes traveled around the circle and found Crowbait. The clan woman sat rigidly upright looking into the distance. Her jaw muscle flexed and quivered.

Lada took a deep breath and looked up at Scar. "This man is now my man," she said and made the sign.

The people beat their hands on their thighs acknowledging the union. Ceda's face was wet with tears.

It is done! Lada thought about the finality of it. *Not at all like the silly girlish dreams. Surrounded by my people; my father standing proudly beside me. Now, my poor father and all my people are gone, slaughtered—and now my life is joined to their murderer,* she thought, blinking back tears.

The men surrounded Scar, slapping his back and, one by one, the captive women came up to Lada and shyly offered their congratulations. Lada hardly noticed.

The next day, the clan set up camp. Scar's decision had been greeted with relief. Lada was footsore, and her heavy pack had rubbed her shoulders raw. All around her the women busied themselves around the new campsite.

Lada was used to the privacy of her family hut and found it hard to get used to the clan's way of living—so close together. She had found a cozy little cove, wedged between two boulders that backed up against the wall. "There is plenty of room for us and a place for you too," she told her mother. "Finally, we will have some privacy."

"Are you sure it will be all right, daughter?" Ceda asked. "The unmated women are always herded together."

"I am Scar's woman, am I not?" Lada said. She gazed boldly about the cave. The other women were busy. Not one so much as met her eye. "You see," she said, with a meaningful glance. She kneeled down and unrolled the new sleeping fur.

She sat back and admired the glossy fur, then picked it up. The thick pelt was soft against her cheek.

"It is truly beautiful, child," Ceda said, beaming down at her.

The auroch's skin had been Scar's joining gift. It was the bull leader's pelt. The slaughter of the herd had taken place early enough in the hot season that the bull had not yet shed his thick winter's coat. Scar presented it to Lada when she came to him and agreed to the joining.

After the confrontation with Crowbait and the clan women, Lada was determined to exhibit her skill. She kept the skin rolled up, and with her mother's help, each night after the evening meal, she worked the hide until it was as soft and supple as doeskin.

She recalled with pride how Scar's eyes had widened in wonder at the fur's softness when she rolled it out in front of him. "Good," he told her, running his hand through its softness. Then, straightening his shoulders, he stood up and walked quickly away.

A few suns later, well before sundown, the men returned laden with meat. Scar marched over to their site—a lopsided grin distorted his face. An entire elk haunch was perched jauntily across one shoulder.

Lada raised an eyebrow.

The grin widened. "We rounded a boulder! The antlers!" he signed and spread one arm wide and almost lost his grip on the meat. "Mine was the first spear," he said, steadying himself.

Lada cupped her hand over her mouth to keep from laughing. She was touched. *He is trying to impress me.* "I love the taste of elk," she said, gazing up at him smiling. She rubbed her stomach, making the clan sign. "I will spit and roast it. Should be enough for one meal," she said.

Scar's brow wrinkled. They communicated with a mix of signs and words, some his, some hers. "Yes," he said, his eyes quizzical. He laid the haunch at her feet and strode off.

Ceda watched him disappear and shook her head. "These white-faced people have no sense of humor," she said.

Using a narrow handblade, Lada punched deep slits into the elk haunch. She reached into her herb bag and pushed dried garlic bulbs into the slits. "There; that should add some flavor!" She turned to her mother. "I've tried making jokes; Scar doesn't even smile—maybe it's my signing.

It is pretty crude, and he finds that funny. When One-ear slipped and fell on his face, Scar nearly choked himself laughing."

"I guess he enjoys seeing others in pain."

"Especially One-ear. It was pretty funny, Mother."

The first days in the new camp had been good. The sun shone and the hunters brought in much meat. They feasted and smoked. Then, one evening, the wind dropped and the setting sun glowed against clouds that spread like a purple bruise across the horizon. Early the next morning, the north wind descended with a full-throated roar, like a she-lion in heat, and the snow came. It was—as her people called it—a hard, flint-knapping snow, with sharp little icy flakes. Lada sat up and stretched. She could hear the rustling sound of the wind-blown snow beating against the stone at the cave's entrance.

Lada threw a bearskin wrap around her shoulders and made her way to the shelter entrance. The snow had doused the fire. She scraped at the snow, blew on the coals and placed some kindling over them, but the wind blew it away. She felt a presence behind her. Scar placed one hand on either of her shoulders, pulled her close and wrapped his arms around her. She sighed and relaxed against the warmth of his bare chest.

"We can do nothing until the Windspirit tires. Come, I will warm you," he said, and led her back to their sleeping fur.

CHAPTER 19

A CLUE

The dawn sun was a deep-red ball in a slate-gray sky. Ejil emerged from the blanket of newly fallen snow like a muskrat from its den. What in summer had been a busy village was now a scattering of frosted molehills dotting a white, featureless plain. Here and there, dark fur-clad shapes popped up like ground squirrels and shook themselves. The air was still, the feather-light snow knee deep; a light wind tickled his ear. Ejil began clearing the snow from the hut's entrance.

Seven moons had waxed full since the first snow. The Season of the Falling Leaves had barely begun, it seemed, when the frigid wind swept down from the north.

A few died. The Ice Season seemed determined to hold the world in its icy grip. Baal and his band of hunters ranged far and wide, returning with more fresh meat than anyone could remember, until the game began to disappear. But the larders were full, and the young ones were sleek and well fed. Everyone was restless from the long days of inactivity. Some prayed to the Sunfather, others to the Mother. The prayer was the same: a hope that the season would break before the coming of the next full moon.

Squinting against the glare, Ejil looked toward the snow-shrouded arch hung above the frozen river, suspended between the earth and sky. Dotted with shrubs in the hot season, its massive, ice-shrouded stonework was almost invisible against the pale morning sky. Dark shapes could be seen plodding across its flat summit, coming toward the village. It was the hunters. Others had spotted them too, and a crowd of villagers rushed to greet and break trail for them. Ejil strapped on his snowshoes and followed.

The brothers exchanged nods as Baal strode by, leading the hunters. The men resembled snow giants, their frosted beards jutting from their hoods, icicles dangling like long, pointed teeth. Ejil felt a twinge of resentment. Breda had been right; Baal had become a favorite among the people. Some shouted his name. He usually waved to acknowledge greetings, but this day he seemed not to notice. His jaw was clamped tightly shut and the rigid set of his shoulders told Ejil that something was eating at him.

Breda saw Ejil and halted.

"Greetings my friend," he said, enveloping Ejil in a bear hug. Baal had needed a scout, and Breda had been pleased to be invited to join Baal's celebrated band.

"Another good hunt?" Ejil asked, his breath billowing out in clouds of steam.

"A bit thin," Breda said as they watched the hunters stride proudly by. A pair of long-legged ibex was strapped by their delicate hooves to a pair of carrying poles; the animals' thick, dappled, brown coats shone in the sharp, gray light.

"You look tired," Ejil said.

"You know your brother," Breda said, raising both eyebrows. "Baal does not return empty handed. We have been out four days and we'd have been out much longer if we hadn't run out of food." Breda jerked his thumb over his shoulder. "We stumbled upon a small herd of ibex yesterday morning. Your brother wields a spear better than any man I ever saw." Breda lowered his voice and glanced around him. "And we found something else," he said.

"What?"

"Man tracks! A hunting party, a good-sized band, two days downriver."

Ejil's heart began to pound. "Fishbellies?"

Breda nodded.

"How many?"

"Six, maybe eight," Breda said.

"Could they be the same ones who murdered our people?"

Breda shrugged. "Who knows? I'm a tracker, not a šamán. Your brother thinks so. He was all for hunting them down."

"And you?"

"Well, that band passed by some time past, and we were out of food and had found no game. The taiga is endless."

"Breda, do you think the women are alive or did they just use and murder them?"

Breda's face clouded.

"Forgive me, Breda, I didn't mean…"

"No, no, you're right," Breda waved a hand in dismissal. "I've thought about it a lot, and I don't think they killed them. You remember how it all started. The kidnapping of Lada and Tule. The war was *all about* the women. They very carefully avoided killing them, except those like our mothers who fought back."

"Why?"

Breda cocked an eyebrow. "You're asking me why a man wants a woman? The men are said to have to have cocks the size of clubs," he said, opening his arms wide. "There were only one or two children in their camp. Remember, I mentioned it at the time, but with everything that was happening," he shrugged, "I wonder…"

"So, what stopped Baal from chasing them?"

"Hunger! The tracks were at least four days old, and they were headed further downriver. The riverbank along that whole stretch floods when the leaves fall. The trees, what there are of them, are thin and scrawny. There's nothing you can use to build a fire."

Ejil drew his parka close and shivered.

"Right! Well, we agreed we would stock up on food, and he and I would go back out and try to find their camp." Breda thumped his chest. "My heart aches to avenge our people."

Ejil placed his right hand over his heart. "When do we leave?"

The scout eyed him.

"Lada is with them."

Breda shrugged. "Right, I'm going to eat and have a sweat. Come along, I'll show you my new tattoo and tell you more about the hunt."

Baal sauntered over. He eyed one then the other. "What are you two talking about?"

"Revenge! I was just telling your brother about the tracks," Breda said.

Baal pulled off one mitten and flexed his fingers. "They haven't come upriver, or we would have seen them, and they can't have crossed over. The ice toward the center is too thin. We will probe downriver until we pick up their trail," Baal said.

"I'll sharpen my spear!" Ejil said and stalked off.

Shrugging off his hooded parka, Ejil gently stroked the wolf's fur hood. It was the sole remains of those things that his mother had made him. He pulled the first of two deerskin shirts over his head. The outer one he wore with the fur facing out. The second, with the fur against his body, he had to peel off. Hanging his garments on a peg, he squatted down next to the two naked hunters. Their bodies were already glazed with sweat. A bowlful of water tossed on the rocks brought forth a cloud of steam. Ejil closed his eyes and sighed. The hut stank of unwashed bodies, burnt wood and rancid fat, but it was good to feel the chill being drawn from his body. After so many moons of cold, he hardly remembered what it felt like to feel really warm.

"So, here's my latest. What do you think?" Breda asked. He raised and flexed his upper arm, eyeing the tattooed image of a bison with his head turned, licking his flank. Outlined in white, the image ran upwards from his taut bicep. Pico had drawn a series of curved lines to represent the beast's shaggy mane, chin and beard.

"Beautiful! I like the way Pico drew his head right so that it pops up when you flex your muscles."

"Yeah, pretty good. I like that too," Breda said, flexing his shoulder muscle again. "I want him to do the other side, but I'm not sure what I want yet."

"I could do one. Whatever you want. Pico has been teaching me," Ejil said.

"Humm," Breda said, eyeing him. "I hear you're getting pretty good."

"Pico says I have gotten very good."

"Alright, let me think about it."

Baal sat hunched over staring straight ahead with his lips twisted in disgust. He raised his fist. "We are going to find those murderers," he said.

Breda shrugged. "On that, I think, we all agree." He drew his forearm across his brow. "The heat feels good. Here!" He handed Baal a flat piece of a deer's shoulder bone and slapped him on the back. "Make yourself useful; scrape my back," he said, winking at Ejil.

Ejil suppressed a grin. He watched his brother eye the scraper as if he had no idea what to do with it. *Baal is growing too used to being a great hunter,* Ejil thought. *It is good to see a needle stuck in his pride.*

Daga joined the group, and the four searchers worked their way steadily downstream for a day and a half looking for tracks. Hopping from one foot to the other, covering ground like a long-legged snow hare, Breda kept several spear-throws ahead. The long shadows of late afternoon had drawn elongated silhouettes on the snow when the scout halted and dropped to his haunches. He beckoned his companions forward. "Found them!" he said.

Ejil squatted beside him; his breath came in steaming bursts. Baal and Daga hovered above them. Baal's restless eyes swept the frigid landscape.

Breda tugged off his mitten, grabbed a handful of snow and squeezed it through his fingers. "Looks like a snowfall here has partly covered the tracks."

"You two jabber like a pair of crows," Baal said. "I don't like the sky. See that rocky outcrop? It's as likely a place to make camp as we'll find, provided we can get that far before dark. What do you say, little brother? Think you can you make it?" Baal asked, his eyes fierce and mocking.

Daga snickered.

Anger sent strength flowing like a river into Ejil's exhausted body. He was tired of Baal's constant taunting. Filling his lungs, he leaped to his feet. He staggered slightly. Hunting had kept Baal, Breda and Daga lean and hard as boiled leather, while he had sat and ground herbs by the warmth of the šamán's hearth. He moved off quickly, his snowshoes churning a path through the newly fallen snow.

Dusk came early. Breda sniffed the air. "You were right, Baal. Storm's almost here."

Working feverously, the four hunters piled snow in a high mound between the rocks. Once disturbed, snow hardens quickly. Daga—the smallest—tunneled into the mound and began scraping out a hollow. Ejil dug in from the top to make a smoke hole. Once he had the drift hollowed out, Daga built a fire and waited while the heat began to melt the snow walls, then put it out. The walls quickly refroze, forming a hard, windproof glaze.

The men crowded in, wrapped themselves in their sleeping furs and hunkered down just as the storm began. They built a tiny fire. There was little to do but talk, sleep, or stare into the pitch-blackness while the wind roared in the smoke hole.

"By the gods, why are we stuck in this miserable place?" Baal asked. "Why do they make such storms? Is it to punish us?"

"The gods have a sense of humor," Breda said.

"Punish us? For what?" Ejil asked. "What makes you think that the gods care about us at all?"

Baal snorted. "Ah, the young šamán speaks. Explain this storm, then!"

"Pelas believed that changes in the weather were part of the circle of life. The sun rises, the sun sets, then rises again. The moon goes through its phases and returns to where it began. The Hot Season, The Season of the Painted Leaves, The Season of Ice, The Budding Season; one follows the other in an endless circle," Ejil said.

"Enough about the gods," Baal said, yawning. "This kind of talk makes my head ache. I'm after finding those murderers. Pelas was a crazy old fool; father often said so."

Daga, who had clung to Baal like a shadow all through the trek but had spoken little, cleared his throat. "Baal's right," Daga said.

"About what?" Ejil asked. "How would you know, Daga? You never met Pelas. He was a very wise man. Do we have any idea if these men we are hunting are from the same band?"

"No, and they outnumber us. We'd have no chance unless we can get help from *our* people," Breda said.

"That's not going to happen while Callas is First Speaker," Ejil said.

"Hah, she may not always be First Speaker," Daga said.

"What do you mean, Daga?"

"Just that! Not everyone is pleased with our Callas."

"The women believe she speaks for the Great Mother," Ejil said.

Baal coughed and cleared his throat. "You spend too much time in the longhouse, little brother. Many of the hunters believe that a woman as First Speaker offends the gods."

"Some of the fishermen, too," Breda said.

Ejil shivered and squeezed his arms against his chest. "Damn, it's cold. How does having a woman First Speaker offend the gods?"

"Everyone knows that the woman serves the man," Baal said.

"The strongest rules by right! As Baal says," Daga said. "As the earth serves the sun, the Sunfather is supreme. The Mother his servant."

"The women are servants? You would never have gotten away with that kind of talk in front of *our* mother, Baal," Ejil said.

"Your mother, you mean. My mother died before you were born."

Ejil's face burned as if he had been struck. He gritted his teeth. "The fact is, among the First People, a woman rules. How do you explain that?" he asked.

"A šamán's trickery! Ask the elder, Mala. He is priest of the Sunfather and…" Daga stopped abruptly.

Baal cleared his throat. Ejil had felt, rather than saw, him make a sharp movement toward Daga.

"It doesn't much matter," Baal announced in a loud voice. "After this storm blows itself out, there will be no tracks to follow."

"Right! Time to get some sleep," Breda said.

The next morning, they emerged to discover a landscape transformed. A burning sun hung like a fiery pendant in a cloudless azure sky. The air sparkled and the Wind Spirit held his breath. Ejil shaded his eyes and searched for familiar landmarks, but where there had once been a flat river shore, the wind had whipped up snowdrifts that appeared to roll, in serried ranks, across a featureless plain.

"Look, the landscape has totally changed," Ejil said. Freezing rain had glazed a thin transparent coating that gleamed like crystal in the Sunfather's glow.

Breda's lips twisted into a scowl. "If we ever had a chance to pick up the trail, that's gone. No chance now."

Baal snorted and kicked at the snow-frozen ground. "This was a waste of time," he said.

The four men sat gathered in a ragged circle. Ejil pulled off his mittens, flexed his half-frozen fingers and eyed his snowshoes. He had been thinking over Daga's words and Baal's reaction. *Something is in the wind; that much is clear.*

He had brought the subject up with Callas as often as he dared but could not move her. He had almost given up hope that their new tribe would help rescue Lada and the other captives. Even after so many moons had passed, he still missed Lada dreadfully. An idea began to form in his mind. *There's some hope if Breda is right about why they were taken.* He stood, stamped his feet and fastened his snow shield across his eyes.

Using spears to steady themselves, they trudged homeward. Struggling up one great snow dune, they breasted the crest only to find another looming up in their path. Late that afternoon, they lucked into a copse of trailing pine. The sharp-needled conifer defeated the artic wind by crawling along the ground like a vine. Ejil knew its resinous wood would catch fire easily and burn hot. Banking the snow into a windbreak, they huddled by the fire. There was little talk. They were too tired. The next day, the sun rose hot and the snow began to melt. The budding season had finally arrived.

CHAPTER 20

A PLACE BY THE RIVER

Holding the slippery body down firmly with one hand, Lada sliced off the fish's head, the tail, and then drew the sharp flint blade across the belly. Flies buzzed around the pile of waste at her feet. She scraped out the guts, sliced the fish neatly in half, extracted the backbone then sliced the filet lengthwise and draped them across the smoking rack. Shading her eyes, she squinted upward. The Sunfather's bright yellow disk burned down on her.

Raising her arms, she arched her back and stretched like a waking lion, then drew one arm across her forehead to wipe away the sweat. A slight breeze off the river ruffled her hair. The hot sun and cooling breeze felt good after the long, cold moons of winter.

They had found the river and the campsite just two suns ago. Lada surveyed the huts the Fishbellies had thrown up. *Hardly enough to keep off the rain,* she thought, wrinkling her nose. The one that Scar had helped her build, had gaping holes in the sides. She shook her head sadly. *Something must be done about this.* Each day she gathered bark, covered the gaps. She found clay by the riverbank, mixed with grass and slathered over the cracks to keep out the wind.

She saw Scar coming toward her. His face was grim—his spear held over his shoulder.

She stood to greet him. He made the sign for her to sit, placed his hand on her shoulder and regarded her belly. "You have eaten well?" he asked, formally. His face showed concern. He had become solicitous since her pregnancy began to show.

"Yes, I have eaten." she said.

"Our hunters found the tracks of a party of Blackdogs a few suns upstream," he signed.

"Blackdogs? Really?" Lada was surprised, though she wasn't sure why. She knew there were other tribes of her people. When she was younger, she had attended a gathering, met and played with other girls her age. "When?" she asked.

He made the sign indicating something that occurred in the past. "They were caught in the big storm. My men followed their tracks and found their camp. There are many, many fires," he said, repeating the sign for fire.

"How far away?"

He made a sign that meant "many days walk." Lada had gotten used to Fishbelly counting. They used their fingers to sign for *one*, *two* and *three*. She wasn't sure why they had no sign for the last two fingers. A single sign that meant *more* was used for any number beyond three. That brought to mind Ejil's counting lesson.

One day, long before her capture, Ejil had tapped her on the shoulder, his face lit up like a sunny day. He was bursting to tell her something. She was used to that. They had always shared each other's secrets. Once she promised not to tell, he had taught her the numbers six to ten. She lowered her head and pushed back the tears. The clan sign for *more* was also the sign for *never*.

"We found another track. A single man. A scout maybe."

"Did anyone see him?"

Scar slammed the butt of his spear into the ground. "No! He passed close enough to spy on the camp."

She felt a stab of fear like a knife in her bowels. Was it the new life within her or the fear of more killing? "Will there be war?" she asked, gazing up at him.

He shrugged. "The clan grows stronger," he said eyeing her distended belly.

Mata had also just become pregnant, though she had not joined with a man and Tule's son had already been born.

Crowbait and some of the clan women remained hostile to Lada. But, by custom, a pregnant woman held high status, and childless women were required to show deference and see to her needs, if required. Being pregnant and Scar's woman had made Lada untouchable.

The winter hunts had been meager. The people were thin, gaunt, and hollow-eyed with hunger by the time they reached the river. A foraging party returned, excited by their news. The journey from their winter cave took almost one full cycle of the moon. By the time they came in sight of it, cracks had begun to appear in the river ice. She was surprised at how quickly a channel appeared.

It was a good place. While the women and the few elders worked building shelters, the hunters cracked the shore ice and waded into the frigid shallows. There were fish, so many fish, that soon there was food in abundance. Tangy, sleek-sided salmon, fat bream and sweet-fleshed trout—in such abundance that even after gorging and eating their fill, the smoking racks sagged beneath the weight.

"What will you do now?" Lada asked her man.

"Keep better watch!"

"Maybe it was a hunting party?"

"Grayhair said they look for our camp."

Lada shrugged. "How can he know that?"

"They want to make war," Scar said, ignoring her question.

"How do you know? Why do you hate the Blackdogs so much?"

Scar spread his hands. "Blackdogs have always been our enemy. Once when my father was leader, we found a good camp. Many Blackdogs came with their spears. They forced us to leave. It had been a long trek. We were weak and had no food. The Blackdogs did not care. We searched for one moon to find another place. The hunting was bad. Many clan died."

"These were not my people."

"They were the same—Mudfaces!" he said.

"These people may want to trade," Lada said.

"Trade?" asked, stumbling over the word. "What does this mean?"

"It is a custom of my people. We give what we have much of for what other tribes have that we need."

He gazed at her thoughtfully. "Yes, I understand. The clan sometimes give gifts, with other clans. Speak more of this."

"Sometimes we gave fish for meat. My people wove baskets that were so tight they held water. Other tribes desired them," she said.

Scar raised an eyebrow and pointed at the basket at her feet. "Like that one?"

She folded her arms across her chest. "I do not lie," she said.

"No, no, I…I…" He glanced around and cleared his throat noisily.

Lada smiled to herself. "It is made of thin willow branches. You must soak it so it will swell. My mother once traded a basket for a nice piece of sharpstone," she said.

Scar's eyes lit up. "He gave sharpstone! For a basket?"

"Yes, our best knapper made my father a handblade."

"Do your people have sharpstone?" Scar asked.

Lada noticed a gleam in Scar's eye that she had not seen before. "Sometimes," she said shaking her head, "but it is very rare."

CHAPTER 21

THE TRADER

Ejil emerged from his hut, flapped his arms against the morning chill, stretched, and turned his gaze toward the river and watched the fishermen working their traps. Squinting through the cool, sunlit mist, he spied a tall, two-legged creature with a hugely deformed body. Ejil blinked and shaded his eyes, and as the apparition drew closer, it resolved itself into the shape of a man with a bulging pack on his back. Bowed forward like a tree in a strong wind, he plodded along aided by a crooked wooden staff.

From the children's gleeful cries, it was clear that the man was no stranger. They surged forward, shouting greetings and dancing circles around him. The man halted; a pair of dark eyes twinkled from beneath a tall, pointed leather cap.

Kokotin raised his hands to his mouth in mock confusion. "Then he extracted a thin swan-bone flute from his ragged parka, put it to his lips, and with big, blunt fingers coaxed a sweet melody from the delicate instrument.

It was a familiar tune, one that stirred in Ejil the memory of a tiny bird, short-billed and plump, that often held forth in the tall spindly pine outside his father's hut. Warm tears rolled down Ejil's cheeks and froze in his thin, scraggly beard which, like a tangle of tiny vines, had begun to form beneath his chin.

Not a young man, the stranger's narrow face was a light brown, craggy and cracked like a cliff face. His eyes grew close together and were edged with a spray of tiny creases. He had a small mouth, a scruffy beard and a long, sharp, vulpine nose. Gray hair sprouted from beneath his cap in a fringe of silver ringlets.

Piping his tune, he led the children toward an open space between the circle of huts and there laid down his pack. People spilled from their huts and clustered around him. "Kokotin!" they shouted, "Kokotin!" Ejil had heard the name of the itinerant trader, one who was welcomed as much for where he had been and what he had seen as for the goods he had on offer.

The trader spread a ratty old sleeping fur face down, dipped into his pack and put out his wares for inspection, gesticulating, making faces, his dark eyes dancing.

There was a flute of carved ivory engraved with tiny deer outlined in black, a small hide-covered drum and a rattle; a double handful of vibrantly colored shells in twisted shapes; chunks of sharpstone, both black and green; nodules of ochre; a woman's vest of softest doe skin, embroidered with dyed ivory beads; a knife of knapped sharpstone set in a handle of carved antler that Ejil's hand ached to hold. Beads, beads carved of bone—beads carved of mammoth ivory and colorfully dyed, and small nodules of red and yellow ochre.

"Please my friends, tonight, tonight I promise to tell all if someone will offer a roof over a poor trader's head."

Shouted invitations came from all sides.

Kokotin raised both hands and blocked his ears. "Many thanks, many thanks. But now my friends, as you can see, I have brought many rare and wonderful things. Show me what you have. Let us trade."

Torches and oil lamps were lit, and a circle formed inside the sacred cave. People were anxious to hear the trader's news.

Ejil listened open mouthed as Kokotin entertained them with his stories—tales of the Great Journey, mountains that rose to the sky; stories of huge white birds with voices that screamed like demented souls, that fished a great lake of saltwater where fish flew and giant waves crashed against the shore with a sound like thunder—a lake so vast that you could not see the end of it even on the clearest days.

A great salt water! Flying fish? I would like to see that place, thought Ejil.

"Kokotin, what news of the hunt?" a man shouted.

"Aha," the trader answered, eyes bulging. "The Mammoth and Bear People sharpen their spears and prepare for the journey to the meeting place. The Hot Season has been long, and the deer herds will be bulging with fat."

A happy murmur passed through the seated crowd. There had been sufficient fish and fresh meat for the people's needs, but as the season warmed. the deep pits that held deer fat were almost empty. The tribe depended on the great hordes of migrating deer pouring south at the beginning of the Season of the Painted Leaves. Each year, the people gathered with their sister tribes at a shallow ford where the herds crossed the river on their journey.

Baal stood. "You come from downriver. What of the Fishbellies? Did you see any sign of them?" he asked. Salat and Daga stood beside him.

"Fish…bellies? Ah, yes, you mean the Paleskins. Yes, now that you ask; I passed a camp five, maybe six suns downriver."

Six suns downriver? He's found them. Ejil's ears perked up.

"Where?" Baal demanded.

"Greetings, friend," Kokotin said with a soft smile. "I don't believe we have met."

"I am Baal, son of Talog, of the Broken People. We know of this Paleskin band. We have followed their sign, but have not yet found their camp."

"Ah, yes, my sympathies. Word of your misfortune has carried on the wind. I met your father years ago, though the Broken People ranged far to the north. Perhaps you did not go far enough. The Fishbellies are camped along a bend this side of the river, the trader said.

"Did you enter their camp?"

"No, my friend. These Pale, er, Snakebellies, as some call them, are dangerous. You cannot speak with them. They wave their hands around and their talk is gibberish. I came on them by accident, and luckily upwind," he said, grinning, eyes dancing. "I climbed a hill and there they were below me. I quickly ducked behind some rocks.

"I was able to see the camp and got a good view of their leader, or so he seemed. Big, ugly fellow—or just *big*, for them. Most are broad and squat, and all are ugly, but his mother should have abandoned this one at birth," Kokotin said, grinning. "He had a great scar ran down the side of his face."

Ejil's palms turned sweaty, his hands shook. *A great scar? Could it be?* His eyes focused on the trader's face.

The people laughed, but Baal raised a hand which silenced them. "The man you speak of is the leader of the pack of murderers who destroyed our people. Did you see any dark-skinned women, women of our people, amongst them?" he asked.

"I can't be sure, Son of Talog, the hill was some distance from the camp. It hadn't been there for long, the camp, that is. The man I saw was with a band of hunters butchering a kill at the base of the hill. There were women, but I did not get a good look; though now that I think on it, some did have dark skin. Sometimes you see a dark one, but most are slimy and pale-skinned. As you say: like the belly of a fish, ha ha! Some have long, stringy hair the color of red ochre."

Baal signaled Daga and Salat. They all stood up and left without another word. Ejil followed them from the cave.

CHAPTER 22

CONFRONTATION

Early next morning, Baal and a grim-faced group of hunters barged into the longhouse. All carried spears. The šamán's two acolytes leaped to their feet and hurriedly inserted themselves between the hunters and their šamán. Ejil knew they were coming. He and Breda had tried to calm his brother down, but Baal would not listen. *Baal wants a confrontation,* Ejil concluded. He did not alert Callas. He sat quietly by the smoking hearth, grinding herbs, and watching.

Callas sat lounging on her bench, chewing on a bone from a platter of steaming meat held by an old woman. "What is all this about?" she demanded. "Why have you come here carrying weapons?"

Baal brushed aside Zula, one of the guards, knocking her off her feet. He strode up to the dais and slammed his spear butt into the floor. Zula picked herself up and raised her spear.

Baal spun on his heel, faced her, and grinned.

"No!" Callas shouted. She raised her hand. "Let him be!" She tossed the half-eaten leg bone back onto the platter and sat back. "What is so vital, Son of Talog, that you trample our customs and interrupt my meal?" she demanded.

"We have important words," he said. "I think you already know! The Fishbellies, Whitefaces or whatever you want to call them! The trader has seen them. They have set up a camp on the bank of the river five suns downstream. There is no doubt. He described their scar-faced leader. This is the same band that murdered our people and hold our women captive," Baal said.

"So, you have found them," Callas said. "Now, perhaps our hunters can resume the task of providing meat for our winter larders."

"I, I tell you they are the same band that murdered our men," Baal stammered. "They butchered our children and made slaves of our women. Now they steal the fish we need to live, their drying racks cover the shore."

"The Mother's bounty is available to all," Callas said, sketching the devotee's sign in the air. Her two acolytes dutifully mimicked her.

Ejil's face darkened. *My Lada is so close. We know where they are, and Callas still refuses to help us. I had hoped but Baal was right; he said that she would never change her mind. Now we have no choice, we must either go around or through her. But how?*

Baal stared open mouthed. "The people say there is hardly a fish in the river. What do we do when the cold winds sweep down from the north and the Season of Death is upon us? Our people will starve!"

"Bah! There are fish enough, and soon the deer herds will stream south and cross upriver. We will have meat in plenty."

Ejil watched Baal and Callas, each eyeing the other like a pair of stags at rut. "Venerable Callas," Ejil said, jumping to his feet. "They hold our people, your kin, as slaves."

"Enough!" Callas shouted, her chins jiggled and her deep voice boomed off the longhouse walls. She stood. "We have spoken of this before. Our tribes separated long ago, and since we found this place, we have lived in peace. Your women were captured in battle. We owe them no debt of honor," she said.

"And, what of the fish catch? Are we to do nothing while they steal the food from our mouths?" Salat asked.

The šamán shook her head slowly back and forth. "Which of you knows these people's plans?" she asked, her gaze slowly roaming from face to face, regarding each of the assembled hunters one at a time. "Do you?" she demanded, her eyes drilling into Salat's.

"All know that the Whitefaces are wanderers," she said flapping a hand in dismissal. "They are stupid and smelly, barely human at all. They never stay anywhere for long. They may be gone before the moon's next quarter. It would not surprise me if they had already abandoned the river. Our adopted brother would have us attack them. He is not concerned for the fishing. He seeks vengeance, and he would sacrifice you," she said pointing to Salat, "and you," she said, pointing at Daga, "and the rest of us to satisfy his bloodlust."

Callas pointed her finger at Baal. "I see into the depths of your heart, Baal, son of Talog. Saving your women is not our task, and though I hesitate to say it because it is a sad thing, they are probably long dead. I shall consult the Mother," she said and sat down heavily.

"And, if they stay and take our fish?" Salat persisted.

"Is your head stuffed with rat dung?" Callas asked. "There are fish in plenty in the river and we must prepare for The Hunt. "If they are still here once we return, we will seek a parlay with them. Our brother tribes await us."

Baal's eyes widened with disbelief. "Parlay?" he sneered. "We too had lived in peace for many years before these pale ones came." He shook his head and spat on the reed strewn floor, propped his hands on his hips, cocked his head and stared up at the šamán perched on her dais glaring at him. "They may go, you say! Kokotin says they have built huts. They will stay as long as there are fish in our river!"

"I will pray to The Mother for guidance," she said.

"Yes, pray; by all means, pray. And while you cower on your knees, hope that these beasts do not decide to attack this village and steal your women as they did ours." Baal strode from the hut.

Ejil gritted his teeth. He and Breda exchanged glances. *No debt of honor? These women are your kin!* His thoughts turned to Lada. *She is alive, I know she is.* Jumping to his feet, he followed the other men out of the longhouse. Baal stood some distance away, shaking his spear, his band of young hunters gathered around him.

Daga was speaking, his voice a whisper. "This is what we have been waiting for, Baal." His eyes burned with a feverish glow. "I understand how you feel; we all do. You heard her. Callas is taking for herself the power that belongs, by right, to the tribal council. She has made a mistake. By custom, a council meets after the coming Hunt to plan for the cold seasons. She thinks she has won. We will prepare. When the council meets, we will be ready."

"Very well, my friends," Baal said, "but remember: before the massacre, I spoke in council and warned our people. But our women, even my own stepmother, preached patience. Breda and my brother were there; they will tell you. 'Wait,' they said, 'there is time.' While we waited, the attack came and our people died. I do not want to see that happen here."

"Baal speaks the truth. We were both there," Breda said, gesturing at Ejil. "We thought we had time to prepare, but the Fishbellies fell upon our camp before we were ready."

Ejil looked around at the eager faces. He recalled the strange talk, that night in the snow shelter. *The young men will support us.' But Callas is stubborn and Callas still rules. I knew it: Baal and Daga are plotting something. They don't trust me, but Breda will tell me.*

"Never doubt it," Baal said and raised his spear aloft. "Those white-faced beasts are your enemies. I have sent four of their warriors to the Shadowlands and my spear hungers for more."

"I too seek vengeance for the death of my father and mother," Breda said. "My Mata is their slave. I will tear out their hearts and drink their blood. This I swear." He slammed his spear butt on the ground.

"Death to the Fishbellies!" Daga roared.

"Death to the Fishbellies!" the hunters shouted and pounded their spear butts against the ground.

CONSPIRACY

On the second night after the quartered moon, as the moon goddess hid from the stars, several men slipped like shadows into the hut Ejil shared with Baal and Breda. First came Tamo, son of Tamo. The second, another elder named Mala who, like Tamo, wore the long gray beard of an elder. A few of the hunters followed.

Baal greeted Tamo. Ejil had not seen the old warrior since he had spoken up for Baal at the Boar feast. He watched the old man as his eyes flickered around the hut noting those present.

"Your words with Callas, Baal, son of Talog, have carried on the wind," Tamo began, speaking formally. "We agree with what you have said. This Whiteface clan is a threat. Just before the leaves begin to turn, the Great Mother sends great tribes of fish upriver to spawn. We depend upon their visit to fill our winter larders. The season is here but the fish are few. These wily white-faced beasts steal the food from our mouths. We have been at peace since almost the time of my father, and the people believe in our šamán's mummery. I am afraid they will remain blind to the danger until they feel the ache in their empty bellies."

"Callas is a fool," Mala said. "She cannot see what is before her face. She is a woman, and because a woman leads us, The First People have become weak. You have faced these men, Baal, son of Talog. We have come seeking your council."

Baal bowed his head for a long moment then faced the two old men. "Venerable Elders, I am sure you know, the beasts that are taking our fish are the same band that destroyed our people. The trader, Kokotin, described their scarred leader. I met him in combat. There can be no doubt, it is the same man. They threaten more than our bellies, they threaten our tribe. We must destroy them, or they will destroy us."

Mala glanced at Tamo. "We thought that is what you would say. We have come to ask you a question, but it is important that what we ask is kept secret," Mala said, his gaze shifting from one man to another.

"I trust these men," Baal said, gesturing around the hut.

"And your brother, the young šamán? Forgive me, Ejil, but you spend much of your time in the šamán's hut. Where do you stand?" Mala asked. His sharp eyes bored into Ejil's skull.

Ejil gritted his teeth and held up his staff. "This was my master's staff. It is all we have left of the story of my people. It belonged to the šamán, Pelas. He died fighting these men. They killed my father and my mother, and they took away the girl I care for. Now they threaten us. I believe some evil hand guides them. I stand with my brother."

Mala raised a hand and smiled. "Good! My apologies, young man, but I had to ask."

He turned to Baal. "You are young and new to our tribe, but you are a blooded warrior. Our young men follow you, and your skill with a spear is known. You have fought these people. We have come to ask you, Baal, son of Talog, to be war chief," Mala said.

"War chief!" Baal lowered his eyes. "You do me great honor."

Ejil eyed his brother, saw his hands squeeze themselves into fists and his jaw muscle dance—watched the other hunters turn to each other and smile. *War chief! Just what Baal wants…what they all want, even Breda.* Ejil felt a stab of jealousy—or was it fear? But he shrugged it off. *Let him be war chief. If we are able to rescue Lada and the rest of our women, it will be worth it.*

Mala waved his hand in dismissal. "Only the council can appoint a war chief. That is why we must keep this secret. As elders, we have the power to nominate you. If you agree, we will propose you at the council, following the Hunt," Tamo said.

"A council should be called now. The people must be warned. The danger…" Breda said.

Tamo shook his head. "We could demand a council, but there is little time before the Hunt. And with Callas against us, the people would not agree. Everyone is excited about The Hunt, or perhaps, the rites which follow," he said, smiling, "particularly the young people. Many of the older people see no threat, and they believe that Callas speaks for the Great Mother and that her magic will protect us! We must bide our time. A council is always called to celebrate The Hunt and plan for the Ice Season. We will act then."

Baal snorted. "We, too, consulted our šamán—a man famous for his wisdom. He did not see the danger, and when it came, we were not prepared and our people died."

Tamo eyed him with a sad face. "I am an old man with more winters than I can count. Every morning I watch the Sunfather rise. In the evening, he disappears from the world. We are born and we die while the gods go on forever. Their ways are far beyond the understanding even of a šamán, but most of the people believe in her."

Tamo is right, Ejil thought. *Callas has ears in every hut, and she hates Baal.*

"How will things be different after the Hunt? Ejil asked. "If Callas learns of your plan, the women will all oppose us."

"Our fishermen are patient, young šamán," Mala said with a smile. "There have been bad patches before, and most will tell you that is the way of it and it will soon get better," Mala said.

"And, when it does not?"

"They will begin to believe, my young friend. They will begin to understand, and they will side with us."

"What of Callas? Will she support us then?"

"She speaks of parlay," Daga sneered.

Mala shrugged.

"She is stubborn," Ejil said.

"We must avoid making an enemy of our šamán. If war comes, our people must be united," Tamo said.

"And while we wait?" Baal asked.

"Is there sign that they have come upriver?" Tamo asked, turning to Breda.

Breda shook his head. "No, none so far," he said.

"Good! So, unless there is immediate danger, we take up our spears and join the Hunt," Tamo said.

"We leave for the Hunt in less than a moon. Scouts must be sent out. Kokotin said the Whiteface camp looked new. They must also prepare for the Ice Season. Continue the scouting. Make a wide circle. If you find sign, Mala and I will demand a council."

Breda nodded. "It will be done."

CHAPTER 24

WINGED SPEARS

Ejil had been thinking about throwing spears with a sling ever since Breda had asked about the possibility. *If one tribe had came up with a way, surely, I can too.*

It had been a frustrating morning. *A spear thrower,* he reasoned, *must be like a rock thrower.* So he had lengthened the cord of his sling to accommodate the spear shaft, but each time he tried a throw, the spear lifted up and spun backwards though the air. He ground his teeth. *Why won't the spear behave like a rock and fly straight?* he wondered. *What would Pelas have advised? 'It doesn't act like a rock, young Ejil, because it is not a rock.'* He smiled at the recollection. He missed the old man. Then, completely unbidden, another idea sprang to mind.

Flies swarmed the bone pile. It lay far outside the village circle. Bones were tossed on the pile where they weathered and dried. Dried bones were more supple than flint and made very useful tools.

Ejil rooted around until he found what he was searching for, the thigh bone of a red deer. It was about the length of his forearm, thick and, he judged, dry enough. He brought it to the hut.

Breda and Baal were gone. *Good! What I don't need is my brother poking around and making fun of me.*

Ejil gazed at the design he had scratched out on a piece of flat slate. Then, working across the bone's knobby end with his flint handblade, made his first crosscut. He sawed halfway through the bone a finger's breadth behind the knobby protrusion that had fit into the animal's thigh, then did the same at the other end where it fit into the lower leg-bone. Inserting a wedge, he tapped gently with his hammerstone until, with a loud crack, the bone split in half along its length.

He slid the butt end of a light throwing spear along the hollow channel until it snugged up against the smaller knob. He gripped the larger knob and, using his other hand to steady the shaft, he was able to hold the spear above his shoulder in the overhand throwing position. *So far, so good.* Ejil faced the open sward that led toward the river and adjusted his stance. The balance felt fine. *Let's hope this works*, he thought, drawing back his arm.

Baal yawned and hefted his throwing spear. He made sure he was last to throw. He always won, and it gave him pleasure to see the looks of disappointment on the faces of his men as his cast flew past the other's best. Either Salat or Tanus usually came in second. *It is important they see that I am the strongest.* Squinting into the sun, he wiped his brow. It was past midday, and the Hot Season was full on. Scraggly bushes and stunted trees stretched from the village to the shadows beneath the lime-stone cliffs, where a narrow band of pines hid from the freezing winds and flourished in the shelter of the high cliffs.

Practice had become serious. Five suns would find them on the trail to the deer hunt. Taking advantage of the fine weather, the elders, moth-ers, and children came out to enjoy the contest, which made the hunters all the more anxious to exhibit their skills.

Baal stepped back from the line, lifted the spear above his right shoulder, retracted his arm, skipped a step forward and threw. The thin shaft arced upward across the sky, came down and embedded itself in the dry earth several paces beyond Salat's, which had been the best throw.

Salat and Breda shared a sour look. Salat shrugged. "As if we didn't know."

Baal's eyes widened. He saw Ejil sauntering toward the group with a pair of throwing spears propped on one shoulder.

"Ho, little brother. What brings *you* here? I see you have brought your spears. Tired of picking herbs and painting pictures on rocks?"

"I have come to give you a lesson, brother, on how to throw a spear," Ejil said, and did a little Pico dance. The hunters and several of the bystanders laughed. People liked Ejil, and he was learning to play to his audience.

"Well," Baal snickered, "you should have come earlier. Everyone has thrown and my cast stands as the one to beat. But I am always eager to learn. I believe we can make room for my little brother. What do you say, men?"

"Aye, let him throw," Salat said, with a wave of his hand.

"I bet he won't beat mine," Daga said.

"Hah, at last, somebody Daga might beat," Tanus said.

Breda's eyes narrowed. He cocked his head, stroked his newly sprouted beard. "Watch out Baal, your brother is up to something."

"What's this?" Baal asked, pointing toward the bone tucked into Ejil's waistband. "Hungry? Bring along something to gnaw on?"

The bystanders tittered and pointed.

"It's a tool I made," Ejil said, evenly.

He put down one spear and pulled the worked bone from his belt. "Now, if you'll all stand back, and watch!" He walked behind the throwing line, slid the butt end of the spear shaft along the bone's concave channel, hefted it, set his stance, skipped a step forward and launched his spear. All eyes followed the spear's path. Indulgent smiles turned to cries of wonder as the thin shaft arced up, up, and up and was swallowed by the cloudless blue sky.

Breda gaped, open mouthed. "By The Sunfather!" he said, shading his eyes. The spear had buried itself upright in the ground far beyond Baal's.

"How did you do that?" Tanus asked. The hunters crowded around to examine Ejil's tool.

"I have been thinking about it ever since Breda mentioned a spear throwing tool he had heard about. I tried throwing a spear with my sling, but it didn't work," Ejil said grinning. "Then I got a new idea. This makes my arm twice as long and adds strength to the cast."

Standing a little apart, Baal stared thoughtfully at his brother. "Let's take a looksee," he said.

The two brothers started toward the spears, everyone followed.

Breda shook his head slowly side to side as they came up to Baal's spear. Ejil's was sticking upright at least three normal throwing lengths further out.

"Good throw," Breda said, clapping Ejil on the back.

"He cheated," Daga said, viciously kicking a stone.

Baal stood rubbing his chin. "The question is, can you hit anything with this, what-do-you-call-it?" he asked.

"That's the same question you asked about my sling. Breda said they called it *a flying spear*. You are the better spearman, brother. Try it yourself," he said, holding out the spear thrower.

Baal's eyes narrowed.

"Go ahead, Baal," Salat said.

Baal looked around. Everyone was smiling and looking at him expectantly. He could see no way out. *I'll kill the son of a dog if he embarrasses me,* Baal thought.

"Yes, try it. Here, take my spear," Tanus said grinning.

"You'll need a lighter shaft that narrows at the far end. Try this one," Ejil said, holding out his remaining spear.

Baal took the tool and spear and scowled. "Alright little brother. How does it work?" he asked as they reached the starting line.

"Here, slot the butt in, like so. That's right, grip the knob tight. Now, set your stance a bit more sideways to the target than normal. That's it! Cock your arm, skip forward and throw as usual."

Baal eyed Ejil and hefted the spear. The thrower's length forced his grip further back on the shaft than he was used to. He tried a couple of practice casts without releasing the shaft.

"That's it," Ejil said.

If you make me look like a fool, you will regret it, Baal thought. He took a deep breath, skipped forward and hurled the spear with all his strength. The narrow shaft arced up and disappeared from sight.

Breda shaded his eyes watching the spear's path. "By the gods," he said.

The hunters raced forward.

Baal's spear stood quivering in the turf far beyond his own best throw and two spear lengths beyond Ejil's.

Daga slapped his chief on the back. "Great throw!"

Baal grinned. He felt good. He was, once again, the center of attention.

"You know what this means," Breda said. "If we meet the Fishbellies in the open, with Ejil's tool, each of us should be able to throw two *flying spears* before they get close enough to use their heavy lances."

Baal caught Ejil's quick nod.

"We'll mow them down like a herd of dumb bison," Tanus said.

The crowd had surrounded Ejil. Everyone was talking at once, waiting for their chance to finger the new tool.

Baal turned Breda's comment over in his mind. *The clever little piece of bison shit has come up with something,* he decided, his mind spinning. He began making his plans.

Baal had never liked the sling. It was something a woman would use. *But the spear! The spear is a man's weapon. Each of my warriors will carry three, two for throwing and one for close in fighting.* He closed his eyes and envisioned the slaughter.

Well, he thought, *enjoy yourself while it lasts, little brother.* He set his jaw, strode over and wrapped his arm around Ejil's shoulder. "Good work," he said. He reached down, grasped the hand holding the thrower and held it up high. The people cheered.

CHAPTER 25

THE HUNT

Ejil stood on the ridge where the First People had pitched their hide tents. He had a good view of the valley and the well-worn trail that led to the shallow ford where the great herd was soon expected to cross. The camp of the Bear People was to the South, the Mammoth Camp to the West, and the tribes mixed on the flat grassy space between them.

The mood was joyous. Friends greeted friends. There were honey cakes and dried sweetberries, smoked marrow, mint tea and much haggling. Flint knappers showed their spearpoints and handblades. A group of women clustered around a bead maker's piles of bone and ivory beads.

Joba, flint knapper of the Bear People, and Vala, a skilled knapper of the Mammoth tribe, showed their finest points. Each craftsman had his partisans. The men stood around arguing whose points were the stronger and held a better edge, but blades and points made by either craftsman were in great demand.

Ejil squatted down next to Daga to view Joba's points, which were spread out on a soft deer hide. Daga was trying to talk Joba into a trade. The young hunter held a delicately formed, leaf-shaped point. Daga hefted it, held it up to the sun, then tested its edge with his thumb. The point was made of tough, dark stone.

"Humm, you used weak stone; this blade will chip," Braga said, holding the point up to the light with one eye closed.

Joba's mouth twisted as if he had tasted something foul. "Gods, give me patience. Use your eyes, boy! See the grain. This is the finest floor stone. I dug the nodule from the seam, myself. You will find none harder." He pointed to Daga's boar-hide sash. "I will trade for that."

Daga clutched the sash and shook his head fiercely. "Never! This is the prize of a great boar hunt, one sung around the evening fires. Boar larger than any man has ever seen. It was a gift from Baal, our first hunter."

"Many speak of my spearpoints and blades around those same fires," Joba snorted. "This one is my best!"

"My fish is cut thick. Sweet bream, smoked over cedar root, juicy and sweet," Daga said.

Joba made a face and shook his head. "I have plenty of fish."

"Humph," Daga said. He gave Ejil a sour look and tossed the blade onto the deer skin, narrowly missing another point

Joba glared at the short hunter, who stood, stalked off and joined Ejil's brother. Baal scowled down at the knapper.

Ejil understood. Baal wanted the blade, but rather than bargain for it himself, had sent Daga. Ejil's mouth went dry. It was beautifully shaped. He had coveted the blade before; now he wanted it even more.

"My apologies," he said.

Joba cocked an eyebrow. "He is your kinsman?"

"No and yes; we are both of the First People, but he is not my blood. My brother and I were adopted into the tribe."

"I have heard. Word of the Broken People travels on the wind. You are the young šamán?"

Ejil's face darkened. "No, no, I…!"

"Humm, you like my points?"

Ejil held up the point and squinted along its edge. Each of the tiny dished knaps was uniform in size and precisely arranged. Reflected sunlight rippled across the point's surface. He had knapped a few points himself, when he could find the stone, but none so fine. Ejil's two spears had only wooden points that he'd hardened in the fire. *With a point like this, a man could hunt anything, man or beast.*

"So beautiful! I wish I could tie it with a cord and wear it around my neck. I have nothing worthy to trade for it," he said, and laid the point reverently down on the tanned hide.

The knapper stroked his beard and cocked an eye. "The shape is that of a leaf from a tree that grows along the river."

"Yes, a laurel. I see that! It is beautiful!"

"And deadly! Almost as keen as sharpstone. You are a šamán? Can you make pictures?" he asked.

"Yes; Pelas, our šamán, taught me some, and Pico also. I can make you a tattoo," he replied eagerly. "Anything you like. A red bison or a cave lion, or…"

Joba shook his head. "And, put it where?" He pushed up his sleeves and held out his arms which were covered in swirling patterns of tiny white dots like smoke curling above a fire. Similar designs covered his face. "It is for my woman. At The Rites, the women dance painted, covered in beads and feathers. Each tries to outdo the others. My woman demands that I paint her, but I make a mess of it. Every year we fight and…"

"She does not like tattoos? I am very gentle."

"She says they ruin her skin, which is soft and very fine. If you will decorate her for the rites, the point is yours!"

Ejil starred at the knapper. "Really? Yes," he grinned. "I will do it."

"I warn you," Joba said, with a lopsided smile, "my woman is not easy to please."

"I will make her happy. She will be magnificent. All the other women will envy her, and after the dance she will come eagerly to your sleeping fur," Ejil said, still grinning.

"No," Joba said, shaking his head sadly, "she will drink honey-water and scratch her itch with younger cocks. But at least I shall have peace around my fire."

Holding his treasure to his chest, Ejil worked his way through the crowd. At one spot he saw a necklace made of fox teeth. *So, delicate! Wouldn't Lada love it,* he thought. *How I wish she was here. I would trade for it. Wouldn't her eyes light up as I fastened it around her slender neck?* Ejil thought about how his brother had praised him over the spear thrower, and what Breda had said about using it against the Fishbellies. *Don't give up hope, Lada. We will be coming for you and all our women, very soon.*

The deep bellow of an auroch's horn sounded through the camp. The mingling stopped. All the young men grabbed their spears and ran down the path toward the ford. Jostling each other for a place, they lined up and waded chest-deep into the frigid river water. Spears held above their heads; they formed a broad corridor out from the shallows into the deeper water. The older hunters held back. There would soon be room once the cold water drove the young ones—blue lipped, teeth chattering—back to the shore.

There was little time to wait. The herd leader, a giant buck with glassy black eyes, his head crowned with a magnificent rack, splashed into the far side of the river. The swift current, swollen by the late season rains, slowed the advancing herd, which stretched back as far as the eye could see. By the time they reached the ford, they were packed so close together that they could not retreat. They made an easy target for the spearmen.

Ejil and Breda stood together, thigh-deep, in the onrushing current. Ejil's first throw was solid. The heavy spear caught a big doe behind its forequarters. The animal's forelegs buckled, and she pitched headlong into the frothing current.

"Good throw!" Breda shouted.

Ejil rushed forward to retrieve his spear and pull the dying animal free of the plunging mass. As he did, a huge stag, dodging the fallen doe, slammed into his chest and sent him sprawling. The frigid water struck him like a club. A pair of strong hands grabbed him under the armpits and dragged him to the surface, gagging and spiting.

"Did I mention it is best to stand well back from the herd?" Breda asked grinning. "Here!" he said, handing Ejil his dropped weapon.

"Best concentrate on the killing and let the youngsters retrieve the bodies," Breda said. He turned back toward the passing herd, and in one smooth motion, brought down a young stag.

They stabbed and bludgeoned until loose entrails and elongated tendrils of dark blood streamed downstream. Piled onshore, the dead and dying animals waited, while the women, arms covered in blood to their shoulders, wielded their flint blades.

While some scraped the fat into leather bags, others quartered the meat and sliced off bloody strips to be hung on the smoking racks.

As night descended, pine torches were lit and the killing continued. Then it was over, the last bobbed tail disappeared into the night. Shaking with cold, the hunters staggered from the frigid water dragging their spears.

The butchering continued. The blood scent had already attracted a pack of Black Spotted Hyena, who slouched just beyond the flickering fingers of torchlight. Carrion eaters fear the fire, but soon the wolves and lions would come, and fire provided little protection after dawn. Finally, as the sun's first fingers creeped over the cliffs, the people packed up and headed back to their camps. Ejil and Breda plodded side by side up the trail.

"A good hunt. I can barely raise my arm," Ejil said.

"Not so good," the scout said, batting away a fly. "I heard Tanus say that the herd was much smaller than last season's."

"Why? They should be fat from grazing on the thick grass."

Breda shrugged. "Only the gods know. But with less meat and fish, there will be empty bellies when the snows come."

"The council must act," Ejil said.

"I am tired of waiting for the council. They are a bunch of old women. I will free my Mata, with or without the council. Baal feels the same. Are you with us?" Breda demanded.

"I feel the same about Lada, and with each moon that passes, I am…" he said, shook his head and wiped his eyes. "Of course, I am with you. The hunters will join us, won't they?"

"Yes. But even so, we need the council's support!" Breda kicked moodily at a pebble along the path. "I have waited so long for Mata. The thought of those beasts touching her." He shook his head. "I must do something."

"The council meets as soon as we get back home."

"Unless Callas finds a reason to put it off," Breda said, shaking his head.

"The elders will insist," Ejil said.

"Ah, yes, the elders. Tamo and Mala talk, but will they stand up to Callas?"

"I believe Tamo will. I know our šamán is stubborn. She hates Baal and she will do everything she can to stop his becoming war chief."

Behind them, flies swarmed over piles of offal and bones. The rich odor of roasting venison rose from the smoking hearths. Some of the hunters were gathered in a knot below the knoll's crest.

"Breda! Ejil! here, 'ave a drink," Tanus said and handed Breda a bulging bladder.

Breda raised the skin and swallowed. "Honey-water. Strong stuff! Where did you get it?" he asked, wiping his mouth. He handed the skin to Ejil.

Tanus slid his forefinger up along his nose. "Itt'ss a ssecret," he said, grinning hugely.

"Yes, and it's been his secret for too long," Salut said, raising an eyebrow. "Here, Ejil, don't fall in love with that skin. Give it here!"

"Tanus' late wife's father is of the Bear People. He makes the best honey-water and he wants Tanus to marry his youngest daughter now that her sister is gone," Salat said.

"Hey, speaking of love, The Rites are about to begin. There's a sweet little Bear girl; she's been giving me the eye since we got here," Tanus said.

"I believe it has already started," Ejil said, pointing to a naked couple copulating in the dry grass. Two young men walked by hand in hand, gazing lovingly at each other.

"Where's Baal? He'll want a swig of this," Breda said and passed the skin.

"It's…strong!" Ejil said, blinking back tears.

Salat squinted up at the sun and passed his forearm across his brow to wipe away the sweat. "He and Daga are meeting with Bear and

Mammoth. Some of the young men are anxious to join the fight against the Fishbellies," he said, eyes wide.

"What fight? The council must make the decision," Ejil said.

Salut nodded, grinned, and winked at Ejil.

"They may not have a choice," Breda said. "I'll have a quick drink, then I'm leaving. We've been away for ten suns. That scar-faced warrior's a canny one. I want to make sure he hasn't had spies watching the village."

"I'm hun-ga-ry," Tanus slurred. "Hey, where's zat skinn?"

"Here, Ejil, take another drink. I hear some of those Mammoth girls are ripe and ready," Salat said, grinning. "Come on, you two, let's go find ourselves a couple of honey pots. My cock's getting hard. Soon it will be so big I won't be able to walk. It's The Mother's will!"

"I need another drink," Tanus said.

"Never mind that," Salat said, grabbing Tanus by the shoulders. "This way!" He gave the drunken hunter a push. "Those girls need us! There is a nice, plump, young one over at the Mammoth camp I don't want to disappoint."

At that moment a girl appeared. She beckoned Salat and propped her hands on her hips.

"You see?" Salat said. He gave Tanus another shove and loped off.

"You going to join the fun?" Breda asked Ejil.

Ejil shook his head. "I don't feel much like celebrating. I'll go back with you." Upending the skin, he took a long swallow, drew his forearm across his mouth and burped loudly. "Ahhh!!!"

"I miss my Mata," Breda said. He grabbed the skin and took a long pull. "That's enough. Come on, if you're coming. It's a long walk. We'd best get going."

"Hold up, I have to decorate a woman for The Rites. It won't take long and I'll be ready to go, Meanwhile have another drink," Ejil said, with a sly smile.

CHAPTER 26

WAR CHIEF

The council chamber was filling. Flanked by her two acolytes, Callas—her speaking stick in one hand, staff in the other—waddled slowly to the speaker's seat and settled herself. She reminded Ejil, who had spent most of the day with Pico, preparing the chamber, of a great spider preparing to spin its web.

Tiny points of light, reflected from cave crystals embedded in the tall columns, flickered like fireflies. The flaming torches, set in niches along the walls, brought the animals drawn in paint and charcoal quivering to life. A mix of smells—fish from the lamp oil, the sharp scent of pine resin of the torches—permeated the chamber.

Ejil noticed the corner of the šamán's mouth lift into a sneer as Baal made his entrance. All eyes followed his tall muscular form. He strode in, eyes straight ahead, and dropped down cross-legged beyond the edge of the hearth, in the midst of his hunters.

Ejil's gaze fixed on Callas. Watching her jaw tighten and her jowls tremble, he could almost read her thoughts.

Pico leaned over and whispered in his ear. "Our šamán never forgets a slight."

Just like my brother, Ejil thought.

Callas struggled to her feet and held up the speaking stick. A hush fell over the assembled tribe.

"Some moons ago, three strangers from The Broken People came among us seeking refuge. Now, we have word of a band of Fishbellies camped downriver. Our adopted brothers tell us that this is the same clan who murdered their men and made slaves of their women. They declare us kin and call upon us to make war and rescue their women.

"This young hunter," she said, pointing at Baal, "speaks of war! He tells us that we should attack these white-faced people and show them no mercy. But, as we all know, young Baal is an angry man. He seeks revenge and he would spill our blood to have it.

"Since before the time of my elderfather, we have lived by this river in peace. Praise The Great Mother!" she bellowed, raising her arms aloft.

"Praise The Great Mother," the people responded.

"Watch carefully now," Pico said, nudging Ejil in the ribs.

"The river has been good to us," Callas continued. "We pray. We make sacrifice to the river spirit and to The Mother. We are happy here. Why should we seek war?"

A soft murmur of agreement rose like a lake fog after the dawn.

"Whenever Callas really wants something, she invokes The Mother," Pico said.

"She's the very image of the goddess," Ejil whispered.

Pico leered back at him, slid one finger up alongside his nose and grinned wickedly.

"All know that Fishbellies are wanderers. They will soon tire of the river; and when they do, they will find a new place. I have prayed to The Mother for guidance, and she has given a sign. We must pursue the way of peace. I say we send a delegation, with gifts, to speak with these people and try to reach an understanding. There need be no killing, give them food and they will leave the river," Callas said, making the sign.

"Yes, peace," several people said and made the sign.

"But if they take the fish from our river when the Ice Season comes, we will starve," a man said.

"'Aren't all people children of The Mother?" an old woman asked. "Is not her bounty available to all?"

"Praise The Mother," Callas said, gazing upward. Her acolytes and most of the assembled repeated the words and made the sign.

Tamo stood. "Baal, son of Talog, our First Hunter and new brother, knows these people better than anyone. We have heard your words, Callas. Now, I would hear Baal's words from his own mouth."

Another man stood. "Let him speak." The people began to chant. "Let him speak! Let him speak!"

Ejil noted Callas' scowling face. *Yes! Let him speak. This is your moment, brother. This is our chance.*

Baal stood, picked his way through the seated villagers, and held out his hand for the speaking stick.

"You all know me," he said in a clear, strong voice. "I was not born among you. As our šamán says, I came with my brother and my friend, the last survivors of The Broken People, seeking refuge, and you took us into your hearts. You adopted us into your tribe; and for that, my brother Ejil, my friend Breda and I will always be grateful," He pressed his right fist to his heart and smiled.

Ejil's heart thumped. Pico was nodding his head approvingly. A soft murmur greeted Baal's words.

"Tonight, I stand to speak to you of a great danger. The trader, Kokotin, has seen the camp of the Fishbellies. You all heard his description of their leader—a scarred man. This is the same man I met in battle. There cannot be two such men. His is the same Whiteface band that massacred our people.

"We did no harm to these strangers. We did not seek them out. They gave no warning and stole away two innocent young girls, in the first bud of their womanhood, to slake the lust of their warriors. The girls' only mistake: to forage unprotected in the woods below our camp. Did they show mercy? Did they seek to parlay? No!"

Ejil's jaw tightened and his hands squeezed into fists. *You are right, brother. These are savages. They deserve no mercy, only death.*

"Our šamán tells us we should offer them meat and fish. We brought back half the venison we expected from The Hunt. If the Fishbellies keep taking fish from the river, where will we find the food to feed our children when the killing winds blow down from the north?"

Pico elbowed Ejil. "Watch her face," he whispered, nodding toward Callas. "Your brother is getting to her, ha ha!"

"We have dried fish to spare, Baal," Callas said, breaking in. "Our larders are full. We will offer the savages smoked meat and fish to supply them for their journey. There is more than enough. And once they are gone, it will be easily replaced."

He turned and faced her. "Easily replaced?" Baal repeated. "What of *our* women, Callas? Don't they matter? Are they so easily replaced?"

While Ejil listened, his eyes roamed the faces in the chamber. He saw women turning to their men with their babies clutched to their breasts, and young men with eyes glued to Baal's face, jaws tightly clenched.

Callas's round face darkened. Her eyes stretched into thin slits. She propped her hands on her hips and glared at the young hunter.

Baal frowned and addressed the crowd. "How about *your* wives and *your* daughters? What if the Fishbellies take them? Will they be easily replaced?" he asked, spreading his arms to take in the whole tribe, his eyes traveling from face to face.

"Your lust for revenge has taken your wits, young man," Callas said. "Fishbellies are wanderers. Why should they attack us? We are strong. Do they even know we are here?" she demanded.

Baal smiled. "I believe I hold the speaking stick." He turned to Breda and handed it to him.

Breda cleared his throat. "The Fishbellies have found our village. I returned early from The Hunt and scouted from the river to the small forest by the cliffs. This morning, by the stream at the edge of the trees, I found the tracks of three Whitefaces."

Breda's words hit like a lightning bolt. The chamber fell silent, then everyone began talking at once. *What, the Fishbellies here?* Sweat broke out on Ejil's forehead.

Callas snorted. "One speaks of a great danger, the other finds signs."

"Salat was with me, Callas," Breda said, his eyes flashing. Drawing himself up, he pointing to the tall hunter. "Is he lying too?"

Salat rose to his feet. "Breda speaks the truth; I saw the tracks."

Baal raised his hand to silence the noise. He shook his head slowly back and forth. "These animals are stealthy. They have not yet come in force, but they have found us. My people saw no sign at all until our girls disappeared and they fell upon our camp like a pack of ravening wolves. Now that they have had a taste, perhaps they seek more girls and women to slake their lust. Will you, any of you, ever feel it is safe for our women to leave the village while the pack circles and waits?"

Mala rose and held out his hand to Baal for the speaking stick.

"The words of Callas, our šamán, are good words—wise words," Mala began. "She councils us to send a delegation bearing gifts and ask the Whitefaces to go. It is a good plan. We love our new brothers, but as she so wisely tells us, it is not up to us to avenge their women," he said and paused.

Ejil was confused. *What is Mala doing? He is supposed to be with us.* He couldn't believe what he was hearing. He gazed at Callas. The šamán's anger seemed to slowly deflate like an emptying water bladder. She sat down; a slight smile played about her lips.

"But Baal's words are also good words," Mala continued, spreading his arms. "These are words we would be wise to heed. By all means, seek a parlay; but what, my friends, do we do if these whitefaces do not accept our gifts? What if they refuse to leave our river? Remember what happened to Baal's people. Who here will ever feel safe with them so near?

"Dalou," he said, pointing to one of the elders who always spoke in support of the šamán. "Your young daughter is a pretty thing. Already, the young men's eyes follow her. Will you still let her go alone foraging for roots in the cool shade of the trees below the cliffs?

"And you, Clea," he said, gesturing to Callas's nephew. "I have seen your wife many times, down on the riverbank, digging cattail roots to make her delicious stews. Will she be safe?"

Clea lowered his eyes and shook his head.

"No, she will not. Must we all, then, hide in our huts in fear of these creatures?" Mala asked.

A strong murmur of agreement greeted his words.

Callas struggled to her feet and put out her hand for the speaking stick, but Tamo was already standing.

"My friends," Tamo said, squinting through the smoke, "as our šamán and our esteemed elder, the Venerable Mala, has said, we should send a delegation to the whitefaces and hope for peace, but we would be fools if we did not also prepare for war."

Ah, now I see. Ejil bowed his head to hide a smile. Callas's face had turned to thunder. *Those two cagey old men set a trap for you, Callas; and, like a dumb hare, you have blundered right into it.*

"To prepare, we need a war chief to train our young men," Mala said as Tamo—ignoring Callas—passed back the speaking stick. "I propose Baal, son of Talog. Baal is a blooded warrior and our first hunter. His skill with a spear is spoken of around the nightfires. Even in the midst of the Death Season when the stinging blast drove us into our huts, Baal led out our hunters and brought back fresh meat. He understands these Whitefaces; he has fought them.

"We must prepare and choose a war chief," Mala continued, "and who better than Baal? I propose that the council appoint Baal war chief, and that we send the Elder Tamo as leader of our delegation to speak with the Fishbellies. Let us appoint three men. Let our venerable šamán choose one man and our new war chief choose the other. What does the council say? Stand if you agree."

Almost everyone stood to signal their agreement. Ejil was filled with joy. *We've done it. Lada, we're coming to rescuing you.* He looked over at Callas. Her eyes spat fire. Her jowls quivered with rage.

CHAPTER 27

PARLAY

The sun was well past midday, and the Fishbelly camp buzzed like a hive of bees. Several hunters trolled the river shallows, spears poised, circling the reeds. With a shout, one hunter stabbed downward and tossed a wriggling flash of silver onto the riverbank. The fish was quickly retrieved by his woman.

Ceda pushed up one sleeve. "Your father always said that the trap must be set in the current with the open end facing upstream and a fence of sharpened branches driven into mud to guide the fish into its open mouth," Lada's mother counseled. A long cone of woven willow branches slowly took shape in her hands. "Be sure your man understands this."

The clan knew nothing of fish traps. Lada had convinced Scar to allow her to build one. She gazed along the length of the trap, admiring her mother's handiwork. "Maybe when they see the fish we catch, they won't be so angry all of the time."

Ceda glanced at her daughter and shook her head. "These women will never accept us," she said.

"The fight at the creek?"

Ceda nodded. "Yes, but before that, too. It is the same with our people. We are different. We will always be outsiders. People don't like that."

A shadow blocked the sun. Crowbait stared down at her, hands propped on her hips. It had been eight moons since Lada's blood flow had stopped. She carried the baby high. "It is a sign of a boy child," her mother had told her.

"I have a task for this slave," Crowbait said, lifting her chin toward Ceda.

"She is busy," Lada signed, stretching to relieve the pressure in her stomach.

"Doing what?" Crowbait demanded, averting her eyes. "What is that stupid thing? I will to use her," Crowbait hissed, her black eyes glittering.

"I will say what she is to do and when she is finished, Ravenhair," Lada said, and made the sign of dismissal. Her stomach tightened. *I am Scar's woman now; things have changed,* she reassured herself.

Crowbait's face reddened. Her thick hands squeezed themselves into tight fists. Turning on her heel, she stalked off.

Lada took a deep breath and smiled with satisfaction. Dropping her eyes, she resumed working the thin branches into the trap frame.

Ceda placed a gentle hand on her daughter's arm. "Have a care, child," she said, gazing at the stocky clan woman's retreating back. "That one knows how to hate!" Her fingers tightened. "Your man comes," she whispered and returned to her weaving.

Four armed warriors had emerged from a grove of spindly trees that lined the riverbank at the edge of the encampment. Scar was in the lead.

Watching him come toward her, Lada had to admit that she was attracted to him—despite his savagery and the scar. The clan's shapeless furs did nothing to hide his muscular body. Lada wiped her hand across her forehead. The clan women knew nothing of sewing with gut and a bone needle. She had offered to make him new, better-fitting clothes, but he had refused. "Husband!" she said.

Scar grunted. He raised an eyebrow at the unfamiliar shape of the fish trap, then squatted facing the two women. The other warriors stood staring down at her.

"Three Blackdogs come toward the camp. We smelled their stink before the sunrise. What do they want here?" He brushed off a fly that had landed on his nose. The flies had come soon after the clan had begun taking fish from the river. Now the tiny pests were everywhere.

Lada's heart raced. *My people, here?* She lowered her eyes and shrugged. "I do not know," she signed.

"All carry spears. A young one carries a staff like a Spirit Woman."

"A šamán?" Lada asked. "Among my people, it is men who speak to the spirits. If a šamán is with them, they have come in peace," Lada said, making the sign for "no war."

"You talked of *trade*," he said, forming the word with effort. Is this why they have come?"

She glanced sideways at her mother. "If Scar will allow me, I will speak with them. They will not fear a woman," she said struggling to maintain an even tone.

"No!" Scar said and slashed his hand down making the sign. The use of word and sign together was a command. Any argument, Lada knew, would only antagonize him. "It is not safe," he said.

Safe? He doesn't trust me. She reached out and gently gripped his knee and gazed up into his face. "You said there are only three? Bring no more than two warriors and me to talk. Scar will protect me," she said.

Scar gazed at her thoughtfully. Gradually, his jaw relaxed and the hard lines around his mouth softened. "You!" he signed and pointed to Greybeard, "and you, Hawkeye, come! You," he ordered, pointing at the other two, "make sure the Blackdog women are hidden, and gather the warriors." His hand, palm down, passed slowly across his waist. The sign meant "keep hidden."

Scar, Hawkeye and Grayhair stood, hefted their spears and set off at a trot. Lada brushed herself off and waddled after them, struggling to keep up.

They did not have to go far. Scar stopped in the middle of a path along the riverbank and glanced up at the sun. Lada arrived panting.

"We wait here!" He motioned to Lada to stand beside him. Greybeard flanked her with Hawkeye on Scar's right. Grinning, Scar spread his arms. "Now, the Blackdogs will not be frightened," he said.

Sometime later, Ejil, Tamo and Daga emerged single file from the shade of the trees into the bright sunlit clearing and halted. The afternoon sun was high on the sky ladder and directly in their faces, and they squinted against the glare. Lada, however, could see them clearly and, with a shock, recognized Ejil.

Ejil? Her mouth dropped open. *Alive? Here? Mother told me they were all killed. If Scar suspects, he will kill them…* She swallowed hard; her heart pounded in her ears. She took two halting steps forward into a patch of shade and pressed a finger to her lips.

"Please, stop where you are! I, I speak for Scar, leader of the Lion Clan. His warriors are close by. Make no sign that you know me. Speak quickly and tell me why you have come."

Scar grabbed Lada by the shoulder and jerked her around to face him. "What did you say?" he demanded.

"You're hurting me!" Lada said glaring. She twisted out of his grasp. "I asked who they were and what they are doing here! Is that not what you wish to know?" She turned back toward the delegation, who stood silently. "Who are you? Why have you come?" she called in a loud voice.

As Mala had suggested, the council chose Tamo to lead the delegation. Baal, in his new role as war chief, had chosen Daga; and Callas, to Ejil's great surprise, had picked him to be the third member. The trip had taken six suns. Now, no more than two spear throws ahead, their enemies stood, blocking their path.

Ejil could now see Lada clearly. The seasons had turned twice since he had last seen her. He remembered a young girl just budding into womanhood. *She is so beautiful,* he thought, gaping at the full-grown woman who stood before him, with the sunlight glinting off a cloud of dark shining hair.

Lada and Ejil locked eyes. He gazed at her swelling stomach. *She is with child.* His whole body tensed. The realization filled him with horror. "Scar believes all our people are dead," Lada said. "If he guesses who you are, he will kill all of you." She turned quickly away.

Ejil swallowed hard, shifted his gaze and tried to concentrate. *So, this is Scar, the warrior who bested my brother.* The Fishbelly stared back at him. *Those dark, hooded eyes hold a strange glint as if he looks at us and sees only prey.*

Tamo raised a hand. He had seen many winters, and the trek to Scar's camp had exhausted him.

Ejil glanced at the elder. The old man cupped a hand behind his ear and eyed Ejil. "What did she say?" he asked.

Ejil took a breath. "Her name is Lada," he said, leaning close. "She was one of the first girls taken. She warns that there are other warriors hidden nearby. She asks why we are here. She says, I must pretend not to know her. Will you speak?"

The old man gestured Ejil forward. "No, you're doing fine. Talk! She must be translating for that ugly brute. Tell them we greet them in friendship. We have come to talk, and we bring gifts, and so forth," he said.

Ejil took a step forward and spoke Tamo's words.

Lada translated. Scar made a quick gesture. "Gifts? Talk? Talk about what?" Scar asked through narrowed eyes. "Do they talk with spears?"

"A man cannot travel unarmed," Ejil said, spreading his hands. "Tamo, I think we must put down our spears," he said, his voice soft.

"What, put down our weapons?" Tamo shook his head. "Tell them we will put down ours if…Oh, never mind! The girl says there are more of them hidden nearby. If they decide to kill us, our few spears will make no difference."

"Daga!" he said motioning to the young hunter. He slammed the butt end of his spear into the soft earth and stepped forward. Daga seemed about to protest, but Tamo moved quickly, and he was left standing alone. Reluctantly, he thrust his spear butt into the ground and stepped up next to the elder.

"Huh," Ejil said, coming back to himself. His mind had turned to Lada, and he had barely heard Tamo's instructions. He quickly stepped forward, retaining only his staff.

Tamo's gesture seemed to mollify the Fishbelly leader. He signed to his men.

One stared back at him, open mouthed.

Scar sneered, stooped, placed his spear flat on the ground and stood tall, eyes glued to his enemies. The other two clan warriors slowly lowered their spears to the ground and stood back up beside their leader.

Tamo untied his deerskin cape, kneeled, twirled it around his head and spread it on the ground with a flourish. Shouldering off his pack, he rummaged through it and placed a carved wooden drinking bowl and a small, finely-knapped obsidian knife on the spread hide. Ejil laid down a handful of pierced shells and a beautifully carved bone spear-tip engraved with a design of swimming fish. Daga added a tiny pendant of a lion tooth, carved of mammoth ivory, and a palm-sized nodule of red ochre in the center of the cape.

Scar stared at the treasures laid out before him, then signaled. Three clan warriors squatted before them.

Lada kneeled down beside Scar and whispered in his ear.

The clan leader nodded.

Ejil watched the girl. He knew from Breda that the Fishbelly language consisted largely of signs. He could not understand the meaning, but the scarred man's attitude was obvious. Ejil was transfixed by the fluid grace of Lada's movements as she translated the leader's words. With effort, he averted his eyes from her swollen belly.

"Scar, leader of the Lion Clan thanks you for your fine gifts," Lada said, and without changing her tone continued, "Ejil, please stop staring! Scar believes all our people are dead. He doesn't trust me. If he thinks we know each other, he will kill you all. Now, smile and nod and tell me why you have come."

Ejil's face darkened. His eyes flicked from side to side. In the distance, he noticed that many of the clan people had stopped what they were doing and were staring at them. There was no sign of the captive women.

Tamo cleared his throat. "Yes, I understand, you, my girl. Tell him I am Tamo, son of Tamo, an elder of our tribe. We are called the First People. Tell your leader that we come in peace as friends."

Lada thought for a moment. "The clan has no word for friend. There is only clan and not-clan." She turned and spoke to Scar.

Scar nodded, but kept his eyes pinned to Tamo's face.

"Scar says, he has met other Blackdog clans. 'When they are strong, they do not bring gifts. They turn their eyes away and spit on the ground. Tell me what you wish to talk about,'" Lada said.

"We greet Scar and the Lion Clan on behalf of our people. We have lived along this river ever since my elderfather's father," Tamo said.

Lada cleared her throat and translated.

"We wish to know, how long will the Lion Clan remain here?" Tamo asked.

"'Remain,' Tamo, son of Tamo?" Lada asked. "You mean here, by the river?"

The elder nodded.

"I will ask."

Scar gazed quizzically at Tamo and shrugged. "When the fish are gone and there is no more meat to hunt, we will go."

Tamo glanced at his two companions and took a deep breath. "This river has been our home for many generations. Our people live on the fish. Since you have come, there are fewer fish. Soon they will be gone."

Scar spread his arms. "Tell them: this is a good place, but when the fish and game are gone, we find another place. That is how it has always been. That is how it will always be."

This is good. He doesn't understand, Ejil thought. *He's not willing to leave.*

"Our ancestors' bones are buried in this earth," Tamo said. "We will give the Lion Clan many gifts," he said, gesturing toward the goods laid out on the cape, "and all the smoked fish and meat the clan can carry, if you will leave the river and seek a new place."

"You have come to say this?" Scar asked, his eye fixed on the elder.

Tamo listened to Lada's translation. He turned to Ejil. "This is not going well," his eyes said.

"Yes, this is what we have come to say." Tamo replied, meeting Scar's eyes.

Scar put his hand on Lada's shoulder, spoke and made signs.

"Scar says, there are many fish in the river. Enough for all. You may sleep here. You will be given food. You are under Scar's protection and no one will harm you. He says he must consult with the Spirit Woman. When the Sunspirit returns, he will speak with you again," she said.

Scar reached down and grasped the knife, scooped up the other gifts and handed them to one of his men. He held up the knife and examined it in the waning sunlight, then tucked it firmly into the strip of hide that belted his waist, nodded curtly to Tamo, and strode off.

Lada, accompanied by two guards, led the three men to a level spot outside the Fishbelly camp.

"You may sleep here; come no closer to the camp. Food will be brought," Lada said. The two guards watched her closely. She spoke calmly and kept her eyes averted.

Ejil could sense her fear. He was astonished at the changes the circle of seasons had wrought; he saw the soft lines of her face, her woman's body, the grace of her movements, and something stirred inside him.

"Can you speak about our women? What of Mata?"

"She is well," she said gesturing toward the place they were to spread their robes. She noticed Ejil stealing a glance at her swelling belly. "Yes," she said, "it is Scar's! Two more of our women are also with child. Tule has a son. We were given a choice. Mate with a man of the clan or live as a slave. Now I must go," she said and motioned to her two guards.

"Can we speak to the women," Daga asked, raising his voice.

Lada shook her head. "No! Scar will keep them away. They cannot be allowed to see Ejil."

Tamo nodded. "I understand."

Ejil watched Lada as she walked toward the Fishbelly camp, the two guards close behind.

That evening, sitting with his companions by the fire and eating, Ejil gazed into the flames. He pictured Lada. Thoughts of his mother and father's happy smiles around other fires crept into his memory and he was filled with sadness. *They are gone. I will never see any of them again this side of the Shadowlands.*

Pelas told him that a man was a spirit living inside a body, like water in a cup. When the body died, the cup was broken, and the spirit flowed out. It fled the body with its last breath and entered the Shadowlands to dwell forever in darkness. Ejil had his doubts. People were born; they died; new babies were born, and the cycle of the seasons went on, seemingly without end. He peered up at the stars spread across the sky.

Maybe those who worshipped the Great Mother were right. A man died, but his spirit was reborn in a new body. In the same way as the world dies when the Ice Season comes and is awakened again in the Budding Season.

Tamo sat chewing pensively. He cleared his throat. "What do you think?" he asked, addressing no one in particular.

Daga hawked and spit. "They call this fish? It tastes like bear shit," he said, and tossed the remains of his portion. It sizzled in the fire. "These Fishbellies will never leave the river. It is as Baal said. We waste time here."

"And you, young Ejil?"

Ejil paused and rubbed his jaw. "Now we know that our women are alive, but I fear Daga is right. These people are wanderers. They are used to taking everything they can before they move on."

"What about this girl, Lada? Do you trust her?" Tamo asked.

"Trust? Her stomach swells with Whiteface filth," Daga said.

Ejil glared across the fire at the young hunter. In the beginning, Daga's attitude had been friendly, almost servile, but gradually as he came to understand Baal's attitude toward his younger brother, he had become arrogant and disagreeable.

Ejil clenched his teeth. "She saved *all* our lives today, Daga! You heard her: if Scar suspects we know they murdered my people, they will kill us," Ejil said.

Daga shook his head.

"We must take care," Tamo said. "The big ugly one, her husband—if that's what he is—is a suspicious brute."

"War is our only choice! We will not be safe until they are all dead," Daga said, his eyes fixed on the leaping flames.

A voice cut through the darkness. "Hello, it is me, Lada."

Daga leapt to his feet, spear in hand, followed by Ejil.

Tamo had made it only to his knees as Lada entered the fire's glow.

"Please, I come alone," she said, and spread her arms.

"What do you want?" Daga sputtered.

"I come for Ejil! The clan's šamán—she is called Spirit Woman—sent me. She wishes to speak with you, Ejil."

"With Ejil, why?" Daga demanded.

"He carries the šamán's staff," she said.

"At this time of night? Where is this Spirit Woman?" Tamo asked, finally gaining his feet.

"In the camp. She has her own hut," Lada said. "Ejil is to come alone."

"Alone? I am leader. If she speaks with anyone, it should be with me," Tamo said. "But I see no reason she should speak with any of us alone. Go back," he said motioning for her to leave, "and tell her my words."

"Venerable Tamo," Lada said, lowering her eyes, her voice small. "I think it would be best if Ejil speaks with her. You, none of you, have anything to fear. You are under Scar's protection. To refuse would be a great insult. Scar believes Ejil is your šamán. He will believe you fear the clan's magic."

"Where are your guards?" Tamo asked.

"Scar wanted to send them, but the Spirit Woman insisted that I come alone."

"Hah, why should we listen to you? Even your man doesn't trust you?" Daga said.

"No," Lada said, shaking her head, "he does not, not entirely."

What is Scar thinking. I must find a way to speak to Lada alone, Ejil thought. "How are the captive women being treated? Are they safe?" he asked.

"Safe?" Lada laughed. It was a harsh bark. "Who is safe in this world, but yes, they are all alive and well enough."

"What is it that swells in your belly? You seem to have survived pretty well," Daga said, sneering.

"Before the sun rose, this day, I believed that all my people were dead. What would Daga have done?"

"You should have died, rather than submit to one of those smelly beasts."

In a rage, Ejil jumped to his feet, but Lada raised a hand to stay him.

"Brave words! Are we not your kin? Has the mighty Daga come to risk *his own death* to save us?" she asked.

The young hunter scowled, turned his head away and spat.

Ejil placed a hand on Tamo's shoulder. "Lada is my friend. I believe she speaks truth. The Fishbellies test our courage. They admire only strength. If you refuse to let me go, they will see weakness," Ejil said.

Tamo scratched his head. "Humm, perhaps you are right, young Ejil. We must show courage—show that we do not fear them." He raised his hand. "Go! But remember, I am the leader. Learn what you can, but make no promises."

The hut was a mound of bark scraps and old hides set across a frame of mammoth bones. It was set apart, behind some rocks from the river.

Lada pulled back the entrance flap and stepped aside. "May The Sunfather protect you," she said.

"You are not coming?" Ejil asked.

"Me? No," she said, with a shudder. "I was not invited."

Ejil hesitated. He would have to face the witch alone. He swallowed, crouched down, and entered the hut. He stood for a moment blinking in the dim firelight. Before him stood a thin, ethereal creature, staring up into his eyes. He shivered. *Where does such a person come from?* Before they left the village, Pico had warned him that Fishbelly sámánok were mostly women. He recalled the old picturemaker's words: "They have the power to see inside a man," the old man had told him.

"Welcome, young šamán. Come! Sit!" The old woman said in Ejil's tongue. She gestured him toward a large, flat rock set on the one side of the fire and scuttled around to the other side of the hearth. A pungent, earthy smell came from the bunched fetishes and dried herbs that dangled from the roof. The clan's totem, the cave lion skull, stared—holloweyed—from a niche on the wall.

Seating himself cross-legged on the warm surface of the hearthstone, Ejil placed his staff across his lap and calmly met the Spirit Woman's eyes. He tried not to show his surprise that she spoke his language. "Why have you summoned me?"

"Have patience, young šamán. We have much to talk about. I have made a brew," she said.

She spoke his people's words without her mouth seeming to move. He had put on a brave show for Lada and his companions, but as he followed Lada toward the Fishbelly camp, his head was filled with fear and strange, grotesque visions of what he might find. Now, meeting this Spirit Woman, seeing her frail body, the fears that had eaten at him seemed foolish. *Why should I fear this old crone?* He asked himself. *A stiff breeze would blow her away.* He began to relax.

"You are very young to be called by the spirits," the old crone said. "Here is tea." She passed him a bowl.

The aroma was fragrant. He took a tentative sip. Bitterness filled his mouth.

"Our šamán is a woman. She is named Callas. I am her apprentice," Ejil said, lying smoothly. He hoped his explanation would satisfy her.

The Spirit Woman nodded. "Why have you and the others come here?" she asked.

"We have come seeking peace."

"Peace? So you say," the crone replied. Her face broke out into a rictus like a grinning skull. "The Lion Clan, too, wants only peace."

Ejil's two hands caressed the smooth, rounded surface of the cup. He lifted it and sniffed, then took another sip. The smell triggered his memory. Pelas had taught him to prepare many herbal mixtures.

The mushroom grew in deep sheltered valleys beneath the trees, its delicate, elongated stem topped with the narrow cap like a woman's nipple. "A brew made from it brings you closer to the spirit world, but," his master had warned, "it also loosens the tongue. Once in its grip, a man can speak only the truth."

The crone's eyes followed as he lifted the cup and pretended to drink. Sweat broke out on the back of his neck and trickled down his backbone. *Now I understand why she summoned me.*

Lowering the cup into the hollow between his knees. "It's good!" he smiled. "What is the talisman you wear?" he asked, pointing at a pendant at her neck.

She followed his eyes, looked down and fingered the amulet at her breast. As she did so, Ejil tipped his bowl spilling the contents. "This is a wolf's tooth," she said. "I'm surprised you don't recognize it. Wolf's tooth is known to keep off evil spells."

Across the fire, the tiny, ethereal figure watched his eyes—her own ancient orbs gleaming, cold as a snake's. Her thoughts filled his mind. He had taken only a tiny sip, but the tea had been brewed strong. He could feel the magic beginning to work its will. His mind was loosening, coming unmoored, like a tree with its roots slowly torn from the ground by a steady, powerful wind.

"Come, speak the truth, young šamán," her voice urged. "Tell me the real reason you have come?"

It seemed a reasonable request. The witch's face lost focus and dimmed, but her spirit clutched at him, her long cold fingers prying at his mind.

"Ah, you have a secret, young šamán. Tell me what it is. Speak!" she ordered.

Sweat broke out on Ejil's brow. His chest tightened. His hand grasped the smooth surface of the šamán's staff as the world began to tilt and teeter. He felt nauseous. His stomach lurched.

Get out, get away, his mind screamed. He remembered Lada's warning: *If this woman discovers who you are, Scar will kill you all.* His mind grew dark, as if he had entered a long tunnel. A misty light beckoned through the darkness. His hand tightened on his staff.

The light expanded. Another presence filled his mind. *Master!* "Remember, young Ejil, life is a constant struggle to control your fear. Fear will take your strength. You must control it, or it will unman you," the old šamán said.

Ejil reached a hand out toward his old mentor. But as he did, the image retreated like a summer's mist and was gone.

The breathing, he remembered. *It saved me during the snow storm! Focus on the breathing.*

He pictured his breath, like a stream flowing in through his mouth, down, curling itself around his center. Then, pausing, like the tide at its peak, it flowed slowly up and out between his lips, cascading down his chin. He pictured it then took another breath, then another.

Gradually, he felt himself calming, his spirit expanding.

The icy fist grasped and tightened. The Spirit Woman's eyes expanded and grew brighter, her brow furrowing with the strain. Suddenly, a flash like lightning. Her grip loosened. Her eyes dimmed. A long groan, like the dying cry of a wounded animal, emerged from deep within that ruined chest. Her body jerked and her head fell forward, lolling onto her wrinkled breast.

Ejil felt a rush like warm honey filling an empty vessel. His chest expanded. His breathing came freely.

He continued breathing long, deep breaths, until finally he rose, pushed aside the hut's door flap, stood up and gazed out into the black night.

He saw the fire. It was a beacon. Ejil's mind filled with gratitude, and he slowly walked toward it.

"That was quick," the elder said, poking at the glowing embers with a stick.

"Really?" Ejil asked. "It seemed like I was gone for a very long time." He gazed up at the sky and swallowed. His throat felt raw. "I will tell you everything; but first, I must get something into my stomach," he said.

Daga hawked and spit into the fire. "Why is Ejil always chosen?" he asked. "He is not even a warrior."

"Hah! Daga, Ejil has killed at least one man, maybe more. It is you who are not yet blooded," Tamo said. "Ejil has the spirit of an old man in the body of a youth. It is a rare thing. Perhaps, as some say, his spirit has lived other lives."

He tossed Ejil a strip of meat. "Eat!" he said. "Then tell us all that has happened. Take your time. Leave nothing out."

"Many thanks, Tamo," Ejil tore off a strip with his teeth and began to chew. "Your words honor me."

Two sets of eyes stared at him from across the fire. Ejil burped. "I guess dinner must wait!" he said. He swallowed the half-chewed meat, took a long drink, and began his tale.

Lada lay awake staring at the night sky through a chink in the hut's wall while Scar tossed and mumbled in his sleep. He had returned late after meeting with the Spirit Woman, then huddled with his warriors until moonset. Her attempt to speak to him brought a malevolent stare and a noncommittal grunt. He had rolled over and gone immediately to sleep.

With the coming of the child, she had accepted her lot. She was Clan, and Scar was her man, but repeating that over and over in her mind did nothing to cure the ache, the hollowed-out feeling in her chest. Something was missing.

How had Ejil and the others survived the killing? What had gone on at his meeting with the Spirit Woman? That old hag! Lada shuddered at the thought. *I must find a way to see him, to talk with him.*

She glanced over at the fur-covered lump curled up beside her. Scar was snoring peacefully, which he did only when he was very tired. She knew his habits. He would sleep through the dawn.

Scar had ordered that no one was to go near the spot where Ejil and his friends were camped. She sniffed. *Well, I don't require a guard to draw water from the stream, and to do so I will have to pass by the camp.* Silently, she rose to her knees and crept from the hut. The air was crisp, and the stars were bright in the night sky. The moon hovered above the horizon. She dipped her head in reverence. All was quiet.

CHAPTER 28

A MEETING OF MINDS

Strange dreams plagued his sleep. Ejil woke abruptly and rubbed his eyes. The occasional spit of flame from the embers of the dying fire pierced the night. He threw a couple of sticks on the glowing coals, stood, stretched himself, and peered through the darkness toward the Fishbelly camp. He could see the glow of a few banked fires, but otherwise all seemed quiet. Then, a shadow appeared, flitting like a moth. It disappeared behind a squat hut shape then reappeared. The slim form told him it was a woman. She seemed to be carrying something and was coming toward the camp. Ejil's heart caught in his chest.

The form took shape. "Lada," he whispered, "I was hoping to speak with you."

The girl glanced around nervously. "Come!" She squatted behind a clump of low bushes and motioned him to join her.

"It will be light soon. I see that awful Spirit Woman didn't turn you into a toad," she said.

He caught a glint of teeth in the starlight. "No," he said, grinning back at her, "not quite."

Lada gazed up at the sky. "I can't stay long. I can't believe how much you have changed, Ejil. There is so much I want to ask you. Mother told me everyone was killed in the raid. How did you escape? How did you find us?"

Lada sat hugging her belly as Ejil quickly related all that had happened to him since the morning of the Fishbelly attack.

"Then you are not here to rescue us?" Lada asked. Her eyes searched for his in the predawn gloom.

Ejil bowed his head. Her face was in shadow, but her voice conveyed her hurt and disbelief. He fidgeted and cleared his throat. "It would start a war, Lada. We argued and begged, but we were sent here to avoid fighting."

"You say these First People are our kin. I remember that. Don't they understand that the Lion Clan murdered our whole tribe?"

"Yes, but they say it is not their blood debt. They mostly care about the fishing. They are hoping that the clan will accept the gifts and leave."

"What about us? Are we not *your* blood?"

"Yes, I have not forgotten, Lada; nor has Baal or Breda, but there are only three of us. Callas, the šamán, is against doing anything that might bring war. She says that you are not her people's problem. If the Fishbellies accept our gifts and decamp that will be the end of it. The First People will not make war to free you."

Suddenly all his scattered thoughts came together in a rush of emotion. *She seems so small, sad and vulnerable.* They had been so easy with each other. *Why is it so difficult to talk to her now?*

He reached out and gently took her hand. "We've tried, Lada; really, we have!"

Lada snatched her hand back. Tears rolled down her cheeks. "Don't you understand? I'm a prisoner here. Since I have mated with Scar, they must tolerate me, but these are not my people. I will always be an outsider. Even my husband doesn't really trust me. I became Scar's woman because…because I had no hope. Then, I saw you and I began to hope again. I should have known better."

"Lada, I'm sorry," Ejil said. There was a pain in the back of his throat. He felt his eyes welling up.

Lada shook her head and used her fingers to snatch away the tears. "What will you do if Scar doesn't agree? What if the clan refuses to go?"

"That will mean war. The people, especially the elders, are fearful with the clan so close, and the young men are spoiling for a fight. That's why Baal was appointed war chief: in case we fail. If there is war, Baal will lead the men. He has sworn a blood oath to free you."

Lada stood up abruptly. "I must go."

Ejil stepped close to her. "What do you think Scar will do?"

"I don't know. Your gifts impressed him. The clan has nothing so fine. The women don't even know how to use a needle."

"What if you spoke to him?"

"And, say what? You expect me to help you? Even if I wanted to, I couldn't do you any good. If I was to tell him I liked your plan, he would grow even more suspicious and distrust me even more."

Ejil gazed at her, stroking his chin. "What if you agreed with him? What if you said it is a trick, that you didn't trust us?"

She cocked her head. "Do you mean I should speak against you?"

"Wouldn't that make him believe you were loyal?"

"Yes, I suppose so, but he would definitely refuse to leave. I thought you wanted me to help you?"

Ejil stepped closer. "Yes, Lada, and no. I want you to help yourself and the rest of our women. I too have sworn an oath," he said, his voice slightly above a whisper.

Lada gazed back at him wide-eyed. Then her lips began to frame the beginnings of a smile. "I will speak to him," she said.

The stars were fading. Tiny fingers of light had already crept over the horizon. She stood up on her tiptoes, kissed his mouth, and hurried off toward the Fishbelly camp.

Ejil touched his lips as he watched her go. His mouth tingled from more than just her soft warmth. *Would it work? So much rests on Lada's slim shoulders. She would be betraying the man whose child she carries. It will mean starting a war.* He took a deep breath, puffed out his cheeks and looked toward the faint glow beginning to form below the horizon, and slowly exhaled.

Scar emerged from the hut wiping the sleep from his eyes. He stretched, sniffed the air. "Fish cakes?" he asked, grinning.

"Sit," Lada said. "Food will soon be ready."

It had been a long night. Scar's head was splitting from so much talk. The Spirit Woman, and two of his trusted men—the talk went on until long after moonset.

"Take the gifts?" Grayhair had urged. "The Blackdogs promise all the dried meat and fish we can carry. There are other places with good hunting. If we stay here, they will bring war."

"Why fear them? The clan killed many Blackdogs," Scar said.

"Yes, but they were asleep. We fooled them. This clan is awake. They watch us. They have many warriors," Grayhair said.

"What does One-ear say?" Scar asked.

"This place is good," One-ear answered. "Hunting is good. Why should we leave?"

"Will the Blackdogs bring war?"

One-ear shrugged. "Only cowards bring gifts."

"You cannot trust the Blackdogs. It is a trick, my son," the Spirit Woman said from across the fire.

Her face seemed changed, older; her eyes were veined in red. Scar was puzzled. The Spirit Woman never changed.

'My son'? Really? I am your son when it pleases you.

"The Blackdogs have brought gifts—fine gifts," he said, fingering the obsidian knife he kept tucked inside his waist wrap. "They offer meat and fish. Where is the trick? You spoke to the young one. What did you learn?"

"He revealed nothing."

"Nothing? His magic was the stronger?"

"A powerful spirit protects him," she said and lowered her gaze.

The boy-šamán has defeated her. Scar felt a mix of emotions. He was concerned that the Blackdog magic was strong. But it came with a sense of satisfaction that even she, the all-powerful woman, the mother who had dominated him, had limits. She could be defeated.

"Very well." He rose, pushed aside the door flap aside and walked back to his hut.

Scar stuffed one of the soft cakes into his mouth. She had mixed the smoked fish with ground acorns and deer fat. Adding a few sweetberries gave it a tang which she knew Scar loved. He chewed with relish. She stood waiting patiently until he finished.

"Good?"

"Good!" he said. He made the sign twice while he licked the tasty grease from his fingers.

"How will Scar answer the Blackdogs?" Lada asked.

He glared up at her.

She propped her fists on her hips and returned the stare. "You will not speak because you do not trust me?"

"You are not clan."

"I am your woman," she said. "Your woman is clan." He could see her face darkening, her anger rising.

Her eyes were steady. *She is proud; she does not hide her eyes like a clan woman.* Still, he had good feelings for this woman, feelings that were new to him. He loved her hair. Clan women never washed their hair—he had not noticed it until Lada. She washed her long, curly hair often and combed it out with a fish's backbone until it shone like sharpstone. He liked burying his face in its softness.

"Then speak, woman!" he ordered, gruffly. "We stay or we take the gifts and leave the river?" he asked, signing slowly.

"We stay!"

His head jerked back in surprise.

"These people are strangers," Lada signed. "I do not trust them. They are not clan. Scar is a great hunter. There are fish in the river. We have meat stored for the Ice Season. We do not need their gifts. Why take the scraps from Blackdog fires?"

"You speak like clan!" he signed, grinning.

She threw back her shoulders. "Am I not Scar's woman," she asked, pointing to herself. "Do you remember your promise? If I agreed to join with you, I would become clan."

Lada's words surprised him. He had been suspicious. She was not docile like a clan woman. She did not understand the customs: *Clan Women do not speak. Men decide.*

He thought back to the time she had attacked One-ear to protect her friend. *Like a wildcat spitting fire,* he thought. "Yes!" he said. "You speak as I speak!"

She lowered her eyes.

"Will the Blackdogs make war if we tell them no?" he asked.

"No! They are cowards. They bring gifts because they fear Scar. They fear the clan," she said.

"Yes," he said. Her words filled him with pride. He puffed out his chest. "Yes, these are good words. This is a good place. There are deer and bison and many fish. We stay here," he said, pointing down at the earth with his finger, "by the river."

"Scar is wise," she said. She crouched down and began clearing away the remains of the meal.

Lada bent her head to the task, but Scar could see a slight smile spread across her lips. He was pleased. *She is my woman,* he thought.

CHAPTER 29

BIRTH PAINS

The pain came in waves. *How long have I been in labor?* Lada wasn't sure, but it had been late at night when the first cramps had awakened her, and now thin shards of daylight had begun to creep in between gaps in the hut wall.

Ceda dipped a doeskin rag into a bowl of cold water and pressed it to Lada's forehead while Tule busied herself about the hut. "Dawn is breaking; it won't be long now," Ceda said.

The Spirit Woman had come and gone. She had mumbled and chanted and burned some herbs that made the women's eyes water. Lada was glad to have seen the last of her.

She clutched at her mother's hand. "Was it this bad for you? With me, I mean?"

Ceda patted her daughter's hand. "Every bit! You weren't anxious to come out; but it's all worth it, you'll see," she said.

"I doubt it," Lada said, with a weak smile.

"Remember to breathe when the next one comes. When the cramps come this close together, it means the baby is near," Ceda said.

Lada felt the blood rush to her face. It felt like some outside force that had invaded and taken over her body. All she wanted was to curl up into a ball and scream as another contraction racked her.

Ceda pulled up Lada's tunic and pushed her fingers between her daughter's legs. "The baby's coming! Tule, bring over that stool and help me get Lada up on it. Hurry, girl!"

Each taking an arm, the two women helped hoist Lada up onto the birthing stool that Ceda had made for her.

Another contraction ripped through Lada's body.

"I see the baby's head. Take a deep breath, dear. And when the next cramp comes, bear down and push," Ceda cried.

"Push, push!" Lada felt an intense burning, like someone had set a torch between her legs. "Ohhh!"

Exhausted but content, Lada lay back. Head propped by a pillow of folded furs, she gazed lovingly down at the tiny creature who was her son. She still couldn't believe he was really hers. His tiny pink mouth sucking at her nipple reminded her of a fish, nibbling at a plant in the river's shallows. Scar stood over her. She saw the joy in her husband's dark eyes.

She had wondered how the child would look. Would he look like her people, or the clan? He had inherited his father's long face, oval skull and soft straight, reddish hair but no sign of a brow ridge. His eyes were dark brown, not like the pale eyes of some clan. His skin was darker, too, more like hers, more the color of tree bark than the river mud. It really didn't matter—he was beautiful and he was hers. Lada's heart swelled with love.

Scar squatted down next to her. He reached over and gently ran the tip of his forefinger along the baby's cheek. Gurgling happily, the infant reached out a tiny hand and grasped at his father's finger—it barely reached half way around. Scar smiled broadly.

Beneath her outward contentment, Lada's mind was troubled. With the baby's birth, she had been engulfed by unexpectedly warm feelings for Scar. *What is going to happen?* she wondered. *Would Ejil's new tribe really attack the clan?* Ejil said so, and what she had told Scar had set it in motion. *What shall I do if they come? What will happen to Scar? Come on, Lada! Stop trying to fool yourself. You know very well what will happen. They will kill him.*

Scar was responsible for the death of her father and the murder of her people. She should hate him, but her newborn was as much his son as he was hers. The love in his eyes warmed her heart and, at the same time, stoked her guilt. Could she return to her people and deny her son a father? *What will I tell him when he gets older and begins to ask questions about his father?*

She looked up and found Scar peering down at her. She could hardly look at him. "You must be starving," she said.

He made the sign that meant she was not to worry. "A man whose woman is giving birth is welcome at any fire," he said.

"What of the Blackdogs?"

"The men watch. There is no sign. You were right. They fear the clan."

Scar's assurance made her feel oddly better. *Ejil's new people care only for their stomachs.* She gazed down at her baby. Happiness, confusion and guilt flickered around her like a moth about a burning torch.

Finally, Scar left, and she was alone with only her mother for company. One by one and in small groups, the clan women, as custom required, had come to view the newborn. Most smiled and made the clan sign for "good," then clucked, giggled and chucked little Efrem under the chin. Near sundown, Crowbait and her friend, called Squinty because her eyes and mouth were squeezed into a perpetual squint, entered the hut. The two nodded curtly to Lada and hardly glanced at the child. Having done as duty required, Crowbait turned on her heel and left, her silent companion behind her.

Lada could hear the two women giggling outside the hut. "Blackdog baby. Not clan." Crowbait's whisper was loud enough for Lada to hear.

Lada caught her mother's eye.

"What did you expect?" Ceda shrugged. "The woman hates you."

"She is saying what they are all thinking," Lada said.

Ceda shrugged. "It's jealousy. Squinty's man left her and joined with one of ours. You are Scar's woman and you have borne his son. None of them would dare speak against you or the baby."

"Yes, but will my son grow up surrounded by hate?"

Ceda frowned and patted her daughter's hand.

"What are our women saying about the delegation?" Lada asked.

"All they know is that men came from another tribe. We were guarded, and none of us got close enough to see anything more. We were told that this new tribe brought gifts because they fear the clan.

"Those who have not joined with a man say little. Those, like you, who have mated, have their own fires to tend. The others say nothing. They know that anyone who does is found out and punished. Even Catya is afraid," Ceda said.

"Catya, really?"

"Yes, and I fear for her, daughter. She was such a bright-eyed, happy girl. You remember. Now, she lives in darkness, hardly speaks, squats by the fire hugging herself and gazing at nothing."

"I know that darkness, Mother."

The corners of Ceda's lips lifted in a feeble smile. "We all do. It is like a deep pit, but you climbed out of it. I fear Catya never will. At first, Crowbait and the others abused her, but she didn't respond. Now I think they believe she is possessed by a demon and they leave her alone." She shook her head as if to shoo away evil thoughts. "What of Ejil? What did he tell you?"

"Ejil's no longer a little boy, Mother. He's tall and handsome, and so kind. I keep thinking about him. When I was younger, I always assumed I would mate with him. Then you told me he was dead…But that night my old feelings for him came back. When I talked about Scar and the baby, he said it didn't matter. 'The baby is yours and Scar is a murderer. You owe him nothing.'"

Ceda reached over and stroked her daughter's forehead. "You bore Scar's child, my dear. It is natural to have feelings for him, but Ejil speaks truth. This is the man who killed your father.

"I've always liked Ejil. He is clever and has a good heart. A woman doesn't ask for much; we need a man who will protect us, treat us well, help with the children and be a good provider. Do you love him, child?"

"Yes, Mother, I think I do." Lada shrugged. "But what difference does it make? He told me that his new tribe would not make war to rescue us."

"But there is hope?"

"Yes. Ejil says the First People are angry. The clan has taken much of the fish from the river. That is why they came and brought gifts. They want Scar to agree to leave the river; and if we do, there will be no war."

"They spoke of war?"

"No, but…"

"And, Scar has refused?"

"Yes mother," Lada said and hesitated. She had told no one about the plan she and Ejil had made. Now, she told her mother all.

"By the Great Mother, I had no idea. That Ejil is a subtle one, and so are you, child. You are playing a very dangerous game."

"I know, Mother. But what else should I do? How else will we ever find our way home?"

CHAPTER 30

INITIATION

Ejil began by setting oil lamps on a small protruding shelf. Holding in one hand a clamshell filled with a mixture of dark clay, charcoal and deer fat, he outlined the horse shape with a flint graver. With his fingers, he rubbed the fatty mixture along the groove. Then, dipping a sharpened charcoal stick in a bowl of viscous fat, he cut in the spiky lines of the horse's mane.

Horse herds, wandering along the river, often stopped to drink in the early morning on the sandy verge opposite the village. Determined to get the line right as Pico had taught him, he made practice drawings, scratched with a flint shard on a flat piece of shale.

Pico had pointed out the section of wall just above the fighting rhinos. "Start there," he instructed.

"But there are already drawings…"

"Scrape them off," Pico said, and waved his hand dismissively.

"But the spirits!"

"Spirits, bah!" Arms flapping like a partridge, the old man broke wind, grinned, and without another word, walked toward the cave's entrance leaving Ejil alone to begin his work.

With a brush of matted horsehair, Ejil brushed the heads and necks with a thin layer of fat. Punching a series of tiny holes in a square of doeskin, he made a pouch, filled it with powdered charcoal and gently dusted the sticky surface to recreate the delicate shading around the animals' necks and muzzles.

The artist stepped back, blinked owlishly, wiped the sweat from his forehead and surveyed his work. All was quiet. The guttering lamplight told him he had been at it for some time.

His thoughts returned to Lada. *The baby must have come by now. I hope she is well. Will the baby change her feelings for Scar? Will it make her care for him?*

Scar had met with the delegation that next morning and refused their offer. "There is much food," he had said, puffing out his chest. The Lion Clan would remain and hunt by the river.

Upon their return, Callas had tried to put off the council meeting. "I must pray for the Great Mother's guidance," she told Baal and the elders. But Tamo and Mala had insisted. "You have five suns, then Mala and I will call the council ourselves," Tamo told her. So, in three suns they would meet. Meanwhile, Baal and his hunters made sure the fear spread.

As Ejil was replacing the lamp wicks, he heard the hollow echo of footsteps. Pico shuffled into the chamber with a leather sack over one shoulder.

"Hallo there," the painter called, cupping his mouth. His words echoed through the chamber. "Still alive, I see. I was beginning to worry—thought maybe the spirits had taken you away."

Ejil rubbed his eyes and shrugged.

Pico pointed at his face. "Hah, you look like a sleepy raccoon."

Ejil held up his filthy hands and walked over to where a freshet of cold mountain water ran from a niche in the wall next to his workspace. He rubbed his hands under the water, cupped some, splashed his face and drank. "Better!" he said.

"You've been drawing all day. The Sunfather was no more than a knuckle's breadth above the horizon when you started, and it disappeared as I entered the cave."

"The horses are finished."

"Finished? Let me see." Raising his torch, Pico moved up close to the wall, cocked his head and made a face.

"My, my, my; very good, my young friend," the old man said, nodding his head vigorously. "Very good, indeed. This last one is the best—beautiful lines. I see you copied the way I laid out my lions. Makes it seem like a small herd racing each other across the plain."

"Yes," Ejil said, grinning. "That was what I was hoping for."

"Well," he said, cocking one ear. "I hear the sound of galloping hooves, ha ha! Now, you are ready for your initiation into the Mysteries. Come!"

"Mysteries? What, now?" Ejil's stomach lurched.

"Yes, now! This is the last step. You must become a true šamán before the council meets. It will give weight to your words. Making pictures draws you close to the spirit world. You are like a fat sweetberry, ripe for the picking. Come along," the old painter said.

Ejil was never quite sure what to make of Pico's words. He inhaled deeply and followed his mentor. *Yes,* he thought, *I suppose it is time,* not really sure he believed it.

The way was dark as pitch. With only the torch to light his way, Pico led Ejil through low passages which opened onto a series of chambers, large and small, as they made their way ever deeper into the heart of the cave.

Tiny stars sparked in the clusters of frozen stone that hung—slick and shining, like wet icicles—from the cave's upper reaches. Some stood alone, upright as tent poles, others, long and slender, clustered in groups. Still others hung down like sharp fangs dripping with venom.

Occasionally, as they made their way into in the cave's dark recesses, Pico would pause and raise his torch to illuminate charcoal drawings and paintings in red ochre.

Finally, the old man halted. "Here," he said, "we will build our fire. The air is sweet, and I believe there is a hole somewhere above that lets out the smoke."

The chamber smelled of musty earth. Other than the echo of dripping water, all was silent. Ejil hugged himself. It was cold, and the air clung like a second skin. He gazed through the gloom while Pico lit lamps set in niches around the walls. They were in a long, narrow, tent-shaped passage that tapered to a small opening at the far end.

The place had obviously been prepared. Wood was stacked against one wall and there was a small pile of torches. The walls were decorated here and there with single drawings. Ejil admired a charcoal engraving of a giant elk. A bit further along, a rhinoceros, an ibex, some horses and a few symbols of the Mother were scattered on the walls. They were simple charcoal drawings and looked quite old. Ejil squatted by the well-used pit and began to prepare a fire.

"You see there?" Pico said, nodding toward a semi-circular archway. "That is the furthest chamber, and the entrance to the world beyond. The walls are thin and the magic is strong. People have been using this cave over many lives of men. The pictures tell of the efforts of other seekers."

While Ejil tended the fire, Pico unpacked his sack. He placed several long-stemmed mushrooms on a flat rock, their pale caps dotted with bright red like tiny drops of blood.

Ejil looked at the mushrooms and frowned. "Wait! Pelas warned me about those. He said they were forbidden."

"Ha ha, yes, he was right to warn you," the old man said, looking up, his normally merry eyes dark and piercing in the firelight. "As with all things touched by the gods, these tiny lovelies are dangerous, very dangerous indeed," he said, and began slicing.

"The tiniest portion of the cap, thinly sliced and steeped in boiling water, will make a brew strong enough to draw you into the netherworld. It is a perilous journey; and I warn you, some who have attempted it have never returned."

Pico raised one finger and grinned. "Luckily for you, you have Pico; and Pico knows what must be done to prepare you for the journey."

"You have followed this path?"

Pico looked up, met Ejil's eye, and quickly looked away. "I have not. What I am telling you, was told to me by my master."

Despite the cold, Ejil could feel sweat along his hairline. "But if you have not…how can you guide me?"

Pico paused bowed his head. "I know how to make the brew, but no one can guide you. All who make the journey travel alone. This is the abode of the Mother. Though many strange things rose up before my eyes and I stood before the entrance to the womb, the lips remained closed." He shook his head, his face hidden by the curtain of braids. "I was not worthy," he said, his voice a shaky whisper.

"You will succeed, young Ejil," Pico said, clearing his throat, "where I have failed, but it will take courage, and it is your decision." He pushed his hair back and lifted his head. A pair of shining eyes met Ejil's; they were rimmed in red.

Shaken, Ejil gazed into the fire and thought back to Callas' story of Pico poisoning the tribe's First Speaker. Pelas had sometimes spoken of his own initiation. It was a journey that must be made before one could be truly called a šamán.

"What about Callas?"

"It is different for a woman."

Ejil considered. He was fearful, but! *With Baal gaining power, things are changing quickly, and soon I may be faced with a hard choice.* Like his father, Talog, his brother often poked fun, but Ejil believed he secretly feared the power of šamán magic.

This was his one chance. If he refused, that would be the end of it. He would never become a šamán. He took a deep breath and made his decision. "I am ready," he said.

"Good," Pico said, placing a steaming wooden cup in front of him. The smell of damp earth was replaced by a sweetish aroma that filled the chamber.

"Drink! It will take some time before you feel anything." The old man reached into his bag and removed a slender flute. It was a beautiful instrument the painter had carved from a vulture's hollow leg bone. "Music will call the spirits while the tea works its magic," he said.

Ejil pressed the cup to his lips and took a sip, then another.

"Drink it all," the old man ordered.

While Ejil finished the cup, Pico raised the flute to his lips. A sweet sound rose as his fingers fluttered and flew up and down the slender tube.

The melody was familiar. Perched in the red berry bush outside Ejil's family's hut, the tiny, brown-spotted thrush sang just before sunrise, its sweet song heralding the start of the Budding Season.

Ejil closed his eyes. Chirps and bright trills, reverberating off the chamber walls, brought back memories: the soft touch of his mother's hand against his cheek, her welcoming smile. An aching feeling of warmth began in his belly and spread upward. His body felt alive, buzzing like the song of a bee. Behind his eyelids, the flutesong summoned forth a scherzo of color: the rich orange-reds of sunrise, the bright blues of the afternoon sky, the pinks and purples of sunset danced about the chamber, and suddenly Ejil was flying.

He blinked. He was the thrush, and the song was his song. He felt the beating of wings and the rush of the wind as he soared up and up, topping a cloud. Night had become day. The sun was a huge, fiery orange ball. Misty clouds, light as dandelion puffs, floated beside him. He looked down and his gaze fell upon a strange scene.

It was a frozen, featureless world. As he watched, a blue mountain of ice swept down from the north and took possession of the earth. It shouldered aside mountains and carved deep valleys while the sun rose and set and the seasons spun by in dizzying succession.

The ice mountain halted and began to weep. Streams flowed down its face like tears and the streams came together and formed a torrent, and the torrent became a river.

Undulating like a snake, it flowed beneath the Rainbow Bridge and through the ice-formed valley. Then, the valley began to green, the village of the Elder People appeared, and Ejil understood how the world he knew had come to be.

His wings beat. He rose higher above the clouds and the earth shrank. He skimmed a rock-bound shore above a great body of water that stretched beyond sight. He glided above glaucus swells, crested and foaming. Then, suddenly everything changed.

He was back in the deep cave. Pico had disappeared. His head spun; his eyes watered. On hands and knees, he retched and puked. Long strands of saliva dripped down his chin. Finally, he stopped and raised his head. This was a different place. Drawings and paintings of all kinds adorned the walls. With a sudden flash of recognition, he understood. *This is the last chamber.*

Looking down at the dirt, his eyes began to penetrate the soil and he saw deep into the earth. Strange things rose up as he went deeper and deeper. His eyes swam, his stomach lurched. Ejil closed his eyes, he could stand no more.

Wiping his drooling mouth with the back of his hand, Ejil sat back on the smooth stone floor, opened his eyes and let them wander about the chamber. One wall was covered with a profusion of charcoal drawings: lions, rhinoceros and hyena. Lions stalked a herd of bison.

Pictures possess great power—the power to steal a man's spirit, Pelas had warned him. Make a picture of a man and the image could affect all men; a family, a clan, a tribe. Its power was impossible to control, and for that reason, drawing pictures of men and women was forbidden.

As his eyes swept the room, animals seemed to emerge from behind the cave walls. *Is there a lesson here? He asked himself. What is its meaning?*

Ejil's mind drifted, and try as he might, he could not focus. The images blurred, the chamber began to spin. He was, once again, engulfed in blackness. He awoke to find Pico staring down at him.

"So," the old man said, "you have returned. What have you learned?"

Ejil struggled to his feet. He staggered once. His head was clearing, but his stomach still churned. His mouth had a sour taste. "I saw so many things, but I'm not sure what they all mean."

"Understanding! That is the work of a lifetime." Pico handed Ejil his šamán's staff and bowed his head. "Your initiation is complete. Welcome Ejil, Šamán of the Broken People."

CHAPTER 31

PRELUDE

"Adding our share of the dried venison from the hunt, our larders are half empty. That is the truth of it," Mala said, his eyes scanning the people's upturned faces. "If the coming Ice Season is a long one, we will begin to starve before the river ice breaks."

Ejil sat twisting his hands together. His eyes darted about the chamber. Shocked into silence by Mala's words, the people eyed each other and murmured uneasily.

He watched Callas. The Lion Clan's refusal had shocked her. "Why?" she had asked him repeatedly. She wrung her hands. "Had this scarred leader understood the offer?" *She has taken a blow, but she will not give up. She cannot admit she was wrong,* Ejil thought.

Many of those who usually supported the šamán seemed unwilling to meet her gaze. Finally, one old woman nodded, stood, and held out her hand for the speaking stick. "This is not a new thing. I remember other seasons when the fishing has been poor and our larders half empty. Our hunters will bring in meat enough," she said.

Daga stood. "Are you a hunter now, woman?" he sneered. "Who can hunt in the deep snow?"

The chamber quieted.

Daga's mother rose to her feet, scowling and pointed a finger at her son. "Is this how I raised you, boy? You insult your mother's sister?

She propped both hands on her hips and glared at the young man. "Sit down!" she ordered.

Daga's dark face turned darker. He stared down at his feet, then sat.

People smiled and nodded to each other, easing the tension.

Salat rose. "Thank you, old mother," he said. Smiling, he reached out a gentle hand. The old woman passed him the speaking stick. "I remember those seasons well. Each sunrise brought another storm howling down from the Ice Lands. Our lodges were buried. We had to dig tunnels between them. We hunters went out, but there was no game to find. Several died of hunger."

Callas stood scowling. "Driving the Fishbellies from the river will not fill our larders," Callas said. "Who will hunt meat when our young men lie deep in the ground covered with earth?"

"The smoking racks groan under the weight of our fish in the Whiteface camp," Tamo said.

"We must take back what has been taken from us," Tanus said.

"I fear, if they come, they will take our meat, kill our men, our babies and the old people, and make our women slaves, as they did to Baal's people." one elder said.

"Who are these young men?" another woman asked, pointing her fingers at the five hunters sitting outside the council circle. "I recognize the markings of the Bear and the Mammoth People."

Baal stood. "These brave men have come to join us if we make war against the Fishbellies. The other tribes know of our trouble. They have heard of our sorrow. They understand that the Fishbellies are a threat to all of us. More will join us if the council decides to fight.

"Our Speaker counsels peace, but what peace and at what cost? We offered our hand in friendship. The Fishbellies spit in our faces. These are not men, they are wolves. They smell fear, and we all know what happens when a wolfpack smells fear."

Baal hesitated, faced the council, and pressed his finger to his lips. "Shhh, my friends, listen! Can you hear it? The howling! While we sit and talk, the wolfpack is gathering and growing stronger. If we do nothing, soon enough it will come for us," Baal said and sat down.

As the echo of Baal's words died, except for the sound of the flickering torches, all was quiet.

Callas labored again to her feet. "Howling wolves?" she sneered. "These Whitefaces have not threatened us in any way. The only sound I hear is that of one young man howling for revenge," she said, her voice dripping scorn.

"I see our First Speaker disagrees. She selected Ejil, our newly initiated šamán, to be part of our delegation. Ejil spoke with Scar's woman and with their šamán. Tell the council her words," Baal said, beckoning Ejil to his feet.

"What my brother Baal says is true." Ejil stood tall holding his staff. "I spoke with Lada. We played together as children. She was one of the first women taken. Scar made her his woman. She told me that Scar believes our gifts were offered out of fear," he said, pausing to allow the weight of his words to sink in. "Lada says he hates our people."

"Yes, and we know what happens to those he hates," Tamo said. "You demanded we talk, Callas, and we have talked. But the Whiteface tribe scorns our talk and our gifts. And a good thing, too. If they had accepted, we would have given too much of the little food we have. What would you have us do now, Callas? Sink to our knees and beg? Or, rather, should we sit quietly and starve? I say no! The time has come to stand on our feet.

"The Whitefaces scorn us because we show weakness," Tamo said casting his eyes over the whole assembly. "You have all heard Mala's words. There is hardly enough food to last us through the Ice Season. Now, time is short. Dark clouds gather in the North. The Sunfather's power wanes. The time for talk is over. We must go to war," Tamo said. "Stand if you are with us."

Callas's eyes darted around the chamber. Most of the people had risen to their feet. She shook her head and sat down.

Daga raised his fist. "W-a-r!" he shouted.

The hunters thrust their fists in the air. "War!"

"War!" the people shouted.

"Baal, our war chief, will lead us to victory! Hail Baal!" Daga shouted.

"Hail Baal!" the people raised their fists and shouted back.

WAR COUNCIL

Baal and his warriors, together with Ejil, Mala and Tamo, squatted in a circle. "Here is the river," Baal said, using a stick to draw a long undulating line in the fine dust that covered the cave floor. "Here, the bridge, the cliffs and here are our two camps," he said, dotting a cluster of tiny mounds.

"This is my plan…" Baal's voice sounded deep and resonant within the chamber. "We divide our men into two war parties. I will lead the larger party along the river toward the Fishbelly camp. We won't hide. I want them to see us. We will act like a hunting party stalking game and work our way slowly toward their camp.

To Ejil, the plan seemed sound. *Baal has thought this through*, he said to himself.

"Breda and Tanus will lead the second party. Breda is our best tracker and Tanus knows the trail," Baal said, nodding to acknowledge the two hunters. "You will travel along the cliffs," he said, pointing to the ridge line, "until you are abreast of the Fishbelly camp. This party will include our Mammoth and Bear brothers," Baal smiled at the tribesmen.

Tamo snorted. "What trail?"

Tanus shook his head. "The elder is right! I have hunted along that ridge many times. The way is passable, but the rocks will slow us down and there are a few crevasses. We may have to circle around to avoid bears and lions that make their dens in those rocks. Walking along the river, Baal, you could reach the Fishbelly camp well before sunset on the fifth day. We will need at least two more suns traveling along those cliffs to come abreast of their camp."

"Could the Fishbellies have watchers on those cliffs? Maybe we should scout it first," Breda said.

Baal grimaced and shook his head. "No, the season is too far along. We must move now. If you find any of those cave rats, you'll have to deal with them."

"I think Scar has watchers camped along the river," Ejil said. "After we left the camp, Fishbelly warriors shadowed us for three suns."

Baal nodded and gestured to Breda.

"I have only seen sign close to the village the one time. I have not scouted that far beyond, but what Ejil says seems likely," Breda said.

"Good!" Baal said, rubbing his hands together. "They may not be watching the village, but they are not far off. They will spot us soon after we set out; I am depending on it. Tanus and Breda, you and your men will leave well before us and go up the back trail behind the forest. Our trap will snap shut on them like the jaws of a cave lion. You and your party will be the upper jaw," Baal said, spreading his arms.

"As we close in on their camp, their vision will narrow; their eyes will see only what is in front of them. We'll allow you two suns. That should be enough time. We will light two fires each night until we get within a day's trek; that night we will make only one. You should be able to spot the fires from the clifftop."

"How hard will it be to get down from those cliffs?" a Bear hunter asked.

"There is an old trail the mammoth herds used to follow to get to the river," Tamo said.

"Yes. We haven't seen the herds this far south since my father's time, but the trail is still there," Tanus said. "It is an easy walk."

"By then we will be maybe one sun from the Fishbelly camp. Scarface will be drawn toward us like a moth to a flame."

"Leaving their camp unprotected," Daga said

"Yes," Baal said with a glance at Daga. "Leaving their camp, food larders and our women with only a few men to guard them. Tanus and Breda, your war party will attack the camp and kill every Fishbelly you find."

"Women, children?" Breda asked.

Baal shrugged. "If they fight back, kill them."

"Tanus and Breda's attack better happen, or we'll be walking right into the middle of a storm," another hunter said.

"Scar may think us cowards, but he can't ignore a large armed party coming right at him," Baal said.

"It is a good plan," Breda said.

"What will you be doing while they are attacking the camp?" Ejil asked.

Baal grinned. "You mean, what will I be doing while *you* are attacking the camp? You know how their camp is set up. You will be with Breda's party, little brother—or should I say, brother šamán?" he said with a laugh. "It will give you a chance to break a few heads with that stone thrower of yours."

The men laughed. Breda slapped Ejil on the back.

Ejil clenched his jaw. "It will be my spear they feel tearing out their guts," he said.

Baal laughed. "We will be the lion's lower jaw," he continued. "Once we are within a sun of their camp, the Fishbellies will either block our way or attack. If they block us, we seek a parlay and delay them until you launch your assault."

"What if they attack you first?" Salat asked.

"So much the better," Baal said, smiling to acknowledge the hunter. "If that happens, Daga will sound the horn." He pointed to the bison horn hanging from Daga's neck. "By then, you should be close enough to hear it. Cut down anyone in your way and come running."

Baal gazed around the circle. "We have practiced over and over. The land is open and flat all along the river. There is no place to hide. They must come at us across open ground where our spear throwers will make the difference. First, we thin them out with our light spears; then, as the gap between us closes, we cut them down with the heavier spears. The few that are left, we will meet breast to breast."

Heads nodded, and there were murmurs of agreement around the circle.

They are all Baal's men now, Ejil thought. He could see how each met his brother's eye. Baal's every gesture exhibited confidence and power and commanded loyalty. Ejil was caught up in it, too. *This is what my brother was born for,* he thought, jealousy fighting with admiration at his brother's accomplishments. *Finally, we will have our revenge, and I will get Lada back. She must have had her baby by now.* He had tried to avoid the painful thought, but it persisted. *Will it look like one of them? Oh well; boy, girl, I don't care. I will adopt it,* he told himself. *As long as Lada and I can be together.* His need for her had grown since they last spoke. Until it had become a great lump in his chest.

"If every man stands his ground, most of those stinking animals will lie jerking and choking on their own blood. The few that survive will probably try to run away," Baal said.

"What if they don't run?" one of the Mammoth warriors asked.

"Then they will do their death dance, wriggling like fish at the end of our spears," Daga said.

"I have one more question," Ejil said. "What if the weather turns?"

"We will all carry our parkas and each man will carry extra meat. Snow or no snow, we will put an end to the Fishbellies." Baal raised his fist. The men cheered.

Baal waited for the noise to abate and continued. "Tanus and Breda, once you have destroyed the camp, your task is to surprise them from the rear. If they try to retreat back toward their camp, you will hear three blasts from Daga's horn. Hold them while the bottom jaw of our trap snaps shut and we shove our spears straight up their asses."

Hooting and hollering, the men danced around the circle pumping their fists and slapping each other on the back.

Baal raised his hand. "Remember, if you hear two blasts, you will know we are under attack. Come running. Three blasts, they are running away. Stand and block them. We want none of them to escape."

"Hail Baal, hail the chief!" Daga said, pumping his fist in the air.

"Hail the chief! Hail Baal!" the men cried out in unison.

Baal held out his hand for silence. "A plan is only a plan. I expect each of you to fight bravely. Death to the Fishbellies!" he shouted, raising his fist.

"Death to the Whitefaces! Death to the Fishbellies!" the warriors repeated and repeated, again and again. The war dance began, and the sound of cheering resounded from the cave walls.

CHAPTER 33

A QUESTION OF TRUST

"What is it, husband?" Lada asked. Since the baby's birth, Scar had stayed close to the hearth.

This morning, before the noon sun, Grayhair and Hawkeye had come to the hut. They were covered in dust and sweat.

Shrugging off Lada's offer of food, Hawkeye had begun signing so rapidly that Lada could not follow.

"Blackdogs! They come," Scar said.

Lada's heart jumped and began thumping rapidly. "A hunting party?" she asked, averting her eyes, trying to control her shock.

"Maybe," Scar said, eyeing her curiously. "Many men. With every rising of the Sunspirit they come closer."

"The talking men?"

"The small angry one," Hawkeye signed.

Daga, she thought. "The young šamán?" she asked.

"No," Hawkeye said.

Lada sighed inwardly. *Surely, if it really was a war party, Ejil would be with them.* She often daydreamed about Ejil coming to rescue her, but now there was Scar's son. *What am I to do?*

Scar had named him Brighteyes, and that was how the clan would know him, but his secret name would be Efrem, in honor of her father. Scar had just shrugged. Grinding her teeth in frustration, she wondered,

Did Scar realize that his son was named after one of the men his people had murdered? Ejil, where are you?

That night, Lada could not find sleep. She listened to Scar pacing back and forth in front of their hut. That evening, the women had been told, "The next sun will bring war."

"Why?" Lada asked, "You said that the Blackdogs were cowards. They are probably a party of hunters," she said, trying to sooth him.

Scar gazed at her with angry eyes. "No!" he said, slashing down with his hand. "The Blackdogs are our enemies. It does not matter why they have come. We will kill them all and take their hearts."

Lada turned her face away. *Finally, I understand. You are a murderer,* she thought and the clouds of confusion cleared from her mind. *Sorry husband, but you started the killing and now you must die, or it will go on and on.*

For Tanus, the trail was familiar; so while he scouted ahead, Breda led the war party along the high cliffs. There were eight in the party. Three, including Ejil from the First People, two from the Bear and three from the Mammoth people. The Sunfather was high on the sky ladder. Big, rounded storm clouds hung as if suspended, dark and threatening. From the heights, the river was a gray worm wriggling across a patched landscape shading toward brown.

As Baal had ordered, Breda's party departed in the early morning darkness. They would have three suns before Baal's party set out. This was only the second time the Sunfather had shown his round face since the trek had begun.

Each warrior carried a thrusting spear mounted with a wickedly sharp knapped point for close in fighting. The points were wrapped in thick bison skin to protect the brittle stone. The men also carried heavy fur tunics and sleeping furs. Most also carried stone war hammers belted at their waists.

Ejil's sling was tucked into his pack, a leather bag of river stones jangled from his belt. Baal's plan had seemed perfect, but now he was having second thoughts. *What will happen if we lose? What if Lada is killed in the attack? If Baal's plan fails, the Fishbellies will revenge themselves on our people.* In the excitement of the moment, the fact that they might lose or be killed had not occurred to him. Now, he thought of little else.

The cliffs were rough and uneven, the trail bisected by huge boulders, wide fissures, and deep narrow gorges. The way was difficult and dangerous, made more so by the weight of the pack each man carried.

Chanting as they trudged along, their song told part of the saga of the Great Journey from their home in the hot lands. All knew the words by heart. There was drought, the rivers dried, the land cracked and turned brown, and the animals disappeared. There was hunger. Names were spoken of places long forgotten that lived on only in song.

Tanus appeared, jogging down trail toward them.

"What do you see," Breda asked, raising his hand to halt the procession.

"Cave bear! A big one!" Tanus said, panting.

Breda rubbed his chin. "Where?"

Tanus held up both hands with splayed fingers. "This many spear throws," he said, and jerked his thumb back over his shoulder. "A female with cubs. Only way forward is past her den."

"No way around?" Breda asked.

Tanus shook his head. "There's a wide gorge," he said, taking a breath. "Couldn't see where it ends, but I remember it pretty well. Getting around it will take at least a sun, maybe longer."

"We don't have an extra sun," Breda said.

"Breda, this is a very big bear," Tanus said, spreading his arms wide.

The scout leaned on his spear and sighed.

"Maybe I could drive her off with my sling," Ejil said.

"More likely you'll end up a meal. Tanus, is there any place Ejil could stand and sling rocks where the bear won't be able to get at him?"

"Maybe! There is a narrow ledge along the side of the crevasse where a man could stand."

"We have bigger problems," Ejil said, pointing toward the North sky. The clouds had blackened and rolled toward them like great rounded boulders filling the sky. The wind began to roar.

Tanus grabbed Breda's shoulder and shouted in his ear. "The gods have turned on us. We can't stay here! The wind will blow us right off this cliff! That defile we passed down trail! We can shelter there. It's narrow, but at least we'll be out of the wind." He grabbed the hunter by the shoulders and turned him around, back in the direction they had come from. Breda yelled instructions to Ejil who passed them to the next man in line. With much confusion, the war party turned and retraced its steps.

Jammed into a space—little more than a jagged crack in the rockface—Ejil stood with the shivering men, their backs pressed against the North side of the defile while above them the storm roared with the voice of a many lions. It was a wet snow, which made a fire impossible. Ejil's thick auroch-hide tunic, though greased with deer fat, clung to him like the skin of a wet cave rat.

Teeth chattering with cold, sleep would not come. Ejil's thoughts led to Lada. He pictured her face. Their last meeting. How her eyes had sparkled in the wolf's dawn after she had kissed him. *Had the baby come? Was she alright?* He felt a stab of fear. Women often died in childbirth. Thinking such thoughts, he finally dozed off. Just before dawn, the storm blew itself out.

The sun rose on a world of gleaming crystal. Ice encased every surface. By the time they had broken their fast, the ice had melted. They resumed their trek.

The Sunfather burned hot, making the path slick and treacherous. Puffy white clouds cast shadows across the valley floor. Ejil's damp clothes steamed and dried on his back. He checked the sun's angle. *We will have to move fast to make up for lost time.*

Tanus, who had scouted ahead, came back smiling. "The bear is gone. I saw no sign of it."

"Maybe the storm drove her deeper into her cave," Breda said.

"She's got two hungry cubs to feed. Sooner or later—probably sooner—she's got to come out," Tanus said.

"Maybe we should stop standing here talking and get going while we still have the chance," Breda said.

Stealthily placing one foot in front of the other, the party passed the bear's den and moved on without incident.

As the westering sun hovered a handsbreadth above the horizon, the party topped a rise and came out on a flat, rocky expanse. Ejil looked around. A few scattered bushes interrupted the field of bone-white rocks.

"It will be easier from here on. Let's go," Tanus said and led off. The whole party fell in behind, jogging along, packs rattling, spears clattering.

Finally, Tanus called a halt. Panting, Ejil bent over and wiped the sweat from his brow. The sun was about to dip below the horizon. He was exhausted.

Ejil stood watch on a knoll with the dark valley spread out below a cloudless sky festooned with stars. With one finger he traced the shape of *The Mother, The Warrior* and *The Snake* and drew a line to *The Father* who always pointed the way north.

He rubbed his eyes and looked down toward the valley floor. Against the dark shape of the river, he spotted a single fire twinkling like a tiny star fallen to earth. *Baal's party must be in position. Tomorrow, we take the trail down the cliffs and attack the Fishbelly camp.* From where he stood, the descent seemed steep and treacherous. *I hope Tanus can locate the trail.* Ejil swallowed hard. He felt his stomach tighten. *I have never fought a man,* he thought.

Ejil's thoughts were interrupted by a sound. He turned his head and saw the silhouette of his friend Breda outlined against the rising moon.

"See anything?" the scout asked.

"Baal's signal!"

"How many fires?"

"One."

"Finally," Breda said, briskly rubbing his hands together. He wrapped his arm around Ejil's shoulder. "Worried about tomorrow?"

Ejil bowed his head.

"Don't worry. Every man gets the shakes and doubts his courage before battle."

"Not you."

"You think not? I break out in a sweat every time I think about what's coming," he said, ruffling Ejil's hair.

Ejil cleared his throat. "Behind you, the Blood Moon rises. The Ice Season will soon be upon us."

Breda gazed over his shoulder. "Aye, as if I needed reminding after last night's storm. The moon is an omen, no doubt. What do your dreams tell you?"

"Nothing! The gods have not favored me since the night of the terrible storm. Last night, I dreamt of meat. I think that was my stomach talking."

Breda squeezed Ejil's shoulders. "You see, nothing to worry about, or the gods would have told you." He gazed up at the sky. "I hope we have come far enough. The sky is clear. Maybe tonight we can get some sleep. I'm looking forward to getting down from these accursed cliffs."

Scar, Hawkeye and Grayhair squatted in the dirt in front of the fire. The Sunspirit stood two finger's breadth above the horizon.

Scar's eyes studied the old man as he made his report. When his scouts had first spotted the Blackdog hunting party, he had shrugged it off. *I am Scar, leader of the Lion Clan. I took their gifts and refused to leave the river, and they slunk back to their camp like hyena with their bellies dragging in the dirt.* But with each setting sun, this new Blackdog party drew closer to the river camp. Scar's eyebrows drew together. *Why have they come?* He bit his lip. *What is their plan?*

"They will be here soon," Hawkeye said, making the sign for the setting sun.

"Another thing," Grayhair signed. "The tall, dark warrior who leads them is the man you fought at the Blackdog camp."

Scar's eyes grew wide. He glared across the fire. "I saw him fall—his body broken on the rocks."

Grayhair shrugged. "He is older and has grown. It is either the man himself or his demon-spirit."

Scar's throat went dry. He recalled his mother's words: "An angry spirit stalks us," she had warned him.

Grayhair shrugged. "He seemed to me to be made of blood and bone."

Could it be true? Scar asked himself. *Had the warrior somehow lived and tracked him here, or was he…?* He studied Grayhair closely. He trusted the old man. *Grayhair always gives good council.*

Could this man be the angry spirit his mother warned of? A single bead of sweat trickled down alongside his ear. They had not spoken much since the meeting with the Blackdog šamán. *She sits alone in her hut, mumbling to the spirits. Should I seek her council?* He peered up at the sun. *There is no time.*

"Hawkeye, go! Rouse the warriors!" Scar croaked.

As he spoke those words, Spearpoint arrived panting and squatted across from Scar. His chest heaving, his body gleamed with sweat.

Scar scowled at the young hunter. *What now?* He had sent him with SquintEye to guard the path that led from the cliffs to the river camp.

"A strong band of Blackdog warriors comes along the high cliffs," Spearpoint signed, fighting to catch his breath. Several hawk feathers were entwined in his shoulder-length hair.

Scar's hand cupped his mouth. "How many?" he signed.

Spearpoint held up the fingers of both hands. "Many," he said. "I made signs to calm the spirits and scouted their fire. They carry heavy spears. The young one with the šamán's staff, he is with them. Soon they will reach the trail that leads down from the cliffs."

Now Scar understood. "You have done well," he said, working to keep his face passive. His eyes sought Grayhair's.

The old man scowled and shook his head. "The black leader divides the pack. Some from one direction. While our eyes are on him, the other pack attacks from behind."

Hawkeye and the other warriors came and squatted around them.

His mind in turmoil; Scar groped for a plan. "Both bands are strong?" he asked.

"Yes, but the one coming downriver—the one led by the demon warrior—is the strongest. Send Hawkeye," Grayhair said, gesturing at the stocky, dark eyed warrior. "Let him choose a few more men. They will block the narrow gap in the trail where the spirits have thrown great handfuls of boulders. It is a good place for a trap. They can ambush the ones coming down from the cliff while we fight the dark warrior here."

"Go quickly!" Scar signed to Hawkeye. "We will block the trail and make the sign for talk. The Blackdogs love talk. We will let them think they have fooled us. Kill the others quickly and come back. Then we will kill the rest."

"What if the Blackdogs will not talk?" One-ear asked. "They have many fighters."

"Did One-ear not kill two Blackdogs with one spear in the fight at their camp?"

"No," the warrior said, tracing the kill scars burned into his chest with his fingers. "More." He puffed out his chest and grinned.

Scar stood and raised his spear. "We are the warriors of the Lion Clan. We will kill the Blackdogs. Go!"

CHAPTER 34

THE RESCUE

"This is the place," Tanus said. It looked well used; the whitish earth was packed hard by the beat of countless hooves. The trail meandered down toward the valley floor, skirting the larger boulders in a series of lazy curves. A light breeze blowing up from the valley brought with it the sharp scent of pine.

"There, that's the camp," Ejil said, pointing at the thin line of gray smoke spiraling up into the air close by the river.

Dividing into pairs, the men squatted and began carefully outlining their eyes with white clay, then smearing each other's faces with red ochre. Using white clay, they drew symbols of The Sunfather, the mother, and clan signs across their cheeks and foreheads.

"Once the men ready themselves, form them up in a single line. Each man should have his thrusting spear ready," Breda instructed Tanus in a soft voice.

Breda kneeled, removed his pack and unstrapped the heavy-shanked lance and quickly smeared his face with red ochre. He stood and handed Tanus a handful of clay.

"I'll take Ejil and scout ahead," he said as Tanus carefully drew black circles around his eyes. "You never know what might be waiting behind those rocks."

Tanus's eyes widened. "What? How long should I wait?"

"You look worried." Breda grinned and slapped the big hunter on the back. "Give us a little bit of a lead. When we are halfway down, follow. This trail is known. Fishbellies may be ugly beasts, but they are wily. I want no surprises."

Breda shouldered his pack. "How do I look?" he asked.

"Fearsome! If your mother saw you, she'd run like the dark spirits were chasing her."

"Good," Breda said. His eyes lit up his painted face.

Joba's beautifully knapped point, shining in the morning sunlight at the end of his spear, filled Ejil with confidence. He rubbed a sweaty palm against his sleeve. *I have never killed a man,* he thought, *standing eye to eye.*

Motioning to Ejil, Breda pressed a finger to his lips. "Keep your eyes peeled and your spear ready, Ejil," he said, his eyes darting from one side of the trail to the other. "Let's kill some Fishbellies." He turned and loped off down the trail. Ejil hefted his spear and followed.

Breda reached a blind turn and hesitated. "Stand back!" He flattened himself against a large boulder, eased himself around it, turned his head, grinned and continued down the path.

Ejil followed as his friend worked his way toward the bottom of the trail. The night before, Breda had listened carefully to his fears. He thought about the pain in Breda's eyes when he told him about Mata and her child. *And, despite everything, this morning he picked me to back him up. He could have picked anyone, but he picked me.* Ejil hefted his spear, gritted his teeth, and followed.

As they reached the bottom, the trail turned level and sandy. A series of boulders, higher than a man's head, flanked both sides of a narrow path. Breda halted and signaled Ejil forward.

"It seems quiet," Ejil whispered.

"Too quiet, if you ask me. Even the birds," Breda said, raising his eyebrows. "I'll go first. Watch! When I reach the other side of these rocks, I'll signal. Follow me." Without waiting for Ejil's reply, he grasped his spear in both hands and stepped through the gap.

A rock whizzed by Breda's nose followed by a spear thrust. A screaming warrior, his hair decorated with feathers, popped up from between two boulders.

Ejil gasped. A well-aimed thrust had almost disemboweled the scout. Only Breda's lightning quick reflexes saved him. He leaped backwards, dropped into a crouch and dodged sideways like a spider.

Parrying a second vicious thrust, Breda rushed forward and slashed the young fighter's throat with a neat side swipe of his spear point. Blood gushing from his neck, the stricken man fell back halfway into a crevice between the rocks.

More war cries pierced the early morning. Hidden warriors rushed forward. A huge, broad-shouldered warrior with a scarred chest attacked Breda. Without thinking, Ejil pulled back his arm and launched his spear.

Narrowly missing Breda's shoulder, the sharp point found its mark, piercing the big warrior's bare chest. Eyes alight with surprise, the man's spear slid from his nerveless hand and clattered to the ground. He dropped into the middle of the path.

Breda glanced back and grinned. Another war cry! He sprang to meet the onslaught of a one-eared warrior who charged straight at him, spear outstretched in both hands.

Breda's blood-curdling cry momentarily stunned his adversary. He drove his spear in the man's stomach, wrenched it out, and buried it in his brawny chest. The warrior grunted in surprise as the slender point slid neatly between his ribs and pierced his heart.

Ejil heard a cry from further up the trail. Tanus and the rest of the war party came running toward them.

Without pausing, Ejil followed his friend deeper into the rocky passage. Blood spattered, chest heaving, Breda stood at bay, backed up against a huge, smooth-sided boulder, facing two warriors who huddled together just beyond the range of his thrust. With two of their men lying sprawled on either side of the bloody path, neither seemed willing to confront the wild-eyed warrior.

"Come on, cowards! Fight!" Breda taunted. He pounded his chest with one hand, grinning with berserker fury. "My spear has not yet drunk its fill. It thirsts for more Fishbelly blood."

At that moment, Tanus, with the rest of the war band at his heels, came screaming through the break in the rocks—painted fiends, eyes burning with blood lust. Ejil saw the fear erupt in the younger Fishbelly's wide eyes.

Ejil's spear struck the young warrior above the ribcage, driving him stumbling backward. He staggered once, then collapsed. Coming from behind Ejil's shoulder, Tanus' spear pierced the older man's thigh. Ejil reached out, wrenched back Tanus' spear, and drove it straight into the wounded man's open mouth. A horrible gurgling sound issued out from deep his throat. He fell backwards, his body, dancing and jerking, fell to the ground.

Ejil dragged his spear from his kill and had halted beside his friend while Tanus and the other warriors finished off the two remaining clan warriors. Breda, his eyes afire, ripped up a handful of dried grass and carefully wiped the blood from his spear. He ran his hand lovingly along the stone point.

A small smile twisted Breda's lips. "The god's have been kind. You have made your first kill, Ejil, and my spear is unhurt," he said in an exaggerated whisper. He winked at Ejil then ran off toward the enemy camp. Ejil screamed a war cry, hefted his spear, dodged around the other warriors and raced after his friend's retreating back.

CHAPTER 35

FINALE

The Fishbelly fighters milled around in a ragged group more than six spear throws distant from Baal and his oncoming warriors. Scar stood a little forward. Behind the men, women and children clustered in front of a group of huts.

Baal's blood was up. He had not expected to get this close to the Fishbelly camp with no sign of Breda and Tanus. *Where is my upper jaw? Something must be holding them up.*

Keeping tight to the riverbank as his left flank, Baal signaled his men. Shoulder to shoulder they moved forward, Baal at the center with Salat and Daga flanking him. Each man held one spear in his throwing hand and two others loosely in the other.

Baal looked left and right, then raised his spear straight up. The line halted.

"They don't seem worried. See, some of them are laughing. They think we are too far away. The one standing forward is making a sign. Looks like he wants to talk," Daga whispered.

Baal grinned. *There he is, the scarred warrior.* This was the man who had occupied his thoughts, the man Baal had dreamed of killing. "Talk? I'll give them talk! Throwing spears!" His shouted order shattered the silence.

Shifting from foot to foot, Daga glanced at Baal. "Uh, there are more of them. Shouldn't we wait for Tanus and Breda?"

"No!" Baal said, grinning madly. "Too late. We will fight them alone."

Looking left and right, he surveyed the line. "Ready!"

Shifting his gaze from side to side, Baal eyed his men with satisfaction as each warrior rammed the blunt ends of two spears into the ground and slotted the lightest into his spear thrower. As they had practiced, the warriors raised their spears and cocked back their arms.

"Throw!" the War Chief screamed.

Each spearman took a quick skip forward and launched. The spears flew upward.

Baal held his breath and shaded his eyes as the spears arced up and were swallowed by the blue expanse of the afternoon sky.

Scar's brow furrowed. *The black warrior does not want to talk?* An icy fear gripped him. *He's grown a beard, but he is the man I knocked off the cliff.*

He watched as his men pranced about, laughing and shaking their weapons. One lifted the flap of his deerskin skirt and wiggled his bare butt at the Blackdogs.

They are too far away, he told himself as he watched Baal's warriors prepare to throw.

"Hah, the black fools waste their spears!" one warrior called out. Another made a face and pointed. Scar stood unsure, watching.

It came like a deadly rain. The spears dropped from the sky, slicing through muscle and bone, sowing havoc among his astonished warriors. Some missed and struck quivering in the ground, but several found their mark, piercing naked flesh. Men screamed in agony. A spear grazed Scar's shoulder, driving him to his knees.

"Flying spears," Scar shouted struggling to his feet. *The Blackdogs are closing in.* Each held a spear, their line unbroken. "Get ready to fight! Kill the Blackdogs!" Scar roared at his men. Ignoring the dead and wounded, he grabbed at those still standing and thrust them into the semblance of a line facing the enemy. Out of the corner of his eye, he saw the tall warrior raise his spear.

"We're close enough now. Use the heavier spear. Aim lower!" Baal admonished his men. The stouter lances arced through the short distance and buried their wicked tips in throats, chests and groins, spreading carnage.

Scar dove to the ground, dodging a spear. He sprang to his feet and surveyed the carnage. *We are lost,* his mind screamed. In that instant, all his plans vanished and he saw his fate. *My mother was right, curse her. The clan is dead. The Blackdog spirits are too powerful.* All around him, the earth was slick with blood and excrement. Most of his men lay scattered across the ground; those that remained unhurt wandered about with vacant eyes. Scar smelled their fear, the stink of panic.

The women and children had gathered at the edge of the camp to watch their men do battle. Lada glanced heavenward. The Sun Father still burned hot in the clear sky, but had begun to descend the sky ladder. Sunset was but a hand's breadth away.

As usual, the women had divided into two groups. The clan on one side. The captives gathered on the other. Crowbait, Rhino and Squinty had armed themselves with spears and clubs. They stood apart, glaring at Lada and her people through narrowed eyes. Lada held her baby tight to her breast. With her free hand she fingered the handle of Scar's gift, the slender sharpstone dagger she had tucked between the folds of Efrem's swaddling wrap.

What will happen if Ejil and his new tribe win? Lada wondered, not for the first time. Though they were afraid to speak of it, most of the captives, she knew, hated their captors. *Most will welcome their freedom, but what about girls like Mata, who are pregnant and those who have babies like Tule and like me?*

Tule stood apart, stooped over, her fingers flickering absently about her mouth. Since she had joined with Spearpoint and had her child, she and Lada had drifted apart. Tule had begun to act like Clan. She began greasing back her hair and had stopped coming to the river to bathe.

Lada dared not share her feelings, lest it get back to Scar. Still, her heart reached out to Tule. She truly loved her man and their young child. *What will happen? What will she do without him?* Lada asked herself. *Baal has sworn an oath to kill all the clan. Ejil told me so. Does that mean the women too? And, what about our babies?* Lada's arms tightened around Efrem.

From where she stood, Lada did not see the rain of spears, but she heard the shouts of surprise and the screams of the wounded, and watched the men fall. Then, she heard a mighty shout and watched as Baal and a mass of screaming warriors, wielding their spears, charged toward Scar and his few remaining men.

Where is Ejil? She could not make out his tall, thin form anywhere among the attackers. She recognized Baal; he seemed different, broader and heavier. But even as a boy he had been tall, towering over most of the grown men of the tribe.

Out of the corner of her eye, Lada caught some movement to her left. Armed warriors, with painted faces, were attacking from behind the huts. Even with the red paint, she recognized Breda. Screaming their war cries, the men bore down on the women. Then she saw Ejil some ways behind Breda and her heart jumped into her throat.

Crowbait had spotted them too. She and her troop thrust themselves between the attackers and the women. *They are badly outnumbered,* but these—Lada knew—were tough, sturdy women. *They know how to wield a spear.*

Crowbait charged one of the oncoming warriors. The man halted, his mouth gaping open with surprise as she buried her spear's fire-hardened point in the soft flesh below his ribs.

Next, another black warrior. Rhino waded in swinging her club back and forth. She rapped his knuckles, knocking the spear from his hands then cocked the club above her shoulder to launch another blow.

The man barely paused; Lada could see the bloodlust was upon him. He plucked out his war axe and rushed forward, blocked Rhino's heavy weapon, with his raised forearm, and split her skull with a single blow. His face spattered with blood and brains, the warrior searched about, looking for someone one else to kill.

"Lada!" Ejil cried, his eyes searching.

"Here!" Lada yelled. Dodging and weaving, she worked her way through the crowd of frightened women who had drawn into a tight knot, screeching like frightened crows.

Grinning, Crowbait blocked her path, spear at the ready.

"You join with Scar. Now betray him," she said, sneering. "Men are fools!"

Lada cringed backward. She raised one arm to ward off a blow. With the other, she clutched Efrem tightly to her breast.

"You want her, Blackdog?" Crowbait screamed at Ejil. She brandished her spear, her face a grinning skull. "Come," she gestured. "Come try! I kill you, then I kill her! You will cook my meat and she will wipe my ass in the Caves of the Fallen."

Lada saw that to Ejil, the big fishbelly woman's few words and hand signs were gibberish, but she stood between her and the man who consumed her dreams. "Ejil, save me!" she screamed. Ejil gripped his spear and moved in.

Crowbait adjusted her spear to chest height. Her black eyes glittered with hate.

"Ejil, look out!" Lada screamed.

Crowbait lowered her head and charged Ejil like a bull auroch. He was taller, but the clan woman outweighed him. He was quick, but her rage made her that much quicker.

Holding the spear shaft in a double-handed grip, she thrust the point forward.

Ejil sidestepped. The sharpened point passed a finger's breadth from his chest.

Crowbait pivoted, reversed, and drove the spear's butt end into Ejil's face, smashing his nose.

Ejil's eyes flooded with tears. He dropped his spear and staggered backwards, hands cupping his gushing nose.

Screaming in triumph, Crowbait shoved him down onto his back. Then, straddling her prostrate victim, she raised her spear above her head with both hands preparing to deliver the death blow.

Fingers clutching at her mouth, Lada watched the confrontation in horror. Suddenly, she realized; *Crowbait's going to kill my Ejil!* Her fingers closed around Scar's gift. She gritted her teeth and ran up behind her tormentor. With a fury driven by her long-simmering hate, she drove the slender blade into Crowbaits thick neck.

Crowbait's eyes shot open. Her snarl turned into a scream. Mouth gaping like a dying fish, her eyes rolled up into her head and she slid bonelessly down on top of her intended victim.

Holding tight to her baby with one hand, Lada kneeled next to Ejil who, with his bloody nose cupped in one hand, was desperately trying to wriggle out from under the female warrior's heavy body. Little Efrem, staring in dismay then terror at the blood smeared-face before him, burst into tears.

Ejil arched his back, and with a mighty heave, levered himself out from beneath the clan woman's body.

Lada and Ejil found each other's eyes, then turned to little Efrem who lay screaming on the ground—tiny fists beating the air—and erupted in laughter, oblivious to the chaos surging all around them.

CHAPTER 36

VICTORY

More than half of his warriors lay scattered like fallen leaves across the muddy ground, wounded or dead. The others stared at him with frightened eyes. Scar watched the Blackdog warrior pump his spear above his head—eyes alight with the battle madness, preparing to attack.

Scar's temples pounded. *The demon warrior has come to avenge the blood of his kin.* The Spirit Woman's words echoed in his mind—his plans were in ruins and with that came the realization. *I have been a fool!* He had sought out his mother the night before, but she had disappeared. *Even she has deserted me*, he thought.

With death sweeping toward him, Scar shouted desperately at his panicked men, but they were beyond hearing. As a body, they turned and fled.

The Blackdog halted before Scar. Their eyes locked. The charging spearmen parted and flowed past the two warriors like an onrushing stream chasing the fleeing Fishbellies.

Twice the great circle of the seasons had come and gone since they last faced each other. *It is him.* Scar's throat went dry. *Is he man or demon?*

Neither ear nor eye heard or saw the slaughter raging about them; their world narrowed to the space between their spear tips. Spear outstretched, Scar circled slowly, blind to everything but his rage and the hate reflected in his enemy's eyes.

Surging forward, Scar aimed a straight thrust at his enemy's gut, but the black demon sidestepped and slammed the shaft of his weapon downward, tearing Scar's spear shaft from his hands. The stone point hit the ground and snapped with an audible crack.

The Blackdog glanced down at the broken spear and grinned. His eyes dared Scar to attempt to retrieve it, but Scar knew better. Raising his hands protectively he backed off. Eyes darting from side to side, he searched for a weapon, but all he saw was defeat and death.

Scar starred at the man, chest heaving, sweat stinging his eyes. The Blackdog warrior stood waiting. *What of my son, Brighteyes? I will never see him again.* Scar squared his shoulders and bared his teeth, spit and roared like a cornered lion. *There is nothing left but to die like a warrior.*

Grinning wickedly, the Blackdog warrior circled right and dropped into a half crouch. As Scar shook his head to clear the sweat from his eyes, the man sprang across the gap that separated them. Scar felt the point's bite deep in his throat.

His hands clutched at the buried spearhead. He staggered once and wrenched it out. A great torrent of blood filled his throat. He coughed; blood spurted from his mouth. Swaying like a reed in the wind, he staggered forward and his world slowly faded into darkness.

Baal regarded the body of his dead enemy. *It had been so easy.* After all this time, Scar, the man who had stalked his dreams, lay on the ground before him, his blood spreading across the ground. Baal almost laughed. He gazed around him. It was over. The Fishbellies were dead and his warriors had begun to cluster around him.

Baal hefted his spear and thrust his arms into the sky. His shout of triumph echoed off the distant limestone cliffs. How often had he conjured this scene in his mind's eye? *Victory!* The taste was sweet as honey in his mouth. "Can you see me, Father? Can you hear me? I have avenged your blood and the honor of our tribe!" His warriors milled around him cheering.

"What do you want us to do, Chief?" Daga asked, his face creased with a broad smile, motioning toward the bloody corpses of dead warriors lying in blood and filth.

"Take their heads," Baal ordered. "Let their spirits wander in darkness. Each man will carry back the heads of the men he has slain. Let the people see the fruit of our victory."

"What about the Fishbelly women and their filthy brats?" Daga asked. The enemy women had compressed themselves into a thick knot and stood off by themselves. Their eyes, when not downcast, gazed toward their captives in mute appeal. The former captives clustered about laughing and embracing their rescuers.

"Separate them. The men may enjoy the women—if they can stand the stink," Baal said, grinning. "Tomorrow, we kill them all and burn the camp."

The warriors thrust their spears into the air and cheered.

"Right, Chief!" Daga raised his right arm in a stiff salute and turned to go.

Baal reached out and gripped his shoulder. "You have done well, my friend. Before you slit the women's throats tell the men put out their eyes. A blind spirit cannot find its way to vengeance."

CHAPTER 37

REUNITED

"What will happen now, Ejil?" Lada asked, as they strolled along the river. The light of the New Moon cut a path through the dark waters and cast a dappled light through the trees' mostly bare branches.

"Tomorrow, we head back to your new home," Ejil said.

"Home! Such a lovely word, Ejil, but I will be a stranger."

"The First People are your kin, Lada. They took us in, succored and adopted us. They will welcome you, and I'll be there to look after you and little Efrem. Everyone will soon learn to love you, as I do," he said, his burning cheeks hidden in the twilight.

She reached out and touched his face. His nose had stopped bleeding, but was puffed up twice its size. *Ejil has grown so much, but in some ways he is still that same boy I laughed with. I loved how we lay in the grass, watching the clouds change shape, talking of our dreams. That seems so long ago. Oh, how I wish I was still that girl.*

"That sounds wonderful, Ejil, but what about Efrem?" she said gazing down at her son's peaceful, sleeping face.

"Efrem will be my son, *our* son," Ejil said.

"Yes, but with his thick brow and pale skin, will your new people accept him?" She shivered. A cool night breeze was coming off the water. She pulled her fur closer. "You remember what Daga said, that night, around the fire?"

Ejil reached for her hand. "Don't worry about Daga; everything is going to be fine," he said.

Lada snuggled up against him. *I want to believe.* But the echo of the hunter's words still troubled her mind.

Early the next morning, Ejil and Breda stood on the riverbank skipping stones. A gray mist rose from the river.

Though he had said nothing to Lada, Ejil was worried. One of the men of the Bear warriors joked loudly to Salat about Mata's pregnancy. Salat laughed. Ejil and Breda both heard it.

"What was that?" Breda called out. He picked up his spear, walked nonchalantly over to the man until they stood nose to nose. Breda looked him up and down. "Something funny about my woman?"

"Your woman?" The man swallowed. Tiny beads of sweat broke out on his forehead and along the back of his neck. The scout's berserker fury on the back trail was already becoming legend. "It was only a joke," he said. "I meant no insult."

"A joke! Ah!" the scout aimed his gaze to Salat, whose eyes quickly shifted. "That's good," Breda said, returning his attention to the Bear warrior, "because soon as we return to the village, I plan to join with her." He turned his back and sauntered away.

Breda walked back to where Ejil was standing. "I heard. That shut him up!" Ejil said.

"Humm," Breda said, running his finger along a long spear scratch across his belly. "I don't like that kind of talk, even coming from one of those dumb Bears." The scout grinned, bent, picked up a flat stone and skimmed it across the river. The rising sun had turned the thin clouds that hovered around the horizon into long streamers the color of blood and berries.

Ejil scanned the muddy bank until he found a likely stone. "What do men like Daga expect? Those women were slaves." He wrapped the stone in the crook of his finger and watched it skip several times across the surface of the gray water.

"Good one!" Breda said. He put his arm around Ejil's shoulders. "Daga!" Breda snorted. "Don't worry about him. I've got my Mata back and you've got Lada and little Efrem. Time we both settled down and bred sons. I'm tired of always eating at other men's fires and going alone to my sleeping fur."

"Alone?"

"Well, mostly!"

"Remember you asked me if I'd had any more dreams like the one the morning before the Fishbelly attack?"

"I remember."

"Last night I had another one. I dreamed we were at council. The First People were gathered around the fire in the sacred cave. Our women were there. Lada, Tule, and Mata had their babies in their arms. Breda, the people turned their backs. No one would speak to us."

Breda faced Ejil, his brow furrowed. "Can you say what it means?"

"I'm not sure. I have lots of stupid dreams, but this one seemed real. I woke up in a sweat, like that other time. I think we should be careful. Some of our people don't understand, and some don't want to understand. Daga is a fool, but his voice is Baal's echo. What my brother is thinking often comes out of his mouth."

"Yes, and now he is an important man, and what Daga hears flows like a stream into your brother's ear," Breda said.

The women were at work tending the cooking fires that had sprung up out of the morning mist. The sharp smell of day-old fish permeated the smoky air.

"Humm…I'll have to have a talk with the Venerable Baal when we get back to the village. That is, if his head has not grown too large to fit through the entrance of our hut," Breda said with a twisted grin.

Ejil laughed. "You may find that our war chief's eye seeks a place with an entrance much larger than our humble lodge," Ejil said.

Breda raised an eyebrow and snorted. "Yes, I believe that is so," he said, shaking his head. He clapped Ejil on the back and they set off back toward the huts.

Ejil spotted Lada. She was kneeling by the fire preparing a meal. Efrem was lying on his back on a doeskin pelt next to his mother. She had gotten her slim figure back. He watched, mesmerized by the grace and fluidity of her movements. Her hair, black as a raven's wing, gleamed in the sun's bright rays.

What joy he'd felt that morning when he awoke lying up against her with his face buried in her hair. It was tightly curled like a swallow's nest and soft like the rich grass that grows in the shade of a tree. It had a smell, like warm earth. Still, he couldn't help wondering, *Is she thinking of Scar? Does she mourn his death?*

CHAPTER 38

EXODUS

Soon after the return of the victorious warriors, the weather turned, and the first of season's storms howled down from the northlands.

For Lada, events moved quickly. A few suns after they settled in the village, Callas slipped away in the dark of night. The following morning, her frozen body was discovered sitting upright by the riverbank. The council met, and Baal was named First Speaker, and Ejil was asked to be šamán. There had been some talk of choosing one of Callas's acolytes to succeed her, but it had been Ejil who invented the spear thrower, applied the poultices, set the broken bones, and mixed the soothing herbs. The people remembered and showed their gratitude.

Lada had joined with Ejil, Mata had become Breda's woman. Tule's sister, Catya, emerged from the darkness and joined with Tanus.

Tule had kept to herself. "When we were taken, she withdrew inside herself," Lada told Ejil. "Then, when she joined with Spearpoint and had her baby, she changed. She became devoted to her small family, and she became clan."

"And now?"

"Once again, her world has been turned upside down. Give her time," Lada told him.

Eventually, the dark days ended, and the first tender, green shoots peaked out from beneath the snow cover. Cracks appeared, and the ice at the center of the river broke. The river began to flow, and the fishermen set their traps and hunting resumed. The Ice Season, as always, had been hard; but with meat added by the hunters, the people had survived.

Breda and Tanus stood outside Ejil's hut. "How many moons have passed since we brought our women to this village?" Breda asked.

"Four, as I'm sure you know," Ejil said, looking up from his work. He was sitting by the fire, just inside the hut he now shared with Lada and young Efrem, preparing a poultice when his two friends arrived. Smiling, he rose and gestured them in. The two hunters settled themselves across the fire.

"No, I thank you," Breda said—with a quick smile—waving away Lada's offer of drink and food. "We have come to speak of a serious problem."

Smiling inwardly, Lada nodded. She had a soft spot for Breda. *He always comes straight to the point.*

"Our women are being shunned," Tanus said.

Lada's scraper paused above the wolfskin pelt stretched across her lap. She and Ejil exchanged looks.

"This is known," Ejil said.

"All the freed women who have Fishbelly babies," Breda said.

"Tule and Bena have spoken of it. Bena too; she is about to join with Maag," Lada said.

"What can we do?" Tanus asked.

"It began with whispers. You remember, Ejil; I laughed about it, but the whispers have grown loud. Now, Baal speaks of gathering together our young men with those of the Bear and Mammoth tribes to create a large war band and "remove the Fishbelly filth from the world," Breda said.

"But where will he find them? There are no more Fishbellies."

"They have grown scarce. In my father's time, we once found sign of a small band, but until Scar…" Breda shrugged and spread his hands.

"What about our babies?" Lada asked, her eyes bright with fear.

Ejil took hold of her hands. "Never!" he said, gazing straight into her eyes.

Lada smiled wanly and gazed down at baby Efrem lying in his basket waving his arms. His dark eyes stared back at her.

She reached down and tickled his chin.

"Baal has changed. I tried speaking with him, but he sucks in the words of men like Daga and Salat, who flatter him, like a hungry babe pulling on his mother's teat. He is drunk with it," Breda frowned and wrinkled his brow. "I do not know him anymore."

"Power is what my brother has always craved. Now he has it," Ejil said.

"I will challenge him man to man before I allow him to hurt my Mata or our child," Breda said.

Lada felt a stab of fear. "Breda—no! Baal has too much support. Even if you win, you lose," Lada said.

"Ejil, you are šamán. You speak for the gods. We have come to ask your advice," Tanus said.

"I am flattered that you have come to me, but…"

Breda cut in. "You are no longer the boy I knew, Ejil. You have grown in wisdom. We have all noticed the changes since you sought the visions in the sacred cave. Everyone sees it, even Baal. I think your brother is a little afraid of you."

"Thank you, old friend," Ejil said, smiling across the hearth. "I have been watching and thinking about this through the dark moons of snow and ice. My brother has a sickness—he has always had it, but now it feeds itself, and it will grow worse. "

"What, then?"

"I believe we have no choice. We must form our own band and leave this place while we still can. Then, we can live as we wish," Ejil said.

For some time, everyone sat quietly around the fire considering Ejil's words. Finally, Breda yawned and stretched his shoulders. "I have heard if you travel south, the weather grows warmer. "I, for one, am tired of the cold and would like to see more of the world."

"Yes, and I would like to see the great salt water and the fish that fly," Tanus said. "Would Baal try to stop us? People have a right to leave the tribe and strike out on their own. That has always been our custom."

"Baal has no respect for custom," Ejil said. "He has already begun to change things to suit himself. I don't know what he will do, but if we are all agreed, it would be best to keep the plan between ourselves," Ejil said.

"The season of the Awakening Moon has begun. Game will be moving north. It is the best time for travel," Breda said.

"Some others may join us?" Tanus asked.

"Yes, I will speak to Bena," Lada said.

"There may be a few others. Not everyone is happy with Baal's leadership," Tanus said.

A few nights later, as the gibbous moon waxed toward full, a short procession, hidden in the moon's shadow, crossed the rainbow bridge.

"They're gone."

"Gone? Who? Speak plainly, Daga." Baal sat in the Long House with Salut and a few of his men. As First Speaker, he occupied it by right.

"Sorry, Chief. Breda, your brother, Tanus, the women and the White-face babies. Ejil's hut is empty. Breda's too. Maag told me about it a few suns ago. They were talking about forming their own band, and they had asked him. I thought it was just talk."

"Just talk?" Baal said, staring a hole in the diminutive hunter. "Why didn't you tell me about this right away? Gather the rest of the men. We are going to find them and bring them back."

"But why, Chief? You've never trusted Ejil, and we're well rid of those women and their filthy pups."

"Shut your mouth, Daga, and do what I tell you," Baal said, his face darkening. "It's that cursed brother of mine. He planned this. We need a šamán to…to explain—to reassure, so people know that our plans have the gods' support. What will the other tribes say when they hear two of our best warriors—and our clever šamán, the man who brought us the spear thrower—have abandoned us? People believe that he is touched by the gods. Tell the men to hurry. We leave before the sun sets."

Daga cleared his throat. "Chief, I have spoken to Penta. Uh, she has been in mourning since Callas's death, but she admires you."

"Penta? She is loyal to Callas."

"Yes, she respected Callas, but Callas is *dead*, Chief!" Daga said, licking his lips. "Penta trained as a warrior and studied under Callas for years. What will she do now?"

Baal snorted. "Join the hunters or find herself a man! What are you getting at, Daga?"

"She told me she, uh, believes in your destiny. That the gods sent you to us to defeat our enemies and lead the tribe. Why not make her šamán? With Ejil gone the people will accept her. I think she wants to be your woman. Penta would be *very* loyal." Daga said, looking around and smiling at the other warriors.

"Humm…" Baal scowled at Daga and drummed his fingers on his thigh. "She would be loyal, you say?"

"You can depend upon it, Chief," Daga said.

Ejil saw Breda running to catch up. He raised his staff and called a halt. The small party gathered around.

"Any sign?" he asked the scout.

"No, nothing. I don't understand it," Breda said between breaths, "I was sure Baal would send a party to bring us—or at least, you—back."

"Well, you brought something back," Lada said, patting the doe draped over Breda shoulders."

"She ran right by me," Breda said.

"Her spirit was ready! Give her here. We will feast tonight."

"Maybe Baal decided that he was well rid of me—of us," Ejil said with a broad smile.

"Yeah, well maybe. I can see why he might feel that way," Breda said, returning his smile.

"How far is it, do you think, to the great salt lake, Breda?"

"Kokotin said three moons, if we keep moving. We should reach it before the last of the brown leaves fall."

Ejil nodded. The thought of a new place excited him. *We are few now, but soon there will be more,* he thought, gazing down at Lada's swelling belly. *Tule is with child as well.*

Just before the Sunfather dipped below the horizon, Lada sat with Ejil on a low rocky ridge where they had stopped for the night. The ridge overlooked a broad shallow valley.

Lada squeezed his hand. "What is it husband? You seem far away."

Ejil turned his head. "Look out there, my love. It is so big. No matter how far we travel, in any direction, there is as much ahead of us as there is behind. It makes me—us, our little band—seem so small. I feel that at any moment, it could swallow us up.

"Does it ever end, husband?"

Ejil shrugged and squeezed her hand. "Who knows! The world is vast. My head aches when I think about it."

"Baal hasn't come after us. Surely, that is good news."

"Yes, it is. I will miss our friends, but I think that we have begun a great new adventure."

"But we are not the first. Others have left their tribe and set out on their own," Lada said.

"Yes, but look at us, Lada. Look at Efrem, Mata's and Tule's babies. We are the beginnings of an entirely new people, not Fishbelly, not Blackdog but with the blood of both. It's like the dawn of a new day."

"We will find a new way, husband, a better way."

"Yes, and perhaps we will find our way to peace."

-- The End --

Also by Richard W. Wise and available everywhere

Redlined: A Novel of Boston

The French Blue: A Novel of the 17th century

http://www.richardwbooks.com

AFTERWORD

The inspiration for *The Dawning* has two sources. The first came from my initial glimpse of the magnificent paintings at Chauvet Cave, located in the southwestern France. Discovered in 1994, and dated between 35–40,000 years BCE, these breathtaking masterpieces are 10,000 years older than the famous paintings at Lascaux and twice the age of the paleoart discovered at Altamira (14,000 BCE). The art at Chauvet demonstrates a sophistication and technical mastery that surpasses even these later works. I was curious about the people who made them. How, I asked myself, could anyone call the culture that produced this exceptional art "primitive"?

My second moment of inspiration came from a question: what happened to the Neanderthals? Small groups of Homo Neanderthalis evolved in and occupied Europe during the Ice Age, from approximately 400,000 years ago. Modern humans, Homo Sapien Sapiens, arrived between 45–50,000 years ago. 5,000 years later, the Neanderthals were extinct. Why? How did that happen?

What of our own ancestors? What were these new arrivals like? How did they live, and how had a preliterate society manage to maintain and preserve the elements of an advanced culture on exhibit at Chauvet, Altamira, Lascaux and other prehistoric sites in Spain and France?

As a history buff, having enjoyed researching and writing one historical novel, *The French Blue*, I decided it would be an interesting challenge to write a pre-historical novel and explore these questions.

Recorded history began with the first writing system, invented by the Sumerians around 6000 BCE. Homo Sapiens, however, evolved and have lived on this planet for 200,000 years. Given our species' progress over the mere 10,000 years of recorded history, is it reasonable to assert that for the first 190,000 years, anatomically modern humans, with brains identical to ours, could do little more than knap stone, wrap themselves in animal hides and grunt?

Preliterate cultures have endured a bad press for centuries. In 1651, Thomas Hobbes characterized the prehistorical state of man as *"solitary, poore, nasty, brutish, and short."* Was this really the case? The prevailing theory suggests that our ancestors migrated out of Africa about 90,000 years ago and entered Europe between 40,000–50,000 BCE. These people lived a nomadic lifestyle in small bands of hunter-gatherers.

Originally, it was thought that hunter-gatherers spent virtually all of their waking hours gathering food; but today's scholars believe that these people worked a 40-hour week (or less)[1] and had far more leisure time than the farming cultures that succeeded them.

The artists of Chauvet obviously had the time, talent and training to create these masterpieces, and despite the thousands of years between the art at Chauvet and the paintings at Altamira and Lascaux, there is a stylistic continuity which is undeniable.

The Venus figurines discovered at other Upper Paleolithic sites are another case in point. These are small, often headless, carvings of women with huge breasts, hips and limbs. The earliest "Venus," carved in mammoth ivory, known as the *Venus of Hohle Fels* was found in Germany and dates to the Aurignacian Period—the same period as Chauvet. *The Venus of Hohle Fels* is also the oldest known example of figurative art.[2] The stylistically similar *Venus of Willendorf,* found in an Austrian cave and dated to 30,000 BCE, is in turn similar to the *Venus of Balzi Rossi* unearthed on Italy's Ligurian Coast (18,000 BCE). Other examples have been found 5,000 miles away in Siberia. As a group, they span a period from 40,000 to 11,000 BCE and an area that includes all of Europe and

---

[1] Deumler, D. G., *Bringing Life To The Stars*, University Press of America (1993) pps. 87, 203.

[2] Some consider The Lion Man, carved of mammoth ivory dated 40,000 BCE and found at Hohlenstein-Stadle, Germany to be older.

a good portion of Asia. Either there was direct communication between these preliterate groupings or an oral continuity—these people had a highly developed culture and a very good memory.

Though the first printed book was produced in 1455, Europe was primarily an oral culture well into the 15th century. There were books, but very few who could read. Like the Iliad, which was memorized and recited around evening campfires from the time of the Trojan War (1200 BCE) until it was finally written down around 762 BCE, the cultural traditions of human societies have been preserved and passed down by bards and tribal story tellers in a tradition that long predates the written word.

In this book, I assume that the cultures that produced the art at Chauvet, Lascaux and Altamira and the Venus figurines were part of an ancient continuity with a formal oral tradition that was systematically passed down from generation to generation. The stylistic similarities of the art allow few other interpretations. These people couldn't write, but like the ancient storytellers and Medieval bards, they passed their knowledge, culture and folk ways down orally for literally thousands of years.

The DNA of modern Europeans contains minor amounts of genetic material passed down from the Neanderthals, a species of man that pre-dates the entry of modern humans into Europe by 350,000 years. Were these people really knuckle-dragging primitives or did they, too, have a well-defined language and culture? Why, after living successfully in Europe for so long, did Neanderthals become extinct after a mere 5,000 years abiding alongside modern humans? In *The Dawning*, I suggest one possible answer to this question, one based upon the history of human behavior.

Archeologists have drawn a number of conclusions about these early cultures, and I have followed these conclusions in some cases, and in some I have not.

According to the prevailing theory, social hierarchies did not come into existence until the Mesolithic Period (8000 BCE). Prior to that, early humans lived in egalitarian groups or clans. Specialists base this assumption on the examination of gravesites and cemeteries. They simply have not found any evidence of social hierarchies in ancient burials. I find this view naively utopian. A lack of evidence is not evidence of lack. In a few Homo Sapien gravesites dating from the Aurignacian Period (37,000-33,000 BCE), we certainly find the evidence of wealth, and disparities in wealth suggest disparities in status.[3] Then, there is human nature. Hierarchies develop in even the smallest human groups. It is simply a part of our nature.

A CLASH OF CULTURES

The Dawning is the story of the clash of two cultures. Note, I do not use the words species or race. All humans alive today are of one "race," and if a male and a female can mate and produce offspring they are, by definition, of the same species. The study of history can be approached from many angles. We may consider it from a political, social or religious or economic perspective; each gives a different slant on the truth. But the one overriding lesson history teaches us is that whenever and wherever two unlike cultures meet, conflict almost invariably follows.

Some have chosen to view prehistory as a sort of paradise of the noble savage in which conflict and warfare did not exist. According to this viewpoint, war and violence are modern inventions. This position is naïve and untenable. It flies in the face of recorded history and what we know of the nature of man. Yes, it is true that there is little direct evidence, but that isn't to say there is none. In the early 1960s, a graveyard discovered in Egypt's Nile Valley at Jebel Sahaba and dated to between 13,400–18,000 years ago, was found to contain the oldest evidence of human conflict yet discovered. Sixty percent of the skeletons

---

[3] Grave goods, specifically thousands of carved beads found in an Aurignacian (34,000 BCE) gravesite of an adult and child buried head-to-head, unearthed at Sungir, in eastern Russia, suggests inherited status and some awareness of a destination after death.

unearthed at Jebel Sahaba show evidence of blunt trauma and/or projectile strikes.[4]

In writing this book, I have attempted to avoid the usual stereotypes. Neanderthals most likely could speak, cared for their sick, buried their dead and even occasionally painted on cave walls. I see them as technologically inferior to modern humans because that partially explains their demise, but I make no attempt to primitivize their speech or that of the early modern humans, for that matter. I assume that both Neanderthals and our direct ancestors stood upright and expressed complete thoughts in what, despite the differing syntax, were complete sentences. I agree with this because how else would we survive at all? People have to communicate, so there has to be a way in which to do so.

Though many scholars now believe that Neanderthals had the power of speech, in this book, their language differs from that of modern humans in that it consists of a combination of words, gestures and signs. In fact, some experts have suggested that all language began with signs and gestures.[5]

Modern language, with its *thumbs up* and other, more expressive signs, retains vestiges of its evolution. As a manual/oral language, it must have relied, to a degree, on facial expressions along with body language to convey meaning. You only have to recall your last visit to a foreign country. You tried a few words perhaps from a guidebook or a long-ago language course, but very soon found yourself making signs and using pantomime to make yourself understood.

Words are tools. They express ideas and concepts. Thus, the existence of words that express certain concepts and emotional states testify to the existence of such. In this book, Cro Magnon speech contains words for *love* and *friend*, but there are no similar concepts and thus no words

---

[4] Crevecoeur, I., Dias-Meirinho, MH., Zazzo, A. *et al.* New insights on interpersonal violence in the Late Pleistocene based on the Nile valley cemetery of Jebel Sahaba. *Sci Rep* 11, 9991 (2021). https://doi.org/10.1038/s41598-021-89386-y
[5] Wade, Nicholas, *Before The Dawn*, Loc. 777

(signs) expressing the idea of friend or the emotion of love in Neanderthal speech. They also have difficulty finding words to express past and future, though they understand both. They express themselves mostly in present tense using simple declarative sentences. Does this make them primitive? Ernest Hemingway might disagree.

As always, the reader will deliver the final judgement as to the value of this work. Enjoy the story.

Richard W. Wise

9 789898 642081 3